VENET

A supernatural thrille:

by

Simon M. Barnes

Acknowledgements

I would like to thank Sue and Alex for their reading and suggestions. Thanks also to Sophie Playle for her good work editing the book and Tom Fletcher for his encouragement. Finally thanks to John Warton for his advice on the technical aspects of diving.

Around her shrine no earthly blossoms blow,
No footsteps fret the pathway to and fro;
No sign nor record of departed prayer,
Print of the stone, nor echo of the air;
Worn by the lip, nor wearied by the knee,
Only a deeper silence of the sea:
John Ruskin

Prologue
The convent of Santa Maria delle Vergini 1508

In the chapel, the Patriarch looked at Elena Erizzo. Such beauty, he thought. There were tears in her blue-grey eyes. He took her right hand, saying, "I marry you to Jesus Christ, son of the Father Almighty, your protector. Accept therefore this ring of faith, as a sign from the Holy Spirit that you are called to be the wife of God." He looked deep into her eyes, and sensed the familiar frisson, as he placed the gold ring upon her finger and felt the touch of her skin.

Later that evening, as he sat alone in the study of the Patriarchal palace on the island of San Pietro, he couldn't stop thinking about her, the softness of her eyes, the whiteness of her neck, and her virgin innocence. He closed his eyes, picturing her looking up at him. A smile crept across his face. He sighed and looked across at the fire blazing in the hearth. It was a month now since he, Aureo Zancani, had returned to Venice to take his position as head of the church. It had taken him ten years to work to this.

Sometimes at night, faces from the past troubled him, floated up in his consciousness, whispering in his head. He'd had to use the lulling properties of the poppy to sleep. Zancani was terrified of what might happen, when this life was over. The fires of hell would be waiting, unless he found some way to suspend the soul — and he had. Haroun had found the book Zancani searched for. It was a forbidden text. All copies were thought to have been destroyed, but one survived, and he had it. It had been copied in the desert fortress of Hassan i Sabbah from the book written by Abdul Alhazred, the necromancer of Sana. This man had the ultimate knowledge of the afterlife. He had the knowledge to prevent the final judgement. The Patriarch knew he could escape punishment, both in this world and the next.

1

Zancani rang the bell beside his chair, and waited for the monk. "Ah Nicolo, there you are. Build the fire up, and bring me a little wine. Then you may retire."

The monk returned with a flask of red wine and a glass and put it on the large oak desk. Nicolo knew the Patriarch, as always, would work into the early hours. He put four logs on the fire, touching a taper to the flames before lighting the thick white candles on the Patriarch's desk. Then went to the window behind the desk, and briefly looked out across the moonlit square to the black waters of the canal before drawing the damask curtains to shut out the night. He bowed to his master and left, closing the heavy wooden door behind him.

Zancani sat for a moment contemplating the glow of the flickering firelight in the wood panelled room. The wood smoke had a sweet smell, almost like incense. He rose, moved to his desk, and unlocked the bottom drawer to get out the ancient Arabic text. It was fortunate he came from a family of merchants who traded in the east. He and his elder brother had been taught the language by their tutor, the Moor. The tutor had quickly seen that he was the clever one, well in advance of his years. He had learnt much more than Arabic from Haroun.

His brother Rinaldo was not stupid. He had what people called low cunning. He continued to expand the family business. Rinaldo was in Tana now, on the Black Sea. The sea and trade had never been for Aureo.

He had paid Haroun a lot of money for the book, almost as much as his brother would pay for a ship, but it was worth its weight in gold. It would allow him to extend his power beyond this world, into the next. His methods before had been primitive. He had had Franceschina buried with a brick in her mouth to stop her speaking after death, and Maria with chains to weigh her down and prevent her rising from her grave. Now, he knew

2

the secret incantations that would keep a soul from transition. These words must be said forever. He knew, too, how to construct the sealed chest. As long as the souls of his victims remained on this earth, he was safe.

He was translating the words from Arabic into Latin. Tomorrow he would give instruction for the chest to be built to the exact specifications laid down by Alhazred. He heard the bell from the campanile next to the palace ring twelve times. It was midnight.

******

Across the water in the convent, in the blackness of her cell, Elena also heard the bell. Her eyes were wet with tears. She did not want to become a nun. She wanted to stay at home like her sisters. She had begged and pleaded with her father not to send her. He had told her it was her duty, as the youngest. For the good of the family, she must devote her life to God. The nuns had told her: "Forget your people. Forget your father's home. The convent is full of unwanted girls like you. There is nothing special about you. There is no money for you, no dowry. That is why you are here. You are ours now. For elsewhere do not hope. You belong to God. "

She would never see the world again. She wiped the tears from her eyes. How could she forget her home, her mother, and her sisters? She wasn't yet ten years old. Why had they done this?

******

The days and weeks passed, and slowly Elena began to get used to the convent routine of prayer and devotion. She did not forget her family but the pain of separation eased, and now the Patriarch himself had started to take an interest in her. He had sat with her in her cell, and held her hand in his lap. "What a sweet innocent you are," he said. "Are you ready to serve your God? Another Saviour must come. You will bring him into the world."

She was overjoyed to be chosen. She longed for the angel to come. She had wanted to write to her parents and tell them the good news, but he said it must be kept secret until the time came. There were evil forces at work, satanic powers that would do anything to prevent the second coming. She must be careful to tell no one.

The Patriarch had brought her a mirror in an engraved silver frame. "It is the finest Murano glass, all wreathed in fairy fruit and flowers," he said. He had hung it on the wall of her cell. It was almost as big as the portrait of her father that hung in the hall at home. She loved it — loved to see herself in the glass. Her mother had a tiny hand glass at home. You could barely see your face in it. But in this mirror she could see from her head down to her waist. And so clearly— it was as if there was another Elena in front of her.

The Patriarch bought her a chest from the palace with an exquisite carving of the winged lion of St Mark on its lid. Below the lion were the famous words PAX TIBI MARCE EVANGELISTA MEUS, Peace Be with You Mark My Evangelist. On the inside of the lid was a circle pattern with strange serpent-like creatures and symbols she did not understand. He told her the wood had come from Ephesus. The symbols were already on it. He had had the emblem of Venice carved on the front to make it Venetian. The chest was lined with lead, and full of silk dresses.

"There is no reason why a nun in her own cell should not adorn herself for Christ," he said, stroking her hair. "You are highly favoured. God has chosen you. Keep this secret my child."

She told no one, but she kept a record. She wrote everything down in the leather bound book her mother had given her as a parting gift, along with the brown coverlet from her bed at home. She wrote when the convent was asleep. She kept the book with the quill pen and ink at the bottom of the chest underneath the dresses the Patriarch had given her. One day, she thought, when her destiny was known, her words would be copied in convents and monasteries throughout the world, and everyone would know how a Venetian girl had been chosen by God. Everyone would read them, and wonder at her story. If only the Virgin herself had put her words down on paper.

Elena sat alone combing her golden hair. It was late afternoon, and the convent was quiet. All the nuns were in their cells. It was the hour of contemplation. A beam of sunlight slanted through Elena's window, and shone on the green of the dress the Patriarch had told her to put on for his visit. They would wait together for the angel to come, and tell her of the holy child she would bear. She could see particles of dust swimming in the shaft of light. A light from heaven, she thought, and turned again to the mirror.

It had been two days since the Patriarch had performed the ceremony and filled her with the Holy Spirit. It had been very painful. It hurt even now. She remembered the sound he made as the spirit passed through him to her. She looked at herself for signs of change, and yes, there was something different in her eyes. She put on the pearl and bead necklace he'd given her. It lay almost luminous against her pale skin.

The door opened. In the mirror she saw the Patriarch in his red hooded robe shut the door. She turned and smiled. He came and stood behind her, and placed his hands on her shoulders. She saw the familiar ruby ring on his finger, and smelt the sandalwood perfume he wore. He pulled his hood down. "God has spoken. It is your time my child." He kissed the top of her head, and unclasped the necklace and put it in the pocket of his

5

robe. He stroked her hair, whispering words she did not understand. She watched in the mirror, waiting for the angel.

Without warning, he yanked her hair and pulled her head back. She dropped the comb. She felt him place a noose over her head. It fell down around her white throat. He began twisting a black ebony stick around and around, tightening the noose at her neck. She pulled desperately at the noose, trying to get her fingers between the rope and her neck. She saw herself in the mirror. Her face was turning blue, her eyes bulged. She wanted to scream but there was no breath. Hot urine ran down her thigh, and pattered onto the floor.

"Don't struggle. Soon you will be in paradise." Zancani twisted the stick again. Spittle appeared at the edge of his fleshy lips and dribbled down his chin. He watched her legs kick in one last convulsion. It was over. He unwound the noose and returned it to his pocket. From his other pocket he retrieved the necklace, and once again fastened it around her neck and stepped back. Her limp lifeless body fell to the floor. He turned to the door and left.

The Patriarch fingered the smooth black stick in his pocket. He did not hurry as he made his way out of the convent. He had no reason to be afraid; his power here was absolute.

In the cell, the body in the crumpled green silk dress lay on the wooden floor next to a puddle of urine. In the mirror, a small circular patch of mist still held the girl's last breath. To the left of that last breath, the door opened. Two monks dressed in Franciscan robes came in. One was big and heavily built, the other, Nicolo, servant to the Patriarch, took charge. He spoke in a commanding whisper, and opened the lid of the chest. The big man stooped down, and picked the dead girl up in his arms. He took her over and laid her in the chest on top of the dresses she would no longer wear and, beneath them, the diary no one would read.

Nicolo took the mirror off the wall and placed it, as he had been told, with the reflecting surface facing down, so it covered the dead girl's face. He shut the lid of the chest and turned the key in the lock. There was a shifting clanking sound as the mechanisms inside moved creating the lead seal.

"The Patriarch wishes for her body to be protected from the sea," Nicolo said. "That is the noise, she must be seen dressed as the harlot she is. Her wickedness in this place of God, Satan is at work my friend, but our master has confounded him."

Together they carried the chest out of the convent down to the canal and a waiting boat. They put the chest in at the front. The heavily built man sat down in the middle at the oars, while Nicolo stepped back onto the land and untied them. He hopped back in and sat at the stern. The big man pulled effortlessly at the oars as they moved away from the convent entrance. It was dark now. He rowed them down the Rio delle Vergini. All was still apart from the steady dip of the oars into the water. They came into the Canale di San Pietro. The campanile towered black over the canal and behind it faint light from the Patriarchal Palace. Nicolo looked up and saw candlelight in his master's room.

The boat glided on, and out into the dark waters of the lagoon. They headed towards the quarantine island of Lazzeretto Nuovo. Some five hundred yards from the shore, where the water was deep, they stopped and sat bobbing up and down in the sea. A crescent moon hung above them.

Nicolo looked around to make sure there were no lights, no other boats. When he was satisfied, he stood up making the boat rock as he moved unsteadily up towards the chest. He felt underneath it to check for the holes the Patriarch said would let the water in and ensure the chest sank.

The big man shipped his oars, and together the two men lifted the chest. With some difficulty they heaved it over the side. It splashed into the sea, floating next to them briefly before the water filled it, and its weight sunk it down into the green silence beneath the waves.

It came to rest on a sandy bed, deep below the waters of the Venetian Lagoon. Inside, the body of Elena was sealed within a watertight lead compartment. Nothing could get in or out. Her soul was trapped.

1
Palazzo Castello di Zancani 2011

Cristofo Zancani sat listening to the rain and the thunder. It was the first storm of the autumn. Soon more would come and the *aqua alta* too. He was in his study at the very top of the house, in the heart of Castello.

Muttering, "What rains," he stood up to look out of the porthole window behind his desk. His head almost touched the ceiling. The ceilings were low up here, and all the windows were round like a ship's. It was his domain. He had all the manifests from all the ships his family had ever owned. It was here he worked on the family history, tracing events back to the time the Zancanis had first begun trading in Cyprus and Alexandria. He looked across the terracotta roofs. The lightning flashed behind the leaning campanile of San Giorgio dei Greci. The storm was right over the city.

He sat back down, deep in thought. He'd had a disturbing call from an old friend telling him an archaeological dig was starting on Lazzeretto, but more worryingly a sonar ship would be mapping the seabed off the coast. An archaeological diver was coming out from England.

Cristofo was one of the few people who knew what had really happened in 1508. He knew what his ancestor had done, and about the bodies buried on the island and the girl sunk in the chest off the coast. Aureo Zancani's crimes had been covered up by the church, and his name discretely erased. It was as if he had never existed, and better that it remain so.

His ancestor had been unspeakably evil, a serial killer who dealt in the black arts. The church had moved him to a monastery, and hidden him there until he died. His body had been returned to Venice in 1578, and buried secretly in the grounds of the Convent of

Santa Maria delle Vergini. A single member of the family had attended the funeral, Rinaldo, Aureo's brother. Cristofo had found an entry written by him, buried amongst the archives.

He wrote about the chest his brother had been buried in. It had a beautiful carving of the winged lion on its lid. Rinaldo would have preferred his brother burnt. He didn't believe his brother deserved a Christian burial. The family were as keen as the church to see the name forgotten. When the convent had been dissolved in the early eighteen hundreds, the body had been removed but there was no record of where or why. Cristofo had spent his life fearing its discovery and the stain it would bring to his family. The Zancani name was not liked in Venice, and the addition of a child killer would do untold damage.

Now, Cristofo feared the archaeologists would find the chest under the sea. He knew it could be traced back to his ancestor. The discovery of an unknown Patriarch would fire their curiosity. He knew how single minded these people could be, once they came upon a mystery. They would leave no stone unturned until the past revealed itself.

His only hope was that the chest had not survived. It had been at the bottom of the lagoon for over five hundred years. The currents would surely have pulled it apart and scattered it over the seabed. But science these days, they would piece bits together. His ancestor might even have had his name carved somewhere on the wood.

Cristofo didn't fear so much for himself, but he feared for his granddaughter Isabella. It would ruin her life. Her name would be forever associated with the perversions of his ancestor, a killer and an abuser of children. People here still believed evil was inherited. They would look at her and see him and his crimes. She was the last of the Zancani, and very precious to Cristofo. He'd lost his daughter when she'd died giving birth to Isabella. He would do anything to protect his granddaughter. Tomorrow he would go again to the state archive in the Frari, and search the records around the time the convent was dissolved and its property given to the navy.

2
Brighton

Penny and Gideon Mantell and their seven-year-old daughter were waiting in the living room of their small terraced house in Brighton. They were surrounded by suitcases. It was early, just gone 5:30, and still dark outside.

Venetia was bubbling with excitement. She'd never been on a plane. She'd never been up before the sun. Her mummy and daddy had told her all about Venice. They'd had had a flat in Calle Erizzo. That was why she had such a funny name. She'd been in Venice, too, when she was very tiny inside her mummy's tummy, and they'd named her after the city. Now she was going to live there, and even go to school there. She was a bit worried about that, but school was weeks away. Soon she would be flying through the air.

"How does a plane get into the sky?" she asked.

Her daddy smiled. "The pilot drives the plane very slowly at first out to the runway, and waits for the signal to go. Then he turns all the engines to full power, and the plane races down the runway so fast the wind catches the wings, and lifts the plane into the air."

She got up and ran up and down the living room with her arms outstretched, making a horrible high-pitched noise. "Like this, Daddy?"

"Don't overexcite her, Gideon."

"Sorry, come and sit down, Ven," he said, patting his knee. "The taxi will be here in a minute."

She sat on her father's knee. He gave her a squeeze, and kissed her on the top of her head. They heard a car outside. "That'll be ours," he said lifting her off his knee.

"Goodbye little house," her mummy said.

Venetia extended the handle of her case. She'd practised this over and over, and practised wheeling it up and down the corridor. She loved her new blue case with its bright yellow flowers. "Goodbye little house," she said, copying her mummy. She wheeled it to the front door. The taxi man took it from her.

"We're going to Venice," Venetia said, as the taxi driver started the car. In the dark she could see her reflection in the window. It looked as if another Venetia was outside looking in on her, watching her leave.

"I took my Mrs," the driver said. "It was carnival. Everyone was in masks. I've never seen so many people. Going for long?"

"Two years. We're archaeologists," Penny said.

"Like Tony Robinson. I love *Time Team*. You digging something up? "

"We're working on the island of Lazzaretto. It was a quarantine island."

"Oh," he said, "don't suppose there'll be many people there." He seemed to lose interest and concentrated on his driving. They came to the end of Southover Street, turned right, and drove past St Peter's church, circled around and headed out of the city.

Thirty minutes later they arrived outside the south terminal. The driver got the bags from the boot, and put them on the pavement. "That'll be thirty quid," he said. Gideon thanked him, and handed over the £33 he'd pre-prepared in his pocket.

"Cheers," the driver said, and to Venetia who was standing by her case. "Say hello to Venice for me."

"Yes," she said looking serious.

"Right," said Gideon, extending the handles of two of the cases, "*Avanti.*" The three of them entered the glass building, and started up the slope. Gideon led pulling two cases. He had his laptop case slung over his shoulder. Venetia followed her parents, pulling her case. It was a long haul up to the top.

"You alright, Ven?"

"Yes, Mummy," she said. She often complained her daddy walked too fast, but today she was so excited she had no trouble keeping up. They got to the top and her mummy and daddy looked at a screen.

"Zone 2 over there," her mummy said.

They queued to go through security, and then entered the vast departure lounge. It was full of shops. "You go and have a drink," Penny said pointing at a Costa, "I'll just have a quick look. You hate window shopping."

Gideon and Venetia went in. They stood at the counter looking at Danish pastries. "Do you want a pastry, Ven? I'm going to have one."

"Yes," she said, pointing at a doughnut.

Gideon ordered a doughnut, a raisin Danish, a glass of milk, and a cappuccino.

"Looks good, eh Ven?"

She took a large bite, and sat smiling and munching. A sugar moustache appeared above her lips. He smiled at her. A surge of love welled up inside him. She was such a sweet girl. He sipped his coffee feeling very content, and took a bite of his pastry.

"Is it really built on water, Daddy? Do the houses float?"

"It's built on millions of poles of wood, hammered into the mud with huge pile drivers." Gideon made a fist, and gently banged on Venetia's head. "Like that," he said, "and the mud fossilised the wood, and turned it to stone, and that's what everything's built on." He smiled at her. "It's a solid foundation, there's no floating. A bit of leaning by the odd tower, that's all."

"It's an upside down forest," she said, "the wood goes down into the ground."

He took a sip of his cappuccino, "You're right. We'll be walking on top of a great petrified forest, keeping everything in its place. What a funny thought."

Venetia was picturing the stone forest in her mind, and a princess riding through it, when her mother arrived.

"Come on you two, our flight's boarding," she said, bending down and wiping Venetia's mouth with a napkin. They followed the signs to their gate and got on the plane. They found three empty seats in the middle.

"Can I sit by the window mummy?" Venetia asked.

"Yes go on then," Penny said.

They watched the other passengers getting on, busily stowing their bags and coats. Venetia looked out of the window. The sun had come up to a bright but cloudy day. There were lots of other planes, and a white van pulling a trolley full of luggage. She could see her own blue suitcase clearly among the others. The bright yellow flower pattern made it stand out. She leaned up against the window, watching until she saw it safely put on the plane. When she turned back, everyone was sitting down. The stewardess who'd greeted them was going up the aisle shutting the lockers. A steward in an orange short sleeved shirt spoke into a telephone asking for a Randall Grant to make himself known. Nothing happened. He shrugged and began a head count of the passengers.

The pilot came over the speaker, saying they should listen to the safety announcement. The stewardess stood at the end of the plane, miming actions while the steward spoke into a telephone telling them what to do in case of an emergency. Venetia listened intently as he told them about masks for oxygen and lifejackets under their seats with whistles for attracting attention. It was all so exciting. She thought she'd like to work on a plane.

Gideon had heard it all before. He was thinking about the work ahead. They would be uncovering Lazzaretto's time as a quarantine station. In the fifteenth century, suspect ships, crews, cargoes and passengers were kept on Lazzaretto Nuova for forty days. The idea had been first thought of in Venice. Indeed the word quarantine came from the Italian for forty *quaranta,* a time considered suitable to isolate disease. Penny would be digging trenches to locate the buildings used to house people held on the island.

Venetians were terrified of the plague. The cargoes were fumigated daily. Even letters were fumigated before being passed to their recipients. They had no idea how the fatal disease was spread. Gideon would be working underwater. He would be diving in the sea around the island, while Penny worked on her trenches.

They were working for Professor Conti. He'd got the money together for the two year project, and invited Penny and Gideon to join. It had sounded perfect. There was

16

nothing in England for them. The money had dried up. Universities were cutting back. Everyone was cutting back. It seemed they'd all been living in a fool's paradise. It angered him that politicians had been borrowing against future generations to fund the consumer boom. It was all just froth anyway, continual growth was unsustainable; the earth couldn't take it. Economics seemed like alchemy to him. They probably had as much idea of what was happening, as the old plague doctor on Lazzeretto. The great roar from the jet engines brought him back from his thoughts, and he felt himself pushed back into his seat as the plane accelerated down the runway. He looked at his wife and daughter.

Penny was gripping the arms of her seat staring fixedly ahead. He knew she had never liked flying, especially taking off. He took her hand and gave it a little squeeze.

Venetia had none of her mother's fears. She gazed out of the window, watching as the plane got faster and faster and left the ground.

"We're in the air, Daddy," she said, as the plane climbed into the sky. Venetia watched the wing dip as they turned. "Everything looks teeny. I can see the road we came on. Will we go past our little house?"

"We'll be up in the clouds soon," Gideon said. "It'll be like fog, and then we'll be up above it. You won't be able to see the ground."

She turned back to the window and, just as her daddy had said, they were surrounded by thick mist that blew over the plane's wings. She could still feel the plane going up. They pierced through the cloud, and were up out of the fog. The sky looked bluer than she'd ever seen it. Below, the clouds were plump and white and fluffy. They looked like great soft cushions. "It's lovely up here," she said.

3

<u>Venice</u>

Venetia looked at the mountains below. They'd been flying over them for ages and now the plane began its descent. "My ears feel funny Daddy."

"It's because the plane's coming down," Gideon said. "We'll be there soon."

She looked back out, and the mountains were gone. Smoke was drifting across a flat patchwork of fields of different browns, and now they were over the Venetian Lagoon. Venetia gazed at all the islands, and the criss-crossing boats. There was a long bridge stretching over the lagoon, with cars and a train on it. She was disappointed. "You said there were no cars, Daddy."

"They park when they get across." Gideon reassured her. "Don't worry. No cars after the bridge."

"It's a pity they built that," Penny said. "Venice'd be better off without all the coach loads. It's turning into Disneyland."

"Oh you're such a snob, but you're probably right," Gideon said smiling.

The pilot told them to prepare for landing. The two flight attendants came up and down the aisle checking seat belts were fastened, then hurried up to the front of the plane, pulled down their seats, and readied themselves for landing. Venetia looked back out. The plane got lower and lower, skimming over the water, and they were over the runway and, with a soft bump, touched down. The engines roared as the plane slowed, and the pilot came on the speaker, welcoming them to Marco Polo airport. He told them the weather was cloudy but dry. It was 16°C and local time was ten minutes past one. Gideon and

Penny adjusted their watches as the plane taxied in towards the terminal building and came to a stop. Gideon stood and eased himself into the queue to retrieve the laptops. They filed slowly off the plane. Soon they were standing on a bus waiting to be driven the hundred yards to the terminal.

"I like flying," Venetia said taking her daddy's hand. "I'm going to work on a plane when I grow up."

"Are you?" he said.

The bus took them in. They passed through passport control and went to wait for their cases. Venetia was the first to spot hers coming down the carousel.

"There's mine, there's mine," she said jumping up and down. "It's beaten yours."

Penny laughed. "I didn't know it was a race."

Gideon got the blue case and presented it to Venetia: "First prize."

He saw their other cases and heaved them off the carousel. He gave Penny hers and led the way through customs and out of the airport. They turned left and trundled their cases along the walkway down to the Allilugana stop. They were in luck: the waterbus had arrived.

"How long will it take, Daddy?"

"About an hour. I'll give Carlo a ring and tell him we're on our way." Gideon had a short conversation on his mobile, then said, "He's going to meet us at the stop."

The waterbus started, and soon they were chugging through a channel marked out by wooden trunks strapped together by metal bands. Each of the markers had a seabird sitting on top. Venetia thought they looked like sentries guarding the way. Penny pointed at a cormorant sitting on top of one. Just as she did, it spotted something and dived into the sea.

Twenty minutes later, the boat slowed and entered the canal delli Angeli. Venetia gazed out at the houses lining the canal. It was just like her Daddy had told her. The streets were made of water. "Venice is lovely," she said.

Penny said, "This is Murano Ven. It's like a little Venice. This is where all the glassblowers lived. They could only leave with special permission."

"Were they prisoners?"

"In a way they were, but it was a nice prison. Look at that lovely house. That must have been a very rich glassblower's home. In the middle ages they were the only ones who knew how to make glass. People would pay a lot of money to look at themselves in mirrors. In their fires, Venetian glassblowers could turn earth and sand into glass. It was like magic and they wanted to keep their secret. We can come over one day and watch them working."

Venetia nodded, and watched as the boat headed up the canal, then in towards a stop. "Murano, Murano," the man shouted. People made their way to the front and got off with their suitcases. The attendant undid the rope, and they were off again. And there was Venice in front of them. They chugged along the water front towards the Fondamente Nove, passing the cemetery island of San Michele.

Venetia had never seen so many domes and spires. In the late afternoon light, the city seemed to be floating on the water. There were shades of pink and grey in the late afternoon sun, soft and dreamy. The houses old and weathered stood together like ancient friends watching the world. Above them, dotted across the city, towers leaned slightly to left or right looking down on the passing scene.

Veneita had a sense she'd come home, a sudden feeling she'd seen this before. Well in a way she had, she thought, she'd been in her mummy's tummy. She pressed her face against the glass of the window, fascinated by everything. A police motor launch raced past them with its blue light flashing. It turned down a canal and disappeared. She saw a barge puffing out smoke. It was piled high with fruit and vegetables, and at the back its owner sat with one hand on the tiller, and the other on a black Labrador. There were waterbuses jam-packed with people, just like the underground in London. They were pulling in and out of stops along the front. Their boat turned, and stopped, waiting for space. The vaporetto in front pulled out, and they moved in.

The water churned as they moved sideways away from the landing stage. "Just Lido, and then it's us," her daddy said. "We'll go there in the summer for a picnic and a swim."

Twenty minutes later, Venetia heard the man calling: "Arsenale, Arsenale." The Mantells got up and retrieved their cases as the waterbus banged into the stop. The attendant threw a rope around an iron bollard and held it tight, keeping the boat close to the landing stage. They got off and there waving at them was Carlo in a blazer and black polo neck. He'd aged a little since they had last seen him. His hair was now grey, though greased and well combed as always. He looked distinguished and elegant. He opened his arms and embraced Penny and Gideon in turn.

"And this must be Venetia," he said smiling at her. There was only the faintest trace of an Italian accent. "Welcome to Venice. What a pretty girl, just like your mother.

21

Come, let me take your case." He led them away from the stop and down a dark and narrow alleyway. As he walked he asked them about their flight.

"Good, no problems at all. Have you started work?" Gideon asked.

"A few minor trenches on the island — nothing significant. We have a sonar boat coming out on Monday to scan the seabed. We'll have a rough idea what's down there when you join us."

They approached Sottoportico Zorzi but did not pass through the covered passageway. They turned right, and immediately left, and came to an open square with a wide canal running along its side. Next to the canal, two small trees had been planted about ten feet apart on little rectangular patches of grass. On one of them, a pug was scraping away at the earth while a woman waited for it to finish. Venetia could see a wooden bridge crossing the canal. Next to the bridge were three stone lions and a great arched entrance with a huge studded door. What a grand place to live, she thought.

She pointed. "Is that our new house with the lions?"

Carlo laughed. "Not unless you want to join the navy. That is the Arsenale, the naval headquarters. You are here," he said turning and walking towards a dark green door with five nameplates. The name on Flat 2 read Mantell. The others were blank. "You have the building to yourselves until the new year," Carlo explained. "The others have not been let."

Carlo opened the door and led them up a stone staircase. On the first floor he unlocked a thick black door and led them in. He showed them a roomy kitchen, a large sitting room with a dining table against a wall, a big dark-green sofa, and two matching armchairs. In front of the sofa was a glass coffee-table with a few guidebooks and a map.

An oil painting of a country scene hung over the sofa. On the right hand wall an ornate mahogany dresser had shelves lined with books. On either side of it, windows looked out on the square and the canal. The light was just beginning to fade, and the sky had a tinge of red.

"And now the bedrooms; this is the master," he opened a door. There was a big double bed with a Persian carpet on the floor in front of it. Another painting of a county scene hung over the bed. "There is a bathroom, en suite as you say," he pointed at a closed door. "And plenty of cupboard space," he waved towards a wall of built-in cupboards. "Come, the other bedroom is across the sitting room."

He showed them a hallway with two doors. "There a shower room and WC, and here," he said, opening the door, "is Venetia's room." It was dark. He turned on the light. There were two twin beds, a dressing table, and two chairs. Two windows looked out across a small alleyway to the houses opposite. A woman had her hands in a sink in a room across the way.

"You can see the people over there," Venetia said.

"You can. I always think two very tall people could shake hands across the calle," Carlo said. "We'll close the shutters for the night." He opened the window and pulled the green wooden shutters in to fasten them.

They went into the sitting room. Carlo asked if there was anything else they wanted to know.

"Where's the nearest supermarket?" Penny asked.

"Ah yes, I've got you some milk, bread, tea, coffee etc — enough for today. The shops are in the Via Garabaldi. Here, let me show you on the map. It's a ten minute walk if you go along the Schiavoni, or five if you go through the backstreets. The Schiavoni is longer but simpler. You'll find everything you need — supermarket, greengrocer, butcher, baker, and of course Venetia's school."

"You've done us proud, Carlo, thank you," Penny said.

"Well, I'll leave you to unpack, and settle in. By the way, there is a restaurant below in the campo if you don't feel like cooking: Da Paolo. It's a good family restaurant and not too expensive. Since tomorrow is Saturday, I'll give you a little tour, my favourite places, and we'll choose some prints to brighten up Venetia's room. Shall we say ten?"

"Yes that would be lovely wouldn't it Ven?" Gideon said.

Venetia nodded shyly.

They said their goodbyes and immediately began exploring the flat. They looked through the kitchen and found they had indeed been well provided for. There were tins of chopped tomato, onions, lettuce, celery, carrots, packets of spaghetti and some delicious looking bread. In the fridge there were two cartons of milk, packets of butter and various cheeses. Gideon found some tea bags. "Cup of tea?" he said. "I'll put the kettle on."

As they sat drinking tea, Penny said, "Shall we eat in or try the restaurant?"

"Let's give the restaurant a go. It's our first night," Gideon said, "we'll treat ourselves. We'll finish tea, unpack, and go down."

An hour later, the three Mantells left the building. Gideon smelt the familiar odour of drains, salt, sea, fried fish, cologne and tobacco. It was a smell he rather liked, and memories of his first trip flooded back. Images of old pink brick, and shadows of water on walls. And he remembered what old Lady Ely had said to him at the Venice in Peril fund raising Carlo had taken them to. 'The city has a power, it draws people here' she told him, 'And the very centre of the web is St Marks. You know, if I stood there long enough, I would see everyone I have ever known. It is magnetic. The water and the crumbling walls suck history in. They remember. Here nothing is forgotten.' He felt his daughter pull her hand from his and go running across to the stone lions.

She went to the largest lion, standing on its own to the left of the entrance. She climbed on the pedestal and put her arms around the lion's neck.

"Look," he said to Penny, "it's Lucy and Aslan."

Penny laughed. "Queen Lucy the Valiant," she called out, "Stay there — photo opportunity." She got her mobile out and took a picture.

Venetia let go of the lion. As she did so, she saw a strange serpent-like shape carved on its flank. She called over to her parents.

"Strange, it looks like a snake. There are other marks in there as well. I wonder what those are," Gideon said. "We'll ask Carlo, he'll know. Come, let's go eat."

They entered the restaurant opposite. A waitress showed them to a table and gave them three menus. Most of the tables were taken. A mixture of languages were being spoken. Gideon recognised French, German, Spanish and loudest, American. He glanced in the direction of the voice and saw a ruddy faced priest holding forth to a party of middle aged women. He was describing a painting in a church.

The Mantells sat looking at the menus. Venetia pointed at hers. "What's *sarde in soar*, Daddy?"

"Its sardine in a sweet and sour sauce, not sure you'd like it, Ven. I think you'd like the fried fish mixture. It's delicious, all from the lagoon, a Venetian speciality."

"No," she said, "I want the *sarde*."

Gideon hesitated. He felt sure she wouldn't like it. It was a grown up taste. But he had seen the look in her face before. She was determined, and she was tired, and he didn't want a scene. "Alright," he said, "but don't blame me."

"I'll have the fried fish, and if Ven doesn't like the *sarde*, I'll swap," Penny said. "I can't decide. I like them both."

"OK, settled," Gideon said, waving at the waitress. He enjoyed practicing his rusty Italian with her. She smiled patiently at him as he ordered the food and a carafe of white wine and a coke for Venetia.

She brought the drinks. Gideon poured the wine and raised his glass. "Here's to us, and our new life."

Venetia and Penny raised their glasses. The food came and Venetia took a bite of her fish. It was a funny sour taste, but she did like it. The fish was covered in onions and raisins.

"What do you think, Ven?" Penny said.

"Yummy," she said.

They had a happy family meal. The owner did his rounds chatting to one table after another. He came and sat with them. He knew Professor Conti. He knew all about the English family who were coming to work in Venice. He made a great fuss of Venetia, especially when he heard she'd had the *sarde*.

"A true Venetian dish, we've been making it since the fifteenth century. The sweetness is the Arab influence our merchants brought back." He asked her if she'd been to Venice before.

"Mummy says I was made in Venice. I was in her tummy."

"Ah, so you are a Venetian. You have come home," he said.

"Yes I have," she said.

He told her he'd been to the school she was going to. Soon she would be speaking Italian like a native. At ten, after cries of 'Grazie' and 'Buona notte', they left the restaurant, and hand in hand walked back to the apartment.

4

Isola di San Pietro

Two miles away, in a small room converted into a chapel, a fifty-year-old woman, Faustina Tarabotti, knelt before an altar and spoke words she did not understand. The altar cloth had once been white but had yellowed with age. The heavy wooden cross that stood on it had come from the convent, where her great great grandmother had lived. She also had been named Faustina.

At first light, noon and evening, she lit the candles and performed the ritual. The Latin she recited had been written down hundreds of years ago. They were prayers of redemption for Aureo Zancani, and she knew them by heart. His body was in a coffin beneath the altar. There was a beautiful carving of the lion of St Mark on its lid. Sometimes she rested her hands on it when she prayed, and looked in dread at the key in the lock. She had never dared turn it. Her mother had warned her: 'Never touch the key. It will burn and turn you to dust. Only the chosen one may open the chest. It must remain sealed until he comes at the end of time.'

When she died, this job, this flat, should pass to her daughter to continue the ritual —but she had none. She did not know what to do. When the convent of Santa Maria delle Vergini had been dissolved, the task had been entrusted to her ancestor. All that remained of the convent now was an arch embedded in the wall of the Arsenale across the canal.

The Tarabottis had lived in this flat in the Calle Frari in the far east of Venice since that time. From its windows, she could see the old Patriarchal palace. Every month an ancient trust paid a small sum into her bank account. It was only just enough to live on, but quite a lot, she thought, when she considered she was only required three times a day. No one even checked to see if she was completing her part of the bargain. She sometimes wondered what would happen if she stopped, and with dread she remembered her mother's words: "Our duty is to a soul in torment. He needs your prayers – stop the ritual and you condemn him to the inferno, where you will join him. Our work is a secret trust. Never speak of it. It would be certain death to reveal any of what we do."

She had never seen her father. She knew nothing of him. Her mother refused to talk about him. She knew no one but her mother. They had never had any acquaintances. They kept themselves to themselves. She continued to live as her mother had taught her. She left the flat to shop and occasionally get money from the bank. This was the only time she spoke to anyone.

She remembered the old fool in the queue at the bank. He talked to her, to the clerk, to anyone. His endless prattle, as they waited to be served, got on her nerves. He was too stupid to see how irritating he was. His mindless pleasantries made her sick. She felt like pushing him aside, but she didn't, she just waited behind him while he talked to the clerk. And when he was finished, he'd always apologise to her and smile. Every time the same — she was glad to get back to the sanctuary of her home.

She spent many hours gazing from her window, gazing out on the melancholy waters of the canal, watching her neighbours coming and going across the bridge. Her mother had warned her not to trust them. When they greeted her on the streets she would mumble a greeting back, but she never met their eyes. Sometimes, when she could not sleep, and this was often now, she would tie her black headscarf around her head and go out into the night. She loved to wander the empty calli, cross the hump backed bridges and walk into the heart of Venice. She walked for hours. It was so silent. The only sounds were her footfalls, cats yowling and the scurry of rats rummaging around in the rubbish left for the dustmen. Once she had walked as far as the Ghetto and into Cannaregio to the Campo dei Mori. The sun was just beginning to rise and in the early morning light she saw the strange turbaned figures and realised she must get back before the streets filled. She had panicked and gotten lost. Gone around and around and found she was back staring at the statue of the moor with the metal nose. Her heart was pounding. People had begun to appear on the streets. She must get home. She clenched her fists and, concentrating, carefully retraced her steps until she was back in Castello and the familiar streets near her home. It was gone ten o'clock when she finally made her way down the Via Garabaldi, past the Fondamenta Santa Anna, and across the bridge to San Pietro. These days she restricted her night time wanderings to Castello. It was safer. She knew every inch, all the calli, all the fondamente, all the campi, and all the rii. In the early hours of the morning it was all hers.

She would continue with the rites and rituals, but she was getting old and must find someone to take her place, a girl who could be taught the words. She would have to be young, someone uncontaminated by the modern world. It would take years to instruct her. She would have to be found soon. Tomorrow, Faustina would devote herself to this task.

She remembered well how her mother had taught her, the beatings when she got words wrong, her mother screaming ferociously at her, and being locked away to relearn, until she was ready to try again. She remembered sitting alone in the room, her eyes wet with tears, as she read the words over and over. She could not remember a time before this.

Her mother had copied the words for her from the original document. This was locked in the ivory casket on the altar in the chapel. It was there now, thirty three pages of the most beautiful handwritten Latin, and she knew it all by heart. What joy she had felt, when she'd finally learned it. She understood then her mother's cruelty. It was the only way. She would use the same regime, and one day the girl would know the same joy.

That night Faustina dreamed she was walking through a field of bright yellow flowers. The sky was a deep blue. She was unbearably happy. She woke in the darkness of her room and knew the dream was important. It was a vision of heaven.

5

Arsenale

Ten sharp, the doorbell rang; Penny picked up the intercom. "Hi, do you want to come up for a coffee? OK, we'll be down in a second." She put the receiver back. "We're off," she shouted, unhooking Venetia's brown duffle coat and her own blue one from the coat-stand.

Gideon put on his old blue Barbour. It was shiny with wear. "You go down, I'll lock up," he said.

Penny and Venetia walked down the stone steps while Gideon found the keys and locked the apartment. He joined them as they were opening the front door, and there was Carlo.

"Good morning to you all. Did you sleep well?"

"Yes wonderfully, so quiet after Brighton. No cars to keep us awake," Penny said.

"I forgot to say: do you see the big chest there in the hall? It has rubber boots for the *aqua alta*. I checked yesterday. You should all find a pair to fit."

"Gosh, will it come into the house?" Penny said

"No, well I hope not. It will flood the campo. The high tides start in October. When one is expected, the siren sounds in St Marks. You can hear it all over the city. The waters will come up into the streets within the hour."

"What happens if we're not at home?" Venetia asked.

Carlo laughed. "You'll get your feet wet. I'm teasing. You always have time to get home. It's a small city, and we are well prepared, as soon as the water comes in, workers erect platforms, so we can walk without getting our feet wet. I prefer to rely on my rubber boots. The walkways are narrow and, although we Venetians understand the etiquette, the tourists do not. You must keep to the right and keep walking – don't stop and stare. Now are we ready for our expedition?"

"Daddy said you could tell us about the snake signs on the lion." Venetia pointed over to the Arsenale.

Carlo beamed at her. "Indeed, that is where our little tour starts. The Arsenale is my favourite spot, my number one in all Venice." He fished something out of his pocket and knelt down next to Venetia. "I have brought you one of my old cameras." He gave it to her and showed her how it worked. "When we come home tonight we'll put your pictures on Mamma's computer. Come take a picture of the ceremonial entrance with the lions."

Venetia pointed the camera and looked at its little screen. In the frame she had the huge dark-green copper doors and the two larger lions on either side. The smaller lions were out of shot. As if on cue two naval cadets exited and, seeing Venetia with her camera, straightened their white gloves and adjusted their caps, posing for the picture. She pressed the button and showed Carlo her first photo.

"Bravissimo," he said, "Show Mamma and Papa." He waved at the two cadets, "Grazie." They saluted and crossed the wooden bridge. He walked over to the single lion on the left and peered at the runic symbols. "Shall we have a photo? Come I'll show you how to work the zoom."

Venetia zoomed in on the symbols, and clicked. "What do they mean?"

"It's runic writing. The creature is a dragon serpent called a lindworm. Viking mercenaries guarding the Emperor of Byzantium carved it on the lion a thousand years ago."

"Does it say, Sven was here?" Gideon said laughing.

Carlo laughed too. "You're not so far from the truth. I can't remember exactly, but something like Asmund, Asgeir and Ivar cut these runes at the request of Harold the tall. It goes on about how they conquered Piraeus, and someone went off with Ragnar."

"What about all the other statues?" Penny said.

Carlo pointed at each in turn. "Justice, Vigilance and, next to Jupiter, Bellona Mars' wife, the goddess of war, and behind her Abundance, and do you see the little bust there? That is Dante, he was here in 1321." Carlo thought for a second. " 'To yet another bridge we made our way – I needn't tell you what we talked about – till on the summit of the carriageway – we paused to peer into another bit of hell, and hear the usual lamentations. It was hot down there and black as your boot. As in the Arsenal of the Venetians – they boil cauldrons full of pitch.' "

"Blimey," Gideon said. "Do you know *The Inferno* by heart?"

"No, no, I memorised the little bit about the Arsenal to entertain my guests – it conjures what the place was like. Wonderful language, 'caulking ships, leaking hulks in dry dock – others slick with new paint, their planks plugged and patched with tow, the climate odoriferous and toxic, — workman hammering at stern and bow, or splicing ropes or fixing oars – boys with buckets dashing to and fro – so here, but heated by God power, not fire, tar glopped and spluttered into the ditch. This the dead black glue of the infernal mire.' Can you picture it? Close your eyes." Carlo closed his eyes.

Venetia copied him, trying to imagine all the ships and all the workers, and all the noise. For a moment she could hear the noise of hissing bubbling cauldrons, and sawing wood. The noise got louder and louder in her head, frightening her. She opened her eyes quickly, and the sound was gone. She looked at Carlo. "I heard the noise," she said.

"Did you? It would have been tremendous. At one time sixteen thousand men worked here. The air rang with the sounds of hammering and sawing, and boiling cauldrons. It was the biggest industrial establishment in the world. Every morning a bell would ring for half an hour summoning the workers to the Arsenale. "

"Where did they all live?" Penny said.

"Mostly in eastern Venice between here and San Pietro. One of the *Proveditori*, a kind of overseer, lived in the house, where you two had the flat when you were first here. Do you remember? It's a short walk from here. Of course it wasn't split into flats then. It was all his – a grand palazzo."

"Of course I remember," Penny said. "We were just married," she ruffled her daughter's hair, "and our Venetia came into being there. What was his name?"

"His name was Ludovico Erizzo."

"I remember the street was the Calle Erizzo, named after him?"

"I think so."

Venetia closed her eyes and whispered the word, *Erizzo*.

Carlo looked at the serious little girl with her brow furrowed in thought. She opened her blue-grey eyes. He pointed up to the top of ceremonial arch. "Do you know who that is Venetia?

She shook her head.

"It is St Giustina. She was almost bewitched by a heathen magician called Cyprian. He conjured demons. Giustina thwarted him by making a sign of the cross. Cyprian in despair made the sign of the cross himself, and his soul was saved. He went on to become a bishop. Giustina became head of a convent."

"Too many stories, Carlo, she'll never get to sleep tonight," said Penny interrupting, remembering both Giustina and Cyprian had been tortured and beheaded. Carlo would quite likely carry on, and give her daughter all the gory details.

"Quite right," he said, "it's time for a break. We'll go to San Marco for a hot chocolate, and then proceed. First we cross the Ponte del l'Arsenal o del Paradiso." He gestured for them to follow. "For the workers to be outside the Arsenal was heaven. This side hell and that side paradise."

They crossed the wooden bridge and walked along to the end of the fondamenta and turned right over a large white stone bridge. It was a fabulous day, cold but with a bright blue sky. The sun sparkled on the lagoon, and across the water was San Giorgio Maggiore. They passed the Danielli and came to the next bridge. It was packed with people blocking the way. On one side, a party of Chinese tourists were standing listening to a guide. On the other, young Americans were taking it in turns to take pictures themselves, with the Bridge of Sighs as a backdrop.

"Scusi, scusi," Carlo said, pushing his way through the throng.

They came to St Mark's square and stood for a moment to take in its magnificence. People were everywhere. "Come we'll be late for our drink, and I have other things to show you. We'll come here one evening, when we can have the square to ourselves." Carlo led them into Florian's, greeting a black jacketed waiter at the door.

"Buon Giorno Professore, come sta?"

"Bene bene grazie."

The man led them into a cosy, narrow and surprisingly empty room. The walls were hung with ornate old mirrors. Venetia had never been anywhere so elegant. She sat down on the red velvet banquette and gazed around the room.

"What do you think, Ven?" Penny said. "Do you like faded grandeur?"

"Faded what, Mummy?" she said.

"Everything is very old and very elegant. The velvet is faded and threadbare. Look at the beautiful gold mirror frames and the ancient glass. Everything is distorted in them, but it all adds to the romance. You can imagine you're back in 1720, couples dressed in silk and taffeta and velvet, sipping their coffee."

Venetia imagined old Venice, and in her imagination peopled the room. She could almost hear their chatter. She pictured a woman in a red velvet gown. Her mother nudged her. A white jacketed waiter stood at the table. Carlo was saying, "Hot chocolate?" She nodded, "Yes please."

"Cioccolata calda per tutti." The waiter left. "Hot chocolate for everyone," Carlo said rubbing his hands together. "Your mother is right. You are in the past here. There," he said pointing at an empty table, "is Lord Bryon with Marianna Sagati, there is Casanova charming a lady in a mask, there is Charles Dickens scribbling a note, and there Ruskin with Effie. Venice is filled with ghosts, but none to frighten you. They hang like magic over the city."

The waiter returned with a huge silver tray held aloft. He put it down on the white marble table. There were four cups and two jugs of dark chocolate. There were also four glasses of water. He poured the chocolate for them. "Bene?" he said.

"Si, si, Grazie," Carlo replied. "Now taste." He lifted the cup to his lips. The three Mantells picked up their cups. The chocolate was thick and delicious. They looked at each other.

"Oh it's wonderful," Penny said, "like a bar of melted chocolate."

"Indeed," said Carlo. They drank and chatted, and refilled their cups. The room slowly filled with little groups, displacing the ghosts of the past. The sound of hushed conversation hung in the air. Where Byron had been with his mistress, an English couple consulted their *Eyewitness Guide*. Carlo told them where he was going to take them. The chocolate had made them all thirsty, and they reached for the glasses of water.

"I wondered why he brought water," Gideon said, downing his glass in one. "Now I know."

When Carlo called for the bill, Venetia remembered her camera. "Can I take a picture?" she said.

"Yes of course," Carlo said. "You take one of us, and I'll take one of you."

She stood up, and looked in the little screen. She had them all in frame. She clicked and took a photo of her mummy and daddy and Carlo. She raised the camera in line with the mirror hanging above her parents. The mirror was covered in black marks where it had aged, but she could just see herself. She looked strange, like someone else. She wanted to take a picture of the other Venetia. She looked at the screen, and clicked.

Carlo said. "Let me have a look." She passed him the camera. "They're good; your parents are a handsome couple, pity about the old man in the picture. I like your photo of the mirror – very artistic."

She sat down next to him, and looked. There was no one in the mirror. "That's funny," she said, "I was in the mirror when I took the picture."

"It's the age of the mirror, and the light in here. I'm afraid the camera is not good enough, but you know young lady I think you have the makings of a good photographer. We'll have to get you better equipment one day. Now, I'll take a picture of you with your mamma and papa."

Venetia sat between Penny and Gideon.

"Say Gorgonzola," Carlo said, pointing the camera and taking a picture of the Mantells. He looked at them and sighed and gave the camera back to Venetia. Penny and Gideon lent over to look at the photo.

"It's one for the mantelpiece," Penny said.

The waiter returned. Carlo paid him and they got up to leave. They crossed the square full of tourists to the other side, where Carlo led them out down a small calle. "This is the Bacino Orseolo, a kind of gondola park." In front of them was a square expanse of water with gondolas queuing to pick up passengers, just like taxis outside a station.

"Are we taking one?" Venetia asked.

"No, they're for tourists," Gideon said.

"It's a walking tour," Carlo added, "but one day maybe you will go in one with your boyfriend."

Venetia giggled at the thought. They followed Carlo, as he led them north into the Campo Manin and down a calle.

"We are coming to the back of the Palazzo Contarini del Bovolo. Come we will look through the bars to see the spiral staircase. Bovolo means spiral in old Venetian." They pressed their noses up against the bars of the gate.

"It's like something out of a drawing by Escher," Penny said. "One of those weird stairways."

To Venetia it was out of a fairy tale. She pulled her camera out, and stuck her arms through the bars to take a picture. She showed the result to Carlo.

"Excellent," he said, "Come there's much more to see, and I've just had an idea." They followed him, as he led through the narrow streets to the Calle del Traghetto. "We are going to look at the Grand Canal and then we will take a ride in a gondola." They all stood looking out on the Grand Canal. Carlo pointed out the Palazzos on the other side,

Grimani, Barbarigo, Marcello, and Persico. "It is all as it was. Look at a Canaletto, and you will see nothing has changed. All names from the Golden Book."

As Carlo talked, a Gondola with eight people standing approached. There were two gondoliers rowing, one at the front, and one at the back. "Aha, here is our ride to the other side. They will take us to San Toma, but we must stand, no sitting." They waited for passengers to get out, and filed on behind Carlo. As he got on, he gave the gondolier a few coins. The gondolier helped Venetia on. She stood behind Carlo. Gideon stood with his feet astride, his hands on Venetia's shoulder. Penny stood behind him, holding onto his waist. The gondoliers pushed off into the canal. They rowed out weaving between other boats, and every now and again stopped to let a vaporetto or water taxi pass. The gondola rocked up and down in the wake, as they waited for the speedier boats to pass. Venetia looked at the sun shining on the water. She squinted, and the water was full of stars sparkling and moving in the light. She opened them, and looked up and down the Grand Canal at all the boats, and all the palaces.

The gondola pulled into San Toma. "We shall now make our way to the Rialto. You must see the fish market, and then I'll put you on a vaporetto home," Carlo said as they disembarked."

"What's the Golden Book?" Venetia asked.

"The names of the ruling families were inscribed in the book in 1325. No family after could join."

"Is your family in the book?"

"No, I'm afraid we came to Venice much later. My ancestor came in 1745, but I know someone who is in the book. A colleague, he is of the Barbarigo family. A very grand family, he teaches architecture at the university. His granddaughter, Sophia, goes to your school. She is a little older than you. I told him about you the other day. He said he'd tell Sophia to look out for you."

"How old is she?"

"She's ten. She's a nice girl. You'll like her."

Venetia wondered about that. Her parents often said you'll like her, but more often than not she did not. Other girls wanted to play with dolls. She liked books and making up stories to play. She had found her best friend at school in Brighton. She wished Lucy was with her. What games they could play.

They walked to the Rialto, with Carlo talking almost all the way. There wasn't a street without some story attached to it. His knowledge was amazing. Venetia decided she would like to be a historian. They passed a stationary shop.

"Pictures for Venetia's bedroom! I almost forgot."

Carlo took them in, greeting the owner, who got a selection of prints and posters. Venetia chose a print of the water entrance to the Arsenale, a poster for a ball at the carnival, a poster for a production of Don Giovanni, and a print of the Doge visiting the Scuola di San Rocco. The owner rolled them up and placed them in a tube. He said something to Carlo and came back with a box of drawing pins.

"To pin them on the wall," Carlo said, giving the box to Penny.

Gideon got out his wallet to pay but Carlo insisted on buying the prints. "A little gift. She has been so good listening to me and walking without complaint. And she has excellent taste too — it's what I would have chosen. I was at that performance of Don Giovanni, sublime. Of course Mozart came to Venice, but that's for another time. We must push on."

They smelt the fish market well before they got there. It was just beyond the bridge, a great covered area next to the Grand Canal. On the wet paving slabs there was metal box after metal box, full of fish, resting on piles and piles of crushed ice. On the stone counters were grey mullet, hake, sole, flounder, turbot, sea bass, brill, and sardines. Elsewhere squid and octopus, and behind the counters fishmongers in rubber boots held up fish for their customers to see, while others worked cutting and filleting.

"What about this, Ven? It's bit different from Sainsbury's," Gideon said.

"Why don't you do your Conte Carlo, Gid?" Penny said.

Gideon nodded. "Good idea, what's monkfish in Italian, Carlo?"

"Cota di rospa, and what is Conte Carlo? I hope it's not some reference to me?"

"No no, it is Venetian though. It's a Carluccio recipe. He said he got it from a Venetian count. Monkfish, parmesan, sage, and potatoes. Simple, but delicious. Why don't you join us tonight?"

"That would be nice, but I'm going to my nephew's. Another time perhaps. Come, we'll get the fish and go to the vegetable market." Carlo did all the ordering, babbling away at high speed and making the fishmonger laugh. A little way from the fish market, they came to the vegetable market.

"How much do we owe you?" Gideon said, as Carlo handed him a bag of potatoes.

43

"Twenty five Euros. I wish, now, I was joining you."

Gideon got out his wallet and gave Carlo the money. "I think we better take a vaporetto back," he said gesturing at the bags.

Carlo took them to the Rialto stop. He put them on the number 1. "Have your camera ready, Venetia. You'll see all the great palaces along the canal."

They sat three in a row with Venetia next to the window, camera in hand, and her tube of prints resting against the seat. As they travelled up the canal, Venetia took photo after photo. When they came to the Salute stop, she saw a woman cross herself. She nudged her daddy. "Why did she do that?"

"What, Ven?"

"She made the sign of cross like in church with Granny."

Gideon thought, and remembered. "It's the church here — Santa Maria della Salute. It was built to thank God for deliverance from the plague. She must be thanking him for good health."

"I think I'll do it too," Venetia said, crossing herself.

The woman saw and smiled at Venetia. Finally they arrived at the Arsenale, disembarked, cut through to the Sottoportico Zorzi and, remembering their right and left turns, came to Campo Arsenale.

"Time for tea and a sit down," Penny said, "And after that we'll put your photos onto Mummy's computer, and Daddy can make supper."

Venetia nodded and held up the tube. "Can we pin these up in my bedroom first?"

"Yes we can, but tea before anything, darling, Mummy needs a rest."

As they sat drinking tea, they heard a rumble of thunder and then another, and another. They were loud and shook and rattled the windows. Gideon got up, mug in hand, to look. A thick black cloud hung over the walls of the Arsenale. It was very low. A flash of lightning lit up the sky behind it and the thunder rolled around the building. Penny and Venetia joined Gideon.

"This wasn't forecast," Penny said. "We got home just in time."

The rain started as she spoke. It poured straight down from the sky. The raindrops seemed larger than normal. They pelted and battered down on the campo. The lightning flashed again, electric white against the black sky, followed by a gigantic clap of thunder.

"It's very close," Gideon said.

"Lucy says God's cross when it thunders," Venetia said.

"He must be very cross now," Penny said, ruffling Venetia's hair. "I'm glad we're safe inside."

6

<u>Torcello</u>

"Wakey wakey," Gideon said, entering the pitch-black of Venetia's room and unlatching the shutters to let the light in. He saw the prints Penny and Venetia had pinned to the walls, while he'd been making the supper, and the storm had raged outside. It had been quite a spectacle, the lightning flashing and the thunder crashing and the lights flickering. Venetia had been frightened but fortunately by bedtime it was over. Today it was bright and fresh outside.

Venetia stirred. There was a knot in her stomach, and she remembered she had a day left before starting school. The dread had slowly been building over the past days. The week had gone so quickly. She had one day left, and she and her mummy were going to the islands. Carlo had said a boat would collect them, drop her Daddy off to start work, and take them to Torcello and Murano. Her mummy said they would take a picnic. The two of them would have a lovely time.

"The boat will be here in half an hour, Ven, don't dawdle. Mummy says she put your clothes ready on the chair."

"Yes, Daddy, I'll be quick," she said as he left the room. She splashed some water on her face, did her teeth and dressed. She joined her parents who were sitting at the table in the kitchen. Her bowl of cornflakes was waiting for her.

"Sleep well, Ven?" Penny asked. "Are you looking forward to our trip?"

"Yes, Mummy," she said through a mouthful.

After breakfast, Penny put Venetia's duffle coat on her and did up the toggles. "Right, you'll do. I'll just get our picnic. You two go on ahead, I'll lock up."

Gideon took Venetia down to the Campo, and across to the canal. "What a lovely day," he said, "Not a cloud in the sky."

A naval launch came down the canal, stopped outside the Arsenale water entrance, and honked. An officer, holding a brown briefcase, stood looking important at the back of the boat. The guard chain was lowered and the boat entered. Another boat appeared under the bridge at the entrance to their canal.

"This is us," Gideon said.

The boat pulled into the side of the canal. "Signore Mantell?" The boatman asked, as he tied up.

"Si si," Gideon said, "un momento." He turned to see if Penny was coming. She appeared with a wicker picnic hamper in her arms and her red handbag slung over her shoulder. Gideon took the hamper, passed it to the boatman, and helped Venetia and Penny on. There was a passenger cabin, with white leather benches, and enough room for eight, four on either side. Its small glass doors were closed. Inside it was lovingly kept. The wood was polished and varnished. The boatman signalled they should go in. They went and made themselves comfortable as he untied the boat and started up the engine. He spun the big black steering wheel and turned the boat around. They chugged slowly up the canal, under the white stone bridge, and out into the lagoon. He turned east and increased the speed so that every now and again the boat bounced up over the waves and came down with a heavy thump.

"We're going fast," Venetia said. "We're the fastest."

47

"Our own private boat — what luxury. I like the decor, very Italian, very dolce vita. " Penny said. "And we've got it all day while Daddy's swimming in all the murk under the water."

"Things are waiting to be found in the murk," Gideon said. "I'll have fun."

"Treasure?" Venetia said.

"Maybe," Gideon stroked his daughter's head. "I'll tell you all about it tonight."

Venetia knelt on the leather bench and looked, out at the passing scene. They went past the Giardini where the Biennale was in its last few weeks. Gideon told her, every country had a pavilion. It was the artistic Olympics.

"We should have gone," Penny said.

"We still could. Most of the stuff 's a bit weird."

Penny laughed. "You're a bit of a philistine when it comes to art."

"No I'm not. Anyway it's not suitable for a seven-year-old. You never know what's around the next corner – some hideous scene of...." He stopped, unsure what to say as the boat turned round the eastern tip of Venice.

They passed San Elena, San Pietro, and on out past deserted islands and ruined buildings. They saw San Erasmo and Lazzaretto, and there just off the coast was a dirty old white motor yacht with *Lanesra Universita di Venezia* painted on its stern. Carlo was on deck. He waved at them.

Gideon got up and Penny followed him out. Venetia came as well. Gideon kissed them goodbye and climbed up a rope ladder onto Lanesra.

Thanks for the loan of the boat, Carlo," Penny shouted up.

"You're welcome, have a good day. Have you got your camera, Venetia?"

She got it out of her duffle coat.

"Promise to go to the top of the campanile on Torcello, and take a picture of all the islands for me."

"I promise," Venetia said.

"Good girl. Now we must get to work," Carlo said, putting his arm around Gideon. "We are in position over an object found by the sonar." They disappeared inside.

"Torcello," the boatman said to Penny.

She nodded, and she and Venetia returned to the cabin. Half an hour later, they were chugging down Torcello's only canal. Penny and Venetia came out of the cabin and stood next to the boatman to get a better view. Using her rudimentary Italian, Penny asked the boatman his name.

"Sono Francesco," he said.

She told him their names.

"Venetia que bel nome," he said.

They passed some vegetable gardens and a few buildings. Straight ahead, towering over the flat landscape was the tower Carlo wanted them to climb. At the end of the canal, Francesco tied up to some moorings next to a restaurant, bearing the legend Locanda Cipriani. He showed Penny his watch and pointed at three. He gestured he would be back then, and helped them off with the hamper.

There were no more than a handful of tourists in the little campo in front of the Basilica. Penny had been before, and loved the quiet and solitude of the place. She loved its very ancientness. She'd worked here as a student archaeologist and they had discovered Roman remains going to back to the 1ˢᵗ century. They'd found evidence of glass working, and a furnace that's structure was Roman rather than Venetian. They had looked at glass from different levels, and seen the transformation from Roman natron-based glass to the later Venetian soda-ash based glass, and the very beginnings of Venetian mirror making. This was where her interest in glass had begun.

She was looking forward to showing her daughter all the things she loved about Torcello. Indeed, Torcello had been named Venetia by the Romans before Venice took the name. Penny had loved the name, and when she found out she was pregnant with a daughter had said to Gideon, 'let's call her Venetia.' She remembered his words as if they were yesterday: 'What a lovely name, a name to conjure with. *Venetia Mantell.*'

She smiled at her daughter. "First I want to take a picture of you sitting on Attila the Hun's throne. He was a barbarian who conquered Rome. People were terrified of him." She took Venetia's hand and led her over to a vast old marble throne. Venetia sat. She looked tiny. There would have been room for Attila himself, Penny thought. She got out her mobile and took the picture.

Venetia got her own camera out. "Shall I take a picture of you, Mummy, on the throne?"

Penny sat down. "I'll do my Attila," she said, raising her fist, and making a savage face. "Attila the Mum."

Venetia giggled. "You're funny Mummy." She took the photo.

Penny got up and came to see the result. "One for the album, Daddy will love that."

"Can we go up the tower?"

"Let's have a walk first, and find our picnic spot. I remember a place. We can leave the hamper there and come back. I don't want to lug it about."

They walked out a little way into the country across a few ramshackle bridges over ditches to a derelict hut. Penny put the hamper inside. "We can have our picnic over there," she said pointing at a little clearing of scrubby grassland. "That's where Mummy did her first dig. We found Roman pottery and coins."

"There's no hole?" Venetia said.

"We filled it in, silly. We couldn't just go around leaving holes all over the place. Come on let's go up the tower, and you can take the promised photo."

They climbed to the top of the campanile, where a huge bell was hanging. "I hope it doesn't ring while we're up here," Penny said looking at her watch. They looked out over Torcello. It was mostly reed marsh and beyond was Burano, with its coloured houses, and Venice itself. The lagoon was very calm. It was a good day for diving, Penny thought.

Venetia walked all around the walkway, looking out over views of marsh, lagoon, and islands, and stopped and took a photo. "Done," she said, showing Penny the camera screen.

"Lovely, Carlo will like that. Let's go and have our picnic."

They retrieved the hamper from the hut. Penny got a rug out, and spread it over the scrub. They sat down to a meal of bread, cheese, apple, and yoghurt. Penny had brought them each a small bottle of mineral water to drink. The great bell at the top of the tower boomed out twelve times just as they began eating. A large white bird flew up out of the marsh reeds in front of them and headed off over the lagoon. It looked incredibly white against the blue sky.

"Look, it's an egret," Penny said. "The bell must have spooked him."

As they ate, she asked her daughter if she was looking forward to her new school. Although Venetia hadn't said anything, she sensed her daughter was worried. Penny wanted to reassure her it would be fine. She didn't want her bottling things up.

"Mummy, I can't speak Italian. I won't understand anything, and they'll make fun of me."

"Course they won't, Ven. They'll all want to talk to you. You'll be the only English girl. I bet they can't wait to meet you. They'll want to practice their English on you and you'll pick up Italian in no time. I guarantee, next year you'll have lots of Italian friends."

Venetia looked at her mother, not saying anything.

"Don't forget Carlo's friend's granddaughter. He said she'd look out for you. Shall I remind him? He could give his friend a ring and say you're starting tomorrow."

Venetia shook her head. "No Mummy. I don't want them to think I'm a baby."

Penny changed the subject. "Have you had enough? I've got some chocolate in my bag." She got out two small Toblerones and gave one to Venetia. They sat, looking out over the reeds, eating the chocolate, while Penny told her daughter about her time on Torcello.

When they'd finished, Penny got up. "Help Mummy put the stuff away, and we'll go look at the Cathedral. We've got an hour. Fourteen hundred years old – imagine. I'll show you the first ever writing about Venice."

They packed away their wrappers and empty bottles, and shook out the rug. Penny folded it up and put it in the hamper. She was pleased to feel how much lighter it was. The two of them walked back hand in hand to the Cathedral. Inside, a small group was gathered around the picture of the day of judgement listening to a priest. Penny recognised him as the American they'd seen in the restaurant on their first night. He spotted her and gave a smile of recognition. She nodded back.

She took Venetia to see the inscription she'd told her about. It was just to the left of the altar. They peered at it, and stood in the middle of the marble floor to look up at the mosaics. Mary was depicted descending from heaven, and the apostles below her walking on reeds, just like the ones they'd seen in the marshes when they'd been picnicking. Penny showed Venetia a Byzantine carving of lions and two peacocks drinking from the fountain of life, then noticed the American and his group had left. They gazed up at the day of judgement covering the whole of the west wall. Venetia was fascinated by it.

"What does it mean?" she whispered. "Look, Mummy, they're worms coming out of their eyes."

"Those are skulls, Ven. In the middle ages they were frightened of the afterlife. They believed they would be judged, and the bad would go to hell. Some people still believe that. I think perhaps your Granny does. Daddy and I don't — not many people do nowadays. I don't think there is a devil or a hell."

"So the bad aren't punished?" Venetia whispered.

53

"Not by the devil." Penny wished she hadn't got into this. It was too complicated to explain to a child. "The police put bad people in prison."

"Supposing they can't catch them?"

"Bad people can't escape what they've done. They live with the guilt and can never be happy," Penny said.

"Why?"

"Because everyone knows what is right and what is wrong."

They stood for a few more minutes gazing at everything happening on the wall. Penny looked at her watch; it was almost three. "We better go."

Francesco was waiting for them. "Ciao, tutto bene?" he said, as he helped them on board. "Murano?"

"Si Grazie," Penny said.

7

Underwater

Gideon put on the dark blue neoprene wet suit to protect himself from the cold, as well as the rubbish that had been chucked into the lagoon, fish-hooks, broken bottles, and God knows what else. Everywhere man went, he thought, rubbish went with him.

He sat on the floor and pulled the fins onto his feet, stood up, and strapped on the belt with the bag of tools, torch and knife. Carlo came over to help him on with the dive tank.

"Hup," he said, as he lifted it onto Gideon's back.

Gideon walked awkwardly out to the deck and along to the stern. Carlo followed him. Captain Cazzano was standing by the roll of line that the divers used to communicate with the boat. Beneath it, engraved on a white metal sign so that no one should be in any doubt, were the simple communication signals.

Line	Tender to Diver	Diver to Line Tender
1 tug:	"Are you O.K.?"	"O.K."
2 tugs:	"Stop change direction take out line"	"Need more line"
3 tugs:	"Come to surface"	"Have located object"
4 tugs:	"Stop" (danger on surface or in water)	"Need help"

Cazzano gave three pulls on the line to signal Gianfranco to surface. Gideon watched the water for the tell tale bubbles and saw Gianfranco come up. Cazzano leaned over the boat and helped him on board.

"Anything?" Gideon asked.

Gianfranco shook his head, "Niente, ma...." He took off his mask, and sat down on deck to remove the fins from his feet and gave Carlo details of the seabed below.

"He says there's a lot of junk, even an old fridge. There are some mounds of sand that might be covering something. He didn't have time to look before he got the signal to come up."

Gideon could feel his adrenalin pumping, as he pulled the hood over his head and put on his facemask. He wanted to get down there. He put his mouth around the regulator mouthpiece and checked it was functioning and ready to go. He smiled at Carlo and gave him the thumbs up. Cazzano fastened the line to him and also gave him a thumbs up. Gideon jumped overboard and splashed into the sea. Beneath the surface, the water had a greenish tinge. He twisted his body and, kicking his legs, headed down towards the bottom, trailing the line behind him.

Visibility was poor. He couldn't see more than a few feet in front of him. He swam along the bottom, feeling with his hands. He loved the slow-moving feeling of weightlessness underwater. He was joined by a party of fish, swimming just above him. He passed the fridge Gianfranco had seen, lying incongruous on the seabed.

He kicked on, and directly in front of him was a slight mound. He swam to it and started shifting the sand with his hand. There was no need for the trowel. As he swept away at the sand, the current lifted it up around him so he looked as though he was working in a sandstorm. He ran his hand over the object and felt something hard and at first smooth, then jagged and sharp. He swept away more sand until he could see. It was a rock, nothing more.

He moved over the seabed scanning for anything, and felt the tugs on his line signalling him to return. He surfaced and clambered back on board. Cazzano helped him off with the dive tank and unattached him from the line.

"Any luck?" Carlo asked.

"Nothing." Gideon heard Gianfranco splash overboard. He sat on deck chatting with Carlo waiting for his turn to go down. They were diving in fifteen minute spells. His time soon came and Cazzano was tugging on the line to call Gianfranco in. Carlo helped Gideon prepare as Gianfranco got back on board.

He removed his mouthpiece, grinning. "I think there may be something a hundred metres left of the fridge. I started to dig away the sand. There's something hard under it. Not rock."

Cazzano attached Gideon to the line. Gideon put in his mouthpiece, jumped from the boat and swam down in the direction of the fridge. He headed left and saw where Gianfranco had started to dig. Gideon worked his hand down into the sand and felt his hand on a flat surface with a raised pattern. He traced it with his fingers. It felt like writing. Perhaps the name of a ship carved into the stern. His heart began to race. Gideon got the torch and shone it on the object. He could see the faint outline of what looked like a *P*. Fascinated he brushed more and more sand away, working as quickly as he could, and through the cloudy water the winged lion of Venice emerged. For a second he just looked then gave three tugs on the line so Gianfranco would come down with a marker.

Where he'd seen the *P*, he could just make out the word *PAX* and, uncovering more saw the inscription *PAX TIBE MARCE*. He looked at his watch. He didn't have much time left. Out of the murk, a diver appeared and gave him the thumbs up. He returned the gesture and shone the torch on the object so Gianfranco could see. Gianfranco placed a weighted line down onto the seabed next to the object, and signalled to Gideon that they should go up. They followed Gideon's line up to Lanesra, surfacing next to the boat. Captain Cazzano and Carlo were looking expectantly into the sea.

Gideon pulled the mouthpiece out. He felt exhilarated. "Fantastic carving of a lion down there," he said, swimming to the ladder. He hauled himself in. Carlo helped him off with the tank and unattached him from the line. Cazzano took the line, and fixed it to Gianfranco, who plunged back in the water, swam away to the marker buoy, and duck dived beneath the surface.

Gideon sat and took the fins off his feet. "I could do with a coffee. I wonder what the carving has come from. It looks well preserved."

"Probably come off a ship? Come, let's get you some coffee," Carlo said. They moved through to the little galley. Carlo shook ground coffee from a red Lavazza bag into the container of a stained and dirty looking coffee pot. He filled its base with water and screwed the two together, lit the stove and put the pot on. It had taken Gideon a while to get used to the strength of Italian coffee, but now he loved it. They talked as they waited for the coffee to boil through.

"It could have come off one of the galleons that anchored off the island during the plague. But the question is, was it thrown off, or did the galleon sink? If it sunk, the sonar should pick up more remains today."

"Gianfranco and I will be able to excavate and get a clearer picture," Gideon said. "I'll take the camera down next time."

The pot hissed and rattled on the stove. Carlo wrapped a rag around his hand, took the handle of the pot and poured out two cups of thick strong black coffee. Gideon added some milk. He hadn't gone entirely Italian. He took a sip of the hot coffee. It was delicious. Everything tasted better after a dive.

They returned to find Cazzano helping Gianfranco on board. "I've uncovered more," Gianfranco said as soon as he had his mouthpiece out. "It looks like a chest. The carving on the lid is very beautiful."

Carlo rubbed his hands with anticipation. "I will contact the university. We must get the salvage ship out as soon as possible to raise it." He pointed at Gideon. "Get me pictures and measurements."

Gideon got the Sealife camera, and prepared himself. When he was ready, they attached him to the line and he splashed into the sea. He swam to the marker buoy and followed the line down to the bottom. It was murkier than ever. He shone the torch on the object. Gianfranco had cleared the sand away from the top. He could see all the words of the carved inscription; *PAX TIBI MARCE EVANGELISTA MEUS*. The chest looked to be about six feet long and three feet wide. The carving of the lion was magnificent. In the watery light it almost seemed to move like a hologram. He took pictures of it from four different angles. He put the camera down, and began to work away with his trowel at the sides to get an idea of how deep it was, and how long it would take to free it. He wondered how much bottom suction there was. The mud and shale, which poured into the lagoon, made a soft bottom. The heavier the object, the more of a vacuum there was sucking it into the mud. It did help preserve though. This wood felt solid. If they could free it of the vacuum without damage, they might be able to get it to the surface intact.

He felt the three tugs on the line and realized he hadn't measured. He got the fibre glass tape out from his tool bag and measured the chest length at 1.8 metres, and its width at 80 centimetres. They'd excavated about 2 foot around the chest, but it was still well embedded. He couldn't help it, but in his head he always thought in feet and inches. He guessed another 2ft to go, but it was impossible to tell. On land, one could remove the spoil from around an object, but underwater it was different. You could remove it, but currents would shift it back in days. He put the measure away, picked up the camera, and headed back up his line to the surface.

"Did you get pictures?" Carlo shouted to him.

He gave him the thumbs up and kicked towards Lanesra. They crowded around him as he switched on the camera and looked at the LCD screen. The pictures had come out well.

"Incredible — so clear. The carving is exquisite. This looks a high status object. It could have belonged to the Doge himself. Did you measure?"

"Yes," he said, giving Carlo the measurements.

"I'll get back to the university. They were contacting the salvage team to see how soon they can come." He went back inside the control room.

Gideon sat down and pulled off his fins while Captain Cazzano helped Gianfranco prepare for another dive. Gideon watched him jump from the boat. He looked at his watch. It was just gone two. He felt hungry. He wondered if Penny and Venetia were having their picnic on Torcello. He left Cazzano at the line, and stepped into the galley in search of food. He found ham, cheese and bread. He made himself a couple of sandwiches, which he devoured and washed down with a can of coke.

Carlo came in. "I thought I'd find you here. They can come out on Thursday. Can you stay overnight on Wednesday so we can get a full day in? The salvage ship is not cheap, and if we can do it in a day, so much the better."

"No problem, I'll let Penny know tonight."

Gideon and Gianfranco did one more dive each, and succeeded in excavating the chest to a depth of a metre. They changed back into their clothes and sat chatting as they waited for the launch to take them back to Venice. The sun was beginning to set when they saw the launch heading towards them. Carlo said he would sleep on board tonight.

"Frightened someone will steal our treasure?" Gideon joked.

"No no, it's as easy for me to sleep here as at home. I have no one waiting for me. And anyway I can keep Federico company." He put his arm around Cazzano. "He has to stay."

The launch came alongside. Penny and Venetia were out on deck and Gideon climbed down to join them followed by Gianfranco. He introduced his diving companion to them and they all went to sit in the cabin. As Venetia sat, Gideon noticed a blue backpack in the exact same pattern as her suitcase.

"What's that, Ven?" he said.

"It's for school," she said, and pulled a glass fish out. "And this is my mascot."

"It's pretty. What a lovely blue. I think he'll be a lucky fish. Did you see him being made?"

"No," Penny said. "We saw a fabulous glass vase being made, would have cost hundreds to buy"

"Let's have a look at your bag," Gideon said. "Has it got compartments?"

"No, daddy."

Gianfranco asked to look at the fish. "Bello," he said, smiling at Venetia. He held the fish up to his eyes. "Que azzuro! What blue!"

"Look there's a secret compartment," Gideon said. "Did you see it's got Velcro fastening?" He undid it. There was a label inside saying made in China. "Suprise, suprise, it's made in same place as your suitcase." He asked Gianfranco for the fish. "I'm putting the fish in the secret place. See if you can find him." He handed the bag back. "Where did you buy it?"

"Venetia saw it in a gift shop in Murano. Should have guessed it was made in China. At least the fish was made here."

"So how was your day?" Gideon asked.

"What about you? I can tell you've found something. You look chuffed."

"You first, I'll tell you all about it later."

"We had a lovely time didn't we, Ven?"

Venetia fidgeted on the seat as she started to tell them about the day. "We saw the day of judgement," she opened her eyes wide. "And skulls with worms coming out of their eyes!"

Gideon raised an eyebrow. "Lovely! What have you been showing her?"

"You remember, Gid – it's in the cathedral – fabulous mosaic."

"Of course."

"That American priest was there, the one from the restaurant."

"We went to Murano, Daddy. And saw men making glass, and a huge furnace, and lots of chandeliers and lots of mirrors. Mummy said mirrors were magic in the old days and were forbidden. They thought the devil watched the world from the other side of glass mirrors. Ladies had to use special water bowls instead of mirrors."

"Mummy knows all there is to know about glass. She is, what we call, a clever clogs." He gave Penny a peck on the cheek. "Dr Goss," he said. He was as proud of her PhD, as she was.

Francesco steered the boat in to Fondamente Nove, and Gianfranco got up to leave. "Ciao," he said. And in faltering English, "Pleased to meet you."

"And you," Penny said. "Ciao."

"A domani," Gideon said.

Francesco pulled away from the fondamenta.

"So what about your day?" Penny said.

Gideon smiled. "Fantastic. We've found a large wooden chest with a carving of the winged lion. We're hoping to bring it up on Thursday. I'll have to stay out on Lanesra Wednesday night."

"Are there beds?" Venetia said. "Can we stay too?"

"No darling – divers only."

Venetia felt the lining of the bag and detected a lump. She peered in, pulled the Velcro apart and got out her fish. "Found it, Daddy. He's coming to school with me. I'll keep him in the secret place."

When they reached the Campo Arsenale it was dark. The street lamps were on and spotlights shone on the statues.

"Nice to be home," Gideon said.

He opened the cabin door to speak to Francesco. Penny and Venetia stood behind him as he explained they would be taking Venetia to school tomorrow. Francesco listened, and seemed to understand Gideon's Italian. He replied and Gideon nodded, saying, "Si, va bene."

"He'll pick us up at nine. We'll eat out shall we? It's been a long day, save cooking and washing up."

Two hours later, they entered the restaurant in the Campo. The smell of pasta and fish made them feel hungry. It was busy, and they waited by the bar listening to the hum of conversation and laughter until the waitress arrived. She recognised them with a smile and took them to a table for four. She passed them three menus and removed the fourth place setting.

"I'm famished," Gideon said. "After a day under the sea, I know just what I'm going to have."

"What, Daddy?"

"*Polpo con patate,*" he said reading from the menu, "and *fegato alla Veneziana* to follow, and tiramisu, if I've room."

"Hmmmm," Penny sighed.

"What's *polpo*, and what's *fegato?*" Venetia asked, scanning the menu."

"*Polpo* is octopus. I saw one this afternoon. *Fegato* is calves' liver. It's served with onions, and white wine, and polenta." Gideon smacked his lips. Diving always made him hungry. "Do you want to try octopus?"

"Yuck," Venetia said. "Too many legs.

"You like scampi. Why don't you have gnocchi with scampi, Ven? That's what I'm having and then we could all have the *fegato*."

Venetia nodded, but continued to read the menu. The waitress returned and asked if they were ready.

"So we're decided?" Gideon said.

Penny and Venetia nodded. Gideon ordered the scampi, his octopus, and the *fegato*. He asked for half a litre of white and half a litre of the house red wine, and a coke. The waitress took their menus and disappeared to the kitchen.

"You're going to town – red and white?" Penny said.

"White with the fish and red to go with the liver," Gideon said, licking his lips.

As they chatted, Venetia noticed the priest they'd seen earlier sitting alone at a corner table. He was eating a plate of spaghetti covered in a red sauce with chunks of fish in it. His napkin was tucked into his dog collar. He had a book open by his plate. She nudged her mummy and nodded towards the man.

"Don't stare, Ven. It's rude," Penny said.

"He must live around here," Gideon said. "I wonder what he does."

They ate their food with relish. Venetia tried some of Gideon's octopus, and pronounced it rubbery. When they'd finished the *fegato,* Gideon asked if anyone fancied dessert. He said he had room. When the waitress came back he ordered three tiramisu. As they waited for the pudding, Penny saw the American priest get up. She smiled at him and he came over.

"Hi," he said, "enjoying your dinner?"

"Very much," Gideon and Penny said together.

"Let me introduce myself: Pat Rice. I'm living near San Zaccaria. I mosey over here every evening."

"I'm Gideon, and this is Penny, and this is Venetia."

"Ah Venetia named after Venice. Well, Torcello. You should have gone, Gideon — great cathedral."

"I had to work, but I've been before. Will you join us?"

"Thank you, yes," he pulled out the fourth chair and sat. "May I ask what your work is?"

"We're archaeologists. We're working on San Lazzaretto Nuovo. I'm a marine archaeologist. We think there's a lot underwater around the island. We found an interesting carving today. Penny starts excavating on the island itself tomorrow, and Venetia starts school – big day for us all!"

"How interesting, I'm on sabbatical from St Joseph's in Baltimore. I'm something of an art historian. I'm particularly interested in depictions of the day of judgement. I have the use of a flat in return for taking specialist art tours. It gives me plenty of time for my research."

"What did you think of the day of judgement in the cathedral?" Penny asked.

"Fabulous – I still have it in my mind," he closed his eyes as he described the picture. "Starting at the top there was Christ on the cross, between the Virgin and Saint John, and below the descent into hell, and the dead rising from their graves. Over the doorway the Archangel Michael weighs the souls on his scales, while the devil stands taking the souls that belong to him, and putting them into a sack. On the right, two angels throw sinners into a river of fire, as the tortures of hell are prepared for the damned, and on the bottom Christ gathers the children around him, and St Peter waits at the gates of heaven. And over the door, the Virgin blessing us."

The waitress appeared with the three tiramisu. "Ah Rosa, un cognac per me per favore." He turned to the Mantells. "Can I get you a degestif, another coke?"

Gideon was tempted, but knew with the dive he should not. "Not for me, thanks."

"Me neither," Penny said.

"And what about you, little one?"

Venetia nodded. "Yes please."

"E una coca cola, grazie," he said. "I've quite exhausted myself with the recollection, such a powerful image, and in those days so terrifying."

"Mummy says the devil doesn't exist."

Penny looked embarrassed.

"Oh, I know not many people believe in him these days," the priest said good humouredly.

"Do you believe in him?" Gideon asked.

"Yes I do. Not a subject for now. You know the name of the bridge across the way going into the Institute of Naval Studies is Ponte di Purgatorio. I walk by it every day." He winked at them. "How's the tiramisu?"

"Excellent," Penny said relieved the subject was moving on.

Pat Rice's cognac and Venetia's coke arrived. He raised his glass. "Here's to tomorrow."

They talked a little more, and the priest got up to go. "By the way, another excellent judgement is in the Hellenic Institute, next to San Giorgio dei Greci, with its leaning campanile — well worth a visit." He smiled at them. "Nice to meet you."

"And you, goodbye," Gideon said, watching the priest leave. "Interesting man," he said to Penny.

"Yes. I can just see him on Mastermind: *and my chosen subject is... The Day of Judgement.*"

Gideon chuckled and called for the bill.

8

Scuola

Gideon opened the shutters to let the light in and saw Venetia was still in a heavy sleep. He bent over and kissed her head, giving her shoulder a gentle nudge. He'd loved her smell since the day she'd been born. It was a warm sweet smell. "Morning Ven." he said, "Time to get up."

She opened her eyes. Her daddy was looking down at her smiling. She'd been dreaming about the stone forest beneath the ground. She had been looking for Lucy's house. For some reason she thought she lived there. She remembered what day it was, and there was the familiar dread in the pit of her stomach. It had been growing every day, and now it was strong. The horrible day was finally here. If only Lucy was coming as well. They could have stuck together, and she wouldn't be the only English girl. But she would take her glass fish. She felt under her pillow for him. She would hold him in her hand, and he would keep her safe. She still felt sleepy; she wished she could shut the day out a little longer. "Can't I have a few more minutes Daddy? I want to finish my dream."

Gideon pulled the bedclothes off. "No you must get up now, and get dressed. We've got to pack your bag and have our breakfast. I'll be back in ten minutes. If you're not ready..." he left, leaving the threat hanging in the air.

Venetia got out of bed and ran the taps in her bathroom. Was there any way out of this? She wondered about pretending to be ill, but knew her mummy would know what the real reason was, and she could tell by her daddy's voice there was no avoiding the day. She splashed water on her face and looked in the mirror. Her golden hair was all tangled from sleep. She brushed it, counting the strokes and went to the bedroom to put on the clothes her mummy had laid out. She was ready before Gideon returned. She didn't like it when her daddy was cross.

They breakfasted together. Venetia started her cornflakes, but today they were soggy and stale and tasted of cardboard. She left half of them in the bowl. Penny asked if she would like some toast instead. She shook her head. All she could feel was the dread; she couldn't eat.

"Get your new bag and we'll pack it," Penny said.

Venetia fetched the blue backpack and returned. Penny put in an apple, a banana, strawberry yoghurt, and a Kitkat. She showed Venetia a white plastic spoon saying, "For the yoghurt." She put the spoon in. She also put in a box of crayons, a packet of pencils and a notepad, and said, "I'm putting in the Italian phrase book. You know how to use it don't you?"

"Yes Mummy."

"Now have we forgotten anything? Did you want to take your fish?"

"Yes, I'll get him." She retrieved the fish from her bed and brought him back. She slipped him into the secret compartment.

"Are we ready?" Gideon said. "I'll get the coats."

He helped Venetia on with her duffle coat and did up the toggles. She picked up the backpack and slipped one arm through its handle and then the other so that it was securely on her back.

"What a sad little figure," he said. "Come on, cheer up. It's not the end of the world. You're going to meet lots of new friends and learn lots of new things. I wish I was going."

She looked up at him and gave him her hand. She didn't want to meet any new friends. She just wanted to stay at home, but she couldn't.

It was another bright autumn day. They walked across the campo to the bridge with the name they remembered: *del l'Arsenal o del Paradiso*. Venetia ran over to the big lion.

"Where are you going?" Gideon said. "No time for that."

She ignored him, and climbing onto the pedestal, putting her arms around the stone lion. "Protect me Aslan," she said, and ran back to her parents. They crossed the wooden bridge and walked along the fondamenta.

"We better take the short cut," Penny said, and they turned left down Campo della Tana, past the empty ticket booths for the Biennale and crossed over another canal. Gideon knew they had to turn right when they saw the communist party sign *Rifondazione Comunista SEZ 7 M Martiri.* At the end of Corte Nova they came to via Garabaldi and spotted children with satchels and school bags. At the school gate Gideon kissed Venetia goodbye. "Don't worry, it'll go in a flash, and before you know it Mummy will be back to pick you up."

Venetia looked up at the dreaded door. There was a bronze carving of a lion above, with his paw on an open book. It gave her a moment of comfort as she felt her mummy take her hand and lead her in. The room was full of children, chattering together. She couldn't understand a word they were saying. There was a woman with long blonde hair standing in the middle of the children. Her mummy took her over to the teacher. Venetia wished she could get out of this room, escape and run back home.

Penny introduced herself."Buon giorno Signora," she said, "Sono la Signora Mantell e questa é mia figlia Venetia."

"Piacere, sono Alessandra Querini, lei parla Italiano?"

"Only un po, do you speak English?"

"Yes I do," the teacher said and smiled at Venetia. "And what about you Venetia? Do you speak Italian?"

Venetia looked down at the ground and said, "No, I've only been here a week."

"We'll soon have you talking like a Venetian. We have put you in Year 1 with the beginners. The lessons will be easy. It will give you a chance to catch up with the language. Shall I take her?" she said reaching out her hand.

Venetia felt her mummy let go of her hand and the teacher took it.

"We'll go and hang your coat up and I'll show you your classroom, and you can meet the class. They have been looking forward to meeting you. You come back at three, Signora Mantell. Venetia will be fine. Say ciao to Mamma."

Venetia looked up at her mummy. She didn't want her to go, but she didn't want to say anything in front of the teacher, and she could see the other children's eyes were already on her. I will not cry, she said to herself. "Ciao mummy," she said in a quiet voice.

"Goodbye darling. I'll pick you up at three."

******

Penny turned and left. She didn't look back. Gideon was standing in the middle of the street waiting. Behind him on a bench across the way she saw an old woman dressed in black. Her head, too, was covered in a black headscarf. She was just like the old women in the Italian films she and Gideon had watched when they'd been trying to learn Italian. Penny didn't think they still dressed like that, but apparently in this part of Venice some did. The woman had two Coop shopping bags at her feet. Penny probably wouldn't have noticed her, but she seemed to be mumbling something to herself and most curious of all, staring straight at Gideon.

"Everything alright?" he asked.

"Yes the teacher seems nice. Don't look now, but there's a strange woman looking at you and talking to herself."

"Where?" said Gideon turning.

"I said don't look."

Gideon glimpsed the woman, who looked down at her bags. "I see," he said. "Probably spotted I'm English."

"Maybe she fancies you?" Penny whispered. "Watch out, she's getting up."

"Well she's only human," Gideon said as the woman picked up her bags and walked away down the street.

Penny laughed. The two of them returned to the flat, got what they needed for the day, and went to wait for Francesco.

The boat arrived, and soon they were out of the canal and speeding past eastern Venice on their way to Lazzaretto Nuovo.

"What a commute!" Gideon said lounging back on the white leather.

Twenty minutes later, the motorboat slowed and came up beside the wooden pilings on the dock. Carlo was waiting. He hailed them as they came out of the cabin.

"Benvenuta," he said when Penny stepped onto the land. "Everything OK? Venetia got to school?"

"Yes fine. I can't help worrying about her, but she'll settle in."

"See you this evening," Gideon called to Penny from the boat, "Home about six I should think. Are you coming out to Lanesra, Carlo?"

"I'll be out later."

Penny and Carlo watched the motorboat, accelerate away, leaving a trail of churned white water.

"I'm itching to get going," Penny said. "What's been found?"

"I'll show you. They found something late yesterday near a pit full of plague victims. It was just outside the walls, on the other side of the island. It was buried separately: the body of a woman with a brick in her mouth."

"My God," Penny said, "Why would someone be buried like that?"

They passed through a solid arched wooden doorway, and entered the grassy compound. A line of mulberry trees marked the way to the tezon, in which the cargos had been stored for fumigation and quarantine. It was a vast building some one hundred metres long, and the only one left intact on the island. Its open arches had been bricked in during the Austrian reign of Venice.

They entered the enormous space. Great thick brick columns about ten feet apart held up the ceiling. It was cathedral-like in its shape and size, but without windows. On the walls, the merchants' ochre painted logos still remained. Three archaeologists dressed in blue overalls were working over a table cleaning artefacts with water.

Carlo introduced them. "Questa é Penny, Cinzia, Bruno, Gina."

"Ciao," Penny said. They went to another table, where the body lay. It had been covered in a white sheet. Carlo pulled up the sheet to reveal the skeleton underneath. The brick stuck out of the skull's mouth. Penny shivered. There was something truly horrible about it.

Cinzia said, "During plague, Venice live in fear. Logic, how you say, went out window? We think they believe she was vampire. They think vampires spreading plague. They put brick in mouth to stop her biting."

"I wish we could take it from the poor creature's mouth," Penny said.

"No, no – is very important," Cinzia said.

Carlo said, "They did not understand decomposition. After death, the body releases a mass of bacterial gases. The decay of the gastrointestinal tract creates a dark fluid, which can flow freely through the nose and mouth. It could easily be confused with blood. They thought this woman was rising from her grave. The stone was jammed into her mouth as a kind of exorcism."

"Is that why she was buried separately?" Penny asked.

"Possibly. They may have thought she would feed off the corpses. It's all theory. Anyway, let's leave these good people to their work. We're beginning a trench outside where we think the lay prior lived. He ran Lazzaretto together with the plague doctor."

They walked across a grassy field. Carlo pointed at an old well. "Look, it has the traditional carving of the lion of St Mark with its paw on the book, but the book is closed, so there's no *pax tibi marce*. It's very rare."

******

Venetia sat in class holding the blue glass fish in her hand while listening to the teacher reading. She did not understand completely, but some words were familiar and she liked the sound of Italian. Her mind drifted back over the morning. It hadn't been too bad; the first class had been maths, and she'd done well. Venetia liked adding and subtracting and had got all her sums right. Then they had some geography and had learnt the names of countries, and their capitals. Now they were doing reading and writing. She'd copied words from the board into her exercise book. Venetia had done it as neatly as she could.

The teacher shut the book with a snap of the covers, signifying they'd come to the end. She said, "Pranzo." The children stood up and started to leave the classroom. Venetia picked up her bag, and slipped the glass fish into the secret compartment. She realised the other children had gone. She didn't know where to go. She looked at the teacher.

"We have a break now for lunch and a rest. Sophia is going to take you to the canteen. Her grandfather knows you, I think?"

"No Signora, he knows Carlo."

"Ah I see, a friend of a friend. She'll be here in a minute. Guess what lesson we have this afternoon?"

Venetia thought for a moment. "Science?"

"No, no science until Year 2. It is English. You will be the star pupil."

A girl appeared at the door. She was a little bigger than Venetia. She was wearing jeans and a black sweatshirt with a picture of Tintin and snowy on the front. She had jet black hair held back by a red Alice band.

"Ah, Sophia, there you are, here is Venetia."

"Ciao, we go lunch," Sophia said with a thick Italian accent. She took Venetia's hand and gave it a tug. "Andiamo."

They left the classroom. Venetia was worried. She hadn't been alone with the other children until now. Sophia had a firm grip on her hand, pulling her along. Venetia wondered about the food her mummy had packed. Should she say anything about it? They entered a dining room and joined a queue. Sophia let go her hand and passed her a plate. "Piatto," she said as if talking to a three year old. When they got to the front, a large jolly woman plonked a portion of lasagne on Sophia's plate. Venetia held out her plate and received a similar dollop. The woman gave them each some greens, saying, "Va bene?"

Sophia ignored her. They joined a group of Sophia's friends. Sophia didn't bother to introduce Venetia. Venetia ate her lasagne and listened to the gabble of the other children. She felt quite alone and wished she could join in but she couldn't. She didn't have the words. Venetia noticed other children getting snacks out of their bags. She got her yoghurt out and rummaged around for the plastic spoon. Sophia snatched the bag from her, pointed at the flowers and said something to her friends. They laughed. Sophia produced the spoon and the Kitkat. She gave Venetia the spoon, unwrapped the chocolate and broke it into four bits, kept one and passed the other pieces to her friends. She took a bite of the chocolate. "Squisita," she said to Venetia, and popped the rest into her mouth. Sophia handed the bag back to Venetia.

Venetia put it on the floor and ate her yoghurt, pretending she didn't care. She thought about getting out the phrase book and looking up 'you are welcome' or some other phrase she'd heard her daddy use. Venetia just wanted the break to be over. It was safer in the classroom. She wanted to get her glass fish out of the secret pocket, and hold it again, but didn't dare let Sophia see.

Sophia and the other girls got up.

"A doppo," was all Sophia said.

Venetia smiled weakly at her, picked up her bag and stood, wondering if she was supposed to follow. Not wanting to be left, she followed the girls into the playground. Sophia pushed Venetia away in the direction of her younger classmates who were playing a game. It was very noisy. Venetia stood on the edge, holding her bag. They did not ask her to join in. Venetia stood for what seemed hours alone. She pretended to be watching the game, but all she could think about was home. No one likes me, she thought. The sadness filled her, and she swallowed hard, trying not to cry, and finally the bell rang for class to begin. She wiped her eyes and followed the children in.

******

Penny was on her hands and knees in the trench scraping away at the earth with a trowel. A student next to her was sieving earth. Penny thought of all the people quarantined on the island: the sailors, the merchants and the pilgrims coming back from Jerusalem. It must have been hard, having been away so long, to wait here with Venice so near. Any sign of disease, and the plague doctor shipped you off to Lazzaretto Vechio to die.

They'd found a substantial amount of pottery during the morning. Penny had used her trusty jeweller's glass and identified it as 15th century. There had clearly been much activity here, but they weren't sure whether they were inside or outside a building. A student brought her something. She got her glass out to study it.

"It looks like a floor tile. We may well be on the inside." Penny gave it back, and looked at her watch. Time had flown. It was almost two. She had been so absorbed in her work she hadn't given Venetia a thought. Now Penny wondered how her daughter was coping. She knew Venetia was pretty self-reliant. Penny carried on working for another twenty minutes, and then explaining she had to go to collect her daughter, gave the students instructions.

"I think we might open another trench up over there tomorrow," she said, pointing at a spot where she thought they might find the wall of the building.

She hurried off to the dock. Francesco was there by the boat on his mobile. He waved as he saw her approach. She got in. It was almost 2:45. She looked anxiously at Francesco, who was having an animated conversation. He terminated the call, untied the boat from the pilings, and jumped in.

"Via Garabaldi, si?" he said, starting the engine and spinning the wheel around in his usual fashion. Twenty minutes later he dropped her on the Ria Schiavoni at the entrance to the Via Garabaldi. Penny ran down the street towards the school. She could see other children with their parents walking home. "Damn," she whispered when she saw Venetia standing alone, holding Signora Querini's hand, the last child to be collected. She hurried to them.

"I'm sorry I'm late, darling." She bent down and kissed her daughter. "Did you have a good day?" She turned to the teacher. "So sorry, I got held up. Everything alright?"

"Yes, Mrs Mantell, she has done very well, and she has a new friend, Sophia."

"That's good. We better let you get on, thanks, arrivaderci."

"Why were you late Mummy?" Venetia said quietly, taking her mummy's hand.

"The boat was late. Shall we buy a pastry for tea?"

Venetia nodded. They went into Pasticceria Majer. Venetia chose a cream horn. Penny thought for a second. She shouldn't really but she had been digging and scraping all day. She deserved a treat.

"Due, per favore," she said.

They left the shop, and turned into the Calle Nuova to take the short cut home.

"Wow, washing day," Penny said, "What a sight."

The two of them stopped to look; hanging from every upper window, suspended from one side of the street to the other, were row upon row of washing lines. They were hung with sheets, shirts, socks, sweaters, pants and knickers of every colour.

"I wish I had my camera," Penny said laughing. "What festoons of colour."

"Festoons," Venetia repeated, laughing too. When they got over the bridge, she ran over to the old stone lion and embraced him.

Penny continued on to the door and unlocked, waiting for Venetia. "You are funny with that lion," she said as Venetia came skipping up.

"He's my protector. He's like Aslan."

80

"Come on, let's go and get the kettle on."

Neither of them noticed the woman in black on the other side of the canal. She watched as the front door shut, turned, and made her way back towards the Via Garabaldi.

Over tea Venetia told her mummy about the lessons. She told her how she'd read to the class in the English lesson. She told her about all the sums she'd got right.

"And did Sophia introduce herself?"

Venetia nodded. "I don't think she wanted to. She's older, and she's got lots of friends."

"Don't be silly. I'm sure she was pleased to. What about lunch? Did you eat everything?"

"We couldn't choose. We had lasagne and a vegetable like cabbage." Venetia made a face. "I had the yoghurt for pudding."

Penny unpacked Venetia's bag. "I see you've eaten the Kitkat, but not the fruit."

Venetia nodded.

At six, Gideon returned. He asked Venetia about her day, and about Sophia. "Gianfranco was quite impressed when I said Sophia Barbarigo was looking out for you. He told me all about her family. One of her ancestors was a Doge and one was a Cardinal."

"Oh, Ven, mixing with the aristocracy," Penny said. "Unfortunately, I don't think you like her do you?"

"She's a bit snotty," Venetia said, "and she can't speak English, so I don't know what she's talking about."

"Don't worry, Ven, you'll soon get the hang of the language. And who wouldn't want to be friends with a clever girl like you?"

They had a quiet evening in. After Venetia had gone to bed, Penny told Gideon about the corpse with the brick in its mouth.

"How extraordinary," Gideon said. "I hope the press don't get hold of it. I can see the headlines, 'Medieval Vampire Found!' We'll be overrun with teenagers."

He stood and looked over the lamp lit campo. A crescent moon hung in the starry night sky over the walls of the Arsenale.

"Children of the night," he said doing an impersonation of Bella Lugosi. "I am hungry for blood." He turned and, stroking Penny's hair, leaned over her and pressed his lips to her neck, letting his teeth touch her skin. He picked her up off the chair and carried her into the bedroom and shut the door. "Come join the undead," he said. "Let me feast on your blood." He gave a maniacal laugh as he laid her on the bed.

Penny said softly, "You are a fool, but you're my fool."

They made love in the moonlit room, and fell into a deep sleep. At midnight the mother of all bells, the Marangona of St Marks campanile, rang out over the city. Then all was quiet except for the sound of water lapping against the sides of the canal, and the echo of footsteps walking away from the campo.

9

Faustina

It was 1am when Faustina returned from her walk. She had stood in Campo Arsenale and heard the great bell ring out the end of the day, and what a day, a miracle: the girl had been shown to her. Faustina had been alerted by the blue satchel with yellow flowers, just like in her dream. Her eyes had been drawn to it as she'd sat on the bench watching the children going into school. It was on the back of a little girl with beautiful blonde hair. And then the girl had turned to look up at her father, and Faustina had seen the absolute innocence in her face. There was something about this girl, something different. The moment Faustina had seen her face she knew. It was as if a distant memory had surfaced. It was as if she had known this girl all her life.

The face had filled her mind. She had begun to shake. She'd been terrified people would notice, but when she'd looked down, her hands were still. The trembling was all inside her. The dream had been a message from another world. A sign, so she would see the yellow flowers. The man she prayed for had chosen this girl to carry on the prayers. She was the one he wanted.

Faustina had gone back to the school in the afternoon, waited outside and watched as one by one the children were collected, until only the girl was left, standing alone with the teacher. She saw her looking forlorn, and almost stepped forward to take her, but her mother appeared, running down the street. Faustina disliked her on sight. She could tell she was not worthy to be a mother. The red hand bag told Faustina everything she needed to know. Soon Faustina would replace this woman and be mother to the girl.

She followed them to the Campo Arsenale, and saw them enter the house across the square. She heard them talking. It was not Italian. It didn't matter. Latin was the language of prayers.

Even now, Faustina could not sleep. She was full of plans; she busied herself preparing her old room. She made up the little iron bed with the new pink nylon sheets she'd bought earlier. She dusted the picture of the Madonna and child above the bed, remembering the comfort it had brought her. She polished the desk at which the girl would sit. She swept the bare wooden floor, and checked the lock on the door still worked. The memories of her childhood flooded back. Almost all of it had been spent in this little room. It was right another child should come and live here. She sat down at the desk, set against the bare white wall, and looked up at the brown leather scourge hanging from the hook. It had been kept there as a reminder to do her work.

She opened the drawer and got the copy her mother had made. The thirty three pages were tied with blue silk ribbon, the same blue as the girl's bag, the blue of heaven and eternity. She untied it, and looked at the first page. She hadn't done this for years. The blue ink had not faded. Her mother's big bold clear handwriting, and all the familiar words were still there. What a journey the girl had before her. There would be tears of pain and joy. Her mother had given her one page at a time. When she'd learnt it and could recite it, the next page would come, and she would learn that, and so on, until after many years she could recite all thirty three pages.

She rolled up the sleeves of her blouse and placed her arms on the desk. She looked at the burns. When her mother had been very cross, and a beating with the scourge wasn't enough, she'd heated a knife on the camper stove and placed it against Faustina's skin.

84

As if some ancient switch had been turned on, Faustina stood and, whispering and mumbling prayers, went into the kitchen. "Deus meus, ex toto corde poenitet me omnium meorum peccatorum, eaque detestor, quia peccando..."

She got the knife out of the draw, turned on the gas, and held the blade over the flame. When it was hot enough, she took it, and held it against her left forearm. The pain was exquisite. She closed her eyes counting, as her mother had done, to thirty. The pain swept through her body, but she didn't cry out. At thirty she took the knife away and sighed with relief. The holy angel of pain must always be overcome. She rolled down the sleeves of her blouse. The pain slowly subsided. It was done for another day.

She sat at the kitchen table, talking. She needed a plan to get the girl away. She would watch every day and see what could be done. She would sit on the bench outside the school, mornings and afternoons. She would see the girl come and go. She need not hurry, the time would come, and she would be ready. Hours, days, years meant nothing to her; they slid away one after another. Her work was with another world.

Faustina felt tired. Now she would sleep. She lay on the bed, not bothering to take her clothes off and fell into a heavy dreamless sleep. Occasionally her snore woke her, and she would look to see if it was still dark. At six thirty Faustina woke, and saw the early morning light. She went into the kitchen and made some porridge. She liked it. It was cheap, it was filling, and it did not take long to make or to eat.

She went to the end room that had been converted into a chapel. It was time for the first of the three services. Faustina crossed herself, knelt before the altar and put her hands on the coffin and could feel his presence. "Grazie per la bambina," she whispered, and began to recite: "Deus, cuius Unigeniti per vitam, mortem et resurrectionem suam nobis salutis aeternae praemia comparavit, concede, quaesumus." Faustina stood, bowed, and lit the candles at the altar. She knelt and again put her hands on the lid of the coffin. Her fingers rested between the letters of the words TIBI MARCE. She began to chant as she had been taught.

Thirty minutes later, it was done. Faustina stood, crossed herself, turned and left the chapel. Her mother would be pleased. Even more so when the chosen girl began learning the prayers. She tied her headscarf on, and left the apartment.

In the streets, the handful of Venetians of working age in the district were going to their jobs. One of the men said, "Buon Giorno, Signora," to her. She mumbled the greeting back. She would have to bring the girl back at night, when the neighbours were asleep. Faustina knew from her night ramblings that after dark San Pietro was the quietest place in Venice. So many people had left and gone to live on the mainland. In the old days, when her mother was alive, there had been other people living in the flats. Now their building was empty, save for Faustina.

She walked with the workers making their way into Venice for the start of the day. In the past, there would have been hundreds. Now no more than seven crossed the bridge. She walked along the side of the Rio Santa Anna. The streets got busier as she got closer to the Via Garabaldi. She saw children walking to school with their parents.

Faustina sat down at the bench in front of the school gates. She didn't have long to wait. She saw the blue satchel and the golden hair. The mother and father were with her. They said goodbye at the gate. She saw them kiss the girl, and turn her towards the school. Her father bent down, and whispered something in her ear. The girl walked slowly into the school. She didn't look back.

10

<u>The Chest</u>

Gideon woke to the sound of screeching gulls. It had just gone seven, but he decided to let Penny sleep a little longer since she always seemed to need more than him. He shaved, did his teeth, and packed his sponge bag for the overnight stay. He wouldn't bother with a change of clothes. He'd be in his diving gear most of the time. Returning to the still dark room, he opened the shutters and looked out. A rubbish boat was tied up alongside the canal. A man in green overalls and thick suede gauntlets trundled a steel trolley off down an alley collecting rubbish.

He heard Penny stirring. "Morning love," he said. "Sleep well?"

"Hmmm," she said stretching and, getting out of bed, padded into the bathroom. Gideon heard Penny start showering, and went to wake Venetia. She was asleep with the little blue glass fish lying in her hand. He kissed his daughter before waking her.

They breakfasted, and walked Venetia to school. The old woman in the black headscarf was on the bench. She was feeding some pigeons with bread she had in a brown paper bag. Gideon thought she must spend a lot of time just sitting on the bench watching. As if he'd somehow glimpsed into her life, he felt a sudden wave of pity for her. There was something awfully lonely about her, but there was nothing he could do, and his mind moved on. He bent down and kissed Venetia goodbye.

"See you tomorrow darling, be good."

Penny ruffled her daughter's hair. "And Mummy will see you at three."

Venetia joined the other children walking through the school gate. Penny and Gideon turned back down Via Garabaldi.

Francesco picked them up at eight thirty. Gianfranco and Carlo were sitting in the cabin.

"I had a call yesterday evening," Carlo said as soon as they sat down. "After you left, another body was found in a grave. It's a young girl. She was weighted down with chains. Another thought to be a vampire. Dio, what were they thinking."

"Weird," Gideon said. "Both girls?"

"Yes, the woman with the brick was between sixteen and twenty. This girl, by the size of the skeleton, can't be more than twelve. It's very strange."

"Where was she found?"

"Not more than ten metres from the other body. Something odd was happening on that island. Did I tell you the TV are coming out, a cameraman and a journalist? We're expecting them at ten. I'll be with them most of the morning."

Francesco slowed the motorboat as they came up alongside the pilings on the dock. Gideon kissed Penny goodbye.

"See you tomorrow, love."

She kissed him. "Hope it goes well."

Carlo, already off, gave her his hand and helped her off the boat. He shouted down at the others. "I'll join you this evening. I'll bring some food and cook."

"A doppo," Gianfranco said.

Gideon and Gianfranco stayed on deck either side of Francesco. It was a clear bright day with a chill breeze blowing across the water. The snow-capped mountains surrounded Venice like a crown. The bracing air off the Dolomites blew straight in their faces, as they motored across the sea. Gianfranco said he would dive first today. Five minutes later, Francesco pulled the motorboat up alongside Lanesra.

They spent the day excavating around the chest, where the harness strops would go. In the late afternoon, they swam down with the harness and strops. They swam over the chest, working out how best to tackle it. Working in unison and signalling to each other, they passed the strops under the chest and connected them to the harness. Finally, they covered the area in terran, a black plastic material, to protect it from the shifting sands.

Cazzano helped them back on board. It had been a good day's work. On the western horizon, a large red sun was almost touching the waves. It would soon be dark. As the sun's rim dipped, they heard the sound of a motorboat and saw Carlo standing by Francesco with two shopping bags. He raised them and shouted, "Spaghetti alla vongole, va bene?"

"Molto bene!" Cazzano shouted back.

"What news?" Gideon asked, as Carlo came on board.

"Penny is uncovering more of the building," he said as they walked to the galley. "The journalists came and interviewed me. They kept trying to put words into my mouth about the vampire. Ridiculous. It's on tonight— glad I won't see it." He put the bags on the counter in galley. "They wanted to interview Penny, especially when I said she was English. I heard him describing her as the beautiful archaeologist from Brighton."

"Hope it doesn't go to her head," Gideon said.

"All publicity is good publicity," Carlo put his arm around Gideon, "and the university needs all the money it can get." He released Gideon, and started to pull ingredients out of his shopping bags. "Now leave me to cook."

Gideon and Gianfranco left to change out of their wet suits. Cazzano climbed up to the room behind the wheelhouse. It had once been a lounge bar, but now had a table and chairs for sit down meals. He put four plates out, cutlery and wine glasses. Lanesra had been a rich man's yacht back in the sixties. He'd entertained Gina Lollobrigida, Carlo Ponti, Vittoria de Sica, and even Sophia Loren during the film festival. The glamour was long gone and Lanesra was now nothing but functional. After years, lying unused in dry dock, she had been put up for sale. No one had wanted her, and in 2001, Carlo had persuaded the archaeology department to put in an offer. They had bought Lanesra at a knock down price, and converted the motor yacht for use as their dive base.

Carlo came up to the dining room with a huge metal pot full of spaghetti and clams. He sent Cazzano down to get bread and wine, and shouted down to the others that dinner was ready. They talked into the night. Although Gideon missed Penny and Venetia, it was good to be in the company of men and talk shop. Carlo explained the process of freeze drying. It was Carlo again who, with his enthusiasm and force of personality, had persuaded the department to buy an archaeological freeze-dryer. He told them it was cheaper and more effective than submersion in polyethylene glycol. It was quicker too; it would take a month for the chest to be dried.

"Freeze-drying is better for the wood," he said through a mouthful of spaghetti, "less possibility for chemical reactions. Polythene glycol left the wood dark and waxy."

"What about the inside?" Gideon said. "Can we see what's inside?"

90

"We could x-ray, but it would take time, and I want to get it straight into the freeze-dryer. I don't want to lift the lid until the wood is stabilised. Whatever is inside will keep. It's been there for centuries. The dryer will keep the chest at minus forty. We've found that temperature best. Whatever is inside will be quite safe."

"I'd love to be there when you lift the lid," Gideon said.

"Sure, you will all come," Carlo said waving his fork at them.

. Gianfranco asked if sonar had detected anything else.

"There are signs of remains scattered all over the area. Some quite large. It could be a ship, pulled apart over time and scattered by the currents. We won't know for sure until you get down there. You're going to have a busy time. But first things first, tomorrow we get the chest up."

Gideon didn't sleep well. The cabin was comfortable enough, but he was used to having Penny by his side. He woke at six and got up to make a coffee and get some food. It was going to be a hard day. The sun was just coming up out of the sea. He was soon joined by the others.

At eight, the salvage ship appeared on their port side. She looked like a small fishing trawler. At her stern was a large red crane. She came alongside, and three men in wet suits came aboard. Carlo introduced everyone. There were two Italians, Roberto and Andrea, and a German Franz. They explained what would happen. The salvage ship had a metal cage, which they would lower to the seabed next to the chest. They would use lifting bags to get the chest up, and into the cage. The salvage ship's crane would then hoist it up. They would be in voice communication with their ship, so there would be no need for the divers to trail lines. Once up, the cage would be secured to the hull and transported to Bacino for landing. Carlo would go with them to supervise this. The chest would be removed from the cage, submerged into a tank of fresh water, and taken by barge to the

university labs in Dorsoduro.

"To work," Andrea said. "We'll meet you under the ship in ten minutes."

The three men returned to their ship. It moved off towards the marker buoy.

Cazzano and Carlo helped Gideon and Gianfranco on with their dive tanks.

"Pronto," Carlo shouted so that they could hear on the other ship. Gideon went off

first and waited for Gianfranco to join him. They swam towards the salvage ship. When

they were near enough, they swam down underneath the hull, and there below was the

steel framed cage. The others divers held on to its sides as it was lowered to the sea bed

next to the chest.

Gideon and Gianfranco removed the terran while the salvage ship's divers got lift

bags out of the cage and secured them to the harness around the chest. One by one, the

valves of the lift bags were opened and, as they inflated the harness, rose and tightened

around the chest. They circled the chest, watching and waiting for it to rise.

Minutes past, and nothing happened. The chest did not move. It seemed the suction

of the seabed was too great. They swam down and shovelled at the sand with their hands.

There was a slight movement. Then, in a cloud of sand, it shuddered and shifted and began

to rise. The divers steered it into the cage and signalled the salvage ship.

The crane lifted the cage up towards the ship. Gideon swam with it towards the

sunlight. The light shone through the water, illuminating the cage and filling it with light.

It would have made a fantastic photo, he thought, and then they were immediately below

the salvage ship's hull and the light was gone.

He helped bolt the cage to the hull for transportation. They checked it was secure and one of the divers gave him the thumbs up. The five men surfaced.

"All OK?" Carlo said.

"Worked like clockwork," Gideon said, as he and Gianfranco climbed on board.

"You may as well get Francesco to collect you," Carlo said to them both. He was in good spirits. "Nothing left to do here today. Take the afternoon off. Why not?"

Ten minutes later, the salvage ship came alongside to get Carlo. Gideon watched the ship disappear towards Venice, and called Francesco.

11

Cristofo Worries

At the state archive, Cristofo discovered that Anzola Boldani, the last abbess at Santa Maria delle Vergini, had been buried next to her brother on the monastery island of San Francesco del Deserto. She wanted to be near him. Cristofo wondered whether she'd left any papers behind, and whether they would still be at the monastery. He'd returned home and made an appointment with the Prior to look at the grave on Friday. He'd then watched the news with increasing dread. He'd heard about the girl who'd been found with a brick in her mouth, and now another girl had been found, weighted down with chains. Both were almost certainly the work of his ancestor. He spent the night in a frenzy of activity, going through paper after paper, gone to bed, and slept fitfully.

The morning brought no respite. He wished his appointment with the Prior was sooner. Things were moving fast. In the course of a telephone conversation with a friend at the university, he'd heard of the exciting underwater find. Yesterday, his granddaughter had told him of the new girl at school, the daughter of English archaeologists. He'd seen the mother on television talking about their work on the island. Her husband was diving off the coast. It would be useful to get to know them. He knew how difficult the first weeks of a new school were. A kind word and the English girl would be Isabella's friend. He went in search of his granddaughter. He wanted to catch her before Aldo took her to school.

"Ah, Isabella, remember you told me about the English girl."

"Yes, Nonno."

"Have you spoken to her?"

"She's not in my class, she's the year below."

"I think you should. It would be nice to have an English friend. She won't have any friends yet. You could be her first. We could ask her here to play. I could make a treasure hunt. Why don't you go to her at lunchtime and say hello. I'll teach you what to say."

"OK," Isabella said.

"This is what you say, 'Hello, what's your name? My name is Isabella. Shall we be friends?' And she will tell you her name and soon you'll be talking away. I'm sure she speaks a little Italian."

Aldo came to collect Isabella and walk her to school. Cristofo kissed her goodbye. "Come up to the study and tell me all about it after school."

Isabella took Aldo's hand and they left the house. Cristofo returned to the laborious task of sifting through his family's past. His thoughts returned to the chest. Was that what they'd found underwater?

12

BancoGiro

Francesco dropped them off close to a plaque commemorating the Caboto's discovery of Newfoundland. Gideon hadn't realised they were Venetian. He took Penny's hand and helped her from the bobbing motorboat. It was the first time he'd been to collect Venetia.

"She won't be out for twenty minutes. Let's wander," Penny said.

They sauntered hand in hand down the wide street looking at the shops. It was a joy to be in a city with no cars. Venetian streets are democratic, Gideon thought, no one can drive by, flashing their wealth in your face.

They looked in the window of a glass shop. Penny pointed at the fabulous coloured sea creatures, and their fabulous prices: "Six hundred Euros!" she said, opening her blue eyes wide, and dropping her jaw in mock astonishment.

Gideon laughed, and led her away. They walked on towards the school past shops and bars. They passed the Coop supermarket, and crossed to the other side to look at the menu outside Giorgione. It reminded him of Gianfranco's invitation.

"I've said we'd meet Gianfranco and his girlfriend for dinner tonight. He wants to take us to BancoGiro by the Rialto. It sounded fun. Do you mind? His girlfriend works in a bank, a highflyer. She's been on at him to meet us."

"No, I'd like that." They arrived outside the school. The old woman in black was sitting on the bench. Penny gave Gideon's hand a squeeze.

He'd seen her. He thought he'd caught her eye. He smiled and nodded, but she looked away. They waited for Venetia. She came out, talking to another girl. They were the same height, though very different looking. Venetia, with her fair hair and complexion was very English. This girl was very Italian. She had short chestnut hair, olive skin, and large brown eyes. Venetia saw them and ran over. Gideon picked her up, gave her a big kiss, and put her down.

Penny ruffled her hair. "Have you made a friend?"

Venetia waved at the other girl, who was being met by a man in a white jacket. He looked like a waiter. She waved back and took the man's hand, and they walked away. "That's Isabella," she said.

"She looks nice. Is that her dad? He looks quite old."

"Don't think so, she said Aldo collects her. He works for her nonno and nonna."

"Her grandparents?"

"Yes, she lives with them."

Gideon noticed the old woman had gone. As they walked back to Campo Arsenale, Venetia told them about Isabella. She was different from the other children. She wasn't part of a silly gang, and she spoke a little English. "She's not in my class. She came up to me at break time, and said, 'Hello my name is Isabella. Shall we be friends?' Her nonno taught her how to say it."

"She sounds lovely," Penny said. "Maybe we can ask her to tea one day after school."

97

"Yes Mummy, and I can show her Aslan." Venetia ran across the bridge to the big stone lion and gave him a hug. She ran back to her parents, who were opening the front door.

"We're going out tonight, Ven, with Daddy's diving friend Gianfranco."

"I'll wear my party dress, shall I Mummy?"

"Black velvet and white lace is a bit fancy for tonight, Ven?"

"Why?" Venetia frowned. "I want to look nice."

"Alright then," Penny said. She looked at Gideon. "You better smarten up as well. Don't want you showing her up."

At seven, they were ready. "What a smart family," Penny said. "We'll need our coats. You're not going to wear that old Barbour are you, Gid?"

"I've nothing else."

Penny and Venetia put on their duffle coats. Penny said, "Your birthday's coming up. I'm going to buy you an overcoat."

They left the flat and crossed the bridge to walk along the well lit fondamenta, rather than the shorter dark route through the alleyways. They came to the Arsenale stop and caught the number one to Rialto. Venetia liked being out after dark. She liked looking at the lights reflected in the water. It was exciting. They moved slowly up the Grand Canal pulling in at every stop. The vaporetto got fuller and fuller, until there was standing room only. As they came in to Accademia, Venetia looked at all the people waiting to board and thought they'd never fit. Then realised she was seeing a reflection in the window of all the people standing on the boat. There were really only three people waiting at the stop.

"I thought there were hundreds of people at the stop, but they were just in the glass," she said laughing. "It tricked me."

They got off at the Rialto, and crossed the famous bridge. The souvenir shops were still open, though the market stalls on the other side had all gone home. They found the Campo San Giacometto and walked along what had been old stockrooms and were now stylish bars, and there waiting for them was Gianfranco with a glamorous woman in a long fur coat. Not what Gideon had expected at all when Gianfranco had told him his girlfriend was a banker. He hadn't seen anyone in fur for years. She looked like a fifties movie star.

Gianfranco greeted them and introduced Laura. They stepped inside and were shown upstairs to an arched room of exposed brickwork and the sounds of conversations and cutlery. The clientele were chic and elegant. The waiter led them to a table next to a window, through which they could see the Grand Canal. He took their coats and disappeared downstairs. They sat, Gianfranco and Laura one side, and the three Mantells the other.

"Oh this is lovely," Penny said. "Have you been before?"

"Yes, we like it. It's amazing to think what it was like. After the market closed, after dark, this was a very dingy insalubrious area. I was frightened to walk here. Now it is the 'in' place to come." Laura's English was perfect with only the slightest trace of an accent. She was wearing a tight fitting dark-green polo-necked sweater, which showed her figure off well.

"Where did you learn English?" Gideon asked. "You speak it better than most of us — insalubrious what a lovely word."

"I studied English at the university in Perugia, and had a couple of years in London with J.P. Morgan. I'm with Banco di Venezia now."

The waiter returned with menus, and asked if they'd like anything to drink. Gianfranco ordered a bottle of prosecco. "What about Venetia?" he asked.

Venetia was gazing out of the window watching the traffic going up and down the canal.

Penny nudged her. "Ven, do you want a coke?"

"Yes please."

"You are at school here in Venice?" Laura asked.

"Yes, I've just started."

"Do you like it?"

"Well..."

"She's just made a Venetian friend, Isabella, isn't that right Ven?"

"Yes."

"Isabella, and what is her surname?" Gianfranco said. "It is such a small city, everyone knows everyone. It is difficult to have secrets in Venice. I'm sure I will know of her family."

"I don't know. She lives with her grandparents."

"I wonder why," Laura said. "Maybe her parents work abroad and they didn't want her to go to a different school."

"We could never leave Venetia in another country," Penny said.

They started to read the menus. There was carpaccio di branzino, which Laura recommended.

"What is it?" Gideon asked

"Raw sea bass. Or maybe you would prefer the baked sea bass, or filet San Piedro, you call it John Dory, or if you're not in the mood for fish, the lamb ragu is very good."

The waiter returned with the drinks, and a plate of olives. He asked if they were ready to order.

"Non siamo pronti cinque minuti," Gianfranco said, and raising his glass to the party, "Alla salute."

They all raised their glasses and repeated, "Alla salute."

The evening passed pleasantly. Laura and Gianfranco were good company, until Laura told them about her job, which stirred Gianfranco.

"Amazing," Gianfranco said. "You wouldn't think a woman trusted with millions would be going to see a medium."

"Not that again," Laura said. "You know, I'm only going to keep Angela company. I don't know why you keep going on about it."

"I just think she's wasting her money, and your time."

"Come on, she's had a hard time, with her mother dying," she looked at Penny. "Men don't understand. Everything must be proved. I know it's probably nonsense, but Angela is convinced."

Gianfranco seemed quite agitated. "The medium's a charlatan, she'll trick Angela into thinking she's speaking to her mother, and then Angela will come every week to talk, and the medium will get a fat fee."

"She doesn't charge, whatever you wish to give. It doesn't matter to me if she is a fake, if it brings Angela comfort that's good enough. She is my best friend. I said I will go with her and I will. What do you think, Penny?"

"I don't know. I guess if a placebo works.... I'm not sure I'd go myself, but to help a friend, I might."

"What's a medium?" Venetia asked.

"It's someone who pretends to talk to the dead. Difficult to explain, darling, they don't really talk to them." Penny looked at the others for help.

"I think we'll change the subject. It's Gianfranco's fault. I don't know why he brought it up." Laura smiled at Venetia. "You will be in Venice for Christmas. How exciting. You know we have snow? Everything changes to white. I will show you where to buy the best Christmas tree."

Venetia's eyes lit up. "We could build a snowman next to Aslan to keep him company."

"Aslan?"

"She calls the big lion outside the Arsenale Aslan," Penny said. "I wonder if we could. It would be rather fun."

"I'm not sure the navy would approve," Gideon said.

"I'll tell you what," Laura said, "when it snows, Gianfranco and I will come and visit and we'll all sneak out after dark and build the snowman, and when the sailors come in the morning they will get a nice surprise. Perhaps we could build a snow lion."

Venetia clapped her hands in delight. "A snow leopard."

They talked on, and noticed other customers leaving. Gianfranco called for the bill and for the first time in the evening the table was silent. Venetia yawned, and leant up against Penny.

"I think we better get this young lady to bed," Penny said.

Gianfranco paid the bill with a card, and they went downstairs where the waiter helped them on with their coats. Outside, it was busy as people began to leave the bars.

"Will you take the vaporetto?" Gianfranco asked. "Laura and I will walk. It's good to work off the meal."

"Yes we will, be nice to walk, but Ven's tired. She's usually in bed by nine. Arriverderci and grazie per la cena squisita."

"Bravo," Laura said, "you speak Italian."

"Feebly," Gideon said.

They kissed goodbye, and went their separate ways. Half an hour later, the vaporetto arrived at Arsenale. Venetia was sound asleep. Gideon picked her up, and carried her off the boat. Penny led the way across the Schiavone into the pitch black of the Calle Forni, to take the shorter route home.

"It's spooky," she said as they walked along the empty alleyway. Their footsteps echoed around them making it sound as if they were being followed. They approached the sottoportico, and turned right.

Behind her, Gideon impersonated the old horror star Vincent Price. "Like one that on a lonesome road doth walk in fear and dread, and having once turned around walks on and turns no more his head, because he knows a frightful fiend doth close behind him tread."

Penny shivered. "Don't," she said, "it's creepy enough without you. You're frightening me, and you'll wake Venetia."

They turned left and a little way on came into the lit Campo. The stone lions looked as if they were guarding the square. Penny sighed. She was glad to be home. She fished in her handbag for the key and let them in. They climbed the stairs, and put the sleeping Venetia to bed.

"What were you trying to spook me with? Poe?"

"No, it was the Ancient Mariner."

13

Faustina Waits

Faustina had been on the bench waiting for the children when both parents had come walking down the Via Garabaldi. The man had smiled at her and nodded in recognition. She hadn't known what to do. For a second she'd felt his eyes on her and looked down at the ground. Faustina hated meeting anyone's eyes, terrified they would see inside her. To avoid suspicion, she'd forced herself to wait on the bench, before getting up to leave.

She'd walked home cursing herself. What had she been thinking? Now the father had seen her, her plans would have to change. Faustina had always thought of herself as invisible. Outside of her neighbours, no one noticed her. But he had.

Faustina unlocked the door of her flat. It was dark, smelt of damp, and remained almost unchanged since the day it had been bought. She entered the bedroom, prepared for the girl, and sat on the iron bed with her head in her hands, sobbing. Her mother was right: she was a stupid stupid girl, and now an even more stupid woman. Faustina took off her coat and sweater, and took down the scourge from the wall and began to flagellate herself, repeating over and over with each stroke: "stupida, stupida, stupida."

The holy angel of pain had come again, freeing her mind from its torments. Faustina felt the blood beginning to trickle down her back. Her punishment was over. She undressed and had a shower to wash the blood from her back. Afterwards, Faustina put on a black robe to go into the chapel to begin the evening prayers. The familiar words calmed her. Trancelike, she repeated them as she had done every evening for the last thirty years. When the service of redemption was over, she bowed before the altar.

Faustina made her supper. Every day at the same time, she chopped up an onion and a couple of cloves of garlic, fried them in olive oil and added a tin of Coop chopped tomatoes. She let them simmer on the stove for half an hour and then put some spaghetti in a saucepan to boil. Seven minutes later it was ready. Faustina drained the spaghetti and mixed it with the sauce. She'd had this same meal every day since her mother had died. It was cheap and it was easy, and it made shopping very simple. There was no reason to change.

As she ate, she thought about the girl and looked at the big bottle of colourless liquid on the shelf. When Faustina had been hysterical, her mother had soaked a rag in the liquid, and held it over Faustina's face until she passed out. The smell of the rag, sweet and sickly, came back to her and that feeling of overpowering nausea. She remembered regaining consciousness, dizzy and weak, and her mother holding a bowl in front of her while she vomited. She'd wiped Faustina's mouth with a flannel, and stroked her hair. Faustina treasured those moments of kindness.

The only way to kidnap the girl was to break into her home. Faustina had been watching the house and knew the girl's bedroom was at the back of the house, facing the dark narrow alley. She knew, too, after midnight the streets were empty and it would be possible to get a stepladder up to the window. It was fortunate she was on the first floor. The ground floor windows had heavy bars to stop thieves.

Every night she'd seen one of the parents close the shutters. These were the same all over Venice, and simply unlatched with a thin knife. She would need to cover the glass with a cloth, to muffle the sound when she broke it. The girl might stir but Faustina would get the liquid-soaked rag over her face before she could call out.

Now the father had seen Faustina, she would need some kind of disguise and thought with the right clothes, she could easily pass for a short old man. Her hair would have to be cut though. Faustina looked in the mirror and held her hair back. She had never been much of a beauty, but, now she was old, there was nothing feminine left in her face. Yes, she could pass for a man. Faustina picked up her scissors, and began to cut away at her thick coarse hair.

14

Laura meets Angela

The vaporetto was hot and crowded. It was rush hour. Outside it was drizzling. Inside there was a damp fug. Laura da Ponte sat squashed to the steamed up window, thinking about the medium. She'd never been to a séance, but had read about them. For Angela's sake, she hoped this woman was convincing. From all reports, it sounded as if she was. Angela had told her the Signora was the real thing. People who'd been swore she was genuine.

Laura was meeting Angela at San Zaccariah. It would take twenty minutes to walk from there to Signora Salvati's house. Their appointment was for seven. Angela's mother had died while Angela had been in America. She hadn't been able to get back, hadn't been able to tell her mother how much she loved her. She'd missed the funeral because snow had stopped flights out of New York and was desperate for one last chance to tell her mother how much she missed her.

Laura had been to San Michele with Angela to put flowers on her mother's grave. She'd watched Angela kiss the photo on the gravestone and break down, crying out 'Mamma Mamma.' It had been awful watching her friend in so much suffering. She'd helped her back through the cypress-lined paths to the vaporetto stop. Angela had leant against her, sobbing all the way back to Fondamente Nuovo. She was inconsolable. She cried every day. Laura knew Angela was barely functioning. She was going through the motions of life, but she wasn't really there. Laura told her it wasn't her fault, but Angela wouldn't listen. It was impossible to penetrate through the grief and the guilt.

Laura pushed her way out onto the deck as the boat pulled in to San Zaccariah. She zipped up her quilted waterproof and saw Angela standing under an umbrella. She disembarked in a crowd, and pushed her way through. They greeted each other and Angela

put her arm through Laura's and held the umbrella to protect them both from the drizzle.

Arm in arm, they crossed the Schiavoni and slipped into the alley running alongside the

church of La Pieta. They headed quickly through to the Campo Bandiera e Moro, and out

on the eastern edge. It was very dark and the drizzle had turned to rain. They crossed a

small bridge, turned right under a sotoportego of cracked and crumbling plaster, through a

courtyard with a wellhead at its centre, and out down a narrow passage. They crossed a

cast iron bridge with a strange pattern of flowers and twisting ivy. Ahead of them, in a

dingy calle, Angela saw what she'd been told to look for: a monkey, a witch, and a pope

suspended from a metal structure next to a shuttered first floor window. The figures were

weird. The pope and witch were dolls, but the monkey had a mummified appearance, as if

it had once been alive. "Look," she nudged Laura. "We're here. This is her house."

They approached the door. Angela closed her umbrella and shook the water from it

as Laura knocked. A middle-aged blonde woman opened the door and welcomed them.

She had a Sicilian accent. She introduced herself as Sara Severi, Signora Salvati's

companion. She took their coats and the umbrella and hung them from hooks by the door.

"Please follow me. The Signora will be ready soon."

She took them through the house. It was dark, and full of religious pictures and

grim wooden carvings of Christ on the cross. In spite of the Christian symbols, there was

something pagan about it, like voodoo, a mixture of the old and new religion. They came

to a sitting room where four other people were waiting. Sara Severi told them to make

themselves comfortable. She asked them if they had any specific questions for the spirits.

A brother and sister in their sixties said they wanted to know if their mother was happy in

the afterlife. An old woman said she wanted to ask her husband about lost money. The

woman with her said she had no questions.

Angela said, "I want tell my mother I love and miss her so much. I want to know she is at peace."

Sara Severi looked at Laura, who shook her head. "I am with my friend. I have nothing to ask." She took Angela's hand.

Sara Severi nodded. "I will see if the Signora is ready."

They sat in respectful silence, a feeling of suspense hanging in the air, no one daring to speak. After what seemed like an age, Sara Severi returned and took them into a candlelit room. It was heavy with incense. Signora Salvati was sitting at a round wooden table. She rose to greet them. She looked seventy, but could have been older or younger. She was small, under five feet with long grey hair and strikingly green eyes. Her skin was lined and very white. She sat down and spread her arms to gesture that they should all be seated.

Sara Severi sat the brother and sister on either side of her mistress. She placed Angela next to the sister and Laura next to the brother. She herself sat between the other two clients, and took their hands. They were all instructed to hold hands and form a circle.

Signora Salvati began to chant, soft at first, but getting slowly louder and more hypnotic. Her head dropped forward almost onto her chest, and her eyes closed. Nothing happened. Somewhere a clock ticked, and time passed. Signora Salvati raised her head and opened her eyes. They looked blank and lifeless. She began to speak in a strange voice that switched pitch from high to low. The room was alive with the expectation of everyone around the table. Something was about to happen

At first, the words made no sense. They were like the wild ramblings of a lunatic speaking at speed, mimicking one voice after another. Hundreds of different competing voices came out of her mouth, fighting for control. Then, almost as if she had found the right frequency on an old radio, she began to speak clearly in old Venetian. She was Polissena Malpiero. She would carry messages between this world and the next. First, a message came from the mother Carlotta, who told the brother and sister to look after each other. They must not worry. She was at peace; next, a message from the husband Davide, confessing to losing the money gambling; and then a message for Angela. Her mother said she knew Angela loved her. Anglela must get on with her life. Vincenzo would propose, and Angela should accept. He was a good man and they would have beautiful children.

Signora Salvati stopped, and all was still. There was a flicker behind her dead eyes, and her head dropped once more. She began to whisper something. Laura strained to hear. Something had changed. There was another presence in the room. Someone else was talking through this strange woman. Signora Salvati raised her head, opened her eyes and looked directly at Laura.

"Beware the man who is a woman, the prompter breathes, the puppet squeaks, the reptile lives." She raised her arm, and pointed a trembling finger at Laura. "You must protect her." She dropped her arm with a bang to the table. She came out of her trance and looked around. She told them it was over. They could release their hands.

"What did you mean?" Laura said. "Protect who?"

Signora Salvati asked Sara Severi what she had said. She listened as it was explained and frowned.

She turned to Laura. "I don't know what it means. They speak through me; that is all. They do not tell me their purpose. Tonight I sensed a disturbance, a shift in the fabric of their world. Something has happened. They are waiting for someone. Is anyone you know close to death?"

Laura shook her head. She looked at Angela.

Signora Salvati rose from the table, saying she was tired and would go to bed. She left the room. Sara Severi took them back to the living room and asked if they would like anything to drink before leaving. She asked for a contribution. Angela gave her a hundred Euros. They got their coats and left. As they made their way to San Zaccariah, they heard a rumble of thunder and the rain got heavier.

On the vaporetto home, Laura asked Angela how she felt.

"She does speak to the dead doesn't she?" For the first time in months, Angela smiled. "Better, much better, Mamma knows I love her. A weight is lifted. Thank you for coming with me. I couldn't have gone alone."

"What did you think she meant when she said protect her?"

"I don't know. Maybe it was a mistake. The message wasn't for you. Maybe she pointed at the wrong person."

Laura looked out across at the island of San Giorgio and saw a flash of sheet lightning behind the church. The thunder rumbled, and the lightning flashed again, illuminating the campanile. The flashing light against the black night was like the flickering of an old silent film. Laura thought she saw something move across the dome, but it was just a trick of the light. She continued to look, her mind turning over what the old woman had said. Was it just theatrics or was their another world? Tonight she could almost believe there was.

The vaporetto headed away from San Giorgio and into the Grand Canal and their stop at Academia, where they parted and hurried through the storm to their separate homes.

15

The Invitation

"Che tempo bruto," Carlo said, "I've never known such fierce storms. The thunder is so loud. We had a lightning strike on the university – the electric surge brought the computer network down. Then we lost power and had to use a backup generator. Quite a panic, but we managed to get it on before any damage to the chest."

"It's awful," Penny said. "I've had the trenches covered in tarpaulin. Work outside is impossible. We've got enough to be going on with inside, cleaning and identifying what we've found."

The weather had not affected the divers. The storms came at night. Gideon reckoned he and Gianfranco would be able to continue until the end of November. They'd found the stern quarter of a galley, which remained intact half buried in the sand. The rest of the galley had been spread over the seabed by the shifting currents. They were investigating the debris trail. There were bits of ship's timber spread out over a large area, and all sorts of other artefacts, pottery, pins, cannon balls and pieces of oar.

On their way to and from Lanesra, Gianfranco and Gideon would talk. They had become good friends, and confided in each other. Gideon told Gianfranco about Isabella. She had come to play with Venetia, and they'd discovered her family's name was Zancani. He asked Gianfranco if he knew them.

Gianfranco thought for a second. "I know of them," he said slowly. "Everyone knows of them. They are a family of great misfortune, almost cursed. Over the last hundred years there have been three suicides in the family. The daughter, it must be

Isabella's mother, died in childbirth. I'm afraid we Venetians are superstitious. The family are left to themselves. We fear catching their ill luck. They live alone with an old couple who look after them. They have been with the family for a long time. They also are avoided. Have you been there?"

"No, we've not been invited. I've spoken to Aldo. He must be one of the couple you mentioned. He doesn't speak English— we sort of communicate. He brought and collected Isabella when she came to play. He seems fond of her. He always collects her from school. I must say she's a lovely girl, and she and Venetia have become close."

"Be careful, Gideon. Don't get involved with them."

"I don't believe in superstition," Gideon smiled at his friend. "You can't catch bad luck, or good for that matter. Something odd I've been meaning to ask you. There used to be an old woman outside the school. I smiled and nodded to her in acknowledgement and she looked away, embarrassed. She's not been there since. Have I broken some sort of code? Is it not done to acknowledge the old?"

Gianfranco laughed. "She probably thought you were going to make a lewd suggestion."

"For goodness sake," Gideon laughed too.

"More likely, though sad, she's probably been taken into a care home or passed away. You say she was old."

"Yes that's probably it."

That evening, after Venetia had gone to bed, he told Penny what Gianfranco had said.

"That's terrible. The family ostracised. No wonder the poor little girl only has Venetia as a friend. Of course it's not a curse, well not in the sense Gianfranco means. Depression can run in families, a gene like any other. And her mother died in childbirth?"

"So he said."

"Well I hope we are invited. I would like to meet them."

Several days later Aldo presented Penny with a letter from Cristofo and Elizabeta Zancani. It was on beautiful headed notepaper with a family coat of arms, a shield with a ship sailing by palm trees. It was inviting Venetia to play on All Saints Day, Tuesday 1st November. There was no school. It was a national holiday. They said Aldo would collect Venetia at 11am from Campo Arsenale, and asked if Penny and Gideon would like to come to collect Venetia at six and stay for a drink. The address was Palazzo Castello di Zancani, Calle dei Preti, and there was a telephone number.

As Penny read the letter, Aldo stood waiting for a reply. Venetia and Isabella were talking to each other in Italian. Venetia looked up at her mother.

"Can I go? Mummy please, there's going to be a treasure hunt."

"Yes, Ven, course you can." She turned to Aldo, "Io telefeno Signore Zancani," she mimed talking on the telephone in case he didn't understand.

"Si, si, bene," he said.

The two girls looked excitedly at each other. It amazed Penny how quickly Venetia was picking up the language. She would be fluent by the end of the year.

"We better get home darling." Penny took Venetia's hand. "Arrivaderci," she said to Aldo, and smiling at Isabella, "Ciao Isabella."

They walked home. The sky was grey but at least it wasn't raining. The aftermath of the storms lay evident in the broken umbrellas, blown inside out and discarded in bins. Venetia told her mother about the treasure hunt.

"Her nonno is working on clues for a great hunt all through the house, and when we've found the treasure, Isabella says there will be a banquet."

"What fun, I wish I was coming. I'll telephone her grandparents as soon as Daddy gets home. It will be interesting to meet them."

Gideon returned at six. The sun was setting earlier and earlier, and the dive day was getting shorter and shorter. He said Carlo had fixed a date for the opening of the chest, the 5th November. "We're to meet at the uni at nine."

Penny showed Gideon the invitation from the Zancanis. "I've already told Ven she can go. Do you want to go for drinks? I can go alone, if you don't fancy it."

"No, I'd like to meet them, and we'll have had the day off so I won't be tired. Will you ring them?"

"Yes I'll do it now."

Penny got out her mobile and telephoned the number on the invitation. "Pronto? Vorrei parlare con la Signora Zancani," she said: "Buona sera, si," and, "What a relief you speak English. Yes, Venetia would love to come, and we'd love to have a drink and get acquainted. Lovely, see you on the first. Yes, All Saints Day."

16

All Saints Day

Venetia had been ready since eight. She'd lain in bed waiting for her Daddy, but he hadn't come, so she'd got up and dressed. She kept looking out to see if Aldo was coming. All she'd seen was an old man in a beret, standing on the wooden bridge by the Arsenale. He was in a short blue quilted coat, leaning on a walking stick and looking over the square directly at their house. There was something familiar about him, but she couldn't think where she'd seen him. The man turned and walked away. He had a strange shuffling walk. Venetia thought he must be very old.

The door of her parents' bedroom opened and her daddy appeared in his pyjamas. "Good heavens, Ven, are you up?"

"What's the time Daddy?"

"It's only eight thirty. You've got hours until Aldo comes. Why don't you watch telly? Mummy and Daddy are having lie in." He passed her the remote control, and returned to the bedroom.

Venetia put on the TV. She sat on the sofa, leaning forward with the remote in her hand, and trawled through the channels for a cartoon. She flicked past a man doing cookery, past some red Indians whooping after a cowboy, and stopped at a channel with school children. It was about a school in Mestre. It was not reopening after the holiday. There had been an outbreak of swine flu. Ten children had caught it. She wondered what it was.

Venetia imagined it coming to her school – not to have to go would be good, as long as she could still see Isabella. Venetia didn't like the other children and would be happy never to see them again. They'd started calling her fish girl, and shouting 'pesce pesce' after her. It started after Sophia had seen her glass fish. They said nasty things about Isabella, too, and made signs of the cross when they saw her. Isabella said not to pay them any attention. She said her grandfather had said the other children were common. He'd told Isabella she was different, and must not worry what others said. She was better than them, and they were too stupid to understand that. "You are like me," Isabella had said. "We are sisters."

The report on the outbreak came to an end and Venetia moved to another channel, and found a cartoon. She settled back on the sofa to watch.

The cartoon finished and her mummy came out dressed in jeans and red Guernsey.

"What's swine flu, Mummy?"

"Why do you want to know?"

"I saw on the telly. A school in Mestre has it."

"It's a type of flu. I wonder if we should get you inoculated. Mestre's not far. I hope it doesn't come here. Give me the remote, let me see if there's anything else about it."

Venetia passed Penny the remote, but she couldn't find anything about the flu on any of the channels. Gideon appeared.

"Ven says she saw something about swine flu in Mestre."

"Yes, Daddy, it was at a school. It's closing."

119

Penny continued, "Do you think we should get her inoculated? We haven't even registered with a doctor yet. We should at least get on and do that."

"Well there's nothing to be done today — everything's shut."

"Do you catch it from pigs Daddy?"

"I don't really know Ven. Just to be on the safe side, I think we'll get you an injection, so you won't catch it."

"Supposing another girl at school catches it. Will they close the school?"

"I don't know."

Penny changed the subject. "Shall we go to the Biennale, Gid? It's the one thing that's open. Fun to look around the pavilions in the Giardini."

"Why not? We'll go as soon as Aldo's collected Ven."

At eleven, the doorbell rang. Venetia looked down of the window and there were Aldo and Isabella. She shouted, "Coming."

Penny put Venetia's duffle coat on her and did the toggles up. "Have a lovely day darling, and we'll see you at six."

Venetia ran down the stairs to the front door. Penny waved down at Isabella, and Venetia appeared. She watched the two girls embrace and go running over to the stone lions. They both climbed on the pedestal and wrapped their arms around the lion with the runes.

Aldo looked up. "Le bambine felice," he said laughing. "Io vado, arriverderci." He hurried off and gathered the two girls up, and off they went down the calle.

Gideon joined Penny at the window. "We may as well go; we'll do the Italian thing, and have a coffee and a pastry in lieu of breakfast."

"Sounds good," she said.

They strolled down the Riva di Schiavone, until it turned into Riva dei Partigiani, and stopped at the cafe Paradiso, drank coffee and had a jam filled pastry, looking out over the lagoon. When they'd finished, they entered the Biennale and, doing their patriotic duty, went straight to the British pavilion to look at the Mike Nelson installation. He'd turned the building into a rabbit warren of dusty low ceilinged rooms, with neglected tools left on tables, and weird implements discarded in corners. It was like wandering through long forgotten deserted workshops.

They poked their noses into the Japanese pavilion, and saw an intriguing animation of a city being taken over by vegetation, and submerged in water. In another pavilion they saw two disembodied heads talking.

"You're very nice, and everything you're doing is very interesting," one said to the other.

The other head said. "No, no, you're very nice, and everything you're doing is very interesting."

They moved from pavilion to pavilion, until Gideon felt his head would explode with all the images he'd seen. In the Russian pavilion he read, '*I wonder why I lied to myself that I had never been here, and was totally ignorant of this place. In fact it was just like anywhere else, only the feeling is stronger and the incomprehension deeper.*' He decided then he'd seen enough. "I don't think I can take any more."

"Me too. I'm all arted out," Penny said.

They walked slowly back through the Giardini. They were approaching the gate onto the street near the school when they heard a wailing siren. It reminded Gideon of the sirens in the war films he'd watched with his grandfather. He smiled at the memory, half expecting to hear the drone of bombers.

"It's the Aqua Alta," Penny said. "Carlo said it gives an hour's warning, didn't he?"

"Can't remember," he said, coming back to reality. "Anyway, let's hurry. It's incredibly loud isn't it?"

They quickened their pace, taking the short cut through to the Arsenale. As they crossed the Ponte del l'Arsenal o del Paradiso, Gideon looked down at the choppy water in the canal. It was coming in fast but still within its banks. There was a foot or so to go before it would go over the top. They crossed the square and went up to their flat. As they took their coats off, Penny said, "I'm glad we're not on the ground floor. I hope we can collect Ven alright. Do you think I should ring the Zancanis?"

"Let's wait and see how high it gets. We've got the wellingtons downstairs, so we should be alright. We'll have to take a pair for Ven."

"OK, do you want some tea?"

"Yes, love some. I'll put the telly on, see if there's anything more about the flu."

He found Canale Venezia with the remote and left it on. He knew sooner or later there would be some local news. Penny returned with a pot of tea and a plate of biscuits. She stretched out on the sofa and put her feet up on Gideon's lap as she drank her tea.

"How long do you think it will take to walk?" she asked.

Gideon unfolded the map they kept on the coffee table and found the Calle dei Preti. He sat munching a biscuit, as he perused the map. "Well I'd say ten to fifteen minutes, it doesn't look far. It's the usual twists and turns, and half a dozen bridges to cross. It's quite near San Giorgio dei Greci, do you remember the priest said there was a good Day of Judgement there?"

"Yes I do."

The local news started on the television. Gideon folded the map up. "Ah, now let's watch this and see if Ven's got it right." He sipped his tea. His Italian was getting better and better, so he could make out most of what was said.

"She's right," he said. "They're saying the flu vaccine is going to be given to children at school. Is that what you thought?"

"Don't know, your Italian's much better than mine. We can ask the Zancanis, they'll know. They didn't mention the Aqua Alta, so I guess it's nothing serious." She got up and looked out. "The water's lapping up around the lions."

Gideon got up to have a look. It still seemed to be coming in. There was a great puddle around the entrance to the Arsenale slowly spreading down the calle. Most of the rest of the campo was OK. "Well it's passable in wellingtons, but perhaps we ought to give them a ring. It may be worse where they are. Will you do it? You spoke to them before."

Penny went into the bedroom, leaving Gideon watching the television. She sat on the bed and keyed the Zancani number into her mobile. Elizabeta answered. She said Venetia and Isabella were having a lovely time, and no it wasn't flooded where they were, but she thought some of the streets on the way might be impassable, if not now, soon. She said, "Cristofo will come and collect you in the boat. That will be safest. He'll be with you in half an hour."

Twenty minutes later Gideon looked out again. It was almost dark and the water was still coming in. Most of the Campo was underwater, though it hadn't quite reached their door. "We'll have to wear wellingtons to get to the boat," he said.

"I'll put our shoes in a plastic bag so we can change when we get there," Penny said.

They got wellingtons from the chest and looked out a pair for Venetia.

"Ready," Gideon said and opened the front door. They stepped straight into ankle-deep water. "I'm glad we're being collected. Some of those streets with no light — you could easily walk straight into a canal."

"I know," Penny said. "Just about guess where the canal is here."

Gideon pointed to a spot, a foot back from where he usually waited for Francesco. "I think we should stand there. It's as close as we dare go."

They waited for a few minutes with the water lapping around their wellingtons watching the moon rise and heard the putt putt of an outboard. A small wooden boat appeared with a white-haired man in a dark overcoat at the tiller. He waved and steered the boat up so they could step in.

"Penny and Gideon?" he asked, getting up.

"Yes, Cristofo?"

"I knew it must be you," he said. "Who else would be out tonight? Take my hand, let me help you in. Sit on either side to balance please." Cristofo sat down at the tiller, and turned the boat back down the canal.

"It's very good of you to come and get us," Penny said.

"Not at all, I like getting my old boat out, especially at Aqua Alta. Every Venetian is a boatman at heart."

"Do you think the water will get much higher?" Gideon asked.

"No, it's almost at its peak. It's not serious; it will start to go down in an hour or so. I remember in November 1966 we had a disastrous Aqua Alta. I had to swim home from a concert."

They came out of their canal into the lagoon. It seemed quieter.

"Are the vaparetti running? I can't see any," Penny said.

"No, many of imbarcaderi, the landing stages, are under water, so the service is suspended. It will resume tomorrow."

They turned right. In the distance, they could see the lights of St Marks. Cristofo turned them in towards the Schiavone, and they passed under the familiar stone bridge they'd walked over many a time, and there in front of them, looming out of the darkness, was the Bridge of Sighs.

"I'm taking you the long way. The water will be too high to get under the bridges the other way. It is the scenic route," Cristofo said. "Let us sit quietly. This is my favourite time. Everyone is at home, afraid to be out. Venice is as it was in the days of my ancestors."

Penny and Gideon held hands as they putt-putted down the canal. All they could hear was the outboard motor, and the water lapping up against the sides of the houses, as the boat turned into a gloomy narrow canal. The only light was from the moon. The buildings on either side seemed even older than usual, and on the point of collapsing into the water. Everything was ravaged by damp and time. They passed under a low bridge inches from their heads. A light shone down on the water from a window high above. Penny looked up to see a crumbling old balcony, next to which two gargoyle carvings hung from the wall, looking down at her. She shuddered, and thought they could easily fall. They moved on. Penny felt as if she was floating through time, as if the present and the past were living together side by side, and breathed a sigh of relief as they turned into a well lit canal, and she could hear the sounds of chatter coming from a house, and the smell of food. Penny had feared the lonely building with the balcony was to be their destination. They turned once again into silence and gloom, through another lonely canal, and again, through another and another. They were in a Venice they had never seen. She had no idea where they were, and yet Gideon had said it was only a fifteen minute walk. They entered another solitary canal, and there in front of them were two lit lanterns on either side of a gothic arch. It was the water entrance into an old palazzo.

"We are home," Cristofo said.

The Mantells looked up at a crumbling pink wall that rose above them, and above the arch they glimpsed the Zancani coat of arms carved in white stone. Above that, a faint light shone from a large window. Before they could take it in, the boat passed under the arch into a cavernous brick boathouse. A lantern hung high from a vaulted ceiling, casting shadows on the walls. Mossy stone steps led up from the water.

Cristofo tied the boat to a great iron ring embedded in the stone by the steps. Penny got their shoes out of the plastic bag.

"We'll just put our shoes on, we'll leave our boots in the boat shall we?" she said.

"Yes," Cristofo said, stepping from the boat. "This is my water garage. In the old days they kept six boats here, but now I just have the one." He took Penny's hand as she stood up, and helped her from the boat. He led her up the steps. "Careful, they can be slippery."

Gideon followed. The brickwork looked fantastically old and decayed, and yet intact. Cristofo unlocked a massive iron door, and with both hands pulled it open. Its immense weight caused an unusual sharp grating sound as it moved on its ancient hinges. He waved them in and, with some effort, pushed the door shut and locked it. He led them up a narrow damp smelling stone staircase. The walls were discoloured and had strange clumps of fungus growing on them. They came to another door. He opened it onto a hall with a magnificent white Murano glass chandelier hanging over an oak table. Penny saw Venetia's duffle coat lying on top of it. Apart from portraits hanging on the walls, the room was empty. At one end was the large window they had seen from the boat.

"Let me take your coats." He took Penny's duffle coat and Gideon's Barbour, and laid them on the table next to Venetia's. He kept his black overcoat on. "My ancestors," he pointed at the walls. "They like to see who is visiting us."

Penny and Gideon looked around at portraits of men from different times over the centuries. She fixed on one who looked a little like Cristofo. He had the same nose and liquid eyes. Penny felt overawed. She knew nothing of her own family beyond her grandparents. She asked, and immediately felt stupid, "Any doges in the family?"

"No, nothing so grand. My family were all merchants; they started by ferrying and selling slaves in Alexandria, where they bought spices to bring back for the Rialto markets. They had an insatiable thirst for wealth, a life of great risk and great profit. Rinaldo Zancani, the man there" — he pointed to a portrait of a powerful looking man in a black fur coat, his hand resting on a globe — "really established our fortune trading in Tana beyond the Black Sea, unimaginable riches for the time, precious stones and silk from China, honey and furs from the Russian forests. By 1600, none of the family needed to work, we could live off the interest. It has not been a blessing. Enough come, the others will be upstairs. We do not use this room any more. We leave it to them."

They moved upstairs into a large lofty room full of faded antique furniture. Here and there over the black oaken floor were patterned oriental rugs. The windows were long and pointed in the gothic fashion. The glass in them was old. The walls were hung with dark tapestries. At one end of the room, a log fire burnt. From a sofa in the corner of the room, near the fire, a woman put down her book and rose to greet them. She was small and thin and had permed white hair. She was elegantly dressed in a tweed skirt and beige cardigan. Her clothes looked English.

"Elizabeta, here are our guests," Cristofo said.

"Welcome to our house, come and sit down, I will ring for Aldo. What would you like to drink? Gin and tonic? It is what Cristofo and I like. We are quite the anglophiles."

"Yes, that would be nice," Gideon said

"Yes please," Penny said.

Elizabeta pulled a cord next to the mantelpiece, and gestured for Penny and Gideon to sit.

Gideon sank into a large threadbare armchair. Penny sat on a smaller green leather chair next to him.

"I will go and get the girls," Cristofo said.

Aldo appeared, and Elizabeta asked him to bring the drinks.

"Now tell me all about yourselves. Venetia, what a charming name, has told me you are archaeologists, and now that I look at you, I remember you from the television, the body with the brick, the vampire, am I right?"

Penny smiled. "Yes that was me. It was an odd discovery. Of course the journalists played it up a bit."

Aldo returned with the drinks on a silver tray, and some olives and nuts. At the same time, Cristofo came in through another door with Venetia on one hand and Isabella on the other. He'd taken off his overcoat. He was in a sports jacket, polo neck, brown corduroy trousers and brown brogue shoes. Like his wife, he was dressed very much in the old English style. The two girls sat on the sofa next to Elizabeta.

Aldo put the tray down on a coffee table in front of them, bowed and left.

"Have you had a good time?" Penny asked the girls.

"Yes Mummy, look what I found in the treasure hunt." Venetia produced an orange coloured glass fish.

"That's lovely."

Isabella produced a clear glass squid, and showed it to Penny.

"What treasures. Did it take you long to find them?"

"We've been all over the house. It's huge. There are lots of old mirrors, like the ones when we had chocolate with Carlo. They make you look funny." Venetia looked at Cristofo. "They've even got their own bridge which goes to Aldo's house. We kept finding notes hidden in between the brick telling us where to look. Sometimes there were sweets, too."

"What fun, I wish I could have joined in."

"Next time I will devise one for us all." Cristofo said. "In the old days, my grandfather used to put messages all over the city for our hunt, but it is too difficult today, with so many tourists. Now tell me what you have been discovering."

Gideon told them about the chest, and how it had been freeze-dried, and would be opened in a few days time.

"How interesting," Cristofo said. "Do you know how old it is, or where it came from?"

"No, it went straight from the seabed to the lab. My guess is 16th century, but all will be revealed once the wood is stabilised."

"Do you have any idea what might be inside?"

"No – Carlo didn't want to x-ray. We'll find out on Saturday."

"I must say it is fascinating looking into the past. I envy you. You must keep me informed. In my own small way I research, but just into our own family. One of the rooms upstairs is full of papers and documents, and ships' inventories, a lifetime's work to sort out, and I have just begun." Carlo got up and rang the bell. "I will get Aldo to freshen our drinks."

They talked more, and Elizabeta suggested they might like a tour of the house.

"Oh yes," Penny said.

"You girls have seen it all. Do you want to do a jigsaw? I have some in the drawer over there." Elizabeta pointed at a wooden chest.

Isabella took Venetia over to the chest and they started pulling out boxes, and finally selected one.

Penny and Gideon followed Cristofo and Elizabeta around room after room of comfortless antique and tattered furniture and ancient blackened mirrors. It was more like a museum than a home, a museum that no one visited. Penny thought it dark and gloomy. An air of sorrow seemed to hang over the house. Penny felt sorry for little Isabella living here amongst all this age. As they went, Elizabeta said how pleased they were that Venetia and Isabella were friends. They spoke of Isabella's mother Catarina, their daughter. She had run away from home when she was sixteen.

"We could not find her. Then four years later we had a call from the Ospedale di Santo Spirito in Rome. She had died giving birth to Isabella. She had given our number to the midwife. The next day we flew to Rome. We brought Isabella and our daughter's body back to Venice. We buried her in the family tomb on San Michele. Isabella is all we have left. She is the last of the Zancani."

"Did you ever find out who the father was?" Penny asked.

"No, we never did, and I think better that we never know," Elizabeta said. "We must keep Isabella from danger. She is so precious to us."

They continued the tour. At the top of the house, they saw the room that Cristofo had mentioned. It was full of pigeonholes stuffed with rolled up documents, and shelves full of old leather-bound books. There were two old globes on wooden stands by a giant desk on which lay an open book. The ceiling of the room was lower than the rest of the house. The windows were small and round, like the portholes of a ship.

Cristofo gestured at shelves around the room. "The details of hundreds of years of commerce; you see, I have my work cut out."

"How old is all this?" Gideon asked. "I'm surprised you've still got it."

"It's a very big house and my family never liked throwing anything away. Rooms just filled up. I found a document dated 1367 the other day."

"Wow, shouldn't it be in a museum?"

"When I've recorded the family history, I will donate it all to the state archive."

They returned to the drawing room, and the cheer of the fire. The girls were still working on the jigsaw. They had only completed a small corner. Penny asked if they knew anything about the outbreak of flu.

"Yes, they are organising mass inoculations at all the elementary schools. We had our doctor give Isabella a vaccination last week. It is dangerous for the young. They do not have our immunity to these things. I'm sure it will be done at the school within the week, but if you like, I can ask our doctor to do Venetia."

Penny and Gideon looked at each other. Penny spoke. "Yes, that would take a worry off. I'll check it's not going to be done at school straight away. Talking of school, I think we better get back, early start. Venetia darling, I'm afraid you'll have to leave that."

"It can stay on the table. You can finish it together next time you come. Perhaps on the weekend, if Mamma will let you?" Elizabeta looked at Penny.

"If it's no trouble. Actually, we're due to go to the university on the Saturday to see the chest being opened. If we could drop Venetia here at ten, say and collect her after?"

"Fine, we'd love to have her again."

"And you can tell us what you find in the chest," Cristofo said, rising from his seat. "I will get my coat, and take you back."

They said goodbye to Elizabeta and Isabella and followed Cristofo down to the boathouse, collecting their coats on the way. In the boat, Penny gave Venetia the wellingtons she'd brought, and they all swapped their shoes for boots. Cristofo started the outboard and they made their way out into the canal.

"I will take us a shorter route now the water is going down. We should get under the bridges."

They passed under bridge after bridge, and through canal after canal, and suddenly found themselves in the canal behind the Arsenale, and there were the stone lions. The water had receded a little.

"I don't know how you find your way around. It's like a maze." Penny said.

"I've been in this city all my life and I've spent a lot of time alone in my little boat. Sometimes, you know," he said, "getting lost is the only place to go. I got lost many times, and now I know every inch of this tired old place. There are many ways here to get to the same place."

The three Mantells got out of the boat.

"Buona notte, see you on Saturday, and don't forget about the vaccination, if there's anything we can do."

"Thank you, Cristofo, and thank you for a wonderful and interesting evening," Gideon said.

Penny whispered to Venetia, who said, "Thank you for the treasure hunt, I had a lovely time."

"You are most welcome, s'ciavo," Cristofo bowed. He restarted the outboard, and turned the boat around. They watched him disappear around the corner of the canal.

"What a house," Gideon said as they walked across the campo, "and what a family. What did you think about the house, Ven?"

"Very old. Isabella's got a four poster bed, and she's got lots of books and dolls, and she's got puppets. Her nonna said we should put on a puppet show."

"My goodness," Penny said, looking at her watch, "it's gone nine. We better get you to bed."

They hurried across the wet campo to their door. Penny helped Venetia to bed, while Gideon got some cold meats and salad out of the fridge. He was feeling hungry. Penny joined him in the kitchen, and they talked about the evening.

"I thought the house creepy," Penny said. "I kept thinking of the House of Usher."

"I liked it," Gideon said.

"Oh I can see you in velvet smoking jacket and embroidered slippers — not," she said, smiling at him.

"I know what you mean, it is a bit Castle Dracu, but they are charming, and such a tragic thing to happen, the daughter dying."

"They obviously dote on Isabella. I just hope everything is alright, and nothing happens to her. It will be very difficult when she is a teenager. I wonder if the girls will keep up their friendship."

"Yes I wonder; I hope so."

17

Brandes Confezioni

The inoculations at the school were to be on Monday 7th, and as it was less than a week away, Penny wouldn't bother the Zancanis. It reminded her Gideon's birthday would be the following Wednesday. She must get him something to replace that old Barbour. She thought a surprise dinner would be fun, and decided to book a table at Paulo's. She'd ask Carlo, Gianfranco and Laura. She wondered about asking Elizabeta and Cristofo, but decided not, remembering Gianfranco's superstitions. It could be awkward. She wondered whether Carlo felt the same — she'd ask the Zancanis another time.

On Friday, Penny collected Venetia from school and they went into Brandes Confezioni, the only men's outfitters on the Via Garabaldi. They found a black overcoat like Cristofo's. It was 150 Euros. Penny thought it expensive, but worth it if she could get Gideon out of the Barbour. It was getting shabbier and shabbier.

She held the overcoat up. "I like it, don't you, Ven? I think we'll get it for Daddy, smarten him up. You can choose a scarf to go with it."

Venetia picked a maroon cashmere scarf, and held it against the black coat. It looked good.

"Oh yes, that goes nicely," Penny said. "Daddy will love it. We'll get some wrapping paper, and wrap them up when we get home. I'll hide them, and we can give them to him on his birthday."

They paid and crossed to the Tabaccaria to get wrapping paper and cards. When they got back to the Campo Arsenale, Penny went into Paolo's and booked a table for six for Wednesday 9th of November. She asked if they could make a cake. Paulo said he would be delighted. She told him Gideon would be thirty six.

She and Venetia wrapped the presents on the floor of the sitting room. Penny loved doing things with Venetia. Once wrapped, they wrote the cards and put them with the presents. Penny hid them at the back of her cupboard in the bedroom. She put her finger to her lips. "Not a word, our secret."

That evening, while Gideon was showering, Penny slipped out of the apartment down to the hall. She rang Carlo and Gianfranco and invited them to the dinner, swearing them to secrecy.

******

At the same time in eastern Venice, Faustina had finished the evening prayers. She undressed, and began to put on the men's clothes she'd bought. She had found them mostly in church jumbles, but she'd got the blue quilted coat new. She'd bought it in Brandes Confezioni, telling them it was for her husband. The padding, and the fact she'd got a size larger, made her look more masculine. She had transformed herself into a small squat old man. She called herself Federico.

The disguise had given her a sense of freedom. She was no longer timid Faustina. For the first time in her life she had gone into a bar and, adopting a low gruff voice, had ordered a brandy. She'd leant against the bar sipping the fierce liquid, watching and listening. The alcohol warmed her. She felt a strange confidence, a glow inside. It was after that she'd invented the shuffling walk. She spent many hours now in front of the mirror practising the low growling voice. Tonight she was going to go to the bar in the Campo Arsenale. She would have a drink, and feel the warmth of the alcohol. Then, she would walk through the little entrance next to the restaurant, which led into Calle Larga, on which the girl's bedroom looked out. She'd investigated it a few days before. Even in daytime the narrow alley was dark. The only person she'd seen was an old woman coming out of the house opposite. With her new confidence, she'd growled a low, "Buon Giorno."

In her youth she'd have been able to use the bars protecting the ground floor window to climb up to the second floor, but now she was old she'd need to bring a small stepladder. She would buy one, light enough to carry, at Il Bottegon. She'd have to leave it behind, once she'd got the girl down. The police might trace it back to the shop, but they'd be told to look for an old man. She would have no need of the disguise after she'd got the girl. The old man would never be seen again.

She entered the bar at eight, and ordered a cognac. She kept her beret on as she stood leaning up against the counter, watching the clientele and listening to their conversations. She ordered another cognac, and felt the glow as she sipped it, and looked out across the dark square to the lit statues of the lions. She recognised the woman she'd seen in the ally walking towards the bar. She came in and spoke to the barman. Her washing machine wasn't working, the water wasn't draining away – did he know a plumber – someone who could look at it. The cognac fired Faustina, and a plan formed.

She remembered the old fool in the bank with his idiot smile, and how he would talk to anyone, *how are you, lovely dress, looking well...* She could do it, too. She smiled, "Scusi Signora." She growled in her practiced gruff voice that she'd been a plumber, perhaps she could look at the machine now, and see if it could be repaired.

The woman saw he was old and not a threat, a kind old man. "Grazie," she said.

Faustina downed the brandy and followed her out into the alley. The woman unlocked her front door, and let them into a small hall. There was a folded wheelchair against the wall. She took Faustina up to her kitchen on the first floor, where she kept the washing machine. Faustina knelt down and saw it was full of water. She took her beret off, and put her head inside the bowl, pretending to inspect, and thinking what to say. She felt around with her hands. "It is the pump, Signora. It needs replacing. I could do it for you if you like. I could come back tomorrow evening."

"Molto gentile," the woman said, and asked how much it would cost. Faustina said she didn't know, but wouldn't charge her for labour; it was a pleasure to help such a charming lady. She asked his name.

"Federico," Faustina said. "E tu?"

"Anna."

"Piacere," Faustina got up.

She asked him if he would like some coffee. Faustina said yes. She was enjoying being Federico. While the woman busied herself preparing the coffee, Faustina looked out of the window, and saw directly into the girl's bedroom, saw the mother and the girl come in. She saw the mother close the shutters. She was almost within touching distance.

Faustina sat drinking coffee at the sturdy wooden kitchen table. She told Anna she lived over on the lido, but it was only one stop away, and the bar in the campo was a favourite. Anna said she would cook him dinner tomorrow for his trouble. What did he like to eat? Faustina wondered whether she would apply the calmer before or after the meal, and said any kind of pasta would be fine. Anna said bolognese was a speciality of hers. She told him she was a widow. The wheelchair in the hall had been her husband's. Her great regret was not having any children to look after her in her old age. She was lonely, no one visited her.

After coffee, Faustina said she would return tomorrow at 8pm with the new pump and some tools. "Buona notte, Signora."

"Buona notte, Federico."

Faustina left and walked home, working out what she would need to do. She'd have to make some excuse about not being able to get the pump. She'd say the shop hadn't had the right one, but promised to get it. She decided she would wait until after the meal before applying the rag. Once the woman had passed out, she would tie her up and lock her in another room. If she turned the kitchen table upside-down, it would make an ideal platform between the two houses. It was designed for two, so narrow enough to go through the window. She'd saw the legs off. Faustina reckoned with knife and screwdriver, it would take no more than fifteen minutes to get into the girl's room, apply the rag, and carry the unconscious girl back across. She would put her in the wheelchair, and have her home well before anyone was up. It was perfect, everything had fallen into place, and there was no need to carry a ladder all the way from San Pietro. She chuckled at the thought of the police searching for an ex plumber on the Lido.

18

The Opening of the Chest

The Mantells walked to the Palazzo Castello di Lanzani, but it took them longer than they'd expected. They came on dead ends and canals with no crossings, passed San Giorgio dei Greci twice, and ended up in a small square off Calle Querini.

"You should have brought the map," Penny said in exasperation. "If we don't find it soon, we'll be late."

Gideon asked a man he took to be Venetian for directions, but he was French, and as lost as they were. Finally, on the point of giving up, there in front of them, as if by magic, was the Calle dei Preti. They had no idea how they'd found it and, feeling relieved, walked down the street looking for the door to the Zancani residence. The street entrance wasn't as grand as the water entrance; the brickwork around the door was strangely asymmetric. They rang the bell, and Aldo came. He opened the door wide and ushered them in, but Gideon explained they were late and must go directly to the university. Isabella appeared behind Aldo and took Venetia's hand. She told Penny and Gideon there would be a puppet show when they came back.

"We'll look forward to that. We must go. Carlo will be wondering where we are," Gideon said.

"Bye, girls," Penny said.

They hurried off and found a sign for St Marks. "It's always easy to get to the centre of the maze," Gideon said. "You're never really lost."

"If you say so, but I'd prefer a map," Penny snapped back.

It was eleven when they arrived. They went straight to Carlo's office.

"Sorry we're late, had to drop Venetia off at her friend's, and we got lost."

"No problem," Carlo said. "Is it the Zancani girl she's with?"

"Yes, do you know them?"

"No, they keep themselves to themselves. I know a little of their history, a tragic story."

"Gianfranco is afraid they bring bad luck."

"Nonsense, don't pay any attention to him, typical Venetian. He's down in the lab waiting for us. The director, Professor Grimani, is coming, so we're on our best behaviour." Carlo winked. "He controls the purse strings."

Gianfranco greeted them in the lab. There were three archaeologists from Penny's dig, and a group of lab technicians in white coats, waiting expectantly. The director had, as yet, not arrived. They all stood together chatting as if at a cocktail party, though the talk was all on the same subject: the contents of the chest. Professor Grimani arrived with Dr Loredan, and a photographer. Dr Sara Loredan ran the university's publicity department.

Carlo switched easily into charm mode. He smiled, joked, and flattered, as he introduced everyone to the director. He instructed the technicians to bring the chest out of the freeze chamber. A technician pressed the red button on the side of the machine to release the vacuum, and undid the door. A blast of ice-cold air filled the room. The four technicians brought the chest out. There was the carving of the winged lion and beneath it the words PAX TIBI MARCE EVANGELISTA MEUS. It was over five hundred years since the chest had last been opened. The bottom of the chest, which had been embedded in the sand, had an intricate pattern of holes.

Carlo called Gideon over. "Perfect, the wood is almost as it was before it fell into the sea. Shall we open?"

Dr Loredan wanted them to wait. She said there must be photographs of the chest, before it was opened, with il Direttore, and Carlo, and with ever an eye for what the media liked, the beautiful English archaeologist. The photographer positioned Penny, Carlo, and Professor Grimani around the chest.

Then there was to be a photo of Gideon and Carlo opening the chest. The two of them tried to lift the lid, but it wouldn't budge.

"It's locked," Gideon said. "You wouldn't think the lock would work after all this time."

Carlo called a technician, who knelt and looked at the lock. He went away, and returned with a box of tools and made a variety of probes into the keyhole. He squirted oil in, and again tried, and they heard the lock move. They heard a mechanism clanking and shifting within the chest. The technician looked up at Carlo, wondering what he should do.

Carlo raised his eyebrows, "Strange, this is no ordinary chest. Come let's try the lid again." Carlo, Gideon, and the technician slowly lifted the lid. There was a gasp when they saw the mummified corpse of a girl inside, with what looked like the back of a framed painting lying on top of her. For a second there was utter silence, and then a burst of noise as they all spoke at once. The technician crossed himself. Carlo lifted the frame from the body and turned it around. His face and shoulders appeared in a mirror, surrounded by a patterned frame.

"Mirror, strange." He gave it to Penny, and knelt to look at the corpse. First in Italian and then in English he said: "It is another girl. The body has been mummified. There is a mark around her neck, above the necklace. There's no sign of water damage."

"How?" Gideon said.

"Extraordinary," Carlo knitted his brow. "It's been designed to keep water out, but for what reason?"

"Some forgotten ritual?" Sara Loredan said.

"I don't know. It's mysterious. It'll be interesting to discover how the mechanism inside worked."

The photographer took a photo, zoomed in on the pearl and bead necklace with the mark above it, and clicked the camera. He asked Penny to hold up the mirror so he could photograph it.

"The frame is beautifully engraved fruits and flowers," she said, "I wonder why it was in the chest with her?"

Carlo asked the technicians to get something to transport the corpse to the lab, where they had the bodies of the other girls. They returned with a stretcher. The body was raised from the chest and placed on it. Penny looked at the poor creature. She wasn't much bigger than Venetia. Her hair still hung over her shoulders onto a faded green dress. It, too, had been strangely preserved.

Carlo knelt, and looked at the chest. He saw the pattern on the inside of the lid. "This is not Venetian," he said. "The serpents, the pattern is foreign." He looked inside. "The compartment must have been watertight. The mechanism we heard is some kind of seal. It's lead lined, but the chest itself is designed to sink – see the holes around the bottom. It's very elaborate."

"Why," Penny said, "why go to such lengths?"

"I think the girl was killed; someone of great power and wealth didn't want this floating to the surface. There's more here, her possessions, more dresses. We must be careful. I will get gloves."

The photographer took photo after photo, while Sara Loredan scribbled away in a notebook. Penny gazed at the mirror. Gianfranco came and looked at it with her. The pattern was beautiful, and unlike anything she'd ever seen. She wondered at its age, and hoped she'd be able to clean and restore it. "It's lovely isn't it?" she said to Gianfranco.

"Fantastic, such craftsmanship, but why did this to happen to her?" Gianfranco shook his head.

Carlo returned with white cotton gloves and large plastic bags. He and the technicians put on the gloves and carefully lifted the dresses from the chest, and placed them inside the bags. There were four dresses of different colours: blue, black, red and yellow.

Sara Loredan pointed in the chest. "Guarda, look," she said breathlessly. There, tucked in the corner of the chest, underneath where the dresses had been, was a book, a quill pen, and a bottle.

Carlo picked the book up and opened it, seeing Elena's faded black handwriting. His face turned white, his mouth hung open, as he peered at the letters. His brow furrowed in concentration. "It's her diary. The letters are very faint, but with magnifying glass I will be able to read them. This is incredible. We will know who she is, and maybe why this happened. She must be from a noble family; the mirror and dresses are very fine."

He asked a technician to get some smaller bags. When he returned, Carlo put the book in a bag. "I will work on this later."

"What a story," Sara Loredan said to Penny.

Carlo picked the bottle up from the chest, bagged it, got the quill pen and also bagged it. He passed Penny a large bag for the mirror and helped her put it in. "I'd love to clean and restore it. It's so beautiful. I think it's early Murano work."

"Of course, mirrors were one of your research projects. You must work on it. Come here on Monday."

"This is so exciting." Penny said, looking around at everyone.

Professor Grimani agreed, said he must be on his way, and thanked everyone for their work.

Carlo and Gideon closed the now empty chest. "It's a miracle these things have been so well preserved," Gideon said. "I've never seen anything come up from the sea in such good condition."

Carlo said, "The seal protected everything inside. The mud and shale have protected the outside. I want to find out everything I can about this girl."

"A historical detective story," Dr Loredan said. "I'll have the press eating out of my hand. Do you think those other girls are connected? The ones in the separate graves, the one with the brick, and the chains — the so called vampires?"

Carlo remembered the marks around the neck. "Did they think she'd been bitten by a vampire?" he said. "Did they use a mirror to see if she had a reflection? See if she had become one? But she would have had a reflection, so why kill her, and place the mirror in the chest? "

"Perhaps someone said she did not," Dr Loredan said. "What I mean is, someone said he had killed her, to prevent her becoming undead. 'Look,' he would have said, 'I have saved her. Her reflection has come back.'"

"A bit fanciful," Carlo said, "Perhaps she was buried with the mirror to show she was not a vampire, so no need of a brick in her mouth. Maybe we can find out what really happened. Everything is exactly as it was, when the chest was sealed."

Dr Loredan looked at her watch. "I must go and do a press release. Keep me informed of progress, I want to know everything." She hurried off with the photographer.

Carlo picked up the bag with the book. "This will tell us more. It's going to be an interesting companion."

"I can't wait to start work on the mirror," Penny said.

"Exciting times, exciting times," Carlo said. "We're done for now. Ciao, have a good weekend, give Venetia my love."

Penny and Gideon left the university and walked over the Ponte Ognisante into the Calle de l'Indorador, with its overhanging medieval buildings, into the Campo Santa Margherita for lunch.

"I wonder what happened to that poor creature," Penny said. "She wasn't much older than Ven, and murdered for a stupid superstition. Do you really think they thought she was a vampire?"

"Don't know," Gideon said.

They had a leisurely lunch. They didn't want to be too early collecting Venetia, fearing they'd interrupt the preparations for the puppet show. It was three when they left the restaurant. They strolled back through Dorsaduro and across the Academia Bridge and made their way into Castello. They were in no hurry and this time, found their way to the Calle dei Preti, without problem. They rang the bell. Maria, Aldo's wife, opened the door and took them up to the living room. Elizabeta was waiting.

"Welcome," she said coming over and kissing them both. "Come sit down, the show is not quite ready. They will come and tell us. Cristofo has been roped in to helping, which of course he loves."

"Do you know what the story will be?" Gideon said.

"No, Isabella and Venetia have written it with a little help from Nonno."

19

The Puppet Show

Venetia was helping with the final preparations in the ballroom on the third floor of the palazzo. It was an enormous empty space which had seen better days. The walls were bare, peeling, and shabby; the floorboards were covered in dust and plaster. All that remained of the room's old grandeur was the high ornate ceiling. A huge black chandelier, fashioned like coral, hung from it. Cristofo had switched it on when they first came in. It had more than a hundred candle-shaped electric lights. He told Venetia they used to be real candles in the days when there had been dancing.

Venetia found it hard to control her puppet. Cristofo had stood behind her, holding her arms, and showing her how it was done. They had rehearsed and rehearsed. She'd felt his warm breath against her cheek as he whispered instructions. Finally she'd got the hang of it, and could do it on her own.

"By George, she's got it," he'd said when she mastered it, and laughed.

Aldo, who was also one of the puppeteers, brought in three high backed chairs for their audience. He placed them in front of the makeshift stage. He called Venetia and Isabella to help him erect a curtain. They slung it from two columns on either side of the stage, and drew it across so all was hidden to the audience. Everything was ready.

Cristofo said they must change into black smocks, so the audience would only see the puppets. "Illusion is everything. Come next door."

Venetia and Isabella followed Cristofo into an antechamber. Its door was built into the back wall of the ballroom and almost invisible to the eye. The room was windowless and empty, apart from an ancient torn leather sofa, whose stuffing was coming out, and a full length mirror on a stand. The black smocks were in a pile on the sofa.

"This is where ladies would come between dances to look at themselves, redo their makeup, and make sure they were at their most beautiful," Cristofo said. He stood between Venetia and Isabella and put his arms around them.

Venetia saw him in the mirror. He looked different as he knelt down to talk to them. There was something scary about him. For the first time, she noticed he dribbled from his thick lips as he talked. The mirror had revealed another side and it frightened her. She didn't want see it, and looked away.

"We will give them a show to remember," he said, and squeezed the two girls. He rose. "Aldo, the smocks."

Aldo brought the smocks, and passed them around. Isabella showed Venetia how to put it on. Aldo gave them a black balaclava each. The four of them were covered from head to toe in black. They looked in the mirror. The only things visible were their eyes and mouths.

"We look as if we're about to rob a bank." Cristofo laughed. "The Zancani gang! Ready? I'll get our audience."

He walked down to the sitting room. "Hello hello," he said beaming at Penny and Gideon, "the spectacular is ready, if you would like to take you seats. Please follow me." He led them upstairs to the ballroom. They'd not seen it on their tour of the house. Elizabeta was ashamed of the state it had fallen into.

The first thing Penny noticed was the black chandelier hanging from the high ceiling. "Wow that's fabulous," she said pointing at it.

"It is isn't it?" Elizabeta said. "It's been hanging here since the 1800s. This used to be a ballroom. We have never used it. Maybe when Isabella is grown up?"

"Take your seats," Cristofo said.

"It's just like a real theatre," Gideon said.

Cristofo switched off the lights, and disappeared behind the curtain. Slowly, Aldo drew the curtains open, and moved off to the side to operate a spotlight. Two puppets about three foot high, dressed in the 18th century fashion of low cut bodices, with tiny waists, and wide hips, curtsied to the audience. Behind them, Isabella and Venetia were dressed in black. You could just make them out when they moved. To the side of the stage was a little easel with a miniature painting. Violin music began to play and the two puppets danced. A third moustachioed puppet appeared, controlled by Cristofo. It had a paintbrush attached to its hand. It danced over to the easel, and began to paint. The music stopped, and Cristofo's puppet beckoned the dancing girls to the painting. Aldo drew the curtain on the scene.

The curtain opened again. The moustachioed puppet was joined at the easel by two male puppets. One dressed in a light blue frock coat, the other in a leather jerkin. The puppets were master and servant. They were controlled by Aldo and Isabella, and in reversal of roles, Aldo was the master. Venetia had taken over control of the spotlight. The moustachioed puppet danced around waving his paintbrush and pointing again and again at the easel. Venetia moved to the side and turned on some music. It was an old recording of Caruso, strange and captivating, a haunting voice from another time. Aldo's puppet had fallen in love with one of the girls in the painting. Venetia drew the curtain across.

The next scene opened with Venetia's puppet sitting in front of a little table with a mirror. The puppet in blue silk frock coat entered. More Caruso played, as the blue puppet fell to his knees in a beseeching pose. The curtain closed.

It opened on a wedding scene. Some Mozart played and the curtain closed. Penny, Gideon and Elizabeta rose clapping and shouting bravo. The curtain drew back, and the four puppeteers removed their balaclavas, and bowed to the audience.

"What a show, terrific," Gideon said, approaching the stage.

"Shall we adjourn downstairs for tea?" Elizabeta said.

"Yes I think we're ready for tea. Aren't we girls?" Cristofo said. "Let us get out of our black clothes. We'll meet you downstairs, and I'll light the fire."

In the living room, Cristofo lit a match and put it to the kindling in the fireplace. Soon a good blaze was going, and he added some logs. He returned to sit. "So tell us what was in the chest."

"It was another girl," Penny said. "The body had been mummified. She was in a green dress. A mirror was on top of her. Carlo thinks she was suspected of being a vampire like the girl with the brick. She has a mark on her neck – he thinks they thought it was a vampire's bite."

"Why?" Elizabeta said.

"It's the mirror. The legend vampires have no reflection?"

"But it would not be possible, for her not to have a reflection in this mirror, unless..." Cristofo stopped.

Gideon said. "Maybe a trick of the light prevented her reflection appearing."

"We found a notebook hidden under the clothes in the chest. Carlo is reading it now. He thinks it may tell us what happened."

"What sort of book?" Cristofo said. "What's in it?"

"A journal, possibly. We'll find out on Monday – Carlo'll be working all weekend if I know him."

"Extraordinary!"

"It might even be in the papers," Gideon said. "Professor Grimani wants to make a big thing of it. He's looking for money."

"Perhaps I should ring him. Maybe I can help," Cristofo said.

Aldo appeared bearing a huge silver tray with teacups saucers plates, and a silver teapot. Behind him, Maria carried another tray of sandwiches, and an old fashioned cake stand.

"Here we are," said Elizabeta, "a traditional English tea for you; we have ham, egg, cheese, or cucumber sandwiches."

They sat eating sandwiches and drinking tea, and discussed the performance. Penny said it was the best puppet show she'd seen.

"So it must be the first you have seen," Cristofo said, laughing.

"No," Penny said, joining in the laughter. "You are very professional. You, Aldo, and Isabella have done it before?"

"We have of course, and Venetia for a beginner was excellent. She had very good control of her puppet."

Elizabeta now offered them cake. There was a Victoria sponge, battenburg, madiera, and chocolate cake.

"You're spoiling us, this is as good as tea at the Grand in Brighton," Gideon said.

Elizabeta cut the cake, and passed it around. "We love our English tea, and this is a chance for us to indulge ourselves," Cristofo said, cutting himself another piece of Victoria sponge.

They talked and ate by the glow of the fire, and finally at seven Gideon said to Penny, "Gosh is that the time? We mustn't overstay our welcome." And to Cristofo and Elizabeta, "Thank you so much, it's been really enjoyable. You must come to dinner with us sometime. We'll fix something up. I'll do something English, perhaps steak and kidney pudding."

They rose and kissed. Cristofo showed them to the door. As he opened it he said, "I'll ring you on Monday."

They walked home through swirling mist. A fog had come down over the city while they'd been having tea, and a damp dismal sheen was rising off the canals and floating into the streets. "It's a bit creepy tonight," Penny said. "A bit 'Don't Look now.'"

"Why don't look now, Mummy?"

"Oh nothing, Mummy's being silly. You did very well with your puppet. Did you practice long?"

"All day till you came. Mummy, can I get a puppet?"

"I should think so, it will be Christmas soon."

They walked to the Campo Arsenale through thickening fog. The moon shone through it, creating a ghostly white light. There was a clammy wintry chill in air. Its touch was cold like the caress of icy fingers. They quickened their pace. There were no sounds except for their own hurrying footsteps. A church bell sounded somewhere and they heard footsteps behind them.

Venetia walked between her parents and, in spite of her daddy having one hand and her mummy the other, she was uneasy. Something was unsettling her, but she didn't know what. She didn't think it was the footsteps behind, but whatever it was, she wanted to get home. It was safe there. She thought about what she'd heard over tea and remembered the photo she'd taken in the mirror. She'd seen herself, and then in the photo she'd vanished. She'd had no reflection. Was there something different about her? Not many children liked her, only special ones like Lucy and Isabella. "Vampires aren't real are they?" she said suddenly.

"No of course not, Ven, just superstition like witches and fairies. What made you say that?" Penny said as they crossed a bridge.

A black figure came out of the mist ahead of them. It seemed to have emerged from nowhere. They'd thought the footsteps had come from behind, but there it was in front. It turned and came towards them. They stopped.

"Hello, how are you? Nice to see you," said a cheery American voice. "I thought I heard English voices."

"You gave us quite a fright," Penny said, recognising the priest, "looming out of the fog like that."

"I'm sorry," he said. "The city is a little scary in the fog, but I rather like it."

"Are you on your way to eat?" Gideon asked.

"I am. What about you? Will you be coming in tonight?"

"No we've just had the most enormous tea with friends, but perhaps tomorrow?"

"Why don't you join me tomorrow? We can get acquainted. Shall we say seven thirty?"

They were now outside the restaurant and back in their own campo. "That would be great, wouldn't it?" Gideon said looking at Penny.

"Yes," she said.

"Good, see you tomorrow. I'll ask them to hold a table." He walked into Paulo's.

"Have a good meal," Gideon called after him.

The Mantells went on to their building and up into the warmth of their flat. It had been a long day.

20
Faustina Gets Ready

Faustina poured the sweet smelling liquid from the big glass bottle her mother used into a smaller plastic bottle. She had two rags, one for Anna, and one for the girl. She put them into her shopping trolley along with the rope, screwdriver, saw, spanner, knife, plastic gloves, and a woollen scarf. Faustina would use the scarf to wrap around her fist when she broke the girl's window.

Faustina had decided she wouldn't eat with Anna. She'd got carried away with the idea of being Federico for a whole evening. It would be hard not to give something away — better to deal with Anna straight away. She would eat whatever Anna had prepared alone, and wait, then break into the girl's room at 1am.

Faustina dressed in Federico's clothes and left her flat at 7:30. No one saw her leave. She trundled her shopping trolley over the bridge into Castello. As she walked unseen through the mist, she could hear chatter coming from the bars of the Via Garabaldi. At 8pm she arrived outside Anna's door and rang the bell. The door opened and there was Anna, smiling.

Faustina lowered the pitch of her voice to the practiced growl, "Buona Sera."

Anna ushered her in. Faustina could smell the rich Bolognese sauce. She explained she'd been unable to get the pump, but it was expected in the next day or two. She would remove the old pump now. She patted her shopping trolley and said all the tools for the job were here.

Anna took Faustina upstairs to the kitchen and said supper would be ready in thirty minutes. Faustina pulled the trolley up to the washing machine. She noticed the shutters in the kitchen had been pulled to for the night. This was good. She'd thought she might have to do it herself. She watched as Anna stirred the sauce, and looked inside the shopping bag for the bottle. Making a show of searching for something, Faustina soaked a rag with the liquid. She got up and stepped quickly behind Anna and pressed the rag hard against her nose and mouth. Anna struggled briefly and passed out, as Faustina knew she would. She'd applied exactly the pressure her mother used.

Faustina tied Anna's hands behind her back and cut the rope and tied more around Anna's legs. She dragged the comatose woman out into the hall, and into the bedroom where she left her on the floor and returned to the kitchen. The spaghetti was in a packet by the cooker. A saucepan of water was just coming to the boil.

Faustina had not eaten meat since her mother had died. It had been served up as a treat once a month. She put her nose to the saucepan and smelt the aroma. When the pasta was ready she drained it and poured the rich red sauce over it. There was plenty of time — at least four hours before she could shift the table out of window and onto the ledge opposite. Faustina would have to give Anna another dose of the calmer before then.

After she'd eaten a hearty meal, she put on the yellow plastic gloves and wiped every surface she'd touched. Faustina knew all about fingerprints from the radio. After she'd done that she opened the shutters and looked across the calle. The girl's shutters were closed and there was no sign of light. She must be asleep.

Faustina looked at her watch. It was 10:30. She cleared the table, turned it upside down and sawed off the legs. There had been no sound from Anna in the bedroom. She'd apply another dose of the calmer at midnight. That should ensure Anna was out until well after three, by which time Faustina and the girl would be safely home. Faustina sat thinking of the life ahead. It would be very different. She would be the mother now.

At midnight, while the great bell from St Marks was still sounding, she re-soaked the rag and went to the bedroom. Anna lay completely still on the floor. Faustina knelt beside her, and lifted her head up so she could apply the cloth. The woman felt cold and lifeless.

"Anna," Faustina said, shaking her. Nothing happened. Faustina put her hand to Anna's mouth to see if she was breathing. She was not. She was just as Faustina's mother had been on that morning. For the first time in her life she'd gone out of the flat alone, wondering what to do. A neighbour, seeing her panic, had asked her what the matter was. Faustina knew she was not supposed to talk to anyone, but this was different. She said her mother needed a doctor. The doctor had told Faustina her mother had had a heart attack. Anna was dead like her mother. Maybe it was better like this – the dead don't talk.

Faustina undid the ropes tying Anna's hands and legs. She'd leave the body where it was. Someone would find it one day. Faustina returned to the kitchen, and put the ropes back in the shopping bag. She took it down to the lobby, and left it by the wheelchair. She looked at her watch. It was almost 1am.

21

<u>The Flu</u>

Venetia awoke. It was very dark. Her body ached, her head hurt, she felt hot, and it was painful to swallow. She wanted to get up and go to her mummy but felt too weak. Venetia wondered if she'd caught the flu. Something was scratching at the window. A rat she thought, trying to get in. Her daddy had said there were rats in the city at night. Venetia struggled out of bed but could barely stand. She must get her daddy before the rat got in. She made it to the door and hung on for support, then turned for a moment, and froze. The shutters were open. There at the window was a face staring in at her. It had something in its hand. It seemed to beckon to her, to wave her towards it. Its mouth was moving. It was saying something, but she couldn't hear what it was. Her legs gave way under her, and she fell to her knees. Desperate, Venetia began to crawl away out of the room. She daren't look back. It took all her strength to inch into the living room.

Penny's eyes snapped open. Her heart was beating too fast. What had woken her? Something was wrong. Had she heard something? Gideon was still sleeping soundly beside her.

She got out of bed and opened the door onto the sitting room. She switched on the light. Venetia lay motionless on the floor. Kneeling beside her, Penny said, "What's the matter darling? What's happened?"

Venetia croaked. "Face at the window. Someone...horrible..."

Penny felt Venetia's head. "You're burning up." Her daughter was delirious. This had happened before. When she'd had a high temperature, she'd hallucinated. She picked her daughter up and carried her to bed. "Lie quietly darling. I'll be back in a minute with some paracetamol. It'll make you feel better."

Penny jumped as she heard the shutter bang behind her. She turned to look. It must have blown open. She opened the window and looked briefly up and down the alley. It was still very misty. As far as she could see it was deserted. The air outside was cold and damp. She pulled the shutters to and re-fastened them. She hurried to the bathroom to get the pills from the cabinet. As she passed the bed, she said to a half-awake Gideon, "I think Ven's caught the flu, she's got a fever, she seeing things. We must get a doctor out."

Gideon got out of bed and followed Penny into his daughter's room. Penny cradled Venetia's head as she gave her a paracetemol and held a glass of water to her lips. "Drink the pill down darling; it will lower your temperature."

Venetia took a mouthful of water and swallowed. Gideon put his hand to her head. It was burning hot. He stroked her hair. It was wet with perspiration. He went out to telephone, and stood for a second wondering who to call. He remembered the Zancanis and found their letter and telephone number. It was the middle of the night, but he had no choice. He listened to his mobile ringing and ringing, and at last someone answered.

"Hello Elizabeta, it's Gideon. Sorry to ring you at this hour. Venetia's very ill – she's burning up. She's hallucinating. We don't know what to do. Could we call your doctor...?"

He went back to Venetia's bedroom. Penny was sitting on the bed holding her daughter's hand. "I called Elizabeta, she's ringing their Doctor and will call me back."

"Good," Penny said.

"I'll go and get dressed," he said.

He'd just finished dressing when his mobile rang. He ran to answer it. "Pronto, yes yes, thank you so much."

Penny came out to him. She whispered. "She's dropped off to sleep. Was that Elizabeta?"

"Yes," Gideon said. "Dr Gabrieli should be here in about half an hour."

"I'll get dressed. Make us a cup of tea, darling."

She dressed and returned. They sat over tea, waiting for the Doctor. It was now three in the morning. The doorbell rang. Gideon pressed to let the doctor in, and switched on the light over the stairs. He waited for the doctor.

"Grazie per venire," he said, "Parla inglese?"

"Yes I speak English," the Doctor said. His English had a strong Italian accent with a hint of American.

Penny was now at Gideon's side. "She's in here, Doctor." She led Dr Gabrieli into Venetia's room. She woke her daughter. "Venetia darling, Doctor Gabrieli is here to see you."

He was a tall thin man in his fifties, with greying hair and a pockmarked face. He was in a brown sweater that he'd pulled over his pyjama top, and a pair of black jeans. He put his bag down on Venetia's dressing table. "Have you taken her temperature?" he asked.

"We don't have a thermometer," Gideon said, "but her head is very hot."

Dr Gabrieli opened his bag and retrieved a thermometer. He shook it, looked at it, and went over to the bed where Penny was sitting holding Venetia's hand.

"Hello Venetia, can you put this under your tongue?" He put the thermometer into her mouth and looked at his watch. He went back to his bag, got out his stethoscope, and put it around his neck. He looked at his watch again and took the thermometer out. He looked at it, "Forty, it is high. Fever is part of the body's defence mechanism. The body creates heat so the foreign organism cannot survive. Fever is a good thing, most of the time. Can I just listen? Can you sit up?"

Penny helped Venetia sit up. The Doctor put the stethoscope to her chest. He listened. "Say thirty nine, please."

Venetia croaked. "Thirty nine."

"Lean forward please." He put the stethoscope to her back and listened. "And again, thirty nine. Thank you." He took off his stethoscope and put it back in his bag. "Open your mouth please, hmm. Do you have stomach ache?"

Venetia nodded.

"I'm going to test for swine flu. I'm going to put something up your nose Venetia. It won't hurt." He put a cotton swab into Venetia's nose, took it out and put it into a bottle of liquid. He watched as the swab turned colour. "It is as I thought. She has the H1N1 strain: swine flu. She will need plenty of rest, plenty of fluids. Standard painkillers from the pharmacy."

"I gave her a paracetemol earlier."

163

"Good, fine, I will notify the school. She's at the Elementare in Via Garabaldi with Isabella?"

"Yes, that's right."

"Has Venetia been treated for Asthma in the last three years?"

"No," Penny said.

"Any other illnesses?" the doctor asked.

"No, she's pretty healthy generally."

He passed Penny his card. "My number. Ring me, if there is any change in her condition."

Penny took the card. "Thank you Doctor, thank you for coming."

"Not at all." He took a bottle out of his bag. squirted liquid onto his hands, rubbed them together and put the bottle back. He snapped his case shut. "Wash your hands as much as possible to prevent spreading the infection. Don't forget: don't be frightened to telephone me. That is what I'm here for. In a week she should be back to herself. I will telephone to see how she's doing."

Gideon showed the Doctor out, and thanked him again. They settled Venetia down and returned to bed. Neither of them slept and at six got up to start the day.

They spent the morning quietly reading and checking on Venetia. At eleven, Gideon went out to the pharmacy in Via Garabaldi and bought packets of Lemsip and a thermometer. At lunch, Penny tried to get Venetia to have some soup, but she wasn't hungry and only managed a few mouthfuls. At six, they took her temperature. It was just over thirty nine.

Gideon remembered the dinner appointment with Pat Rice. "We're supposed to be meeting the priest tonight. I don't know his number. I'll have to go down, and tell him what's happened. We can't go."

"You go," Penny said. "I'll stay."

"Are you're sure?"

She nodded. "I wasn't that keen anyway."

"OK," he said. "I quite like him, think he's interesting. I'll go."

At seven thirty Gideon went down to the restaurant. He saw Father Rice sitting at a corner table. "Hello," he said sitting, "I'm afraid it's just me. Venetia has the flu, and Penny's staying with her."

"Oh I am sorry. There's quite an epidemic. Schools have been closed. But I'm sure Venetia will be fine, the first three days are the worst in my recollection. Now, what will you have? I have a hankering for meat, steak and chips."

"Sounds good, I'll join you."

Father Rice called Rosa over and in flawless Italian ordered two steaks, chips and vegetables, and a carafe of the house red.

Over the food, Gideon told Pat Rice about the chest, the mummified corpse, the notebook, and the vampire theory.

"What a fabulous story. I can see why the media are interested. Vampires have a strange pull, particularly with teens these days. I suppose it's that they're not of this world, more exotic than the boy or girl next door, and of course dangerous."

"You don't think they exist?"

"Certainly not, they are a fiction, but all things have a basis. Some people can take your soul. By the way, did you get to see the Judgement at the Hellenic institute?"

"No we haven't had a chance."

They continued to talk, telling each other their histories. As an atheist, Gideon usually felt ill at ease with clergymen. Pat Rice didn't have that affect on him. Maybe it was the wine and the food. There was something he'd always wanted to ask a priest, but never had the chance, and now he felt he could. "I've had this question for a long time; I hope you won't mind me asking. If our God is a loving God, why does he send people to hell?"

"I've been asked that before. The biblical picture is that sin separates us from God, and the ability to receive or give love. I saw this in the drug addicts in Baltimore. They had no interest in anything but their next fix. Complete disintegration of personality, and as time passed they needed more and more heroin. Then isolation set in, as they began to blame everyone but themselves for their problems. How often have I heard 'No one understands, everyone is against me.' A common image of hell is fire and fire disintegrates."

He looked thoughtfully at Gideon, "I'm sure you have seen the kind of disintegration, self-centredness creates. We know selfishness, and self absorption leads to bitterness and envy; to paranoid thoughts, mental denials and distortions. Imagine when we die we don't end, but spiritually our life extends on into eternity. Hell is a soul living like this forever." He took a gulp of his wine. "Our conversation has taken a rather serious turn, forgive me."

"Not at all Father, I started it. It was very enlightening. I'm afraid I don't believe in God or life after death. I do believe in heaven and hell, here on earth though."

"What a shame. But you are young, there is plenty of time, and you may change your mind. God believes in you." Pat Rice smiled warmly at Gideon, who suddenly felt slightly uncomfortable. He didn't know what to say. He looked at his watch. It was gone ten.

"Is that the time? I ought to get back. Penny's had a long day. I'll get the bill." He waved at Rosa and mimed bill writing.

"No let me," Father Rice said. "You are here at my invitation."

"No no, this is my treat," Gideon said putting his credit card down on the bill Rosa had brought.

"Thank you. We must do this again when Venetia is better, and it will be my treat. I have a week of Texan ladies in front of me, the Daughters of the Alamo on an art tour. They've spent a week in Florence, and now they come to Venice. They arrive tomorrow. I meet them at the station at midday, and from then until Sunday for my sins, I am their guide."

Rosa reappeared with the credit card machine. Gideon put in his number and confirmed the transaction. The two men got up and saying "Buona notte" to Rosa, made their way out of the restaurant. They stood outside for a moment and shook hands.

"Give my love to Penny and Venetia, and say I hope she gets well soon. I will say a prayer."

"Thank you, Father. Good luck with the Texans."

"Yee ha," he said chuckling. "Ciao Gideon, thank you for the dinner." He turned and walked back down the calle, whistling 'Home on the Range'.

Gideon smiled at the departing priest. It had been an interesting evening. He let himself quietly back into the flat. Penny was sitting reading in the living room.

"Hello," he whispered. "How's Ven?"

"Sound asleep. How was your evening?"

He told her all about his conversation. "He is a charming man, very spiritual."

"Well he would be, he's a priest," Penny said. "Nothing else to think about."

22

Faustina Returns

Faustina had arrived back at 2am. The fog had been thick, almost impenetrable, but Faustina did not need to see, she could walk these streets blindfold. She had come so close to getting the girl, been about to break the glass and open the window, when she'd seen a light go on. She'd panicked, scrambled back into the kitchen, pulled the table in after her and closed the shutters. In the dark, she'd waited, her ears straining to hear. She'd heard the girl's window open, and the shutters being pulled back.

When she'd thought it was safe, she'd hurried downstairs, got the shopping trolley, and crept out into the calle. She'd had the presence of mind to take the front door key with her. If she was lucky, she would be able to use the house again. Unless the woman had some appointment, she was unlikely to be missed. Faustina would give it a couple of nights, and let things settle.

The girl had seen her. Would her parents believe her? Faustina knew she'd managed to get the shutters unlatched without leaving a scratch. She'd simply slipped the knife in between a gap and lifted the latch. They'd think they'd not been shut properly and blown open. It was lucky she hadn't actually got as far as breaking the window. No, the parents would think the girl had imagined it. They might check on their daughter for a couple of nights, but they'd soon relax.

The girl had looked at her. Their eyes had met and Faustina knew more than ever that this girl was special. Faustina had beckoned to her, thinking she too understood their destiny. But the stupid girl had been frightened. Next time she would not be Federico – she would be Faustina and the girl would see it was her new mother.

Although Faustina had been tired after everything that had happened, she'd kept to her routine and said the morning and midday prayers. In the early afternoon, she'd walked by Anna's house to see if there was any sign of disturbance. Everything was as it had been. She checked no one was looking, unlocked the door and slipped in. She went to the bedroom. Anna still lay on the floor. All was fine. She could still use the house. Next time she would succeed. She wouldn't have Anna to worry about. She wrapped the black headscarf around her head and left the house.

She walked by the bar, head held down. It was a pity not to go in and have a warming brandy, but Federico was gone. She missed him. She missed wearing the beret and the blue quilted jacket. She missed being someone else.

As she walked down the Via Garabaldi, she wondered where the children were. They would normally be walking home from school. She saw a notice pinned to the door of the Scuola Elementare. It said due to an outbreak of swine flu, the school would remain closed until further notice. She stood in front of the door for a good five minutes staring at the words. Did the girl have flu? Was that why she had been restless? She would be weak and vulnerable. Faustina needed to look after her. Deep in thought, she returned to San Pietro.

23

__Sleepwalking__

At six thirty, Penny checked on Venetia. She was awake, so she took her temperature. It was down to 38.7.

"No school for you today, darling. We'll have a quiet time together."

Venetia nodded. She settled down into the bed. Penny tucked her up. There was no point going back to bed. She washed and dressed.

At eight thirty, Gideon went out to wait for Francesco. Penny telephoned Carlo.

"Carlo, Venetia's got flu. I won't be able to come in this week. I'll have to stay here."

She heard the excitement in his voice. "Of course of course, listen I have been working on the book. The girl's name was Elena Erizzo. Do you remember I told you Ludovico Erizzo lived where you and Gideon first stayed? It's probable he was her father. She wasn't there when she was killed, she had become a nun. My God, she was barely ten. She was in the Convent of Santa Maria delle Vergini. Somebody was grooming her, to use the modern term. Something unspeakable was going on. She wrote that the man told her she was chosen by God. It sounds as if he convinced her she was to be another Virgin Mary, the mother to a holy child."

"That's horrible," Penny said, "But the dress, that wasn't a nun's habit? And who told her these things? Do you know?"

"The man who killed her. God knows what else he did. She wrote, he told her to dress for God. God wanted to see her beauty. He must have been a priest of some standing to be able to come and go in the convent, and be allowed alone in her cell. There is more to read, maybe she will reveal his name. I have a date, June 1508, it was at the top of a page, very faint, but it gives me something to go on. I should be able to find out more. I'm going to the Convent this afternoon."

"Is it still there?"

"No, it was suppressed and given to the navy two hundred years ago. They demolished it, but bits of the garden remain, a few outhouses, and an arch where the old water entrance was. It's bricked up and embedded in the wall of the Arsenale near San Pietro. I've just telephoned them to get permission to look around. I want to get a feel of where she was. I have a real sense of her from her book."

"Is it near here?"

"No, it's at the far end of the Arsenale on the Rio delle Vergini. But look, I'm getting Francesco to take me in the boat, we will be passing by. Why don't I drop the mirror off with you? You can work at home while you look after Venetia."

"That would be great."

"A doppo. I'll get back to Elena's journal."

Penny took the opportunity to tidy the flat while Venetia rested. She made Venetia chicken soup for lunch, and was pleased to see her eat it. After lunch she read 'Rhymes without

Reason' to Venetia. It was an old favourite. She knew that the familiar was comforting when one was ill. When she felt poorly, she reread Georgette Heyer's regency romances.

They giggled together at the picture of the Greenland whale in Aunty Mabel's nighty, and Uncle Paul of Pimlico and his seven cats as white as snow. When she finished the book, she asked Venetia if she wanted to rest. She nodded, and settled down into the bed. Penny went back to her dusting and polishing. At four, the doorbell rang. It was Carlo and Francesco. She buzzed them in. Carlo came carrying two plastic bags, followed by Francesco bearing the mirror wrapped in cloth.

"Dove?" he whispered, looking for somewhere to put it down.

"Just put it on the table," Penny said, pointing at the table in the living room.

Carlo put the bags on the floor next to the table. "Your work tools, and cleaning chemicals," he whispered. "How is the patient?"

"She's sleeping, but I think she's a little better. Would you like a coffee or anything?"

"If it's no trouble." He pulled a newspaper out of the bag. "Have you seen this? We're front page news."

She took the newspaper from him as she led them into the kitchen and sat them down. There on the front page of *Il Gazzettino* under a huge headline, which she translated as Mysterious Murder, was the picture of her, Carlo, and Professor Grimani in front of the chest. "Wow," she said, "I've never been on the front page before. Can I keep this for my scrapbook?"

"Yes, I brought it for you. I have my own copy. Dr Loredan has been working the press. There is even talk of a television documentary; Grimani is talking five figure sums."

She filled the coffee pot up and put it on the cooker to boil through. "Gosh, do you mind? It'll interfere with our work."

"We'll have to put up with it. I've just had a call from my office – a pathologist came to look at the body. He thinks Elena was strangled – the mark around her neck wasn't what I thought. He says it looks like a rope.

"Have you been to the convent?"

Carlo pulled out a notebook from his pocket and showed her a rough sketch of the convent arch embedded in the wall. "You can't tell from my picture, but it's the Virgin and Child flanked by St Mark and St Augustine, the founder of the order to which the nuns belonged."

Penny saw below the sketch he'd written in capitals SPES ET AMOR GRATO CARCERE NOS RETINENT S.M. DELE VERZENE. "My Latin's not what it was," she said. "Well, it never was actually. What does it say?"

"It says hope and love keep us in this pleasant prison." He sniffed. "The convent records will be in the state archive at the Frari. I've made an appointment to go there tomorrow." He looked out at the fading light. "We must go. Francesco will be on overtime if we're not careful." He winked at the boatman. They both got up to leave.

"Ring me tomorrow – keep me up to speed."

"I will of course." The two men left and Penny checked on Venetia. She was still asleep. She thought about taking the mirror out of its cloth, but decided to wait until

173

Gideon got home. It wouldn't do to damage it. She heard Venetia call. She was complaining her head was hurting. Penny made up some Lemsip and got her daughter to drink it.

"Lie quietly and rest, Daddy will be home soon."

Gideon was home by six thirty and anxious to find out how his daughter was.

"Hello Daddy," she said quietly smiling.

"How are you feeling, little one?"

"A bit better, my head doesn't hurt. Mummy gave me medicine."

"Good." He sat on the bed, and told her about his day. "It was very cold out at sea, bitter east wind straight off the mountains. I wish I'd been tucked up in bed like you."

Penny said, "Let's take your temperature again." She put the thermometer under Venetia's tongue. It read 38. "It's still a bit high."

"I do feel better, Mummy. Can't I get up and watch television?"

"Well, I suppose it wouldn't hurt. You can lie on the sofa, with a blanket. Come on then, let's get you up."

Gideon got Venetia's dressing gown and put it on her. He carried her to the sofa.

"What's that on the table?" she said.

"That's the mirror from the chest Daddy found at the bottom of the sea. Carlo brought it for me to clean. I'll start tomorrow. I want Daddy to help me get it out of its wrapping."

"Shall we do it now?" he said.

"Why not?"

He held the mirror up while Penny took the cloth wrapping off. "Just lie it back down on the table," she said.

"Can I see, Mummy?" Venetia said getting off the sofa, and not getting far before Gideon picked her up and carried her over. She looked at the mirror.

"What do you think, Ven? It was at the bottom of the sea for five hundred years. I bet it's one of the oldest mirrors in Italy."

"It's beautiful. I wonder who looked in it."

Penny shivered, remembering its history, and spoke before Gideon could. "I expect it was a princess. It's such a lovely mirror. Look at the patterns on the frame. They're silver fruits and flowers, do you see? I'll clean them tomorrow, and you'll see them better."

Gideon took Venetia back to the sofa and put the television on for her. He flicked through the channels and found an old Hollywood film, with knights at a tournament. "How about this, Ven?"

She nodded, and snuggled up in her blanket. He saw her put her thumb in her mouth, as she used to when she was little. He smiled at her.

Penny covered the mirror with the cloth to protect it. "Shall I make us all an omelette? We can eat it in here."

Venetia nodded, with her thumb still in her mouth. Gideon said he'd like that. She went off to the kitchen and he sat next to his daughter. Penny brought the omelettes in on a tray. He helped Venetia sit up and eat hers. She finished it.

"You're getting your appetite back?" he said.

"Yes, Daddy. I was hungry.

They all sat watching the television. Sir Lancelot was stuck in quicksand, and his horse was pulling him out. When the film finished, Penny said she thought Venetia ought to go back to bed. Gideon picked her up and took her back to her room.

Penny followed. "How are you feeling, Ven? It's been over four hours since you had medicine. You could have another Lemsip?"

"I'm alright, Mummy." She snuggled down into the bed. Penny tucked her in.

"Goodnight sweetie," her daddy said.

"Goodnight darling," her mummy said, and turned off the light.

Gideon turned off the television. "Shall we sit in the kitchen? We won't disturb Ven there."

"OK. I think she's on the mend," Penny said. "Have you seen *Il Gazzettino* today?"

"Gianfranco bought one out to the boat. You are photogenic; Gianfranco said all the men of Venice will be talking about you. It's quite a story — murder, mystery, intrigue, and vampires. This will run and run, as they say."

"Carlo said there's talk of a TV documentary. He's found out her name was Elena Erizzo. He thinks she might have lived in the building where we stayed after we were married. Do you remember he told us a Provedatori of the Arsenale, Ludovico Erizzo, lived there? Her father, he thinks. He's going to the state archive tomorrow to research."

"Wow," Gideon said, just as Penny had. They talked on, sitting at the kitchen table, mostly about their work. Penny told Gideon she thought the mirror would take two to three days to clean.

Penny's mobile rang. She put her hand over the speaker and mouthed, "Cristofo." She listened, as he asked how Venetia was. Penny told him. Then he asked if she had heard from Carlo – had he found anything out. She told him everything Carlo had said. "No no, he doesn't know – he's going to trawl through the archives. Yes, I will. Bye."

"Gosh, he seems quite agitated about it. It is shocking, but it was a long time ago."

"I can understand why. The corruption of children is vile," Gideon said.

At ten, they decided they would have an early night. They checked on Venetia. She was sleeping soundly.

They went to bed and read, and at eleven turned off the light. Penny fell asleep almost immediately. Three hours later, she woke. Her heart was beating fast. Something was wrong. She thought she heard something outside. It was very faint — an unfamiliar sound. She listened hard — a faint scratching noise. She got up to check on Venetia. She opened the bedroom door and turned on the lamp by the sofa. Venetia wasn't there. Penny crept into her daughter's room. She was safely asleep in bed.

Penny checked the shutters hadn't blown open again, and returned to the living room. A cold breath brushed against her cheek. There was an icy damp chill to it, like wind blowing off the lagoon, and a smell she couldn't place. Gideon must have left a window open. She looked but they were shut. She wondered where the sudden cold draught had come from. She checked the kitchen windows, but they also were shut. She went back into the living room and saw the cloth covering the mirror had moved. Half of the mirror was exposed. Next to it was Venetia's blue glass fish. She looked at it puzzled. That hadn't been there. She put the cloth back and sniffed the air. The smell was gone.

She stood thinking. Could Venetia have got up, looked at the mirror, and gone back to bed? That was the only explanation. She returned to bed and lay awake thinking. She wondered whether Venetia might have been sleepwalking. Penny used to sleepwalk as a child. Her parents had found her in front of a cupboard trying to open it. As far as she knew, Venetia hadn't before, but the fever might have something to do with it. She remembered that she'd heard a sound before getting up —a faint scratching sound. Penny fell asleep and dreamed of Elena writing with quill pen in her convent cell.

When she next woke, she heard Gideon washing in the bathroom. She remembered the night's events but not the dream. It was just gone seven. She got up and opened the shutters to let the light in, and went into the living room. The mirror was still covered by the cloth. She picked up the fish and put it back on her daughter's dressing table. Venetia was stirring.

"How are you feeling?"

"It hurts to swallow, Mummy."

"Does your head hurt too?"

"A bit. My eyes hurt."

"I'll get you some medicine. Do you want me to leave the shutters for now?"

"Yes," she said quietly.

Penny helped her daughter sit up and drink the medicine. "I think when you've had this, you should try and get some more sleep. Did you get up in the night? Do you remember?"

"No Mummy. I was awake for a bit, I'd been dreaming about the puppets. I didn't get out of bed. My dream was all in Italian."

Gideon came in. "How's the patient?"

"She's going to have a little sleep, and then I'll get her some breakfast."

Gideon kissed his daughter. "See you this evening, get lots of rest."

They went to the kitchen. Penny told Gideon what had happened in the night. She didn't mention the cold air she'd felt against her face, or the strange smell. She thought she must have imagined them. The windows had all been shut to keep the warmth in and there was nowhere for the air to have come from. She had, after all, just woken up; maybe her senses were slightly off. She wondered now whether the draught could have come under the front door.

"I think you're right," Gideon said. "She was sleepwalking. The fish definitely wasn't there last night. It's a bit worrying. I mean, could she walk into something and trip up, or even walk out the door, fall down the stairs?"

"I don't know. I don't think so. I never came to any harm. I think I'll ring the doctor."

After Gideon had gone, Penny called Dr Gabrieli and told him Venetia's temperature was fluctuating. He said it was natural with flu. She told him she thought her daughter might be sleepwalking. Again he said it was not uncommon particularly in the 4-

179

12 age group, and particularly if the child had a fever. He asked her if she had sleepwalked as a child. When she said she had, he said the behaviour was often inherited. She said Venetia had moved a cloth in her sleep.

"Sleepwalkers can do all kinds of things," Dr Gabrieli said. "They can dress, undress, move furniture; there is even a case of a man driving a car. I don't know how much you know, Signora Mantell?"

"Not much really," Penny said. "Is it dangerous to wake Venetia?"

"No, I suggest you try guiding her back to bed. Another misconception is that sleepwalkers cannot harm themselves. This is not true. They often trip and injure themselves. I think you should lock the windows and your front door at night— those stairs. Don't leave anything on the floor she might trip on. It might be wise to lock the kitchen door — knives, cooker, etc all dangerous."

"Right, yes."

"Hopefully, once she's over the flu, these episodes will end. By the way, sleepwalking generally happens two to three hours after the child has fallen asleep. When does Venetia go to sleep?"

"She's usually asleep by nine."

"In theory, the walking will happen between eleven and midnight. Is there anything else?"

"No, thank you Doctor. It's been helpful."

"Good. I will call you at the end of the week to see how she is. Goodbye Signora Mantell."

Penny said goodbye. She took the cloth off the mirror and looked deciding where to begin. She got the brushes and laid them out on the table next to the mirror. Carlo had also provided her with orange sticks, cotton buds, cotton wool, several pairs of cotton gloves, cloths, and a fine silver liquid cleaner. Before starting, she checked on Venetia, who was still asleep. She got her jeweller's eyeglass. She would need it for the slow painstaking work ahead. She flexed her hands together, stretching her fingers before putting on a pair of the cotton gloves, then selected the smallest of the brushes and began.

She had been working for about niney minutes when she heard Venetia. She asked if she wanted anything and told Venetia she'd started on the mirror. Venetia said she would like a boiled egg with soldiers. Penny opened the shutters to let the light in, and made the breakfast.

After Venetia had finished her egg, she asked if she could get up and watch her mummy working on the mirror.

"It won't be very exciting." Penny looked at her daughter. She was so pale. "Venetia, I have been talking to the doctor. I think you have been sleepwalking. You took your blue fish into the sitting room last night. You don't remember, do you?"

"No, Mummy."

I used to sleepwalk when I was your age. You might wake in the night and find yourself out of bed. It's nothing to be frightened off. Just go back to bed, or come in to Mummy and Daddy's room. I'm going to lock the door through to the kitchen tonight. The doctor says it's dangerous."

Venetia wrinkled her brow. "How could I get up when I'm asleep? I wouldn't be able to see where I'm going."

"I know, that's why we have to lock the doors. You might fall over something. Anyway, now we know, Mummy and Daddy can listen out for you." She helped her daughter on with her dressing gown and carried her into the living room. She showed her the portion of the silver she'd cleaned.

"It's a bunch of silver grapes isn't it Mummy?"

"Yes it is. Come on, let's get you on the sofa and I'll get your drink." She got Venetia some apple juice and, putting her eyepiece back in, returned to her work.

Venetia watched from the sofa, occasionally asking what her mummy was working on. After an hour, she asked to go back to bed and to have her glass fish. Penny carried her back to bed and got the orange and blue fish from the dressing table. Venetia put them on the pillow and said she would have a little nap. "I want to dream I'm diving with Daddy down in the sea."

Penny remembered Gideon's birthday tomorrow. She would have to ring everyone and cancel the party. There was no point in keeping it a secret from Gid anymore. She would pop down to the restaurant and tell Paulo what had happened.

Later that afternoon, the phone rang. It was Carlo. "Just ringing to keep you informed; I've been to the archive. Elena was Ludovico's daughter. She was the youngest of his children, and she did live in your old building until she was nine. He and his wife Mariella had five daughters. He could not afford her dowry, so she went, as was the custom then, into a convent. According to the convent records, she escaped with a man. The abbess wrote she was possessed by the devil. In a sign of contempt, she urinated in her cell before she ran away. Her lover, it says, helped her escape with her possessions in the chest. Well, we know what really happened. She was strangled."

"Do you think the Abbess believed that, or was she covering up what really happened?"

"The church certainly hides the sins of its priests. She may well have known what really happened."

"You haven't found out who killed her?"

"She does not name him. I will go over it again. There must be something. How are you getting on with the mirror?"

"It's coming on nicely."

"And how is Venetia?"

"A bit better, but I think we'll have to postpone Gideon's birthday party. Venetia's not going to be up to going out."

"That is a shame. How about I ring Paulo, and have him prepare something and bring it up to the flat? After all, he's right there below. What do you say? And if Venetia is feeling a little better she might join us?"

"Do you think he would?"

"Of course, leave it to me. We will come at 7:30 as planned, and I will ask Paulo to bring the food at eight. Does that sound like a good plan?"

"Wonderful."

"Good good, I'll let you get on. Ciao, see you tomorrow."

She checked to see if Venetia was awake. "Hello darling, how are you feeling? Do you remember tomorrow's daddy's Birthday? And we were going to have a surprise party downstairs?"

"Yes, Mummy."

"We're going to have the party here now. Carlo's fixing it. You might feel well enough to come and sit for a bit, and you can give Daddy the lovely scarf you bought. Don't forget, it's our secret."

Venetia nodded. "I could come in my dressing gown."

"Let's concentrate on getting you well for tomorrow. The more you rest today, the better you'll feel tomorrow."

24

The Mirror

Gideon climbed the stone steps to their apartment and opened the door as quietly as he could. He found Penny leaning over the table in the living room, brush in hand, cleaning the mirror. She turned when she heard him and put down the brush.

"Hi," she said, as he kissed her on the cheek.

He looked at her work. She'd cleaned a quarter of the mirror. "It's looking good," he said. "How's Ven?"

"Asleep. Go have a look while I pack this away."

Gideon found Venetia awake. On either side of her on the pillow were her two glass fish. "Hello sweetie, how are you feeling?"

"I had a nice sleep and a dream about diving in the sea. There were lots and lots of fish, all different colours."

He sat down on the bed. "Sounds just like diving in the Red Sea. We'll go there one day and we can dive together. Perhaps when Mummy and Daddy have finished the work here, we could take a holiday."

"Could we take Isabella? She'd like diving."

"I don't think her grandparents would let her. It's a long way."

"Has Isabella got flu as well?"

"No, she had the injection, she's protected."

"Could she visit me?"

"I don't see why not. I'll get Mummy to give her granny a ring."

"Can I come and lie on the sofa again?"

"Come on then, let's put your dressing gown on." He put it on her, and picked her up. "Ven was wondering if Isabella could come and visit," he said as he put Venetia down on the sofa. "I said you might give Elizabeta a call."

"Yes, I will. Good idea. I rang Dr Gabrieli about the sleepwalking. It's quite common apparently. It's inherited — I'm afraid she gets it from me."

"Can she come to any harm – did he say?"

"He said to lock the kitchen and the front door. I was wrong: sleepwalkers can harm themselves."

"I'll lock everything before we go to bed."

"Dr Gabrieli said she'll most likely sleepwalk two or three hours after she's gone to sleep. I'm going to stay up and see."

"I'll keep you company."

They put Venetia to bed at 8:30, and she was asleep before 9:00. Penny and Gideon sat quietly reading, waiting for their daughter to leave her bed. At midnight nothing had happened. They heard the great bell from St Marks ring out twelve times.

Penny kissed Gideon. "Happy Birthday, darling. Sorry it's not going to be much of a day for you, what with Venetia."

"Thank you – what, no presents?"

"Well there might be a little something – you'll have to wait and see."

"I'll lock up. Is there anything you want from the kitchen?"

"No. I'll make sure there's nothing on the floor."

In the kitchen Gideon got himself a glass of water. As he drank, he looked out onto the Campo. There was a mist again, cloaking the square in an eerie light. It was the season of mists. He heard brisk footsteps echoing on paving stones below and saw a naval cadet walking hurriedly towards the Arsenale entrance. He watched the man key in a code to open the door. Gideon locked everything up and joined Penny in the bedroom.

"I'll leave our door open shall I?"

"Yes. Don't leave your shoes on the floor - she might trip if she comes in."

They fell into a heavy sleep. Outside, the mist thickened, turning to dense fog. The Marangona struck twice and the sound of the bell echoed across the sleeping city. Venetia dreamt she was a puppet on a stage, her lips moved, but someone spoke for her. Her eyes opened, and she rose from her bed and walked silently out of the bedroom and stood in front of the covered mirror. She felt her arm being lifted and her hand close around the corner of the cloth. She dragged it off the mirror and onto the floor.

In the mirror, a girl was sitting on a stool in front of another mirror, combing her golden hair. The mirror was identical to the one in front of Venetia and she could see the girl's face in it, and the room behind her. The walls were white and there was a small bed with an embroidered brown coverlet. A big wooden chest stood against the wall in a corner. Next to it was a plain black door. She knew she was dreaming. In real life mirrors reflected what was in front of them. This mirror was showing her another room, in another place.

She saw the door creep open and a man enter and stand behind the girl. He was in a red hooded robe. His back was to her, and she couldn't see his face. He was much bigger than the girl. His shoulders appeared in the mirror above the girl, but nothing more. She watched as he put a rope over the girl's head and began twisting a black stick. The girl looked as if she was screaming, but there was no sound. Her face was wrenched in pain. She was trying to pull at the rope. Venetia clenched her hands. She didn't like this. She wanted to wake up. She wanted this to stop.

She saw the girl fall to the floor. Still there was no sound. The man turned. She saw his face. She had seen it before in another mirror. His fleshy lips moved, and spittle appeared at the corner of his mouth. His voice was as dry as dust. He spoke in archaic Venetian, but she understood every word.

"A secret between two people," he said, and his black eyes looked into hers, "will only be kept, if one of them is dead."

The man melted from the mirror, leaving the room empty, except for the body of the girl in the green dress. She rose and came towards Venetia. Her white face was pressed right up against the glass. Her lips moved. She spoke slowly. Her voice was very soft.

"I know you. I know your name. We have been waiting for you." She dissolved into air, and came through the mirror. An ice-cold breath brushed Venetia's face, and a voice whispered from inside her. "I am here, we are one."

Venetia felt the warm trickle of urine on her leg. She woke, and saw herself in the mirror, and behind moonlight shone through the reflection of the living room window. There was nothing else there. She looked down, and saw a puddle on the carpet. Her body felt wet and cold. She knew something had happened but she didn't know what it was. She opened her mouth wide and let out a piercing scream.

Penny and Gideon woke, and simultaneously stumbled out of bed. "Oh my God, what is it?" Gideon said, as they rushed to their daughter.

Venetia was standing bolt upright next to the table. There was a look of absolute horror on her face. All the blood seemed to have drained from her. Her eyes were blank.

Gideon stood for a second in shock. "What's the matter, darling? What's happened?"

"I've weed on the carpet." She started to cry, and whimpered, "What's wrong with me, Mummy?"

Penny wrapped both her arms tight around Venetia and kissed her head. "Don't fret darling, it's the flu making you do this. You're soaked with sweat. It's not your fault. Let's get a new nighty and put you back to bed."

Gideon kissed his daughter. He tasted the damp cold salty sweat on her forehead. "You were sleepwalking, sweetie. You were probably dreaming you were in the loo."

"I was scared when I woke, Mummy. I was looking in the mirror. I was cold. I saw myself, and I was frightened. It looked like someone else. I saw someone else in the mirror."

"You must have been having a nightmare. Can you remember what you were dreaming? Was the girl in your dream? Was it one of those girls at school?"

"I can't remember. I don't think I was dreaming."

Penny took Venetia into her bathroom and washed her. "There, you'll soon feel better," she said, patting Venetia dry with a towel. "Do you want some talc, make you smell nice?"

Venetia nodded. Penny shook on some Johnson's talc, and rubbed it gently. "You smell lovely and fresh. Now lift your arms up, and I'll pop a clean nighty over your head." Penny took Venetia back to her bedroom. Gideon came in.

"Would you like some hot milk, Ven?"

"Yes please, Daddy."

"I'll check your temperature while Daddy's making the drink. Your temperature must have shot up. You were soaked with sweat." She looked at Gideon, "I wouldn't mind a hot milk too, Gid."

"OK," he said, "coming up."

Penny put the thermometer under Venetia's tongue and sat on the bed watching the second hand of her watch. When two minutes were up, she took the thermometer out. "I think you're on the mend darling. Your temperature's back to normal."

Gideon came in with three glasses of hot milk on a tray and a plate of biscuits. "Midnight feast, cookies," he said passing Venetia her milk. He offered her a chocolate chip cookie. She took one and sat up eating it and drinking the warm milk.

"Her temperature is normal," Penny said. "Not that I'm a doctor, but I think she may be over the worst."

"She does look better." He looked at his daughter. "The colour's come back to your face, Ven. You gave me a terrible shock in there. You were white as a sheet. Is the milk warming you up? Do you feel a bit better?"

"Yes, Daddy. I like midnight feasts." She gave him back the empty glass.

"3am feast, actually," he said, putting the glass on the tray. "You settle down now and get some sleep. Sweet dreams, little one."

She pulled the blanket up around her. Penny and Gideon kissed her goodnight, and switching off the light.

"Help me put the mirror in the kitchen," Penny said. "I don't want her coming and looking at it again."

They leaned over the mirror, and saw a small circular patch of mist. "Look," Gideon said, "Ven must have been leaning right up to it in her sleep. She's left a mark where she was breathing." He wiped it with the sleeve of his pyjamas.

They carried the mirror into the kitchen and put it on the table. Penny got the cloth from the floor in the living room. She covered the mirror. "We better sponge the carpet."

"I'll do it. You go back to bed," Gideon said. He filled a bowl with water and squeezed in a bit of detergent. He took it in and, kneeling, rubbed at the wet stain. When he'd done, he returned the bowl to the kitchen and locked up.

"Everything secure?" Penny said.

"Yes, all locked. Let's hope she settles now."

25

<u>The Party</u>

"What do you want to do today, darling?" Penny asked after Gideon had gone. "Do you want something to read? Don't forget Daddy's party tonight."

"I'm sleepy."

"Not surprised after last night." Penny tucked Venetia up.

She returned to the mirror. Gideon had helped her get it out of the kitchen before going to work. She fixed her eyepiece and, as a matter of routine, intertwined her hands, stretching the fingers, before putting on the cotton gloves to start. She was about to select a brush to clean more of the silver when she decided to take a closer look at the glass itself. In order for a smooth surface to act as a mirror, it must reflect as much of the light as possible, and absorb as little as possible. The mirror's surface must be perfectly smooth, so the light's rays are not scattered. This mirror was not perfectly smooth and its reflection was not perfect.

She bent over it, scanning the surface. It looked as if it had been made using a combination of the old 14th century glass bulb technique, and a thin sheet of reflecting metal. It was a hybrid. She remembered from her research that the first near perfect mirrors began to be made on Murano towards the end of 1507, and Elena had had the mirror in 1508. Her heart quickened as she wondered if this was an early attempt, a prototype. She would love to take it apart and study it more closely. If she'd had the tools, she wouldn't have been able to stop herself. She would ask Carlo tonight if she could.

She worked for the rest of the morning. At lunchtime she looked in on Venetia. She made them ham lettuce and tomato sandwiches. She sat on the bed, and the two of them munched on their lunch.

"You're looking much better, Ven. The sleep has done you good. Do you remember last night?"

"I remember sitting in bed having lovely hot milk, and Daddy saying he was worried about me."

"You don't remember pulling the cloth off the mirror, looking in the mirror?"

"No."

"Do you remember any dreams?"

"No, Mummy. Have you finished the mirror yet?"

"Nearly, I want to take the back off and have a close look at the glass. It's very exciting, Ven. I think it may be one of the first tries in a new way of mirror making. If it is, it's unique. There aren't any others left."

"Can I have a look?"

"OK, put your dressing gown and slippers on." She took Venetia's hand.

Venetia gazed at the silver surround. Her mummy had cleaned it beautifully. She could see all the silver fruits and flowers winding around each other. "It's so pretty."

"It is lovely, isn't it?"

Venetia looked in the glass. She hardly recognised herself. Something stirred inside. She mumbled very quietly. "Jèristu onto."

"What was that, Ven?"

"Don't know, Mummy, don't know why I said it. It just came out of my mouth. It must be something Isabella says. Can't remember what it means. I'm getting good at Italian; sometimes I dream in Italian. Isabella's nonno says I will be fluent."

"I think you will, too. You know much more than me. I think I'll try to finish the mirror before Daddy gets home and we can give him his presents. Do you want to lie on the sofa and watch telly while I work?"

"Yes, Mummy."

Penny flicked through the channels, stumbling on a film of Mozart's Marriage of Figaro. The familiar overture was playing. It was a recording of a production at La Fenice. "You'll love this, Ven, the music's wonderful."

Venetia settled on the sofa to watch. Penny put on her white cotton gloves, and began cleaning the last of the frame. The work, the music, and having her daughter close made her happy.

Three hours later, the mirror was finished. Venetia was fast asleep on the sofa and the opera had come to an end. Penny stood back and admired her work. She was very pleased with it. She would show everyone tonight. She put the cover back over the mirror, and switched the television off. She retrieved Gideon's presents and put them on the coffee table.

Venetia stirred and rubbed her eyes. She looked at the presents on the table. "Will Daddy be home soon?" she said.

It was just gone five and already dark. Penny said, "He'll be back in an hour. We'll have a nice cup of tea and give him his presents."

"What about a cake?"

"Paulo is making one – it's coming up with the food tonight. Don't forget," Penny put her fingers to her lips, "shhh, secret."

Venetia's stomach tightened. There was something frightening about secrets. She couldn't remember. She must keep this secret. She nodded at her mother, and slowly raised her finger to her lips.

"Shall we give you a little wash and put on a clean nighty so you can come out and say hello?" Penny took Venetia into the bathroom and washed her at the basin. She looked through the drawers and selected a warm cream flannel nightdress and put it on Venetia.

"Daddy said Isabella could come?"

"Oh yes, I forgot I was going to ring. I'll do it now."

While Penny phoned Elizabeta, Venetia watched for her daddy.

"Elizabeta and Isabella are coming to visit tomorrow, and Cristofo might come as well. He's very interested in the mirror," Penny said, putting her mobile back in her handbag.

"Goody. Look, Daddy's coming."

They watched Gideon getting out of the familiar launch. The mist had been replaced by a damp drizzle. He saw them up at the window and waved. Behind him the boat turned back up the canal. He crossed the wet campo and was soon in the dry with his family.

"Happy Birthday," Penny and Venetia said as he came in. He saw Penny was holding a big package wrapped in blue paper. Venetia had a small package wrapped in paper with a pretty fish design.

He took the presents, and kissed them both. "Thank you, what a lucky man I am. Now which shall I open first? I love the fish on the paper, Ven. I'm going to unwrap it carefully so I don't spoil it." He unwrapped the present, making sure he didn't tear the paper. "Oh, that's lovely." He tied the maroon scarf around his neck. "Just what I need, now that winter's here. And what have I here? I think I might know what this is." He pulled the wrapping paper off and smiled. He held the overcoat up against himself. "Thank you."

"Try it on," Penny said.

He put it on. "It's a good fit."

"You do look smart," Penny said.

He looked. "Yes I do, smart as an Italian. Thank you." He kissed them again. "Shall I make something for our supper?"

Venetia looked at Penny. "No need," Penny said, "I've ordered a take away from Paulo."

"Good heavens, I didn't know he did that."

"Oh yes, well he does now. We'll have a lovely family dinner. Ven's feeling a bit better and is going to stay up."

At 7:30 Gianfranco, Laura, and Carlo arrived together. Gideon was showering to freshen up after the day under the sea. When he heard the bell, he assumed it was Paulo with the food.

Penny greeted them at the door. Laura was in her fur coat looking like a film star, Gianfranco handsome as ever, and Carlo elegant as always. Carlo presented Penny with two bottles of champagne.

"I'll get some glasses," she said. "Will you open a bottle? Gid will be out in a minute."

They all stood in the kitchen as Carlo opened the champagne and poured it into five glasses. Venetia appeared in her dressing gown and slippers.

Carlo beamed. "Ahh, la bambina, how are you?" He picked her up, and gave her a big smacking kiss on her cheek. "Will you join us in a toast for Papa?"

Venetia nodded. "I've had flu. I'm better now."

"You better not have champagne. I'll pour you some apple juice." Penny got some juice and poured some into a wine glass. "She said the most peculiar thing today, when we were looking at the mirror *Jèristu onto*. She doesn't remember where she learned it, or what it means. She thinks Isabella must have said it."

Carlo smiled. "How quaint, it's old Venetian dialect. It means *you are clean now*. Her grandparents are old, and eccentric from what I gather. They probably still speak it. It's good to think the old words live on."

They heard Gideon come out of the bedroom. They all picked up their glasses. Penny took an extra one for him.

"Surprise," they said, holding up their glasses. "Buon Compleano, Happy Birthday."

Gideon took his glass of champagne, laughing. "What a nice surprise to have my friends here." He downed it in one, and asked for another. Then he opened his presents. From Carlo he received a Venetian cookery book, and from Gianfranco and Laura a CD of Monteverdi's Vespro Della Beata Vergine recorded at the Basilica in St Marks. "What treats," he said. "I shall play Monteverdi while I cook."

The doorbell rang. Penny let Paulo in with three of his staff. They laid out a feast on the kitchen table. Paulo explained what he had brought, pointing as he went, while Carlo translated. There was anchovy and chick pea crostino, chopped chicken liver crostino, arancinii, potato and parmesan crocheta, spinach and parmesan and soft egg pizzetta, goats cheese, roasted grapes and walnut bruschetta, fritto misto, calamari, cuttlefish and ink risotto, duck ragu, a plate of cold meats, cauliflower, grilled polenta, and a dish of roast potatoes with rosemary.

"It's what we call *cicheti* " Carlo said. "It's like the Spanish tapas, but better, a little of everything delicious." He smacked his lips. "I hope you like it. If not, I am to blame, not Penny. I chose it all, with help from the maestro." He nodded towards Paulo, who bowed, whispered something to Carlo and left. "It is my other present to you — a Venetian feast."

"It looks fabulous," Gideon said. "Shall we tuck in?" He got plates and passed them around.

They piled their plates and returned to the living room to eat and talk. Laura sat next to Venetia and engaged her in Italian. Carlo, Gianfranco, Gideon, and Penny talked shop. When they had finished, Carlo got out his mobile and rang a number. All he said was, "Pronto," and smiled enigmatically at everyone, got up and left the room. Minutes later, he returned with Paulo bearing a large cake with thirty six burning candles. They all started singing happy birthday, as Paulo put the cake down on the coffee table.

"You have to make a wish, Daddy, when you blow them out."

"Do you want to help Daddy?" Gideon said.

"You must do it alone, or the wish won't come true, é vero Venetia?" Laura said.

Venetia nodded. "It's true, Daddy."

Gideon took a huge breath in and stood over the cake. He blew all the candles out, and wished his daughter a happy life. Everyone clapped. Gideon cut the cake and Penny passed it around. It was orange and almond flavoured.

When Venetia had finished her cake Penny said, "Time for bed now, Ven. Isabella's coming tomorrow, and you want to be awake for her. Say goodnight."

Venetia put her plate down. She was tired now. Sleepily, she said goodnight.

"Come give Daddy a kiss."

She kissed Gideon. Carlo held out his arms, and she kissed him. Laura got up and kissed Venetia saying, "Buona notte, bella bambina." Gianfranco blew her a kiss, and Penny took her to the bathroom to clean her teeth, and then to her bedroom.

"In you get. I'm going to shut your door so we don't disturb you. See you in the morning, night night." Penny switched off the light and shut the door.

When she rejoined the others, she saw Gideon was showing them her work on the mirror.

"Bravissimo," Carlo said. "It's looking good."

"Thanks. I've discovered something. Here, put on my eyepiece and look closely at the glass. She handed it to Carlo. He put it on. "Do you see?" she said. "It's been made using a combination of the old 14th century glass bulb technique and a sheet of reflecting metal."

He bent over the mirror, peering closely. "Oh Dio," he said. "I think you're on to something. What a find, if it is."

"I want to take the back off and see exactly how it was made. I haven't got the tools here."

"Let me see the back, can you hold it up for me?"

Penny held the mirror, while Carlo looked at the back.

"Yes, I see. They have used blocks of wood at the corners to hold the back. They are nailed in." He peered closely, and pulled at one of the blocks. "I don't think you can pull the nail out without damage. There is room for the thinnest of cutters. Just cut the nail off. I will send Francesco tomorrow. He can do it for you. We'll put the mirror back together at the lab.

They talked and drank late into the night. Laura said she was impressed with Venetia's Italian. "She's almost fluent, you know, and you've only been here, what is it, nine or ten weeks. She has some odd old fashioned phrases, but that's her friend I suppose."

"The Zancani," Gianfranco made the sign of the cross.

"Don't be ridiculous," Laura said. "He is so superstitious."

"How can a family have such misfortune, there must be a curse. I wouldn't want to be them."

"You shouldn't believe all those old stories," Carlo said. "Lord, it is almost one. We must leave these good people. Paulo will come tomorrow to clear up and get his dishes." He got up, followed by Gianfranco and Laura.

"Thank you so much for organising the meal," Penny said.

"Yes, thank you. Best birthday meal I've had," Gideon said. He got Laura's coat, and helped her on with it.

They kissed their guests and saw them to the door wishing them a goodnight, and then they were alone. Gideon kissed Penny. "Thanks for the party, darling, really good, complete surprise."

"To bed," she said. "I'll just cover the mirror. We can't put it in the kitchen tonight, it's a complete tip, and I'm too tired to sort it out. Will you lock up in case of sleepwalking? I think I'll leave her door shut tonight. She knows if she wakes she can open it. She seems much better, don't you think?"

"Yes, she did, she's so sweet; they all loved her, particularly Laura. She talked to Ven all evening." He locked the door through to the hall and kitchen. "Do you think the sleepwalking will stop, now her temperature's normal?"

"I hope so, but we'll keep locking just in case."

Penny took Gideon's hand and led her husband to their bedroom with a mischievous smile, shutting the door behind them.

26

<u>The Bank</u>

Laura da Ponte yawned. It was 6:15am and it had been a late night. She had a long day ahead. She worked as a trader. Her job was to monitor the movements of the world's exchanges and make trades for the bank. She worked in a 14th century building looking at a flickering electronic world on two computer screens at her desk. At the touch of button, she could make or lose millions.

The merchants, who'd owned this house, would have made voyages across real seas, to real countries, to make their fortunes. How the world had changed, yet stayed the same. She remembered her history, and how in 1499 an accumulation of malign events brought the banks down. First the banks of the Garzoni family and the Rizzo brothers failed, then the bank of Lipomano went down. It was known then Venice was haemorrhaging money, and the city lost its credibility with the world. It was happening again and there was a rumour an Italian bank would go the way of Lehmanns. Her bank was sound, but one never knew... if she got it wrong, well it didn't bear thinking about.

In truth, the whole of Europe was in trouble, especially what the Anglo Saxons labelled PIGS – Portugal, Italy, Greece and Spain. She believed Italy was essentially sound. The land of Ferrari, Armani, Versace, Alfa Romeo would always be able to sell to the world. Italy would recover, but she doubted Greece could. She felt guilty sometimes, but it was her job, and there was money to be made in volatility. Venetians knew all about risk and fortune. She wondered what 2012 would bring. The Mayans said it would bring the end of the world, and strangely the idea appealed to some. The web was awash with end of the world sites. She didn't want to die in a catastrophe, but she didn't want to continue doing this job. There was too much stress. She wondered if Gianfranco would ever propose. She'd love to have children – just be a mother.

She thought about Venetia. She'd found her enchanting, and been amused at how quickly the little girl had picked up a Venetian accent. She guessed she was learning most from her friend Isabella. Gianfranco really did think misfortune could be spread like flu. He'd told her about it on their way home last night. Old wives tales, she'd said, and asked him if he really thought the Mantells would suffer through their friendship with the Zancanis. All he'd said was, 'I hope not.' He was quite logical in everything else, and had refused point-blank to come to the séance. He said it was rubbish; the dead could not talk through the living. Laura wasn't so sure anymore. For a second last night, she'd thought she was talking to someone else other than Venetia. Was Venetia the one she had to protect? Salvati's words had been so odd, 'the prompter breathes, the puppet squeaks.'

What was she thinking? The girl was possessed? She fixed on the business of the day. She'd shorted Greek bonds and it was time to buy back.

27

San Francesco del Deserto

Cristofo wanted to see the mirror, but it could wait. The Prior had rung cancelling Friday's appointment and suggesting today instead. He left his study and told Elizabeta he wouldn't be going with them after all. Half an hour later, he was steering his way through the back waters of Venice, past the hospital and out into Canale delle Fondamente Nuove. He passed around San Michele, towards the green island of San Francesco del Deserto.

Prior Vittorio was waiting for him. "Welcome, you have come to see the grave of the abbess?"

"Yes. It was kind of you to let me come." As the Prior showed him through the grounds, Cristofo asked, "I wondered if she left anything?"

The Prior looked puzzled. "What do you mean? It was over two hundred years ago."

"I am interested in Santa Maria delle Vergini and the reasons for its closure. I wondered if she might have left any documents?"

"It is possible – there is much stored here – we could have a look after."

They walked through cypress paths into a little orchard, where they found her grave. Cristofo read the writing on the gravestone. She had died in 1807, a year after the convent had closed. They paid their respects.

The Prior took him into the monastery. "Only seven friars remain now," he said as they went down into the cellars. "I don't know how much longer we will survive. So many empty rooms."

The cellars were piled high with books, papers, chests, old furniture, and the dust of centuries. Cobwebs hung over everything.

"Do you know where to look?" Cristofo said.

"If she did leave anything, it will be there." He pointed at a corner of the room. "I suggest we start there."

They spent two hours searching and found nothing. Cristofo thanked the Prior for his time and returned to Venice to wait for Elizabeta.

28

Universita di Venezia

In the department of archaeology, Carlo had almost finished Elena's journal. He sat with the open book in front of him, as he wrote the translation by hand into his notebook. He would type it into the computer later. The story of the girl and the chest was more and more intriguing. Experts in the department were still examining the lead-lined chest. The mechanism inside had never been seen before. It was incredibly complex. The lead closed to create a watertight seal. The circle pattern, on the inside of the lid, with its serpent symbols, was of Arabic origin. Its significance had not been discovered. One of his colleagues had seen a similar pattern in a medieval book of magic.

He looked down at Elena's writing. There was only one page left. It was the last thing she'd written before she died. It was hard work, her handwriting was scratchy, and there were many crossings out. He picked up his magnifying glass and read, making constant use of the dictionary of old Venetian at his side. *The pain when the Holy Spirit entered was excruciating. The Patriarch told me it would be so. I must not cry out. I must endure the pain. It was a sign I was entering a higher spiritual level. Only then could I become the mother of God. He gave me a holy cloth to put in my mouth. He told me to bite on it, as the spirit entered. The spirit was in him, and he would pass it to me. He said I must be naked. He lifted his robe and covered us, and he pushed it into me. It hurt him too, for he struggled not to show pain. A strange sound came from his mouth, as the spirit passed through him to me. I bit on the cloth. I am with holy child.*

There it ended. Carlo stared into space. He picked up the telephone and called the director's secretary.

"Conti here," he said, "I'd like to see the director tomorrow morning. Is he free? Good, 10am."

He called Penny. "Ciao, Francesco will be with you this afternoon to help with the mirror. I've come to the end of her journal. She says it was the Patriarch. My God, this will cause a scandal. A Contarini was Patriarch then – the family are still in Venice. Keep this to yourself. I'm seeing the director tomorrow."

29

<u>The Visitors</u>

Venetia woke feeling well and got out of bed. She found her mummy clearing up. She had loaded the dishwasher and was wiping the table in the kitchen.

"Ah there you are, darling," Penny said. "Did you sleep well?" She felt Venetia's head. "You don't feel hot. You're on the mend."

"Shall I get dressed, Mummy?"

"Yes darling, Isabella will be here in an hour. I think we better tidy your room and make the bed."

Venetia washed and dressed herself, and came back for breakfast. The kitchen was spotless, and the dishwasher was humming and gurgling away. While Venetia ate, Penny tidied the bedroom. On the dot of 11:00, the doorbell rang. Venetia looked and saw Isabella and her granny. She waved down. "It's Isabella," she called.

Penny buzzed them in. The girls embraced, and Venetia asked if they could go and play.

"Of course, darling, you two go. We'll have coffee shall we?"

"I have brought some pastries." Elizabeta passed a bag to Penny. They sat talking in the kitchen.

"Carlo's found out more about the girl. Hard to believe that she actually lived in the house Gideon and I had a flat in after we were married."

"This happens in Venice. The present bumps into the past. It's always around us, but I must say, you living there, and your husband discovering the chest. It's as if fate brought you back."

"It is curious, and Venetia was conceived in the building," Penny said, "so she lived there too."

Venetia and Isabella came in and showed Penny two beautiful puppets. Isabella's puppet had chestnut hair and was dressed in a red ruffled dress. Both puppets had white faces and red lips. The one Venetia was holding was dressed in a lovely blue brocade dress. The puppet had blonde hair.

"Isabella says I can have her. Her name is Venetia, and Isabella's is called Isabella. They are us in the puppet world."

"How kind, are you sure? They look old and rather precious."

"Yes, Cristofo was insistent. He said Venetia must practice puppetry while the school is closed. Have you heard? They're not reopening until the 21st." Elizabeta picked up the plate of pastries and offered the last two to the girls. They laid their puppets on the table and took the pastries.

When they'd finished, Isabella put her chestnut haired puppet down on the kitchen floor and manipulated the strings so it moved. "Hello Venetia," she squeaked, "are you feeling well?"

Venetia put her puppet down and squeaked back, "I am quite well, thank you." The two of them walked the puppets back to the bedroom.

Penny showed Elizabeta the mirror and explained her theory. She got Elizabeta to look through the eyepiece.

"It's fantastic. I wish Cristofo had come. He wanted to, but was called away. He would be so interested. I'll tell him all about it when I get home."

"I would like him to see it. You must come to dinner. I don't know how much longer I'll have it here. We're taking it apart today, and over the next day or two I will study how it was made. I'll ring you when I know what's happening."

"Yes, we'd like to. I'm sure we'll be free. We don't have many engagements these days."

There was a commotion from the bedroom. Venetia shouted, "Copa i Zancani, copa i Zancani."

Isabella screamed and came running out crying. Elizabeta stood up to comfort her. She took her in her arms. "Che cosa é successo tra tu e Venetia?"

Penny went to the bedroom. Isabella's puppet was on the floor in a heap, its strings all tangled. Venetia stood above it, making her puppet jump up and down on Isabella's while she repeated, "Copa i Zancani, copa i Zancani."

"What on earth is going on? What are you doing? You've upset Isabella."

Venetia dropped the strings and the puppet fell to the floor. Her face was strange. She looked blankly at her mother. Her eyes had lost all depth. Her mouth clamped shut, then opened and closed without a sound. Then, as if she had come out of a deep sleep, she focused, and her eyes returned to normal.

"I don't know. I don't know what happened. We were playing. I saw Isabella in the mirror at the dressing table. It wasn't her – she was different, and words came out of my mouth." She put her head in her hands. "I don't feel well, Mummy. My head hurts."

Penny felt her daughter's forehead. It was burning hot. "I think you've overdone it. I'm putting you back to bed."

"Isabella said she doesn't like me – her nonno told her to be friends – she didn't want to, she only spoke to me to please him."

"Don't be silly. I'm sure she didn't mean it – it was because you were nasty to her. Lie on your bed. I'll tell them you're not well." Penny returned to the living room. "I'm sorry Venetia's not herself, her temperature's up again. I shouldn't have let her get up."

Elizabeta asked. "Where did she learn the word *copar*, Isabella? Do you know what it means?"

Isabella shook her head.

"I'm so sorry," Penny said.

"I'm sorry too." Elizabeta said. "We better go."

"Let me get the puppets."

Isabella gave the blonde puppet back. "It is Venetia's."

"Are you sure you still want her to have it?"

Isabella nodded and packed her puppet into her backpack. She got off her granny's lap. Elizabeta got up, and Penny showed them to the door.

"What does *copar* mean?" She asked.

"Isabella, go and kiss Venetia goodbye. You can give her the puppet."

Isabella took the puppet from Penny's hand. When she had gone, Elizabeta said. "It is old Venetian for kill. She was saying kill the Zancani. I think one of those evil girls at school has taught Venetia. I don't think she knows what it means."

"Venetia used another phrase the other day, *Jèristu onto.* Carlo said it was old Venetian; I thought it was something Isabella had taught her."

"I shouldn't think so. Those children, who come from the social housing, speak a dialect that has kept a lot of old words. That's where she's picked it up. It's like me learning English in your East End. They're a tough bunch. So much bullying and -" she stopped as Isabella returned. "We'll leave you now. I will ring tomorrow to find out how Venetia is."

"Goodbye," Penny said closing the door, and going back to Venetia. She tucked her into bed and took her temperature. Penny frowned. It had gone up to thirty nine.

Venetia snuggled into the crisp clean sheets. They smelt of the soap powder her mummy used. "Can I have my fish, Mummy?"

Penny picked up the fish and put them on Venetia's pillow. Venetia tucked her puppet under the blanket. "We're all going to have a sleep now, fish, puppet and me," she said.

"I'll shut the shutters so it's nice and dark. I'll come and see you when Daddy gets back." She left Venetia in the darkened room.

Venetia put her thumb in her mouth. She remembered Isabella's face in the mirror, and she remembered how her own had changed too. Why did they look different? She remembered her mummy saying the devil watched the world from the other side of the glass. She got up and turned the mirror on the dressing table to the wall. She got back into bed, returned her thumb to her mouth, and fell asleep.

30

<u>The Paper</u>

Francesco arrived shortly after three in the afternoon with the rubber tipped pliers and special cutters. Venetia was still asleep. Penny shut the bedroom door so they wouldn't disturb her. She took the cloth off the mirror and together they lifted it off the table. While Francesco supported the mirror, Penny spread the cloth over the table on which they put the mirror face down.

"Here goes," she said and gripped the left topmost wooden block with the pliers. Francesco picked up the cutters, and applied more and more pressure to the exposed nail until with a snap, he cut through. Penny jerked upwards as the block was freed.

They repeated the process at each corner and lifted the back off the mirror. Inside was a thin sheet of black tin and a scrap of folded paper. She looked at Francesco, and raised an eyebrow. She put on her cotton gloves and picked the paper up. Her heart raced as she unfolded it, wondering what it would reveal. She couldn't make the writing out, and realised it was a mirror image. "Mirror-makers joke," she said, turning the paper around so Francesco could see.

He shrugged; he didn't understand her. She put the paper down and lifted the tin up and turned it around. It was a reflecting surface, but quite what it was made of she wasn't sure. There were elements mixed with the tin.

They lifted the glass out of the frame. The glass had reflecting metals mixed into it too. It was going to be an interesting couple of days. She thanked Francesco for his help, "Good Heavens, time's flown. Grazie mille, arrivederci," she said not wanting him to be late out to Lanesra.

215

He left and Penny checked Venetia. She was still fast asleep. Penny picked up the scrap of paper and walked to her bathroom. The mirror there, like an actor's, was surrounded by little light bulbs. She got the paper out and held it up to the glass. There were twenty lines scrawled in blue ink on the yellow paper. At the top, she could make out *Memoria nos defendit sapientes,* and right at the bottom a date MDVIII ADI VII IVNIAS. Next to it the words: *Patriarch Aureo Zancani.* She peered closer and frowned. Had there been a Zancani Patriarch? She couldn't remember. Surely Cristofo would have mentioned it. She didn't think Zancani was a common name. Penny put the paper back in its bag, and phoned Carlo.

"Carlo, hi, buona sera. We've taken the mirror apart. There was a note inside the frame. It's in mirror writing. I can't make much of it out, but at the bottom, it looks like Patriarch Aureo Zancani. Was there a Zancani patriarch?"

She could almost hear him thinking at the other end of the line. "No, I'm sure there wasn't. I must see this. This Zancani could be the murderer. Could he have lied to her about his position? I'm coming round."

Thirty minutes later Carlo arrived with a magnifying mirror and a list of patriarchs. Penny showed him the paper, and they sat down together to decipher. In the new mirror, the writing was clearer.

"It starts, *memory protects the wise,*" Carlo said. He scanned the other lines working out a translation from the Latin. "It is a description of the inauguration of the new patriarch. It says something like, *on the afternoon of June 6th the patriarchal barge carried Cardinal Zancani over the peaceful waters of the Grand Canal, stopping in close vicinity of the golden cathedral of St Mark. All the bells of the city announced the joy of the multitudinous throngs lining the canals and crowding at the windows of the palaces. They waved their white flags beneath the rich marble balconies, and shouted prolonged choruses of jubilation as the Cardinal in his scarlet robes passed by.*" Carlo stopped for a moment working out the next line. "*Midst such festivity, did the humble Patriarch enter the city of the Venetians. Tomorrow morning he will celebrate Solemn High Mass, and address his first words to us. I, Federico Manin made this perfect mirror with mercury and gold. On the...*" Carlo looked at the roman numerals and looked at Penny, "*...7ᵗʰ June 1508, I will present it to Patriarch Aureo Zancani.*"

He put the paper down, and showed Penny the list of patriarchs. She looked at 1508, and saw the name Lodovico Contarini. Four months later he was replaced by Antonio Contarini. "What does it mean? There's no Zancani. Is it just fiction, but why make it up?"

"Odd indeed. We knew the mirror must have been owned by someone important, and I think we can safely say it was a patriarch, but why was it in the chest? Was this Contarini really Zancani? Did he kill the girl, or did someone else get hold of the mirror?" Carlo put the paper back in the bag. "I'll take this if I may. Much to think about. And the mirror, gold and mercury?"

"Wow," Penny was flushed with excitement. "I could phone Cristofo and ask him if he knows anything. He's never mentioned a patriarch. He's researching his family's history. He's got masses of old documents."

"No wait. Let me see what I can find out. "

They heard Gideon at the door. "What are you two up to? You've found something, haven't you?"

They told him, and showed him the paper in the mirror so he could see the writing. Carlo put the paper back in the bag. "I must go, things to do, places to be. Let's keep this between us for now. There is something very odd about this non-patriarch. My mind is telling me cover up, but 16th century cover up, and they knew how to do it in those days."

As they saw Carlo out, they heard Venetia stir.

"Awake at last," Penny said, and noticed the mirror turned to the wall. "Why have you turned the mirror around?"

"I don't like it, Mummy. I see things."

"Don't be silly. You're supposed to see things." She turned the mirror back. "I know you said Isabella looked odd, but your head was hurting and your temperature was high. I shouldn't have asked Isabella to come."

Gideon kissed his daughter and felt her forehead. "Feels OK now," he said.

"I feel fine, Daddy. Look what Isabella brought me." She held up the puppet. "Her name is Venetia, like me."

Gideon held the puppet. "She's pretty, but not as pretty as you, Ven. She's beautifully made. Can you make her walk?"

Venetia took the puppet back and got out of bed. She stood up holding the strings and made the puppet dance.

Penny said, "Now, don't overdo it." She felt Venetia's forehead. "Sit and we'll just check." She took Venetia's temperature. It was back to normal. "Come on then, let's get your dressing gown on if you're getting up. I think we better have supper in the kitchen. I've got the mirror in bits in the sitting room."

"By the way," Gideon said, as they ate, "Laura and Gianfranco have invited us for 21st of November to join them for the feast of Madonna della Salute. Apparently the city builds a pontoon bridge across the Grand Canal to the church. They go every year."

"What time?"

"Gianfranco suggested meeting outside the Gritti Palace at five, and we can all walk across the pontoon together. There are lots of sweet stalls outside the church. Sounds fun doesn't it, Ven? You'll be better by then."

"Yes, let's go, as long as Venetia is better," Penny said.

After dinner, Venetia asked to stay up and watch television. She said she wasn't tired. Penny agreed to let her stay up a little later, as she'd had such a long sleep during the day. They couldn't find anything to watch, so Gideon suggested playing the CD he'd been given for his birthday. "It's music for angels," he said.

Venetia lay on the sofa with her head on Penny's lap. Gideon put the CD on, and waved his arms like a conductor as the baroque music filled the room. He joined them on the sofa, putting Venetia's feet on his lap. They sat quietly listening, until at ten they noticed Venetia had fallen asleep. Gideon carried her to her room and put her on her bed. Penny carefully took her dressing gown off, trying not to wake her, and tucked her up for the night.

"She seems much better, doesn't she?" Gideon said.

"I don't know. Her temperature shot up after she'd been playing with Isabella. We mustn't let her do too much too soon."

31

Dr. Gabrieli Returns

Venetia rose. She was the puppet. Strings were pulling her up off the bed. She picked up her brush from the dressing table and walked silently into the living room. She removed the cloth from the dining table and pressed the palm of her hand on the surface of the mirror's glass. It was like a sheet of ice. An arctic current streamed through her body. She looked at herself in the mirror. Her face was as white as death. She began to brush her hair, counting the strokes. "Uno, due, tre..."

Without the reflecting sheet behind the glass, her image was bent, like a face in the house of fun. She felt something tighten around her neck. She continued to brush her hair. It got tighter and tighter. She couldn't breathe. She dropped the brush and screamed but nothing came out of her mouth. There was no breath left.

A patch of mist began to form and spread across the mirror. Her face melted into the background. A dark shadowy shape moved through the mist, out into the room, and floated above her. Something stroked her hair. It was cold against her scalp and for a second she smelt a cloying scent. She shook violently with the cold and her teeth chattered. She fell, and lay motionless on the carpet. A stream of warm urine ran down her thigh. She jolted awake from the nightmare, shivering. She was wet. She had weed in her sleep.

She wasn't in bed. She was lying on the floor of the living room. She'd wet the carpet like a baby. Venetia didn't want to wake her parents — didn't want them to know she'd wet herself again. Exhausted, she crawled to her bedroom, found a clean nightdress and took the wet one off. It lay on the floor next to her feet. She pushed it under the bed.

Her mind was in a fog as if the mist from the lagoon had crept inside her. Without thinking, she put on the clean nightdress and climbed into bed.

Venetia fell asleep, and found herself in a church surrounded by women in black. Venetia knew them all. They began to sing. It was beautiful, like the music her daddy had played. She looked down at herself, and saw she, too, was dressed in black. She sat up in bed, and began to sing. "*Avie Maria stella, Dei Mater alma, Atque semper Virgo, Felix coeli porta.*"

Penny woke. She sat up, and listened hard. Venetia was singing — there was no doubt about it. She got out of bed and hurried across the living room. She could hear it clearly now, it was Latin. She heard Venetia sing, "*Mala nostra pelle.*" She switched on the light. Venetia was sitting bolt upright, her mouth open wide as she sang, "*Monstra te esse Martrem.*"

Penny stood stunned. Venetia didn't know Latin. She stepped towards the bed to wake her, and stopped. Gideon must see. She ran back to wake him.

"Gideon, quickly it's Ven."

"What," he mumbled.

"Venetia, quick."

He got up and, half awake, followed her. Venetia was still sitting up singing. Her eyes were glassy and staring. She sang, "*Virgo singularis, Inter omnes mitis, Nos culpis solutes.*" She lay back down on the bed, turned, and pulled the covers up. They knelt by the bed and looked at their daughter. She was fast asleep.

Penny switched off the light and they returned to bed.

"What's happening to her? I'm frightened. She was singing in Latin," Penny said, looking up at Gideon.

Gideon put his arms around her. "The words were from the music I played. Strange what the brain can do." He looked at her quizzically. "You didn't think something supernatural was happening, did you?"

"I don't know. For a moment, I thought of the murdered girl. She was a nun and..."

"Don't be silly." He put his arm around her, and snuggled close. "Let's sleep."

Penny lay awake, next to Gideon, who'd begun to snore. I supposed Gid's right she thought, but it was very odd. She'd talk to Venetia in the morning.

Penny got up at six thirty. She hadn't slept well. She switched on the light in the living room and noticed the cloth on the floor. Venetia had been sleepwalking again. She picked the cloth up and saw her daughter's handprint on the surface of the glass. Still holding the cloth, she went to Venetia's room. She was sleeping soundly. Penny returned, and put the cloth back over everything on the table. She wouldn't leave the mirror here again. She'd work on it today, and keep it in the kitchen overnight. She'd ring Carlo and see if it could be taken back to the university tomorrow. She wanted it out of the flat as soon as possible. It wasn't logical, but there was something in the mirror affecting her daughter.

She stood, thinking. She'd read somewhere, a theory, inanimate objects could record powerful events, echoes and vibrations coming back from the past. It was something like vinyl recording. It explained why certain places had a reputation of being haunted. Events played out over and over forever. She pictured the arm of an old record

223

player reaching the end, and automatically lifting, and returning to the beginning. In her head, the scratched recording of Carusso they'd heard at the Zancanis, played.

There wasn't any point discussing her fears with Gideon or Carlo. They would poo poo her, and persuade her there was nothing. She didn't want to be persuaded; she just wanted the mirror out. She returned to the bedroom to find Gideon getting up.

"She's been sleepwalking again. She's had the cloth off the mirror. Do you think we should ring Dr Gabrieli?"

"Not really, he seemed to think sleepwalking was quite common in her age group, didn't he? We should only call him if it's an emergency."

"We must put the mirror and its bits in the kitchen tonight. I don't want her touching it again. She seems to go to it whenever she sleepwalks. What do you think that's about?"

He sat on the bed in his pyjamas. "I don't know. It's weird. Maybe she just brushes the cloth as she walks by."

"I don't think so. Her handprint was on the mirror this morning."

"I suppose the table is the first thing you'd walk into, coming from her room. Don't forget she is asleep, so she bumps into it and fumbles with whatever is on top. We'll just have to make sure there is nothing on the table overnight. Have you looked in on her?"

"She's still asleep."

"I'd better get on," he said, fingering the stubble on his face.

Venetia was still asleep when Gideon left. Penny took the cloth off the table and surveyed the mirror and its parts, deciding where to start. She put on her cotton gloves, put in her eyepiece, and picked up the sheet of metal to see if she could work out what it was made from. Looking closely, she could see flecks of gold.

"Buongiorno, Mamma."

Penny jumped. Venetia was standing in the doorway in a blue nightdress staring at her. "Hello, darling, how are you feeling?"

"Sto bene," Venetia said.

"Don't be silly, Ven, let's talk in English. Plenty of Italians to talk to without practicing on Mummy. I thought you were wearing the pink nighty last night?"

"Was I?"

Penny felt her daughter's head. She didn't seem hot. She gasped. "Oh my God. There's a rash around your neck. What happened? I'm going to call the doctor." She studied Venetia's neck. It was red with scaly bumpy patches, a bit like nettle rash. "Does it hurt?"

"No, Mummy."

"Does it itch?"

"No Mummy."

She carried Venetia back to bed. "You lie down while Mummy makes the call." Penny found Dr Gabrieli on her contacts list. While she waited for him to answer, she thought about the girl in the chest they suspected had been strangled, and now Venetia had a mark around her neck.

"Hello Dr Gabrieli, it's Penny Mantell. Venetia's developed a rash around her neck. I'm worried... no she doesn't have a temperature, well I don't think so. She seems OK, except for the rash. Thanks, see you in an hour."

She returned to Venetia's bedroom. "The doctor's coming. Are you sure you feel ok?"

"Yes, Mummy."

"Alright, but you better stay in bed for now. I'll get you some cornflakes and a cup of tea."

She brought the breakfast in on a tray, and sat and watched as Venetia ate. "Did you sleep alright last night, darling? I think you must have been sleepwalking. You pulled the cloth off the mirror."

"Did I?" Venetia said as she munched on her breakfast. "I don't remember anything." She looked at the puppet lying on the pillow beside her. "Venetia the Puppet hasn't moved. She's been asleep all night."

Dr Gabrieli arrived punctually at ten. "Good morning, Signora Mantell," he said as he came in. "Let's have a look at the patient."

He went into Venetia's room. Penny was relieved to see him. There was something confident and calming about him. He put his bag down beside Venetia's bed and sat next to her. As he leaned over to open the bag, Penny saw the pink nightdress under the bed. She watched him get out a spray, and squirt it on his hands and rub them together.

"Hello, Venetia. Your mamma says you have a rash, can I see?" He looked closely at her neck. "I like your doll, she's a puppet isn't she? And I think I know where she came from: Signora Zancani?"

Venetia nodded, "Isabella gave her to me."

"Have you taken Venetia's temperature today?" he asked.

"No, she doesn't seem hot," Penny said.

He placed a thermometer under Venetia's tongue. While he waited, he wrote on a pad. He took the thermometer out and looked. "Good," he said. "Normal, nothing to worry about." He looked at Penny, and got up off the bed. "She has ringworm, a fungal infection." He tore the page off the pad. "A prescription for some cream, it should help clear it up." He put his things back in the bag.

Penny felt a little foolish now she knew the mark was ringworm. What had she been thinking? Supernatural strangulation. It was crazy. She hesitated and asked, "Could I have a word before you go?"

"Of course," he said, following her to the kitchen. "I know it looks bad, but there's really nothing to worry about. It's a common skin complaint in children. The fungi thrives in warm moist areas. The fever will have caused Venetia to sweat and, being in bed, the conditions would have been ideal. You must wash her sheets and nightclothes daily, and apply the cream. The rash should clear up in a couple of weeks. You don't have any pets?"

"No, we don't."

"Good! They can catch and spread it. I would wash the puppet's hair, by the way, and any of Venetia's combs and brushes."

"Right. The thing that's really worrying me, Doctor, is the sleepwalking. She's still doing it. Last night I heard her singing. I went into her room, and she was sitting up singing a hymn in Latin. It was music we played earlier, but she'd never heard it before, and she was sound asleep. Then this morning, I discovered she'd moved things around on the table next door, and she changed out of her nightdress and put another one on. And she doesn't remember a thing."

"Strange indeed, but as I told you sleepwalkers can do the most extraordinary things. Does Venetia have headaches? Is she abnormally tired during the day?"

"She was very tired yesterday, and she does get headaches."

"Do you know when in the night she is sleepwalking?"

"Not certain, but it's later than you thought."

"I think perhaps we should get an EEG. Can you bring her to the hospital on Monday?"

Penny nodded. "Yes, what are you thinking? What will happen?"

"I honestly don't think there is anything wrong, but I would like to check for epilepsy, just to be sure. It's a simple procedure. At the hospital, they will put some sensors on Venetia's scalp, which will transmit the electrical signals produced by her brain's neurons to a computer screen. I will ring to confirm the appointment and time later today."

"Should I keep her in bed?"

"No no, the flu has cleared. Fine for her to get up. Some fresh air might be good, but don't let her do too much, and remember hygiene. Ringworm is very contagious." And as if to emphasise the point, he got out his hand wash. "Was there anything else?"

"No, Doctor, thanks." She saw him out.

"Doctor says you can get up, darling. We'll go out together later, and get the cream for your rash. Mummy's got to wash all your things," Penny said, "even puppet Venetia's hair." She knelt down and got the pink nightdress from under the bed. It was slightly wet.

Venetia flushed. "Mummy, it was in my sleep; I woke up, and I was wet."

"Don't worry, darling, everything's going in the washing machine. Let's pull the sheets off."

They stripped the bed and, after Venetia had dressed, they put both nightdresses and sheets into wash. Then together they took the dress off the puppet, and hand washed it in the basin. Penny let Venetia wash the puppet's hair with shampoo. "There," she said, "puppet Venetia's nice and clean."

Later in the morning, they got the cream from the chemist. Doctor Gabrieli phoned and said the appointment was for 10am on Monday. He said they should take the vaporetto to Ospedale, but not enter through the main entrance, next to the stop, but take the first left over a bridge into Fondamenta dei Mendicanti. He would meet them there, at a side entrance. Venetia was likely to be in for three to four hours.

32

The Hand of Elena

Penny remembered a line of Eliot, *the troubled midnight and the noon's repose*. In daylight things did become clearer. But there was no repose. There was nothing supernatural in the flat, just the possibility Venetia was epileptic. She'd never had a seizure. Could it just come on? Penny wished she'd asked the doctor more.

She hadn't bothered to phone Carlo. She'd be at the hospital all day Monday with Venetia, so wouldn't finish the mirror until Wednesday. Penny decided to do a couple of hours before Gideon got back. She put on her cotton gloves and removed the cloth. There was Venetia's handprint staring back at her from the glass.

She picked up a cloth, and rubbed over the handprint. As she removed it, she froze in horror. On the inside of the glass was an identical print. Venetia's left hand had been on the outside. The faint print on the inside was a right hand. It would have matched perfectly, like the palms of two hands coming together to pray. Her mind was in turmoil. It could not be. There was no way Venetia could have lifted the glass, and placed her hands on either side of it. It was too heavy.

Penny stood rooted to the floor, staring at the print on the inside of the glass. She couldn't move — couldn't breathe. She was having some kind of panic attack. Her heart was pounding, thumping in her chest. Was this what a heart attack was? She couldn't die now. Her life had barely begun, and Venetia and Gideon needed her. She fought to control and calm herself. She closed her eyes and kept them closed. Her eyeballs beat like pulses. She gripped the table and, began breathing slowly, in and out, and in and out, as she'd been taught when she'd been giving birth to Venetia. She felt her heartbeat slow. She opened her eyes, sat down and put her head in her hands.

"Elena," she whispered. It is Elena's hand. "Don't be stupid," she said out loud. She looked again at the mirror. It was still there on the inside. How could it have got there? It was a child's handprint, and it was not Venetia's. Penny trembled. She couldn't think of a logical explanation. This was not the print of a living hand. It was the hand of Elena and Elena was trying to contact Venetia. The two hands had touched through the glass. She had to get the mirror out of the flat. She would need Gideon's help. She couldn't do it on her own. It could wait down in the hall until Carlo could send someone to collect it. It must not remain anywhere near her daughter. It was dangerous.

Her hands were shaking as she got her mobile. Her voice trembled. "Carlo – yes, I can't work on the mirror here anymore." She stuttered, "I'm frightened. A print's appeared on it. I know it doesn't make sense, but I think it's Elena's."

"Is someone playing a joke? Venetia?"

"No, definitely not."

"I will come now. Francesco can help me take it back when he brings Gideon. Be calm, I won't be long."

He called Francesco and told him to go out to Lanesra immediately to collect the divers. He phoned Gideon. His mobile was off. He tried Gianfranco and got through. Gideon was underwater doing the last dive of the day. He told Gianfranco he was worried about Penny and asking him to tell Gideon. He called a water taxi. He didn't have time to walk or use the vaporetto service. Fifteen minutes later, he paid the driver 60 Euros and stepped off the motorboat onto the Campo Arsenale. He could see Penny standing at the window waiting for him. He hurried across to the door. She'd already buzzed it open. She was standing at the top of the stairs, pale with the shock.

He put his arms around her. "There's nothing to worry about, I'm sure there is an explanation. Is Venetia alright?"

"Yes, thank God, she's asleep. I'll show you the handprint and you can see for yourself." She freed herself from his embrace, and led him into the sitting room. For a second, she thought: it won't be there, and he'll think I'm going mad. But it was still there, faint as before, but clearly a handprint. "Look," she said.

He looked, and bent closer to the glass. "It is a child's hand. Are you sure Venetia couldn't have done this? Could the glass have been turned the other way at some time?"

"No," she said firmly, "Venetia's print was on this side. I cleaned it off, and saw the other print." She put her hands together to show him. "They were matching, touching."

"Let me have your gloves." He took her cotton gloves and put them on, and lifted the glass until it was upright. It was heavy. "No, she couldn't have lifted it and put her hands either side." He put the glass back down. "Come into the kitchen, I think you could do with a cup of something sweet. You have had a shock. I'm sure there is an explanation for this."

"A cup of tea would be good, but I'll make it. What about you?"

"I'll have tea too."

They sat in the kitchen. Penny was slowly recovering. "Thank you for coming so quickly, Carlo."

"Not at all. Gideon should be home soon. I sent Francesco out after you called. Look, do you think the print could have been there all along? I mean, without you seeing it. It is faint, and maybe when the reflecting sheet was behind the glass, the print wasn't visible. You only saw it after you had taken the mirror apart and cleaned Venetia's print off. It could explain why Venetia put her hand there. She saw it too."

"It's possible I suppose, but how did the print get there?"

"There is only one answer to that. You were right, it is the dead girl's handprint, but she put it there when she was alive. It is not the hand of a ghost."

"How could it have remained on the glass?"

"I don't know but I want it to stay on there. What a story," he smiled at her. "Imagine a five-hundred year old print, the hand of Elena."

They heard Gideon on the steps with Francesco.

"What's happened, love?" Gideon said, coming into the kitchen. "Gianfranco said something frightening." He put his hands on her shoulders and knelt and kissed her. "Are you alright? Ven alright?"

"I found a handprint on the inside of the mirror. I thought it was a ghost's hand, what with Venetia behaving so strangely yesterday and the rash around her neck."

"Rash?" Gideon said.

"It's ringworm, I had Doctor Gabrieli out, long story — what a day," she sighed. "Carlo thinks the print I found is the dead girl's, but put on the glass when she was alive."

"Yes I think so, and maybe the last thing she did." Carlo spoke in Italian to Francesco, and then to the Mantells. "We'll pack the mirror up and take it away. You come

233

in when Venetia is better and back at school. You are not to worry, Penny. There is plenty of time for the work."

They all helped with the packaging of the mirror parts, and took them down to the boat.

"Bye, Carlo, thanks again," Penny said.

Gideon took Penny's hand and they walked back to the flat. "No wonder you were scared. Five-hundred year old handprint would have spooked me. How are you feeling now?"

"Better, but I was terrified, petrified. I was convinced I was having a heart attack. I've never been so frightened. I guess Carlo is right, but I'm glad he's taken it away. I'm sure Venetia can sense something in that mirror."

When they got back in, Venetia was awake. Gideon sat on her bed and looked at the rash around her neck. It looked to be oozing slightly. "That looks nasty, Ven, does it hurt?"

"No," she said, "it feels hot, but doesn't hurt."

"It's time to put more cream on. Let's give you a wash first, and you can get up if you want, and sit with Mummy and Daddy. We could play Scrabble." Penny took her into the bathroom and gave her a basin wash, and dried her thoroughly before applying the cream. She helped her dress, and the two of them joined Gideon in the sitting room.

Venetia looked around. "Where's the mirror?"

"Carlo's taken it to the university. The rest of the work will have to be done there. It's too difficult here." Penny didn't normally lie to her daughter, but she didn't want her to know the real reason. They passed a quiet evening together playing Scrabble and eating pizza. While they played, Penny's eyes were constantly drawn to the mark around Venetia's neck.

At nine, Gideon's mobile rang. He answered it, and said, "Yes, she's here." He passed the phone to Penny. "It's Laura."

"Hello?"

"Penny, how are you? Gianfranco told me what happened. Carlo phoned him. Something's been on my mind. I didn't want to say anything, but now..." Laura hesitated.

"What is it?" Penny said

"The other night, when I was talking to Venetia, she used odd bits of old Venetian. I sensed I might be talking to someone else. Gianfranco says I'm crazy, shouldn't bother you, but, look, I know a medium, Signora Salvati, she lives quite near you. Would you and Venetia come with me? She could tell if there was something."

Penny looked across the table at her daughter. No, she couldn't take her to a medium, ridiculous to think of it. "No, Laura, I don't think so. I don't believe in that kind of thing."

"Sorry Penny, I shouldn't..."

"No no, you were only doing what you thought was right."

"Forgive me, and we'll see you on the 21st for the Salute?"

"Yes, we're looking forward to it, ciao." She passed the mobile back to Gideon.

"What was that about?"

"Nothing really, tell you later, we must get on with the game. It's late. It's my turn isn't it?" She looked down at her letters and saw she had PPUEPSA. She saw a T on the board next to a double word score, which she could join to. She made the word PUPPET, and smiled at Venetia. She counted the score. "Nine and double word, ha, eighteen. That puts me in the lead."

When they finished the game, it was almost ten. Penny won, Venetia came second and Gideon last.

"I beat you, Daddy," she said.

"You did, I got terrible letters."

"Poor workman always blames his tools," Penny said. "Come on, young lady, bedtime." She took Venetia to bed, while Gideon put the game away.

"So what was it?" he asked, when she came back.

"Laura wanted me and Venetia to go to a medium with her. She said she thought, well, that a spirit was talking through Venetia."

"You're not going are you?"

"No, of course not."

"Good, that sort of thing makes me cross. It feeds on the gullible and stupid. I'm surprised at Laura. She's very bright. Why on earth does she believe in all that?"

"People aren't always logical, you know."

"I suppose. Tomorrow's Saturday. What shall we do?" he said, changing the subject.

"How about going over to San Giorgio Maggiore to look at Anish Kapoor's ascension? Cinzia at the dig said it's fantastic. It's a column of rising smoke from the floor of the basilica all the way up to the vaulted ceiling."

"That sounds good. I'd like that. Do you think Ven's up to it?"

"Dr Gabrieli said fresh air will do her good. As long as she doesn't overdo it."

"That's a plan then. Shall I lock up for the night?"

"Yes, I'll get ready for bed while you do that."

Gideon locked up and peeked in on Venetia. She was asleep.

He was soon asleep, too. Penny lay awake by his side, thinking about the hand. It was on the inside. The dead girl couldn't have put her hand there, unless she'd taken the mirror apart. Carlo hadn't thought it through. Just before sleep came, a terrible idea crept into her head. *Elena was on the inside of that mirror. Did I release her, by taking it apart?*

33

Bad Dreams

Gideon dreamt he was down deep in the sea. There was a pounding on his chest. He had to surface, but knew it was dangerous to come up too fast. He swam slowly towards the light. As he broke the surface, he heard his daughter's voice. "Non andro, Papa, non andro."

He woke. Venetia was sitting on top of him, pounding on his chest with her fists. He grabbed them and sat up. "What are you doing?"

Penny switched on the bedside lamp

Tears were streaming down Venetia's face. She was whispering, over and over. "Non andro."

"What is it darling?" Penny said. "What's the matter?"

Venetia looked into Gideon's face. Her eyes were blank and glassy. There was nothing behind them. "Tu sai male."

"What?" He looked at Penny.

"She's asleep. Look at her eyes. I'm going to wake her." Penny leant over and shook Venetia. "Wake up, Ven, you're having a bad dream."

Venetia's pupil's dilated. "Non andro, Mamma."

Gideon put his arms around his daughter and tried to hug her to him, but she pushed him away. He looked at her. She was very white. He knew what was going to happen, but was too slow. Thick vomit shot out of her mouth, spattering regurgitated pizza over his pyjamas. It smelt foul. He felt it hot and wet against his skin through the cotton.

"For Christ's sake," he said, as he tried to lift her off him.

She woke. Her eyes focused. She looked at him and Penny. "Sick," she said, and threw up over the bed.

Gideon lifted her off him, got up, and carried her to the basin in their bathroom. Penny followed and took over, while Gideon took off his sick spattered pyjamas.

Venetia stood over the basin. She swallowed. "I don't feel sick anymore," she said.

"Are you sure darling?"

She nodded. "Can I have a drink of water, nasty taste."

"Course, rinse out your mouth here." Penny cupped her palm with water, and put it up to her daughter's mouth.

Venetia swished the water around and spat it into the basin.

"Come on, let's get you cleaned up." Penny took her daughter and got her out of the nightdress. She washed Venetia's face and put on a clean nightdress. Taking her hand, they went back to the other bedroom and got the keys to the hall. Gideon joined them as they went to the kitchen. They sat at the table and Venetia drank a glass of water.

"Does that feel better?" Gideon asked.

"I didn't mean to be sick over you, Daddy."

"I know, darling. Why were you saying I won't go? You were saying it in Italian. Were you dreaming about going back to school?"

"I don't know, Daddy. I can't remember dreaming anything. I just woke up, and I was in your room, and I was sick."

They put Venetia back to bed. Gideon locked up, and he and Penny returned to their room. "I'm sure she was having a nightmare about school," he said. "Do you think she's being bullied?"

"It's possible." Penny looked at the bed. "We'll have to change the sheets."

Penny got some clean ones, while Gideon stripped the bed. The smell of the sick was overpowering. They cleaned up and, exhausted returned to bed.

"We'll have to talk to the teachers. Anyway let's try to get some sleep," Gideon kissed Penny goodnight. "At least I don't have to be up early tomorrow." He turned over on his side.

34

Signora Salvati Speaks

Penny hardly slept. She kept waking and looking at the clock. First it was 1:50, then 2:15, then 3:20, then 4:40. She kept thinking about Venetia begging not to go and beating Gideon's chest. Not to go where, though? She wasn't convinced it was school. Venetia seemed to have settled in now she had Isabella. She thought of Elena. She would have begged her father not to send her to the convent. Was it Elena talking through Venetia? All her reason told her it couldn't be and yet there was something different about her daughter. A mother knew. How could she find out? She remembered Laura and resolved to call her in the morning.

At six, she gave up all attempts at sleep, and got up. She dressed as quietly as she could, took the keys from Gideon's bedside table, and crept out to check on Venetia. She was sleeping peacefully. She made a mug of tea, and sat thinking. She had to leave Venice for her daughter's safety. Gideon could remain and finish his work, but she and Venetia would return to Brighton. She knew she wasn't thinking logically. She was acting on pure instinct. She knew she would be letting Carlo down, but what else could she do? She was a mother. Her duty was to protect her daughter. Nothing else mattered.

Penny wondered how early she could phone Laura. She decided to try at seven. She went back to the bedroom and got Gideon's mobile out of his jeans. He was still asleep. She knew he wasn't going to be pleased. Best get it done, before he woke. Back in the kitchen, she retrieved the last number to call his mobile, and pressed enter. Penny watched the connecting signal.

A sleepy voice answered. "Pronto?"

"Laura it's me, Penny. I've changed my mind. I do want to see Signora Salvati, I'm frightened. I think Venetia may be..." Penny didn't want to say the word. She searched for another. She whispered it. "Possessed." Her voice cracked, as she continued. "By Elena the murdered girl. You were right, she says strange things, and she keeps speaking in Italian. Gideon says nightmares, but it's more than that. Do you think we could see her today? It's urgent. I think something terrible might happen."

At the other end, Laura listened. "I will ring her now and see if she can see us. Did something happen last night?"

Penny told Laura everything. "I don't know what to do. I think we may have to leave Venice."

"It may be nothing. It may be bad dreams like Gideon says. Let's wait and see what Signora Salvati says. I will ring you."

An hour later, Gideon joined Penny in the kitchen. "Have you been up long, love?" he asked.

"I couldn't sleep, I'm worried about Venetia."

"I didn't leave that there, did I?" he said, seeing his mobile.

"No, I borrowed it. I wanted to get Laura's number. I phoned her."

"What, it's not 8:30 yet, and it's Saturday. What are you thinking? You haven't changed your mind, have you?"

At that moment, the phone rang. He reached to get it, but Penny grabbed it before he could. "Yes," she said. "Eleven outside San Giovanni in Bragora, OK, see you then.

Thank you." She looked up at Gideon. "I'm taking Venetia to see Signora Salvati. I just want to be sure there isn't more to this."

"Are you mad? Of course she'll say there is more to this. That's her job. That's how she makes her living. I didn't think you were stupid enough to believe in all that mumbo-jumbo."

"Laura believes in her, and Laura is not stupid. Venetia's behaviour over the last few nights hasn't been natural. There is something unnatural going on here. There is something different about Venetia. I feel it."

He frowned, and narrowed his eyes. "And you think it's supernatural, you think our daughter is possessed. Any moment her head will start revolving."

"No, but all the Italian, all the sleepwalking, and I've sensed something in the flat, sudden stirrings of cold air."

"You're imagining it. She's becoming bilingual, she dreams in Italian. She's going through natural changes. There's nothing odd about it. I won't let you take her. It's insane."

Penny was close to tears. She hated arguing. "Not all things are sane, Gideon. I am taking her." She fixed her eyes on him. "You can't stop me."

He picked up his phone and called Gianfranco. "Hi, is Laura there? Oh! Well she's arranged to take Penny and Venetia to the medium. I don't like it. You'll call her, thanks." He put the phone down.

Venetia came into the kitchen in her nightdress. She looked at her parents and wondered what was happening. She'd never heard them arguing before.

Penny got up. "Come on, Ven, let's get you dressed. How are you feeling?" She took Venetia's hand.

"Fine, Mummy. I don't know why I was sick in the night. I'm hungry. My tummy feels empty."

"We'll get you something to eat. We're going to meet Laura later. You like her don't you? Tell you what, why don't we have an Italian breakfast in a cafe, hot chocolate and pastries, on the way?"

"Is Daddy coming?"

"No, it's a girls' outing, just you, me, and Laura." Penny heard the phone ring and listened. She heard Gideon say:

"Thanks for trying. Yes, a doppo." He turned to Penny in the doorway. "If she doesn't hear from you, she'll be outside the church, as arranged. Go if you want, but if it makes things worse, you know who I'll blame. Why don't you just ring her, say you've changed your mind?"

"I won't change my mind, and it won't make things worse. I'll know if the woman is a fraud. And if she isn't, she will know what to do." She went back to dress Venetia.

"Let me just put some cream on your rash, darling. You can borrow Mummy's pink silk scarf. It'll hide it. We don't want people looking."

"Will people think I've got a nasty disease, like plague?"

"No of course not, just people do stare," Penny said, applying the cream to her daughter's neck.

244

Gideon came in. "OK go," he said. "But I'm still going out to San Giorgio. I'm sure I'll have a better time than you."

"We're having a girls' day out," Venetia said.

"Has Mummy told you where you're going?"

"We're having Italian breakfast and meeting Laura."

"And you're going to see a ridiculous lady, who pretends to see things, and talks piffle."

"Yes that's right, it'll be fun," Penny said fixing Gideon with her 'don't say any more' look. She took Venetia into the hall and put on her duffle coat. She put her own on, and got her handbag. "See you later," she called back as they left the flat.

Outside, it was a bright cold November day. The air was crisp and fresh and a light easterly breeze blew across the campo. They could hear the water slapping against the sides of the canal. Hand in hand, they walked away from the Arsenale, crossed the Rio delle Gorne, and made their way through the backstreets towards the Campo Bandiera e Moro, where the church of San Giovanni in Bragora stood. Penny knew a cafe just off the square, where they could get a hot chocolate and something to eat. They crossed through the square, passing some boys kicking a football up against a wall, and went down a side street to the cafe. There were customers standing at the bar. They walked through to an empty room with a low beamed ceiling and walls hung with black and white photos of Venice. Penny put her red handbag on a table by the window. Venetia sat down on a beige banquette facing the empty room. Penny sat opposite her. They had just over an hour before their meeting, time for her to explain the real nature of their visit.

The waiter came. "Bella mamma e bella bambina che desiderate?"

245

Penny wasn't in the mood to be charmed. She ordered two hot chocolates and a selection of pastries.

"Si subito," the waiter replied. Five minutes later he returned with a plate of jam filled pastries, madeleines, and biscuits, and two mugs of steaming chocolate.

"What shall I have first?" Venetia said stroking her chin in pretend thought, just as Isabella did. "I think the little cake."

Penny sipped her drink. "Now, darling, Laura is taking us to see a woman who can sense things we can't. Spirits of things past. Do you know what I mean? Have you ever felt, or seen, anything like that in the flat?"

"You mean a ghost, Mummy?"

Penny looked at her daughter. "I suppose I do."

"No, I haven't. Do you believe in ghosts?"

"I didn't think I did, darling, but I don't know. Maybe it's just this city. People keep saying it's full of ghosts, but I think they just mean history."

When it was time, Penny paid the bill, and they walked back to the square, which, apart from pigeons, was now deserted. The boys had taken their ball and gone. Penny saw Laura standing in her fur coat in front of the church. They crossed towards her and, she seeing them, waved and came to meet them. "Ciao, how are you?" she asked.

"We're fine aren't we, Ven? Looking forward to our little adventure."

"Daddy says the lady will talk piffle."

Laura frowned. "No, Venetia. The Signora does not talk piffle. Your daddy and Gianfranco do not understand. We women are more sensitive." She looked at Penny.

"I'm sorry. Gideon's got himself in a state about this."

"Don't worry – I understand," Laura said and, looking at Venetia, "You must listen to Signora Salvati."

Laura led them out into a street on the north-eastern edge of the campo. They turned left down a calle, crossed a small bridge, turned right under a sotoportego of cracked and crumbling plaster, through a small courtyard with a wellhead at its centre, and out down a narrow passage. Someone had scrawled indecipherable graffiti on the walls below its name, Calle Bosello. Penny knew she would never be able to find this place on her own. It was another Venice hidden from sightseers. They crossed a strange cast iron bridge, and passed a large brown dog sitting guarding an arched entrance.

They went down a dingy calle. Ahead of them, Venetia saw the weird figures hanging from the metal structure. "Look," she pointed.

"We're here," Laura said. That is Signora Salvati's house. Don't ask me about those."

Penny looked up, and saw the monkey, witch and pope, and wondered what she had let herself in for.

Laura knocked on the door.

Sara Severi, Signora Salvati's companion, opened the door. Laura had spoken to her earlier, and explained why they needed to come. She welcomed them and showed them in through rooms of dark religious pictures and carvings, to the room with the round wooden table. As before when Laura had come, the room was heavy with incense and, as before, Signora Salvati was sitting at the table waiting. She rose to greet them. She was not much taller than Venetia. She took both of Penny's hands, and looked deep into her eyes.

Penny had never seen such green eyes. She felt the woman was looking inside her mind, as one might look through a cupboard searching for something. She squeezed Penny's hands, saying something in Italian. Laura translated.

"She says, keep looking in her eyes."

Laura spoke to Signora Salvati, who nodded, and released Penny's hands. She took Venetia's, and repeated the process. As she let go of her hands, she smiled, and beckoned them to sit at the table. She wanted Penny and Venetia to sit either side of her. Laura sat next to Penny, and Sara Severi sat between Venetia and Laura. Signora Salvati raised her head, looking upwards, and spoke. Penny understood some of the words, spirits, lost, souls, and saints, but not much else. Then Signora Salvati began to chant. Her head dropped forward and her eyes closed.

Venetia was afraid of what was to come. She looked at Penny.

"It's alright, darling," Penny whispered and squeezed her daughter's hand.

Signora Salvati raised her head, and began speaking in a strange voice. Her eyes were tight shut. The sound of the voice changed, and became higher in pitch. Suddenly she opened her eyes wide, and stopped speaking. They sat in silence for a minute or more, and she released their hands, and stood up and crossed herself. "Si," she said, and sat down.

She nodded at her companion who let go of Laura and Venetia's hands. Penny understood it was over. She looked at Laura, who smiled at her comfortingly.

248

"Che ha successo?" Laura asked.

Signora Salvati asked Laura to translate. She spoke slowly occasionally stopping to allow Laura time to work out the correct English.

"There are two spirits attending your daughter. They are attracted to her. One is very strong; she is Elena. She can enter your daughter. They mean no harm. You understand, Signora Mantell, there is no death, only transition to another state. These souls are not aware they have passed on. Their lives were cut short. They are living in a dream state, seeking salvation. They believe Venetia can help them cross to the next world."

"Why do they need Venetia? Can't they go?" Penny asked afraid.

Laura asked Signora Salvati. She just shook her head. Venetia turned towards Signora Salvati and start talking. It was Venetian dialect.

Penny heard her say Elena Erizzo. She shuddered. What had she done? Gideon was right, she had made things worse. Just as suddenly as she'd started, Venetia stopped.

Signora Salvati asked Laura if she'd understood the old Venetian. Laura nodded. She told Penny what had come from Venetia's mouth.

"I am Elena. I speak for us. Franceschina cannot. The monk put a brick in her mouth. We are waiting for another. When she comes we will be strong. We three cannot go to the light, until it is done."

Penny struggled to take the words in. The spirits of Elena and the girl with the brick in her mouth were here in this room. Elena spoke through Venetia. Elena was inside Venetia. Penny felt weak, her head was spinning; she tried to get up, but fell forward onto the table, and blacked out.

249

When she came to, she was lying on a sofa. Signora Salvati's companion was sitting beside her, wiping her brow with a damp cold flannel. Laura and Venetia were standing looking down at her. Behind them was a large sombre wooden carving of Christ on the cross.

"I'm sorry," she said, "I don't know what happened. Could I have a glass of water? Un bicchiere d'aqua, per favore?"

Sara Severi got up to get the water. "How long was I out?" Penny asked.

"Just a couple of minutes, are you alright?" Laura said.

"Is Signora Salvati here?"

Laura pointed. "She's over there."

Penny sat up to look at the medium. She was sitting on an old red velvet armchair stroking a Siamese cat. The eyes of the cat were green just like the woman's. "Can you ask her if the spirits would follow us, if we went back to England?"

Signora Salvati sighed and spoke at length. She gestured at Venetia. Penny caught the word *importante* but could understand nothing else. The words all ran into each other. She looked anxiously at Laura. Eventually the Signora stopped.

Laura said, "She says they cannot leave Venice; she says the spirits are good. They will not harm Venetia. But she says there is another. An earthly presence, a real and physical danger to your daughter. She says you must never let Venetia alone."

Sara Severi returned with a glass of water, gave it to Penny, and sat on a chair next to the medium.

Penny drained the glass. "What does she mean by earthly presence?"

250

Laura asked, listened to the reply and said, "She says there is a person in Venice who wants Venetia, and this person will harm Venetia. She does not know if it is a man or a woman."

"Seems to me, the sooner we get away the better."

Signora Salvati became agitated, the cat jumped down of her lap, as she spoke urgently to Laura.

"She says you should not. The spirits mean you no harm."

Penny sat silently for a second. "I will think about it. Shall we go? I've heard enough. I need some fresh air, it's stuffy in here."

Laura thanked the medium for her help. Signora Salvati nodded and, looking at Venetia, said, "Non si preoccupi, stara bene."

Penny got up. She saw her handbag had been put on the floor next to the sofa. She picked it up, and took Venetia's hand. Sara Severi showed them to the door. Laura looked in her purse, found a 100 Euro note, and gave it to her. "Grazie," she said.

The three walked back down the calle. "You must let me pay," Penny said.

"No," Laura said, "it was my idea."

"I'm out of my depth, don't know what to believe." Penny said. "Do you believe her, Laura?"

"I do believe there is another world, and she can see it. I didn't before I met her. I don't think the other world can harm us. It's just there."

"If we are being haunted, I want to get us away. It's this place. This wouldn't, couldn't happen at home in Brighton."

Venetia looked up at her mother. "You mustn't worry, Mummy. The Signora said everything will be well."

35

Ascension

Gideon sat in the kitchen, fuming. "Bloody woman," he said. Why did Laura have to interfere with his family? Things were bad enough without the addition of a load of supernatural quackery. He stood up, put on his Barbour, collected his camera and stuffed it in a pocket. He set off to walk down the Schiavoni to catch the vaporetto. The trip would calm his temper.

If you weren't in the mood, the alleys of the city could be claustrophobic, but Schiavoni was open to a wide expanse of lagoon and sky. It always gave him a sense of freedom. His mood lightened a little. He was sure Penny would see sense, and see how stupid she was being. And as for Venetia, well, he'd try to persuade her it was Laura's odd idea of entertainment. He planned to take photos of his trip. He'd put them on his laptop, and show them what they'd missed.

He arrived at San Zaccaria, bought a ticket for the vaporetto, and waited with a mixed group of tourists, jabbering in different languages. The boat arrived and banged against the landing stage. He waited for them to board before getting on and stood outside for the crossing with his legs apart to help balance against the movement, and his hands plunged in the pockets of the old blue Barbour. He liked the feel of the engine under his feet and the breeze in his face. Five minutes later, they pulled into San Giorgio. There in front of him was the magnificent Palladian church. Gideon took a picture of the outside. He wished Penny and Venetia were here to share it with him. He climbed the steps into the serene and spacious interior. The Kapoor installation was in the centre of the nave; a vortex of white smoke rose to the vaulted ceiling of the basilica. It was miraculous, like ascension into heaven. Sometimes he wished he believed, it was a solid foundation to life, but he didn't and neither did Penny. If they had, she would have gone to a priest instead of a medium. He stood looking at the column of smoke and wondered how it worked. He saw a large extractor fan up in the ceiling and assumed it was sucking the smoke. Suddenly, the smoke broke, swirled, and the column was lost. He took a picture of smoke drifting randomly up from the floor. The extractor kicked back into action and the column was reformed.

Was it timed to switch off intermittently? Gideon read about the installation. The language of art took some getting used to. It said: 'The work had taken on a new form to respect the spiritual consecrated space.' He saw a quote by Kapoor: *"In my work, what is and what seems to be often become blurred. In Ascension, for example, what interests me is the idea of immateriality becoming an object, which is exactly what happens in Ascension: the smoke becomes a column. Also present in this work is the idea of Moses following a column of smoke, a column of light, in the desert."*

Gideon decided he'd go up the campanile. While he waited for the lift, he was joined by four American women. He could tell they were from the south, maybe Texas. He remembered Father Rice and his daughters of the Alamo art tour, and wondered if this was them. He was going to ask, but then thought better of it. He didn't feel like talking.

The views from the top were spectacular. He could see right over the city. It was spread out below him. He could even see the Arsenale. He took photo after photo. He walked around and looked down on the cloisters of the monastery and across to the fabulously luxurious Cipriani with the only swimming pool in Venice. He squeezed past the American ladies saying "Scusi" and gazed across to the islands of San Servolo and San Lazzaro. San Servolo had been a lunatic asylum, but was now used by the university. The other island was an Armenian monastery. Byron had studied Armenian grammar there, when he wasn't swimming across to the Lido or chasing women about Venice. What a life, Gideon thought, and took the lift back down.

Gideon had one last look at the rising smoke, before going out to walk the tiny island. He passed a small marina full of boats bobbing on the water. The wind was blowing through the rigging, knocking the ropes and tackle against the masts and making a pleasant sound. There was no one around. He smelt a breath of pine and came to a forest. It was fenced off and the gate in was locked. "Damn," he said out lout. It would have been good to walk with his thoughts through the green pines. Gideon turned to make his way home. As he waited for the vaporetto, he thought about the American priest.

When he got back across, Gideon had a pizza at a restaurant opposite the San Zaccaria stop. After lunch, as a treat he bought Friday's Telegraph. It would be a comfort to read a familiar English paper. Once home, he settled on the sofa and read, waiting for Penny to return. She would be pleased; she liked the crossword. They could do it together. He'd reached the sports pages, when he heard footsteps on the stairs. Gideon folded the paper and got up to open the door.

"Hello," he said, looking at them and trying to gauge what had happened. "Did you see the medium?"

"We'll talk about it later." Penny said. "I'm going to make some tea. Do you want some?"

"I'll do it," he said. "You get your coats off and relax. I've got some great photos to show you. I got the paper if you want to have a look; it's in there."

"We heard ghosts," Venetia said.

"Ghosts, I don't think so. I bet she had someone hiding, making noises and moving things around to give you a fright."

"Nothing moved, Gideon," Penny said. "Signora Salvati was the only one talking. There were no tricks." She didn't tell him what Venetia had done.

Gideon could tell there was something else. Penny was on edge. He changed the subject, deciding to ask her later when Venetia had gone to bed. "Go on you two, sit down and I'll bring tea."

In the kitchen, he made a pot, set it out on a tray with some cups and took it in to the living room. "There we are. I'll get my laptop while it brews and transfer my pictures. I wish you could have seen the church and the ascension installation."

He downloaded the pictures onto the laptop and put it into slideshow mode. Penny and Venetia watched while they sipped their tea.

Venetia pointed at his picture of the installation. "It's going to the light. It's going to heaven."

Gideon looked at Penny and raised an eyebrow. She shrugged. The pictures moved on to his views from the campanile. When they'd finished looking, he turned the laptop off and picked up the paper. "Shall we do the crossword?"

"Go on then," Penny said, "read me a clue."

"Book unravelling ethnic treachery, 7, 2, 3, and 3," he said.

Venetia got up. "I'm going to play in my room. I don't like crosswords - they're boring. The clues don't make any sense, they're piffle."

"*Catcher in the Rye*," Penny said. "They're cryptic. You'll like them when you're older."

"What's cryptic?"

"It means obscure, the real meaning is hidden. You have to unravel the clues to find the answer. *Catcher in the Rye* is a famous book, and the letters for *Catcher in the Rye* were hidden in ethnic treachery."

"Oh, like a secret?" she said quietly.

"Sort of, yes," Gideon said, as he read out another. "Distillation made by member of religious community around Chartreuse primarily, 7 letters."

"I'm going to play with puppet Venetia."

"OK, darling," Penny said.

They heard Venetia begin playing, and the squeaky voice she gave the puppet.

Penny took the paper from Gideon, and whispered. "She is possessed. Signora Salvati said there are two spirits with Venetia. One of them spoke through Venetia. It was the girl in the chest, Elena. I'm really frightened, Gid. I've got to take Venetia away. I'm going to get us on a flight next week, after the hospital."

Gideon didn't know what to say. He couldn't believe what was happening. "What do you mean, 'spoke through Venetia'?"

"I remember what she said word for word. I'll never forget it. 'I am Elena. I speak for us. Franceschina cannot speak. The monk put a brick in her mouth. We are waiting for another, when she comes we will be strong. We three cannot go to the light, until it is done.' Do you see now they must be real? The girl with the brick is the other spirit. The one they found on the island. There was another body wasn't there, weighted with chains? I have to get Venetia away from here before they gain strength. I think they are going to take her with them."

Gideon struggled to think of a rational explanation. "Could the medium have hypnotized Venetia without you knowing? Was Venetia ever out of your sight? Salvati would certainly know all about Elena, and the girl with the brick. It's been in all the papers. She could have made Venetia say those things."

"Venetia was never out of my sight. Signora Salvati also said that there is a person in Venice who wants to harm Venetia."

"This is nonsense. She's just making it up. I wish I'd come with you. I'm sure she's tricked you somehow. Could you have been drugged? Did you drink anything there?"

"No, Gideon, I didn't. What happened, happened." She wanted to shout at him but was still whispering because of Venetia. "Why don't you phone Laura if you don't believe me?"

"I will. I'm sure something's gone on here, and it's nothing to do with spirits." For a moment he wondered whether Laura was an accomplice, was mixed up with Salvati, but that was ridiculous. She was a rich banker, why would she be mixed up with a fraudulent medium? And even if it was true, what possible motive could she have? He went into the bedroom to phone. He closed the door behind him.

"Pronto Laura, it's Gideon. What's going on? Penny's come back in a terrible state. She thinks spirits are speaking though Venetia. She thinks it's the girl in the chest. Are you trying to drive us from Venice?"

"I'm sorry, Gideon, but I believe it is true. Your daughter is being used by the dead girl. I felt it the night of your party. I don't want you to leave, of course I don't. You are our friends. Why don't you come to see Signora Salvati yourself? I could take you tomorrow."

"You're all mad," Gideon said, and ended the call. He rejoined Penny. He was fuming. "She's as mad as you." He'd stopped whispering and in a ghostly voice said: "The spirits are coming to take you away."

"Shhh for God's sake Gideon, I don't want Venetia upset."

"God's got nothing to do with it. I'm going for a walk. I need to clear my head." He put on his Barbour, and slammed the front door behind him.

36

Flight Booked

Penny listened as Gideon's footsteps faded away from the campo. She switched on her laptop and waited for a connection. She'd decided what to do the instant he'd slammed the door. She scrolled through to the 16th November on the website and chose the flight leaving at 12:15. She delved in her handbag for her purse and credit card. As she typed in the details, she felt something on her shoulder.

"Are you leaving us, Penny?" It was the squeaky voice of the puppet.

Venetia had never called her Penny. She felt the hair on the back of her neck rise. It wasn't her daughter talking. She tried to remain calm. "We're both going, darling, on Wednesday. You're not well, and I want to get you back to England. We can see Granny and Grandpa, and Lucy. Won't that be nice?"

"I must stay in Venice, Penny – we cannot leave." Venetia squeaked and manipulated the puppet on Penny's shoulders so it was stroking her cheek. "You are a silly mummy."

Penny felt cold inside. "Stop it, Ven, I don't like it. Take it off my shoulder."

"You go, Penny – you're not well – I am quite safe here. We won't tell anyone about our little talk – it will be our secret." The puppet raised its hand and put it to Penny's lips.

Penny's heart started thumping. It was happening again, another panic attack. She snatched the puppet from Venetia and flung it to the floor, fighting for control of her breathing. In out, in out, her heart was still pumping wildly. Her hands were trembling.

Her daughter's voice changed. It was Venetia again. Elena had gone. "What's the matter, Mummy? You look funny."

Penny whispered, "Nothing, darling." It was difficult to breathe, but the thumping in her chest was slowing. Her heartbeat was returning to normal. She felt exhausted.

"Do we have to go? I don't want to leave Isabella, and what about Daddy? Is he coming?"

"No, Darling, he'll come back later. He's got to finish his work. We'll get Isabella to come and play on Tuesday, and I'll ask her granny if she can come and visit us in Brighton. We can show her the Pavilion and the pier, and take her out on the downs. She's probably never seen the country. That will be something to look forward to."

Venetia picked the puppet off the floor. "Yes, Mummy. Puppet Venetia will come on the plane. She's never flown before. She says we must go and see what we need to take."

"You've got plenty of time, four whole days."

Venetia went back to her room. Penny could hear her talking to the puppet about Brighton. It was creepy. She had to get rid of it somehow before they left. It certainly wasn't coming to Brighton. It was horrible. She hated the squeaky voice.

She returned to the screen. She had to fill in her passport details, and it would be done. Nothing was going to stop her taking Venetia, not Gideon, not Carlo, and not the spirits. They were trying to frighten her off. She must remain strong. They could not physically harm her. Her mother always said, '*Sticks and stones may break my bones, but words will never hurt me.*' They were trying to get into her mind. She wouldn't let them. They were vapour, just air, and she was flesh and blood. As long as she was strong, as long as she stuck to her plan. She would not let anything get in the way. She would not let Venetia sleep alone. She could sleep between her and Gideon in the double bed. She made one last check of the details. The flight was leaving on the 16th at 12:15, check in closed at 11:35, so they would need to take the 9:29 boat out to the airport. She closed down the laptop and looked in on Venetia. She was playing with the puppet.

"Venetia," she said, "Mummy's just going to make some calls, and then we can have a game of Scrabble together."

She'd call Carlo first. She wouldn't be able to get anyone at the school until Monday. She'd call them then and tell them Venetia would not be returning. Then, she'd call Elizabeta and tell her they were leaving.

"Pronto, hi Carlo. Look, I'm really sorry but I'm taking Venetia back to England. I'm not happy with her staying here. Really sorry to let you down like this, but you know, I wouldn't if it wasn't serious. I've booked us out on Wednesday."

Although it was Saturday, Carlo was at the desk of his office in the university. "Penny, this is a shock. What about Gideon?"

"He'll stay, he'll complete the contract," she said, although she realised she had no right to speak for him. She just guessed he would.

"I'm sorry. We will miss you, and you'll be hard to replace. Look, I won't advertise for anyone until December. If you change your mind when you get back to England, you can come back to us. What about that?"

"That's kind, Carlo, I don't deserve it."

"Penny, of course you do. Will you do something for me before you go? Could you phone your friends the Zancani? I've been through the state archives and letters of the time, and can find nothing on Aureo Zancani. If he really was Patriarch, it's inconceivable there should be no record. But perhaps they have some knowledge? It's a long shot, but could you try them? I'm beginning to think either Elena or the killer made the name up."

"Sure, I was going to ring them and let them know. I was hoping Isabella could come and see Venetia before we go. I'll do it straight away. I'll ring you back if they know anything. Ciao, and Carlo, thank you."

She ended the call and paused for a moment, working out what to say, before retrieving the Zancani number from her contacts. She pressed call, and listened to the ringing, waiting for someone to pick up. Cristofo answered.

"Ah, Penny," he said. "Good to hear that English voice. I expect you want Elizabeta?"

"Yes, but I wanted to ask you something. Carlo's been working on the dead girl's writings we found in the chest. She mentions Patriarch Aureo Zancani, but there is no official record of him. We wondered if you had any ideas, any family record?" There was silence at the other end. "Cristofo?"

"No," he said. "I have never heard the name. If he existed, he is not of my family. There have never been any patriarchs with our name. The girl must have made him up. Perhaps she was writing to entertain her friends in the convent."

"I suppose. Carlo thought the name might be made up."

"Yes. Well many people invent and embellish their lives. She wouldn't be the first. I will get Elizabeta for you."

She heard him put the telephone down, and walk slowly away. She'd wanted to tell him they were leaving, but he hadn't given her a chance. She waited for over five minutes, and remembered the size of the house and Cristofo's age. Elizabeta might be in some far off recess. Eventually she heard Elizabeta's voice.

"Penny, how are you?"

"Not good," she wondered whether to tell Elizabeta the truth, and decided not. "Venetia hasn't been sleeping well. She keeps sleepwalking. She's unsettled by something, and one thing and another, I want to get her back to England. We are leaving on Wednesday."

"Oh no, Isabella will be so upset. Have you spoken to Dr Gabrieli?"

"Not today, he doesn't know we're going. He's arranged for a scan at the hospital on Monday. I'll let him know then. If they do find something's wrong, it's better we're back in England for treatment. My Italian is so bad. I want to be sure I understand what is happening. Could Isabella come and play on Tuesday morning — chance to say goodbye? It'll be our last day."

"Yes, Aldo can walk her round to you. What time?"

"Shall we say 10 o'clock? I'm sure the girls will keep in touch. They're such good friends. Perhaps Isabella could visit us in England in the summer?"

"And Venetia could come and stay here, too. It won't be so bad if they know they will see each other again."

"Yes," said Penny, but she knew full well she would never let Venetia return.

37

Faustina Prepares

Faustina returned just after six, having spent the day at Anna's house. She'd shut the door to the bedroom, where the body lay. It had become unsettling seeing it as she pottered around. She'd thought it best that neighbours heard movement in the house. At lunchtime, she'd heated a tin of soup and clattered pans about as she looked for a saucepan.

She'd kept the shutters of the kitchen closed. There was a crack in the wood that enabled her to look out. She could see right into the girl's bedroom. She was pleased the girl was on the mend. The flu was finished; she'd not been in bed, like before. Faustina had seen her playing with a puppet on the floor of her room. Faustina had never had anything to play with. The girl wouldn't need anything either. Their work was everything.

Faustina had seen the unsuitable mother. She could see she was what men liked. Her eyes were lined with black makeup to attract them. The world was an evil place. Her mother had told her that, told her to beware of the devil and all his temptations. The girl was pretty, but hers was an innocent beauty, the look of an angel, not a painted harlot. It was as well Faustina was going to get her away from this, saving her from damnation. If the girl stayed, she would become a painted woman of dirt like her mother.

She planned to take the girl in the early hours of Tuesday morning. It was the anniversary of the date her ancestor had received the work from the abbess, the 15th November 1806, two hundred and five years ago. It was propitious. Nothing would go wrong. On Monday morning she would do a big shop. She would buy enough pasta, porridge, and tins of tomato to last them a month. She wouldn't need to go out again until the girl had submitted to her will. By then, she would be the mother.

In the chapel, she began the evening prayers. She sensed restlessness in the air, a stirring, as if the spirits in the other world she prayed for were whispering. They were waiting for the girl. That was it. When Faustina finished, she made her supper. After tomorrow night, she thought, she would never eat alone. It was exciting to think of the new life. How different from these days alone.

38

<u>Father Rice</u>

It was dark when Gideon returned to Campo Arsenale. Paulo's was open. As he made his way around the restaurant to the apartment building, he peered through the window to where Father Rice usually sat, and there he was, leaning over a plate of pasta. As he went to pour himself some wine, he glimpsed Gideon, and turned. He smiled and waved. Gideon waved back, retraced his steps and went in.

"Hello father," he said going up to the table, "may I join you?"

"Sure, pleased to have some male company, a week of the daughters is enough for any man. Can I get you anything?"

Gideon looked at the plate of pasta, and felt hungry. "I'll have what you're having."

Pat Rice waved at Rosa. "Un altro vongole, per favore."

"Si subito."

"And how is your family? Penny, Venetia?"

"I need to talk to you. You know Venetia had the flu?"

Pat Rice nodded.

"The fever's disturbed her sleep. She's been sleepwalking, having nightmares, and talking in her sleep. She talks in Italian. Penny thinks there's more to it than there is. She's very wrapped up in the work she's doing. She's restoring the mirror we found in the chest with the dead girl."

"Yes?" The priest looked at Gideon.

"Twice, while still asleep, Venetia has moved the cover off the mirror. Penny thinks she is possessed by the dead girl. A friend persuaded her to go to a medium, and the medium said there were spirits with Venetia. Penny's terrified something is going to happen. She wants to take Venetia back to England."

Gideon's food arrived. "Eat your vongole, let me think. For one terrible moment, I thought you were going to ask for an exorcism." Pat Rice's eyes twinkled, and he smiled. "Seriously, though, Gideon, you must remain calm. You should not be angry with Penny. I can see why she might jump to the conclusion she has. I wish she had come to me, instead of going to the medium. As they say, it is what it is."

Gideon ate, relieved he'd confided in Father Rice.

"You know the scriptures warn us not to consult mediums, but to inquire of God. Our souls belong to him; to tamper with them is very dangerous." The priest pointed his fork at Gideon. "They are quite clear. If those who practice the dark arts had any power, beyond being deceivers, it is most definitely not a gift from God." He looked up, closed his eyes to concentrate. "This is what Deuteronomy has to say: 'When you come into the land, which the Lord your God is giving you, you shall not learn to follow the abominations of those nations. There shall not be found among you anyone, who makes his son or his daughter pass through the fire, or one who practices witchcraft, or a soothsayer, or one who interprets omens, or a sorcerer, or one who conjures spells, or a medium, or one who calls up the dead. For all who do these things are an abomination to the Lord.'" He looked directly at Gideon. "You and Penny don't play with Ouija boards or the occult I hope?"

"Good grief no, not at all," Gideon said.

"I wonder, may I come and see Penny, when we've finished eating?"

"I wish you would," Gideon said.

After the meal, Gideon took Father Rice up to the flat. It was getting late, and Penny had begun to wonder what had happened to him. He was supposed to be making the supper. Her heart sank when she saw the priest come in behind Gideon.

"Hello Penny, how are you?"

"Not so good father," she said.

Venetia came out of her room to see her daddy. She was in her nightdress.

Pat Rice saw the red mark around her neck. "Hello Venetia, how did you get that nasty mark around your neck?"

"I've got ringworm."

"Ah, the Doctor's been?"

"Yes he has," Penny said coldly. "What were you thinking?"

"Do you use the local guy, Dr Martino?"

"No, Dr Gabrieli," Gideon said. "The Zancanis recommended him."

"Right," he said. "Is there anything I can do Penny? If you want to talk, I am a good listener. You can tell me anything. Here, let me write down my number." He got a pad out, scribbled his number down and passed it to her. "Anytime," he said, looking at her for a sign she might want help. "Well, I guess I better go."

"Yes, I think you better," she said. "Venetia and I are leaving on Wednesday, so I doubt I'll have time to take you up on your offer." She looked at Gideon. "I booked a flight while you were out."

Gideon wished he hadn't brought Pat Rice. "Goodbye Father. Sorry," he said as he followed him to the door.

Father Rice put his hand on Gideon's shoulder. "You know you can call me anytime, or catch me downstairs."

"Yes, Father."

39

<u>Ospedale</u>

It was a miserable weekend. Gideon feared for the future. He had to stay in Venice to finish the work. He owed it to Carlo. And, anyway, was unlikely to find anything in England in his field. They needed the money. The mortgage on the house in Brighton had to be paid and now his would be the only income. He was frightened he and Penny were being torn apart. He still loved her, but she had become so strange. He wondered if she was having a breakdown. Was Venetia safe with her? Penny kept telling him that it would all be alright once she got back to England. He hoped it would, but he'd ring his parents and ask them to keep a close eye on her. Luckily, they lived nearby in Lewes and liked nothing better than visiting their granddaughter.

Venetia was now sharing their bed. Penny did not want her left alone at night. Gideon woke on Monday, and looked at his sleeping wife and daughter. He loved them so much. He got up and went into the bathroom to wash and shave. When he'd finished, he woke Penny.

"It's 7:30, love," he said.

"Thanks." She nudged Venetia. "Time to wake up, darling. We've got the hospital today."

Penny got herself and Venetia washed and dressed and joined Gideon. They breakfasted together, and he got his stuff to go down to the boat for the morning pick up.

"Hope all goes well and they don't keep you hanging about," he said, ruffling Venetia's hair and bending to kiss her goodbye. Instinctively, he would have kissed

Penny, but after the rows of the weekend, he felt odd doing it. He pecked her tentatively on the cheek.

She looked sadly at him. "See you tonight. Have a good day."

"Yes," he said, "you too."

From the window, they watched him get on the boat and go into the cabin. The boat turned and went down the canal. Venetia waved but he didn't see.

"Do your teeth, Ven, and I'll come and put some cream on your rash."

Penny rubbed cream on to Venetia's rash. "It's looking much better. We'll put a scarf on again shall we?"

Venetia nodded. Penny got a blue silk scarf and tied it around Venetia's neck to hide the red mark. "Right, Ven, duffle coats on."

They walked to the Arsenale stop and Penny bought two returns to Ospedale. Five minutes later they boarded the 41, and chugged off into the lagoon. They found two seats inside. It was evident by the passengers the boat was bound for the hospital. At San Elena, an old couple got on. The man's arm was in a sling. They made their way towards the seats in front of Penny and Venetia and stopped. The woman looked at Venetia, and crossed herself. She tugged at her husband's arm and they walked on past to the back of the vaporetto.

Venetia looked to see the scarf was still in place. She frowned. "Why did that woman cross herself when she saw me?"

"Nothing to do with you, darling. She must be taking her husband to hospital, she's probably saying a prayer."

The boat stopped at San Pietro di Castello, then Bacini, Celestia, and finally arrived at Ospedale. Penny took Venetia's hand and they joined the throng of people waiting to get off. Some were carrying bags of fruit and magazines for the sick. They filed off. There were four yellow Ambulanza motorboats moored outside the main entrance. The automatic doors had a big red cross on them. They kept opening and closing as people went in and out. As instructed, Penny and Venetia walked past the main entrance, on over the bridge and down the Fondamenta dei Mendicanti to the side entrance. Penny was relieved to see the familiar face of Dr Gabrieli.

"Buon Giorno," he said. "Tutto bene, we can go straight in. By the way, your priest called me to ask about Venetia. He was concerned."

She interrupted him before he could say more. "Not our priest, he's a friend of my husband." Penny was going to add that he'd got no business calling, but didn't. She'd take it up with Gideon later. Rice didn't trust her. What did the stupid American think she was doing?

They took a lift to the second floor. The hospital was busy. There were patients being wheeled about in chairs, and white coated staff with stethoscopes walking briskly down the corridors. They came to the EEG room and were met by a man in a white tunic and white trousers. A black badge on the pocket of the tunic read Dr G. Raphael. Dr Gabrieli introduced them. He explained what was going to happen.

Penny watched as they seated Venetia and attached flat metal discs to her scalp. These electrodes would pick up the electrical signals from Venetia's brain and send them to the EEG machine. When everything was in place, the machine was switched on, and Dr Gabrieli asked Venetia some questions, starting with her name. He made her do a few basic exercises, lifting her right and left leg, and her right and left arm. Finally he gave her a pad and asked her to write a sentence and draw a picture. When she'd done that, he asked her to add fifteen, twenty one, and seven together, and multiply the answer by six. She wrote it down on the pad, and worked out the answer. "Two hundred and fifty six," she said.

"Clever girl. Let me have a look at your drawing. What is it? What are all those lines going up from the figure?"

"It's my puppet," Venetia said.

Penny looked over Dr Raphael's shoulder at the wavy lines produced on the computer screen. It was odd to see her daughter's thoughts graphically transposed. The whole test took about thirty minutes. When it was over, Dr Raphael said something to Dr Gabrieli, who began taking the discs off Venetia's head. "Mrs Mantell, would you and Venetia go and wait? There is a cafe on the ground floor. I will come and find you."

"Yes," she said. "Have you found anything?"

"No, Dr Raphael is going to print out the results and have another look, but at first sight everything looks normal."

Penny took Venetia and, following signs on the walls, found their way back to the lift down to the ground floor and the cafe. She bought a coffee and a bottle of juice for Venetia. They sat at a table waiting.

"What did my thoughts look like, Mummy? Were they pictures?"

"No, darling, just lines going up and down."

Half an hour later, Dr Gabrieli came and sat down. "Dr Raphael would like an MRI scan, if that's OK?"

She looked in the doctor's face to see if it revealed anything. "Why? Have you found something? What's wrong?"

"Don't worry; nothing to be concerned about. He's detected a slight anomaly. He just wants a scan to check. It's a completely harmless procedure, though I should warn you the scanner is very noisy."

Penny wasn't sure whether she believed him. "How long does it take?" she asked.

"In all, about forty-five minutes, but she won't be in the tunnel more than ten minutes." He turned to Venetia. "You must lie very still when you are in the scanner tunnel. There's nothing to be afraid of. We can talk to you through an intercom.

Venetia nodded. "Shall I pretend to be dead?"

"That will be very still indeed," he said. He raised an eyebrow, and looked at Penny.

"What does the machine do?" she asked.

"It's called Magnetic Resonance Imaging. Have you ever had an X-ray?"

"Yes," Penny said.

"Like X-rays, the scanner produces a picture of the inside of the human body, but it uses magnetism and radio waves and not harmful radiation. Venetia is going to have what we call a T2 brain scan. Shall we go? Dr Raphael is waiting for us."

As they ascended to the third floor, idea after idea ran through Penny's head. Did Venetia have a tumour on the brain? Could that explain her behaviour? Would they have to operate? Penny looked at her daughter, and squeezed her hand. "Please let it be alright," she whispered to herself.

In the MRI unit, Venetia was asked to undress down to her underclothes. Dr Gabrieli explained the metal zip and buttons on her jeans would affect the machine. He helped Venetia onto a table in front of the machine and asked if she was comfortable.

Penny watched as the table moved and her daughter disappeared into the tunnel. The machine started making alarming metallic bangs and clanks. She could see it vibrating. She heard Dr Gabrieli over the intercom reassuring Venetia. Five minutes later it was over.

"What a brave girl," Dr Gabrieli said. "Not a sound, much better than my grown up patients. You get dressed. We're done." He turned to Penny. "We should have the results later in the day. I will telephone you."

"Thank you, Doctor. I meant to tell you earlier, we decided on Sunday to go back to England. Can the results be sent to our doctor there?"

"Yes, there will be a fee, but yes of course if you give me all the details."

"I'll email you his contact details when we get back to England."

"OK. Can you find your way out?"

"Yes, we can follow the signs. We're good at Italian now."

"Si, a doppo," he said.

They took the vaporetto back, but got off at Giardini and, because Venetia had been so good, stopped for an ice cream in the Cafe Paradiso as a treat. Afterwards, they walked through the gardens down to the Via Garabaldi, past Venetia's school, and then home to Arsenale.

Back at the hospital, Dr Raphael was puzzled. The EEG patterns had been the usual alpha and beta waves. The alpha turning to beta when Venetia had been processing information and doing the arithmetic and answering Gabrieli's questions. But when she had shown the doctor her drawing, there had been two abnormal spikes, and a brief surge in electrical activity as if the girl was having a seizure, though she had appeared quite normal. It was these spikes that had made him want an MRI image of Venetia's brain. He feared she might have a tumour. The scan had shown something he'd never seen before. There was a white shadowy mist on the left side of her brain. He could not understand it. He telephoned a specialist, explained, and said he would send the scan for him to look at. He rang Dr Gabrieli and said he would like Venetia to come in for another scan.

Gabrieli told him the Mantells were leaving. "Non é possible, tornerranno a Inglaterra Mercoledi."

He rang Penny. "Buona sera, Signora Mantell. Dr Raphael wanted Venetia to have another scan, but I explained you were leaving on Wednesday. It's important I talk to your doctor in England. He should arrange for Venetia to have another scan as soon as possible. Do you have his details?"

Penny was now really worried. "No, I can get them off the web. What is the matter? What did Dr Raphael say? Tell me, Doctor – I want to know. What's the matter with her?"

"He's not sure, to be honest. It might be a fault with our machine. A specialist is looking."

"Is it a tumour?" she said, dreading the answer.

"It is a possibility – there is a shadow on the scan. I will send everything to your doctor as soon as we know. Now, will you ring me, as well as sending his details? You've got my number and email on the card?"

"Yes, I have." She ended the call. She didn't want to talk anymore. Her mind was in turmoil. Her stomach was churning with fear for her daughter. She pictured the lump growing in Venetia's brain. Why was this happening to them? They should never have left England. The sooner she and Venetia got back to Brighton and saw Dr Ross, the better.

Venetia had been listening at the door. "What's a tumour?"

Penny tried to hide her emotions. "It's a sort of lump. Dr Gabrielli thinks it's a mistake on the machine. Don't worry, darling. If it is, they will take it out in England. The doctors will put you to sleep, and when you wake it will be gone."

"In hospital?"

"Yes – there's a special children's hospital in Brighton."

"I think there is something in my head – it feels funny sometimes." She returned to her bedroom.

Penny sat down at her laptop. She thought of the scalpel cutting out the growth. She Googled Kemptown Surgery and got Dr Ross's email address and the telephone number of the surgery. She sent them to Dr Gabrieli and, as requested, called him on the mobile. She returned to Google and looked up 'tumour' and read everything she could. It was terrifying.

She shutdown the computer and sat at the table looking out of the window and listening to her daughter playing with the wretched puppet. This city she had loved had turned and become a thing of nightmares. She only had Tuesday to get through, and she and Venetia would be away. She heard the sound of a motor boat coming down the canal. It was the university launch bringing Gideon home. She watched him get out and walk across the campo. She saw him look up and wave, and quicken his step. Then she heard him on the stone stairs and seconds later the lock of the door. She turned to meet him.

"How did it go?" he said.

Venetia came running out of her bedroom. "Daddy," she said, going up to him with her arms open wide.

He whisked her up into his arms, kissed her, and put her down.

"Well what about the hospital? What happened?"

"I went into a dark tunnel, and there was lots of noise and they took a picture of the inside of my head."

"Sounds a bit frightening."

"I wasn't frightened, Daddy. The doctor said I was braver than his grown -ups."

Penny interrupted. "Dr Gabrieli rang. He's contacting Dr Ross at home. He wants Venetia to have another scan. He said they detected a shadow on her brain. Possibly a tumour, it might have been a fault with the machine. They're not sure."

"What does he mean fault with the machine? That's stupid. What's the point of scanning on unreliable equipment? Dr Gabrieli didn't say anything else?"

"No, he didn't say anything else, only that your friend Rice called him to check up on us and make sure we're not harming Venetia ourselves."

"Did he say that?"

"Not in so many words, but I think it's pretty clear don't you? Why else would the man ring our doctor?"

"I don't know. I'm going to shower and change."

The evening passed much the same as the last two days. They were civil with each other, and nothing more. After Venetia had gone to their bed, Gideon said, "I'll sleep in Venetia's bed tonight, so I don't wake you. I'm going to make an early start."

"Good, I think I'll turn in now," Penny said. "It's been a long day. You better get your clothes and washing stuff."

He took his shoes off and crept through the bedroom to the bathroom. Venetia was already asleep. He decided he wouldn't bother to shave, so just took his toothbrush. He picked up his clothes, and whispered good night to Penny. He closed the door quietly behind him. He stayed up a little longer with his thoughts, then looked at the time and calculated it was only 8:30 in England. He called his parents.

"Hi Mum, Penny and Venetia are coming back on Wednesday. I wondered if you and Dad could pick them up. Flight gets in at 13:30. Venetia's not been well and I'm a bit worried about Penny, too. She's been under a lot of strain recently."

He listened as his mother asked him question after question. It was good to be able to talk to her. She told him she knew someone who'd had a tumour removed from her brain successfully. She'd returned to complete health. She said of course they would pick Penny and Venetia up, and if Penny wanted, they could come and stay with them. He ended the call feeling better. He hoped Penny would stay with his parents.

He locked the door through to the hall for the night and went into Venetia's room. He put his work clothes on a chair and the keys to the hall down on the bedside table next to Venetia's glass fish. The puppet was lying on the pillow. He put it on the dressing table and noticed the print of the Arsenale Venetia had put up, and thought how happy they'd been in those first few weeks. Now everything had changed. He got into bed and lay awake for a long time. The smell of Venetia was still on the pillow. He breathed it in and switched off the bedside lamp.

40

Night Journey

Penny woke with a jolt. She was freezing. An icy blast of air surrounded her. The temperature had plummeted in the few hours she'd been asleep. She thought about getting an extra blanket from the cupboard but didn't want to wake her daughter. She was getting colder and colder. She wondered if she could, without disturbing Venetia. The room was pitch-black. She thought she might be able to feel her way to the cupboard. She opened her eyes and sat up to see if she could make anything out. Her heart stopped in sheer terror. The hairs on the back of her neck stood up. There was something in the room. She felt death pressing its bony finger against her spine. Something breathed on the back of her neck. It was cold and dead. The horror — she wanted desperately to shut her eyes and not see.

A shimmering yellow-green light filled the room. It had an electric glow. Penny didn't seem able to move. She watched, as invisible hands pulled the blanket off the bed. She tried to grip the sheet to her, but a force pulled it from her and onto the floor. Some unseen weight pinned her legs down to the mattress. She was paralyzed in ice cold terror.

The light grew in intensity and formed a shape that moved and hovered over her daughter. She saw her daughter sit up and rise from the bed. She looked as if she was floating over the floor. The yellow-green light surrounded her. Penny opened her mouth to scream but no sound came out. She had no voice. The air was being sucked out of her lungs. She couldn't breathe, she was suffocating – she was going to die.

She knew it was a nightmare. This couldn't be real. She needed to wake herself. From childhood, she remembered being told that if you die in a dream, you die in real life as well. She must wake or she would die. She clenched her fists and pressed her nails into the palms of her hands, digging deep into the skin. Yes, she could feel it, yet she could still see the horror in front of her. She was awake. Everything was real. She saw Venetia open the door. She was hovering an inch above the floor. The yellow-green light followed her out of the bedroom. Penny struggled against the force holding her to the bed, but it was too strong, crushing her legs.

She tried to scream out for Gideon, but nothing came out of her mouth. The ice air was creeping through her skin. She could no longer move her fingers – they ached. The cold was unbearable. It was howling and screaming, all around her, like an arctic storm. She couldn't think – flashes of white light – sheer panic. Her body was overwhelmed. It closed down and she sank into blackness, floating down a long dark tunnel into deep emptiness. The lights were gone. The nightmare was gone. Everything was black. It was over.

Outside, a voice within Venetia spoke in archaic Venetian that she understood. "Tis time," it said. "We are three." Venetia felt the strings pulling her. Her limbs were so light, she could barely feel them. She moved through the sitting room to her bedroom. Silently, she took the keys from beside her glass fish and picked up her blue backpack from the floor. She picked puppet Venetia off the dressing table and put her in the bag and left to unlock the door. She turned the key in the lock and opened it. She moved into the kitchen and opened the knife drawer. She looked down at the shining knives and chose the sharpest of them all, a gleaming carving knife she'd seen her daddy use. She slid it into the secret compartment and pushed the Velcro together. She closed the bag and put it over her shoulder. In bare feet and nightdress she left the flat and floated down the white stone stairs. She opened the front door onto the deserted Campo. She did not feel the cold of the night.

The moon cast a silvery light through the night mist down on the little girl in the white nightdress. She had her blue backpack with its pattern of yellow flowers hung over her shoulder. She walked towards the Arsenale. As she did, she heard a bell ringing. The campo was suddenly alive with whisperings. Strange colours and shapes rose out of the canal and moved in mass towards the entrance of the shipyard. Swarms of ghosts brushed past her like the wind through trees, forms and faces from the past risen from their graves. The voice within her spoke. "Do not be afraid. You are seeing through our eyes. They are spirits like us. Here, all time is one, endless, they must go on forever, until they enter the light. They come from the deep, where things that might have been and never were, are always wandering. It is the bell summoning them to work."

Venetia looked up at the statue of St Giustina on top of the arched entrance. The voice spoke again. "You will be like her, have strength. Demons cannot hurt you." Venetia made the sign of the cross. The bell stopped ringing. All at once she could hear banging, hammering, cauldrons boiling pitch, and the sounds of voices shouting. She turned and crossed the bridge. The yellow-green light shimmered around her, sometimes darting forward to show her the way. The sounds of the Arsenal faded as she moved like a ghost through the Campo della Tana, crossed the Rio, and turned left. The streets were alive with the shadows of the dead. She walked down the Calle Nuova into Via Garabaldi and on to the Fondamenta Santa Anna. No one living saw her, as she passed through the eastern quarter of the city. She walked through a parallel world.

She entered Salizada Stretta. "We are nearly there," the voice said. "Be strong." She walked through Campo Ruga like a spirit from another world and came to the white

284

stone bridge in Ramo San Daniel. She took the ten steps up to its summit and turned to look across the water of the Rio delle Vergini to the old arch. From beyond the walls, she heard the sound of singing. It drifted across the water. She had forgotten and remembered how beautiful it was. The yellow-green light hovered around her and for a long time she stood, as if in thought. Then she opened her mouth, and whispered the words. "Spes amor grato carcere nos retinent." The yellow-green light swirled and twisted above her head, forming a column. She looked up with her mouth wide open and sucked it into her body. Her feet felt the touch of the cold stone.

Venetia woke. She was staring across a canal at a white plaque embedded in a high wall. She had no idea where she was. She had never seen this place before. She looked for her mummy and daddy but they were not there. She was in her nightdress. She looked down at her bare white feet on the stone of the bridge. What was she doing here? Was she awake or asleep? She was frightened. She heard a woman's voice calling to her: "Bambina, bambina venga."

41

November 15

At midnight, Faustina wrapped the headscarf around her head. She would go first to the bridge in Ramo San Daniel to pay her respects to her ancestor. Faustina did this every year on this date. Then she'd walk to Anna's house and get the girl.

Faustina walked out of her building and into the swirling mist. She could just make out the lights on the bridge across into Castello. The city was asleep. Into Campo San Pietro and over the wide lamp lit bridge — all was quiet in the fog white night.

Then, she heard two cats yowling and hissing at each other, as she approached Ramo San Daniel. Through the mist, she thought she saw the yellow flowers of the girl's backpack. Faustina looked harder. It was the girl, standing on the summit of the bridge, gazing across the water at the old convent arch. She was dressed in white and was barefoot. With the mist hovering around her, she looked like an angel. Faustina had had hallucinations before. They were signs from God, and she thought this was another. Faustina hurried towards the girl, expecting her to vanish. Then she heard her crying. She was calling for her mother.

Faustina called out to her. "Bambina, bambina venga."

The girl looked at Faustina. Tears were running down her cheeks. "Please, I'm lost. I live in Campo Arsenale – my mummy and daddy are there."

Faustina didn't understand. It didn't matter. The girl had been delivered to her. The man she prayed for had done this. Her mother had told her he had great power. It must be so – he had brought her to the convent to take on the work. She took the girl's hand. "Venga Mamma e Papa sono li," she pointed over the bridge.

She gripped Venetia's hand and took her back over the bridge. "Mia figlia," she said, "tu sai venuta." She looked up to heaven. "Grazie, grazie."

42

<u>San Pietro</u>

The old woman's hand gripped Venetia's. It was hard and rough, not soft like her
mummy's. The woman looked like a witch and the grip of her hand was too tight. Venetia
wanted to pull away but then she recognised her. It was the woman who'd sat outside the
school. Her mummy and daddy must have told her they were looking for their daughter. It
was going to be alright. She walked with her over a big bridge into a deserted square. They
came to an old grey building. The woman took her inside. Surely her parents weren't here?
Perhaps the woman was going to telephone for them to come. She felt the woman pulling
her as they went up a dirty staircase. The woman unlocked a door and they went inside.
Venetia smelt a strange musty smell of age in the dark corridor. It wasn't nice. The woman
took Venetia into a room, turned on the light and pointed at a bed.

Venetia sat down on the iron bed. She saw the picture of the Virgin Mary holding
the baby Jesus. It made her feel safe. The old woman must be good. "Are you going to
telephone my mummy?" she said. "Chiamare mia Mamma." She held her hand up to her
ear pretending to call.

"Si si," the old woman said. "Fa freddo," and opened a drawer, and got out an old
jumper and gave it to Venetia. She watched as Venetia put it on over her nightdress. She
pointed at Venetia's feet, and produced a pair of socks. She came over, knelt and rubbed
Venetia's cold feet, before putting the socks on. She stood up and nodded. "Tutto bene."

The old woman took the backpack off Venetia's shoulder, looked inside and pulled
the puppet out. "Bambola," she said smiling and giving it to Venetia. She stroked

Venetia's hair, and put the backpack down on the floor. Then without a word, got up and crossed to the desk, where she took some papers out tied together by blue ribbon.

Venetia watched the woman leave the room. She heard the key turn in the lock. Did she think she would run away before her mummy and daddy came? Maybe she thought Venetia had run away from home — children did.

But something wasn't right. The woman wasn't like other grownups. Fear crept into Venetia's stomach. She swallowed and looked around the bare white walls, taking in the room. And saw the brown leather whip hanging from a hook. She had no idea what it was. A few feet to the left of the whip, set deep in the thick walls, was a small barred window.

Venetia was very tired. She longed to curl up and go to sleep. She pulled the blankets down and got into the bed. It wouldn't hurt to have a little rest while she waited for her mummy and daddy. She put puppet Venetia next to her and pulled the sheets up over them. The sheets and pillowcase were pink nylon. They felt scratchy against her skin. She put her thumb in her mouth and closed her eyes.

She woke at first light and wondered where she was. She looked at the barred window and remembered. How long had she been asleep? Where were her mummy and daddy? She could hear someone humming and the sound of a saucepan being stirred. She got up and tried the door, but it was locked. She got back into bed and stroked the puppet's hair.

"They'll be here soon, don't worry," she said. "It's morning." She heard the key turn in the lock.

The old woman came in carrying a tray. "Maria, buon giorno."

289

"No, I'm not Maria. I'm Venetia. Where's my mummy?"

The woman sat down on the bed next to her, and put the tray between them. She'd taken her scarf off. Her hair was short ragged and unevenly cut. She reminded Venetia of someone else. Venetia watched as she put a spoon into a bowl of grey sludge.

She smiled. "Buono," she said and pushed the spoon into Venetia's mouth. The stuff was revolting. Venetia wanted to spit it out, but swallowed it in a lump. Venetia shook her head.

"I don't like it. Where's my mummy? Have you called her?"

"Si, Maria, mangia." She tried to force another spoon in.

Venetia pushed it away. "I'm not Maria. I'm Venetia. I'm going." She knocked the tray to the floor and struggled out of bed.

"Stupida," the woman said. She raised her hand and slapped Venetia across the face and pushed her back on the bed. She struck her again across her cheek "Stupida bambina, stupida bambina."

Shocked, Venetia raised her hands to her face. Her cheek was ringing with pain. She'd never been hit before. Her parents never hit her. Petrified, she peered through her fingers at the woman, who just nodded and wagged her finger, and got up. Venetia heard the lock turn.

The pain in her cheek eased. She looked around again. It was hopeless. She would be trapped forever in this horrible place. Tears streamed down her face. She was a prisoner. She cried like she'd never cried before, great wrenching sobs. There would be no help. She would be here for the rest of her life. Her mummy and daddy would never come.

The woman was an evil witch. In Hansel and Gretel the witch wanted to eat children. She fattened them up. Venetia now remembered where she'd seen that face – it had been at her window. This witch had been watching her all along.

Outside, Faustina could hear the girl's sobs. She would have to be taught her name. The knife would have to be heated over the camper stove. Faustina knew how to deal with indiscipline. Before nightfall, the girl would say the words. "Sono Maria."

43

The Search Begins

The alarm on Gideon's mobile started buzzing at 6:30. He woke, stretched, and got out of bed. He noticed the keys had gone from the bedside table. Penny must be up. The puppet had gone too. He wondered if Venetia had had a disturbed night and went to find out what had happened.

As he walked into the sitting room, he saw the door to the hall was open. He looked to see if Penny was in the kitchen. She wasn't, but the front door out of the apartment was ajar. She must be taking the rubbish out. He wondered if Venetia was awake. He stopped in shock when he saw Penny alone in the bed. The blankets and sheets were lying in a heap on the floor. There was no sign of Venetia

"Oh my God, where is she?" He shook Penny, shouting, "Venetia's gone." But she wouldn't wake. He shook her again and again, until her eyes opened. They looked glazed and far away. She looked drugged. He repeated, "Venetia's gone – vanished!"

"What?" She sat up and turned to look next to her. Her hands grasped her head. "Oh no, it was real. They've taken her."

"What was real? Who's taken her?"

"The dream, the room was full of light, something pulled the blankets off and Venetia was floating."

"For God's sake," Gideon said. "I'm going out to look for her. She's opened the front door. She's outside. Get up and pull yourself together."

He ran into the campo in his pyjamas, looking left and right, and shouting. "Venetia, Venetia." He walked up and down the canal staring into the water, his body tense, ready to jump in if he saw her. It was still dark and he could see nothing on the surface. People were beginning to make their way to work. Someone stopped to ask what the matter was. He described Venetia to the man. He ran through the calle onto the wide Schiavoni but there was no sign. He was frantic and ran back to dress.

While he'd been out, Penny had dressed. She looked awful. He could see she had been crying. "I'll call the police," he said. He put his arm around her. "We'll find her."

"I swear, Gideon, I saw her surrounded by green and yellow light. That's why I thought I was dreaming. The spirits have got her. The shadow the doctor saw – it's Elena. They've taken Venetia. We'll never see her again. We should never have come here."

Gideon tried to calm her, but wasn't sure anything he said was getting through. "You're not well Penny. You saw her sleepwalking, that's all. I wish I hadn't slept in her room. You need to see the doctor."

He rang 112 for the Carabinieri and told them his daughter was missing. They asked him if someone could have broken into the flat. He said he thought she had gone out alone. He told them about her sleepwalking. He didn't say anything with Penny standing next to him, but was petrified Venetia had walked into the canal and was lying at the bottom. They said they would send an officer.

Penny looked in the bedroom and called out. "She hasn't got her clothes. She's in her nightdress, unless she got something from her room, but she would have woken you. I'll look." She walked past Gideon into Venetia's room and checked the drawers. She came back with tears running down her face. "She's not taken anything, she'll be freezing. She hasn't even got any shoes on. She'll die out there."

Gideon did his best to think. His mind was full of images of Venetia. "Once the police have been, we need to get out looking," he said. "I'm going to get dressed."

In the bedroom, he telephoned Dr Gabrieli and told him about Venetia. "Doctor, I think Penny's having some sort of breakdown. She thinks spirits have possessed Venetia. She's hallucinating. She says she saw lights around Venetia. You need to see her."

"It sounds like a panic attack. I will come immediately. I'll be with you in fifteen minutes."

Gideon went into the kitchen and gulped down a mug of coffee. Penny was sitting staring vacantly into a mug of tea.

"I know what I saw, Gid," she said. She looked at the palms of her hands, and saw where she'd dug her nails in. "Look," she held her hands up to show him. "I wasn't sure if I was dreaming. I dug my nails in to see if I was awake."

He looked sadly at her. "What you think you saw. The doctor's coming. He'll give you something to calm your nerves."

"You think I'm mad." Before she could say anything else, the doorbell rang. It was the Carabinieri. Penny said very little. She nodded as Gideon explained about Venetia's sleepwalking. He told them she was in her nightclothes, without anything on her feet. He begged them to start searching, said she would die of cold, if she was not found soon. The officers asked for a photo of Venetia.

While Penny went to her laptop to print out some recent photos, the officers looked for any sign of a break in. They asked if anyone else had keys to the flat. Gideon said, as far as he knew, only the landlord; it had all been arranged through Carlo and the university. They said a search would begin immediately. The photos would be circulated to all their offices in the city. As they left, Dr Gabrieli arrived.

Gideon offered him a coffee, but he said he'd just had one. Gideon asked, "Could this have anything to do with the tumour, I mean, would it make her act oddly?"

"I don't think so. Not so soon. We're not even sure it is a tumour."

"I'm going to look for her. I'll walk to the school. It's a route she knows."

"Good idea, a familiar walk is most likely."

Gideon left. Dr Gabrieli asked Penny about the lights she'd seen around Venetia. She told him about the dream. She told him everything she could remember of the events leading up to the visit to Signora Salvati.

The doctor listened and, when she'd finished, sat silently for a minute looking at her. "I must be honest, Signora Mantell, I do not believe in the afterlife. I believe you are suffering from acute anxiety. It is the worry about your daughter. It is one of life's most painful experiences. One in ten suffer; you are by no means alone. Have you had palpitations, elevated heart rate, difficulty breathing?

"Yes, but it's because of what I've seen. I'm terrified."

"It is a symptom of panic attacks. The victim is cast into a state of terror, all rational thought processes cease during this time. Do you feel butterflies in your stomach, trembling, pins and needles, or numbness?"

"Yes," she said. "Last night pins and needles down my spine, and I felt numb and cold, so cold. Now, I feel exhausted, as if I'd taken a sleeping pill. I'm worn out – I feel as if I'm in a dream. I have to find my daughter."

"Are you taking anything?"

"No, Doctor."

He reached into his bag and brought out a bottle of pills. "I have brought some Benzodiazepine. Take one in the morning and one at night. It will help inhibit the nerve signals and calm you without making you sleepy. You should feel much better. But you need to see a specialist. I will write to your doctor in England so he can arrange something when you get back." He unscrewed the top. "You may as well start now." He passed her a pill, and put the top back on the bottle.

She put the pill in her mouth and swallowed it. "There," she said. "Now I'm going to search for Venetia."

"Better to stay here. She may return home. Let me have a photo. I'll put it up in the surgery. The more eyes we have looking."

Penny printed out another photo and gave it to Dr Gabrieli. He put it in his bag and snapped it shut. "Ring me if you need anything, and let me know when you find Venetia. I think your husband is right. She has walked to school in her sleep. Sleepwalkers often repeat their daytime routine."

He left. It was now 8:30, and the sun was up. Penny tried to compose herself and think. She wondered if she was having a nervous breakdown, and if she would know if she was. The mad don't know they're mad, she thought. What she had seen last night had been so real. What on earth was happening? She was a woman of science. I must think clearly,

296

she told herself, and remembered Isabella's visit and jumped at the idea Venetia had gone there in her sleep. She rang Elizabeta.

"Hi, Venetia isn't with you is she?"

At the other end, Elizabeta frowned. "I thought we were coming to you?"

"Yes, you were. Venetia disappeared in the night. You know she was sleepwalking? Behaving a bit strangely?

"Dio," Elizabeta said.

"The doctors found a possible tumour on her brain when she had the scan. I think it's affecting her. We found the front door open this morning and there's no sign of her. I thought she might have made her way to you."

"What a terrible thing. No, she is not here. Where could she go? I will send Aldo out now to search the streets between you and us. What else can we do? Oh the poor child."

"I don't know what to do," Penny said. "It's hopeless."

"Isabella and I will go out looking. I will send Cristofo searching in the boat. Have you contacted the police?"

"Yes, yes, they have Venetia's photo." Through the window, Penny saw Francesco standing by the boat, waiting for Gideon. "Oh God, I have to ring Carlo."

"I'm sure she'll be found. Ring me as soon as you know anything," Elizabeta said.

"Yes, bye." Penny waved at Francesco. She hurried to the launch and in Italian tried to tell him what had happened. She told him she was going to ring Carlo and asked him to wait.

"Carlo, something dreadful. Venetia disappeared in the night. We think she opened the front door in her sleep and walked out. She's completely vanished. Gideon is searching for her. We've called the police."

"I am coming to you now, and I am bringing the department. We will search till we find her. Is Francesco with you? Let me speak to him."

She passed the phone over and listened as Francesco said, "Si, si si. Subito." He passed the phone back to her. "I go look in boat." He jumped back in the boat, started the engine and went back down the canal.

Ten minutes later, Gideon returned from his search. "Any news?" he said.

"No, Carlo is coming with more people to help search, and the Zancanis are searching the streets around their house."

"The police are stopping the vaperettos out on the lagoon. I saw one of their motorboats with its light flashing, stop one, then move on, and stop another. Everything's being done. We'll find her."

Half an hour later, Campo Arsenale was full of archaeologists. Penny passed out photos of Venetia, while Carlo went from person to person, issuing instructions as to who was to search where.

Penny saw Gianfranco talking to Gideon. She wanted to ask him if Laura was home, but daren't in front of her husband. He was still furious with Laura. She'd ring later, when she was alone. She wanted Laura to take her back to see Signora Salvati. If what she'd seen last night was real and Venetia was possessed, Salvati was the only one could help. The only one who might know where Venetia was.

44

Cristofo Searches

At the Palazzo Castello di Zancani, Elizabeta had already sent Aldo out in search of Venetia. She went to Cristofo's study and found him sitting at the desk, peering through a magnifying glass at an old yellowing document.

"Venetia's gone missing. They found something in the scan on the poor child's brain. You remember I told you she acted oddly the other day? She's gone from the flat, disappeared. I told Penny you would take the boat out and look."

He looked up from his work. "Of course, when did she go?"

"She walked out in her sleep. Since the flu, she's been sleepwalking, and now this new discovery. Penny is frantic. I've sent Aldo out, and Isabella and I will search too. We will look around the school. Isabella said she might go there."

He put on the tweed jacket he'd hung at the back of the chair. "I'll go straight away. I'll take my mobile, call me if she's found, otherwise I'll keep looking until dark."

He went down to the boathouse, picking up a pair of black leather gloves and a warm grey scarf, which he knotted at his neck. He also pulled on a fur hat which covered his ears. He knew it made him look ridiculous, but it was cold out on the water, and at his age he didn't care what he looked like. He climbed into the boat, started the outboard motor, and steered out through the arch into the day.

He went from canal to canal, scanning the water, dreading what he might see. An image of Venetia floating face down in a canal came into his mind. He tried to erase it, but the picture of the floating body kept coming back. Whenever he passed a tied up boat selling vegetables, he described Venetia and asked them to look out for her. He asked them to pass the word amongst their customers.

One name kept creeping into his mind, *Aureo Zancani*. How long had it been, since Penny had asked him and he'd denied any knowledge? And now another girl had disappeared. He felt it was at the centre of a labyrinth, where all time was one. How could it have anything to do with what was happening now?

As he passed through the waterways of the city, all his ancestors seemed to merge within him, until at dusk he found himself in the Rio delle Vergini. He cut the engine below the plaque commemorating the convent. This had been their water entrance. There was no way in now; thick high walls surrounded, and protected the naval base. He looked up and thought of what had happened here. He sensed Venetia was near. He restarted the engine, turned the boat around and went out into the Canale di San Pietro. He saw the leaning campanile towering up in front of him and the old Patriarch's palace behind. He steered the boat into the side of the canal and tied up to a black iron ring embedded in a flagstone next to stone steps.

Light was fading and the sky had a pink tinge. As he stepped off the boat, the lamps on the path to the cathedral flickered on. He walked hurriedly into the empty cloister of the deserted palace. He could almost feel the presence of his ancestor hanging heavily over this place.

"Venetia," he called out, and his voice echoed around him. Nothing stirred, no one came. He walked all the way around, looking in shadowy corners, but there was no sign of her. He walked the streets behind the campanile but there was nothing, and it was now dark. He had seen no one. He knew few people lived here and they were shut in their houses for the night. The area was known to be the quietest in Venice. His mobile rang. He pulled it from his pocket. It was Elizabeta. He hoped she'd have good news.

"What news? Has she been found?"

"No, Cristofo. Have you found anything?"

"No, nothing. I've asked around, but no one has seen her."

"Prior Vittorio has been. He left you a box. He said he thinks it is what you were looking for. It is labelled Le Vergine 1806."

"What's inside?" Cristofo said.

"He didn't know. There is no key. You'll have to break it open. He said to do with it as you will. He doesn't want it back. Aldo has taken it up to your study."

"I'll get back. See you soon." Cristofo hurried past the cathedral to the boat, started the outboard motor and headed out of the canal to take the shortest route home. What, he wondered was in that box? He steered by instinct, turning in and out of the waterways, hardly noticing where he went. And then he was outside the palazzo, steering through the arched entrance.

Aldo had turned the great lantern hanging over the domed ceiling on. He looked at the shadows of the water on the walls and climbed up to the iron door and heaved it open. He walked through the dark passage to the hall of his ancestors. Tonight, more than ever, he felt their eyes on him, as he passed through to reach the floor above where Elizabeta would be, and there she was on the sofa with his granddaughter. The fire was blazing in the hearth.

"Have you spoken to Penny since this morning?" he asked.

"I don't like to," Elizabeta said. "I'm sure she would have rung if Venetia had come home."

"Please ring, Nonna," Isabella said. "I don't want to go to bed until she's safe."

"Alright," she got up and dialled Penny's mobile. "Penny it's Elizabeta, any news?" She listened, put the phone slowly down, and returned to the sitting room. "No she has not been found yet. It's terrible to think of her outside alone at night."

"Can we go out again and look?" Isabella said.

"No, we have to let the police look tonight. It's too dark."

"She will be OK, won't she?"

Elizabeta looked at Cristofo. Her eyes said 'she's dead isn't she?'

"I hope so, cara," he said. "We will look again tomorrow. I'm going to my study. Have Aldo bring my supper there. I want to look inside the box."

45

The Search Continues

At first light on Wednesday, police divers began searching the Rio del Arsenale, the canal in front of the Mantell's flat. Penny sat at the window in her dressing gown, glass of water in hand, and watched as they rolled backwards off their boat into the water. She twisted the cap on the Benzodiazepine and put one on her tongue, took a swig of water and swallowed. An image of a diver with Venetia's body in his arms flashed across her brain. She couldn't bear it.

She stood up, closed her eyes, and thought about Venetia. "Where are you darling?" She emptied her mind. She had a sudden positive jolt – a strong feeling Venetia was alive somewhere near. She turned to Gideon. Her eyes were alight.

"She's alive. I feel it. I'm going out to search. Will you phone the airline – tell them we're not flying?"

"Yes. I'll call my parents as well. I haven't told them." While Penny dressed, Gideon called Easy Jet and then steeled himself to speak to his parents.

"Hello Mum, Venetia's missing... yesterday... the police are searching... I don't know... No you stay there, no point in you coming out... " A surge of sorrow welled up within him and he couldn't carry on. "Sorry Mum, I've got to go... I'll call you soon as I hear anything." He ended the call, sat down, put his head in his hands, and started to cry.

Penny returned dressed and saw Gideon slumped over the table. She put her hand on his head and began stroking his hair. He stood up and they hugged each other tight.

"She was such a beautiful child," Gideon said.

"Don't say *was*. She's alive. I'm certain of it. I would know if she was dead, a mother knows." She smiled at Gideon and wiped the tears from his eyes with her fingers. "I'm going now," she said. "Call me if there's any news. Don't give up, Gid."

"No," he said and watched her go.

When she was out of sight of the flat, she called Laura. She wasn't answering. Penny left a message to call. She carried on to the Via Garabaldi, stopping at the shops she and Venetia had been in. Many of them had police posters of Venetia in their windows. Penny sat on the bench outside the school, where she and Gideon had seen the old woman. She sat for a long time remembering Venetia, her first steps, her first words, her first day at school.

She walked on and asked directions. She wanted to see where the convent had been. She found it and stood on the bridge, looking across at the white plaque. She gazed at it, reading the words carved into the stone. SPES ET AMOR GRATO CARCERE NOS RETINENT S.M. DELE VERZENE. She raised her head and looked up above the walls. "Where are you, darling?"

In the late afternoon, she found herself on an iron walkway on the outside of the Arsenale. Under the walkway, a choppy sea lapped up against the thick pink brick walls. She could not remember how she'd got here. She'd walked and walked, not caring where, just letting instinct take her. Every now and again, she'd stopped strangers and showed them a photo of her daughter. She'd knocked on doors where she'd heard people inside and asked them. No one had seen Venetia and Laura had not returned her call. The sun was beginning to set – she needed to get home. She saw the Bacino vaporetto stop and waited alone for a boat to take her around to the other side of the city.

When she got back, the police divers had gone. There were no boats on the canal. She found Gideon watching television.

"They found nothing," he said, as she came in. His voice was flat and weary. He switched the television off.

"I've been up to the end of the Via Garabaldi and beyond, knocking on doors, but no one has seen her. Where on earth is she?"

"I wish I knew. There is nothing we can do. I feel so helpless."

"I saw the plaque where the convent was, where Elena was murdered." She burst into tears, and sobbed. "Oh, God, I wish we'd never come here." She sat down heavily on the sofa next to Gideon.

He put his arm around her, and they sat in silence. The doorbell rang. Penny wiped her eyes. "Will you get that, Gid?"

He went to the intercom. "Yes, come up, Father, I'll buzz the door." He went to wait at the top of the stairs and brought Father Rice in.

"I'm so sorry, we have been praying at the church for her return. Is there anything I can do? Would you like to pray?"

Penny heard her phone go in her handbag. She looked at the screen. It was Laura. She let it go to answerphone. "It can wait," she said. The last thing she wanted was the priest hearing her asking for the medium.

"I would like to pray," Gideon said. "But it's been so long I've forgotten how."

"Come back to the church with me. Penny, will you come?"

"No, Father," she said. "I will not pray to a God who let this happen." She looked fiercely at Gideon. "Besides, someone has to stay in the flat in case she comes back."

"I know," he said. "I'll get my coat, Father."

The two left the flat. Penny felt like shouting after them. "Caught another fish, father."

46

Faustina Begins the Lessons

Venetia held her puppet close. "I'll look after you," she said. "We've got each other."

The puppet squeaked in Venetia's voice: "Don't let her hurt me."

Venetia heard the lock turn and the old woman entered. "Buona sera, Maria, cena."

"I'm not Maria, you witch." She saw her chance. There was a gap between the witch and the door. Venetia, with the puppet in her hand, ducked low and darted past Faustina, who lost her balance and fell crashing to the floor. The tray went clattering across the room.

Venetia ran into the corridor. Ahead of her, she could see a room with candles burning. She turned, looking for the front door. It was at the end of the dark corridor. She ran towards it, fumbled desperately with both hands on the handle, terrified she'd be caught before she could get away. It turned and she pushed the door open and found herself on a stone landing. She saw the stairs to her left. She went to go down them and was on the second step when she heard the woman behind her. It was too late. A heavy hand yanked her hair. She lost her footing and fell backwards. The woman dragged her by her hair and bumped her back up the stairs.

Venetia screamed. "Help – aiutami, aiutami!" But no one came. She clutched her puppet to her, as she was pulled back to the room, screaming and shrieking with pain. The woman picked her up and stuck her face into Venetia's. It was wrinkled and horrible. There was hair on her chin. Her teeth looked rotten and her breath was rancid.

"Nessuno sense, bambina," she said, and dropped Venetia on the bed. She left, locking the door behind her. Venetia sat on the bed with her knees drawn up to her chest, hugging her puppet. Tears ran down her cheeks. In her mind she could see her mummy. "Oh Mummy, please find me."

The door opened again. The woman had a small blue camper stove in one hand and a knife in the other. She put the stove down.

"I don't want anything, you witch. You want to fatten me up. You're going to eat me." Venetia sobbed.

The woman looked at her and shook her head. She looked down. The blue backpack was next to her foot. She kicked it under the bed and snatched the puppet from Venetia.

"No," Venetia screamed, "don't cook her."

"Ora io sono Mamma," the woman shouted. She lit a match, kneeled beside the stove, and turned the gas on.

Venetia watched in terror for her puppet. She heard the whoosh as the woman lit the gas. There was a bright blue flame. The woman held the knife to it. She seemed to be counting. Venetia heard her reach thirty. Then she stood, holding the puppet in one hand and the knife in the other. She put the knife against the puppet.

"Don't," Venetia tried to grab the puppet.

The woman stepped back. She laughed and continued to hold the knife to the puppet. She said in an imitation of Venetia's voice. "Sono Maria." She dropped the puppet onto the floor. She knelt again to the flame with the knife and counted. She got up and sat on the bed and grabbed Venetia's arm. She pushed up the sleeve of the jumper to expose the flesh.

Venetia screamed even before the knife touched her skin. The woman started counting, "Uno, duo, tre, quattro, cinque..."

Venetia screamed and screamed. The burning pain was intense, getting more terrible as the count increased.

The woman pointed the knife at Venetia's mouth and mouthed 'Maria'.

Venetia understood what she had to say. "Sono Maria," she whispered.

"Ed io sono Mamma." The woman leaned down and heated the knife over the flame again, mumbling to herself. Venetia whimpered pitifully. She applied the burning knife to another spot on Venetia's arm, and began to count.

Venetia screamed. She knew what the woman wanted her to say but she wouldn't say it. The pain grew and grew burning at her skin. Before the witch reached seven, Venetia whispered, "Mamma."

"Bene, bene." She smiled and took away the knife. She stroked Venetia's hair and got up. She picked everything off the floor and put it back on the tray and left the room.

Venetia got off the bed. The pain on her arm was beginning to subside. She picked up puppet Venetia. Her dress was burnt brown where the witch had put the knife. She hugged the puppet to her. "Poor Venetia," she said. "We'll switch the light out. The dark will be better." She switched the light out and lay on the bed. The room was completely black. No light came through the window. Tears streamed down her face, as she thought of her mummy and daddy. She would never see them again. They would never find her in this place. She got up off the bed, and began banging her fists on the door and shouting louder and fiercer than she'd ever shouted. Someone must hear and come.

She heard footsteps coming towards the door. It was the woman back. Before she could get away, the door banged into her and knocked her to the floor. The woman's big rough hand grabbed her hair, while the other forced a rag over her face, covering her nose and mouth. Venetia felt sick. The smell of the rag was overpowering. It was sweet and sickly. The room began to spin and she passed out.

47

Penny Calls Laura

Two miles away, Penny got her mobile and returned Laura's call. Before she could say anything, Laura spoke. "Penny, it's terrible, I've just heard. I've been in Milan. Has anyone seen anything?"

"No, there's been nothing. The police have been searching. We've all been searching. She's vanished without a trace. I want to see Signora Salvati again. I'm sure Venetia is alive somewhere and Signora Salvati might be able to find out where."

"I'll call her now. I'll switch to conference, hang on."

Penny recognised the Sicilian accent of Sara Severi. She listened, not understanding, but hearing Venetia mentioned several times. She heard Laura say arrivederla. "Will she see me?" Penny asked

"Yes," Laura said, "she will see us at six tomorrow. Can you meet me in Bandiera e Moro as before, say 5:30. I will come straight from the bank. Take care, Penny."

It was nearly ten when Gideon returned. "God sorted it out?" Penny said challenging him, as he came in.

He didn't want to argue. He couldn't. He was so tired. "No, but it's good to talk to someone."

"I'm going to see Signora Salvati tomorrow. You've got your mumbo jumbo, and I've got mine." She waited for a reaction.

"I'll come with you. I'd like to see her," was all he said.

Penny looked at him. "Are you sure?"

He nodded.

"OK, we're meeting Laura at 5:30. I looked through Venetia's room while you were out. Her backpack's gone. I can't find it."

"She didn't leave it at school?"

"No, I'm sure I saw it in the room on Monday after the hospital. She must have taken it with her."

"Is anything else missing?"

"The puppet's gone too."

"Did you call the police?"

"No, I thought you could do that when you'd finished praying with your friend!"

"OK," he didn't rise to the bait. He called Detective Rossi, who was in charge of the case and had left his mobile number with instructions for them to call day or night.

"Pronto, si, my wife's discovered Venetia's backpack is missing. It's blue with yellow flowers. Yes she must have taken it with her. She bought it on Murano. And also a puppet her friend Isabella Zancani gave her. Yes I have their number: 0415227207. OK si, arriverderci."

"He's going to have a description put out on the news. I'm going to bed," he said, "I need to rest, shut my eyes."

"Sleep would be nice," Penny said.

48

<u>The Light Comes</u>

At around four in the morning, Venetia woke. An ice-cold breath brushed her cheek and the voice she'd heard before whispered from inside her. The strings were moving her arms. She rose from the bed. The blue backpack rolled out from under the bed and lay at her feet, open. She took the knife from the secret compartment and dragged the chair over to the side of the door and stepped on to it. She waited poised, with two hands wrapped around the knife's handle and her arms high above her head, ready to strike. She waited for a long time, absolutely still. Her arms were held by invisible strings. They were so light she could almost be a ghost.

In the kitchen, Faustina prepared the porridge. When it was done she put it on a tray with the camper stove and a knife. Maria would see the knife and know what was good for her. It would be a long day. By the end of it, Maria would have four lines by heart.

Faustina walked to the door and put the tray down in order to unlock the door and turn on the light. She pushed the door open and stepped in. The room was full of a shimmering green-yellow haze. Something ice cold brushed against her neck. She reached for the light switch and, as she turned it on, she saw the girl looming above her. She saw the knife. It was surrounded by flashing blinding white light. It was coming down at her. Time slowed. She raised her arms to protect herself — it was too late. She felt the cold steel enter her neck. Strangely, there was no pain. She staggered back and tried to pull the knife out, but could not. Blood was spurting from her in a fountain of red. The girl was standing on the chair smiling benignly at her. Her nightdress was covered in blood.

Faustina staggered forward in an attempt to pull the girl off the chair and fell to the floor. She crawled towards the chair on her hands and knees and reached to grab a leg and pull it over. She got her hand around a leg of the chair. The blood was pouring out of her so fast that she had no strength left. She knew she was dying. She had failed her mother. She had failed the man. She had ruined everything. She pulled weakly at the leg, but it didn't move. She reached up for the girl's leg. "Maria," she whispered hoarsely, and her fingers reached for the girl's ankle. Before she could wrap them around, she fell back on the floor. A roaring sound came from the chapel, a sound from the depths of hell. Faustina died in terror thinking of what was to come.

Venetia stepped down from the chair. She was covered in blood. The room was awash with thick red blood. It meant nothing to her. She followed the noise down the corridor to where she saw candles burning. She entered room that had been converted into a chapel and walked to the altar. The noise became louder and more dreadful. The coffin below the altar began to shake as Venetia opened the ivory casket, took out the papers and untied the blue silk ribbon. The candles flickered, and a crimson shadow rose through the lid of the coffin like smoke. It moved in the air and its dreadful shape hung over Venetia, as if to strike. Three angelic voices rose through Venetia's mouth and filled the chapel with a heavenly sound. The roaring noise ceased, but the crimson shadow remained swirling around her.

"Sancta Maria, ora pro nobis, Sancta Dei Genitrix, ora pro nobis, Sancta Virgo virginum..." She sang as she took the first page, and held it over the flame of a candle at the altar. As it caught fire, she released it. It floated, twisting turning and burning in the air, and dropped blackened ash to the ground. One after another she burnt the pages until there were none left.

49

No2 San Pietro

Thursday morning, Detective Rossi called to say they'd bought an identical blue backpack.

He asked if Gideon and Penny would record an appeal for information. They agreed, and a

police launch collected and took them to the local TV studio in Mestre. Everyone was

kind. They could feel their pity as they were shown to their seats. They sat next to

Detective Rossi at a desk in front of a television camera. On the desk, Rossi had a blue

backpack with the yellow flower pattern. It was exactly the same as Venetia's. He showed

the bag to the camera. Penny spoke emotionally in English, begging anyone who knew

anything to come forward. Her words were translated for the audience. At the end, she

broke down and cried.

Gideon repeated a simple appeal for information in Italian. He managed to hold

himself together. The piece was to go out on the lunchtime and evening news.

"Va bene?" Rossi said. "You were very brave. The phones will soon be ringing.

One call may bring us something. Thank you, we'll take you back home now."

At the same time, Cristofo was sitting in his study. He had brought a lamp to the desk to

help him see. It was a grey day and not much light was coming though the porthole

windows above. He had worked his way through most of the papers in the iron box. They

had belonged to Abbess Anzola Boldani and were an account of the last days of the

convent. He'd almost given up hope of finding anything, when he came upon a page with the name Zancani. It was uncanny how it stood out. How his eye had gone straight to it. He read slowly, occasionally referring to his Latin dictionary.

Aureo Zancani had died in a Fransiscan monastery in Le Marche in 1516 and had left ten thousand ducats to the convent for prayers. He had transcribed them himself while he had been in the monastery. They had been delivered to the convent in an ivory casket, along with the money, and his body in a wooden chest. He peered through his magnifying glass, hardly believing what he was reading, as he worked out the Latin nouns, and their endings and placements, to get a rough approximation of the sentence meanings.

I, Anzola Boldani, last Abbess of the convent Santa Maria delle Vergini, will ensure the prayers we have been paid to say, will continue. With the help of our banker Jacomo Sanuto, I have purchased rooms at No2 Calle Frari in San Pietro. Sister Faustina Tarabotti has been instructed. A trust has been set up to pay a monthly sum to the sister and those that come after her.

Cristofo scratched his head. How long could this have gone on for? Could they have kept it up for five hundred years? It seemed unlikely, and the coffin with his ancestor's body – might it be there in a cellar? It could be, he thought. He looked at the page he'd just read, folded it and put it in his pocket. He would go immediately to San Pietro. He looked for Elizabeta and Isabella, but they had gone out. He put on his tweed jacket, scarf, gloves, and fur hat and went down to the boathouse. He was soon on his way. It was a mild but damp day. There was a slight drizzle in the air. He took his fur hat off and stowed it under his seat as he headed out onto the lagoon, and increased the speed of the boat. It bounced over the waves. He found the drizzle and spray on his face refreshing. He licked the salty water from his lips. He saw the Giardini and turned the boat in under a bridge and slowed. He went under another bridge and into the Canale di San Pietro and, as before, tied up alongside the stone steps. He walked through the deserted square and turned to the right of the campanile and followed the street behind it. There on the left was the Calle Frari.

He looked down the street and saw a large No 2 painted in white over a doorway. It was a two storey house split into flats. He peered through a window into a long abandoned room. There was nobody living on the ground floor. He pushed at the front door. It was unlocked and he entered a hallway. He saw stone steps and climbed them to see if anyone lived upstairs. They were dirty and smelt of old cooking. On the next floor, there were three doors. One still had a name below its bell. It read **Tarabotti.**

"Dio," he mumbled and rang the bell. There was no sound from inside. He began to think no one was in, when the door opened. There in front of him was Venetia. Her nightdress was covered in blood. She was very pale and her eyes were blank and lifeless. He dreaded what he might find. He stepped inside and shut the door.

She looked at him with dead eyes and spoke, but it was not her voice that he heard. It was old Venetian dialect. It took him a second to work out what she said. "You know who I am."

He shook his head.

"I am Elena."

He had a sense of déjà vu, a sense he was continuing some story he'd started long ago in a dream. It was very familiar.

50

The Spirits

Penny and Gideon met Laura at 5:30 in the Campo Bandiera e Moro. Laura was surprised to see Gideon.

"Ciao Penny," she said, kissing Penny, and then Gideon. "Gideon ciao, I'm glad you're coming."

"I wanted to come," he said.

He sounded cold and distant. She led them through the narrow alleys to the dingy calle, where Signora Salvati lived. The stuffed monkey, doll and Pope still hung above the door. She walked quickly to the door and knocked. Gideon didn't notice the figures. His mind was elsewhere.

Sara Severi let them in and showed them straight through to the room with the round wooden table. Gideon smelt the incense and wondered whether they were burning some mild intoxicant to relax their clients and make them more susceptible. Signora Salvati rose to greet them. Gideon was struck by her looks. She looked like a wizened old child He towered over her. He put his hand out to shake hers and pulled it back awkwardly by his side when she did not respond. He felt her green eyes looking up into his. She knows I don't believe in her, he thought. She beckoned Penny and Gideon to sit either side of her. Laura sat next to Penny, and Sara Severi next to Gideon. They joined hands around the table, and Signora Salvati began to chant. Her eyes closed, her head dropped forward, and there was silence.

Gideon waited for something to happen. He wanted to keep his wits about him so he'd be able to see any trickery. He could hear the clock ticking from another room. Time passed slowly and no one spoke. He looked at Penny. She had her eyes closed. He felt the Signora's grip on his hand tighten. He turned to look at her. Her head was upright, but her eyes too were shut. They opened. The startling green eyes pierced into his. They were boring into his brain. She's trying to hypnotize me, he thought, and fought against it. She shook her head.

"Niente," She said. "Non posso." She stood up and left the room.

Sara Severi spoke to Laura. Penny could understand she was apologising. She recognised the words 'mi dispiace,' said over and over.

Laura turned to them. "I'm sorry, Signora Salvati has not been successful. They will not tell her where Venetia is. It is a very painful process for her. She cannot try again today. They want us to go now."

They left the house and walked back to the square. Laura asked if they would like to join her and Gianfranco for dinner. Gideon said they should return home. He didn't feel up to company. They parted, Laura going towards the Rialto to meet Gianfranco, and Penny and Gideon back to Arsenale. They didn't speak. Gideon suspected Signora Salvati of being a fraud. He thought she'd realised he'd see through her performance, tried to hypnotize him and failed.

51

__The Body__

The white nightdress was soaked in blood. Cristofo knew he was talking not to Venetia, but to his ancestor's victim. She had possession of the girl. As her hand moved towards him, he saw a flash of electric white light. He looked for a knife but there was none. Instead she clasped his gloved hand and led him along the corridor. He saw a tray on the floor in front of a door. She led him into the room. An old woman lay on the floor with a knife sticking into her neck. The white walls of the room were spattered with blood.

"What have you done?" he said.

He listened to the unearthly voice coming out of the little girl's mouth. Again they were old Venetian words. He struggled to make sense of them. "This is the end. We have finished – we are free." She let go of his hand and stood motionless, starring fixedly at some unseen object.

"Venetia?" he said, looking at her eyes, trying to get a response.

She said nothing. Her eyes were lifeless. There was nothing behind them. She was in some sort of trance. He looked around the room and saw the backpack on the floor near the bed. Lying next to it was the puppet he'd given her. He stepped around the body and picked it up. Its dress had a burnt brown mark on it. He picked the bag up and put the puppet inside, and began to think.

He pulled the blanket off the bed and laid it down over the blood on the floor next to the body. He knelt on the blanket, put his hand to the woman's head and pulled the knife from her neck. He put it in the bag. He knew he must wipe every surface in the flat. No one must know what had happened here. He found a cloth, and went meticulously from room to room wiping everything. She followed him, her blank eyes watching everything he did.

At the end of the corridor, he came to a candlelit room. There was an altar with a heavy wooden cross on it, and in front of that an opened ivory casket. He could smell burnt paper. Below the altar, he saw a coffin-like chest and knew it was Aureo Zancani. On the floor around the chest were the blackened remains of paper. He walked slowly forward and wiped the casket. He knelt and looked at the chest. There was a carving of the lion of St Mark on its lid and a key in its lock. He turned it and heard a clanking mechanical movement inside, like the shifting of the iron door in his boathouse. He waited for the sound to stop, and opened the lid a fraction to peer in. He saw the skeleton of his ancestor. The black holes in the skull, where the eyes had been, seemed to be looking at him. He could not draw his eyes from them. He felt his ancestor's power, such malevolence. It belonged somewhere beyond humanity, beyond the grave. He couldn't take his hands from the lid of the chest. They were stuck. He couldn't pull away. He was locked in the grip of something frightful. It was trying to communicate with him.

Something made him open the lid wider and he saw a black leather book lying on his ancestor's chest. Two bony hands lay on top of it. He glimpsed an Arabic word written in gold. The body beneath was dressed in a red robe. It seemed to stir within the coffin and move, as if to rise. He smelt a musty smell of sandalwood. One bony hand left the book, and scraped against the side of the coffin. He heard a dry dusty croak come from inside, ancient and horrible.

Flesh of our flesh.

Red smoke seemed to curl out of the mouth of the skull. It formed into to two faint thin lines and entered Cristofo through his nostrils. He stepped back in terror and dropped the lid with a bang that echoed through the flat. Heart thumping, he left the room. He had to get out of this house. He went back to the kitchen where he'd left the blue bag. He would sink it into the lagoon. He looked for a weight and saw an iron on a shelf. It would do. He dropped it into the bag. His heart was still beating at his chest, pounding away almost in his mouth. He dreaded turning and seeing the creature behind him. He kept telling himself: it is dead, it cannot harm you. He wanted to leave but there was more he had to do. He had to get rid of the blood on Venetia.

She was still gazing blankly at him. He took her hand and walked her to the bathroom. He took off her nightdress and lifted her into the bath. He saw there was a sponge. He turned on the shower and washed her down. He saw the burn marks on her forearm. "What happened?" he said.

She stood without saying anything.

Cristofo looked at the water running down her naked body. A terrible lust came over him. He wanted press his mouth against her face, and take her hand to his stiff penis. He reached down to unzip his trousers.

"Stick it in her. Fill her with your power. You are a Zancani. Nothing is forbidden."

His ancestor was in him. He shut his eyes and lifted Venetia out of the bath. He must not look at her. He reached for a towel and wrapped her in it. He searched the flat for something for her to wear. He kept repeating to himself, "I am Cristofo, I am Cristofo."

In a drawer in the room where the body lay, he found a girl's dress. It was old-fashioned. Venetia said nothing. He put the dress on her and stuffed the nightdress into the blue bag. He put the backpack, over his shoulder and looked cautiously out of the front door. It was dark now. He picked Venetia up and carried her out of the flat. He shut the door quietly and went down the steps. He breathed a sigh of relief, as he left the building. He got back to his boat. Panting with the effort, he helped Venetia on board, untied, and yanked on the starter to get the motor going. He did not turn back the way he'd come, but went straight down the empty canal past boatyards and cranes, and out into the lagoon. Straight on would have taken him to Lazzarote Nuovo. He turned right towards Certosa. He cut the engine where he knew the water was deep and dropped the blue bag overboard. It splashed into the water and sank to the bottom.

It was very dark. He could not make Venetia out. She was just a shadow at the front of his boat. He sat thinking. His heartbeat, thank God, had returned to normal. He could not take Venetia home – no one must know. He would leave her somewhere she would be found. Would she remember him – he hoped not. It would take time and by then he would have done what he had to do. He would return to the house in San Pietro and burn it to the ground.

He restarted the engine and steered back where they had come. In the dark, they passed into the Canale San Pietro, turned right into Rio delle Vergini, under the towering Arsenale walls, left under a stone bridge and finally came into Rio della Tana. This was where he would leave her, half way between her school and her home. Someone would find her – she might even instinctively find her way back.

He cut the engine, and drifted into the side of the canal. He stepped to the front of the boat, rocking it as he did, and picked Venetia up. The warmth of her body again stirred the beginnings of desire. Quickly, before it could take hold, he placed her onto the fondamenta.

"Go home, Venetia," he whispered.

She said nothing.

He could not look at her anymore, had to get away. He started the engine and turned back down the canal.

52

<u>The Lion</u>

Gideon was watching *Midsummer Murders*. Penny had already gone to bed. The familiar English programme had been dubbed into Italian. When it finished, he turned the television off, and walked slowly over to the window. He wanted to look at the stone lion outside and remember his daughter. He leaned out, and there she was with her arms around the lion. He couldn't believe his eyes. It wasn't possible. Was he also going mad? He leaned out further. It was Venetia. There was no doubt about it.

"My God, it's her." His heart jumped. "Venetia!" he shouted, and ran out down the stairs three at a time and across to the lion. She heard him coming and let go. He scooped her up in his arms and kissed her. "Where have you been? We've been so worried." He looked into her face. She looked blankly back at him. He carried her back towards the flat and saw Penny at the bedroom window.

She met them on the stairs and took Venetia from him. He could see tears of joy in Penny's eyes. "Oh, darling," she said, carrying Venetia into the flat. She sat down on a chair in the kitchen with Venetia on her lap, kissing and hugging her.

"She's in shock," Gideon said. "I don't think she knows where she is."

Penny stroked Venetia's hair. "It's Mummy, darling – you're safe – you're home."

Venetia put her arms around Penny, but still said nothing. As she did, Gideon saw the burns on her arm.

"Look," he pointed at them. "What happened?"

Venetia started crying. Penny hugged her tighter. "It's alright, it's alright."

"I must call the police, tell them she's back," he said. He found his mobile. "Someone's had her in their house. That dress – that's not hers. She was in her nightdress when she left."

Penny looked, seeing it for the first time. "It's horrid. Let's take it off and put something of yours on, while Daddy telephones."

Gideon phoned Detective Rossi.

Twenty minutes later three police launches, blue lights flashing, tied up beside the canal. Two of the boats were Carabanieri, the other Polizia Locale. Detective Rossi and a policewoman make their way across the square to the flat, leaving ten blue uniformed officers waiting by the launches. Gideon had seen them arrive and opened the door.

He told them how he'd seen her by the lion. "I looked out and she was just standing there, holding the lion's neck."

"Did you see anyone?" Rossi asked.

"No – not a soul – I ran straight down."

"Did Venetia tell you anything?"

"No. She hasn't spoken a word. I think she's in shock – there are marks on her arms. They look like burns."

"The police doctor is on his way. In the meantime, can Maria talk to Venetia?" He gestured towards the policewoman, who put her hand out to shake Gideon's.

"Yes, of course," he said shaking her hand. "My wife's just changing her clothes. She was in someone else's dress."

"We better have that," Rossi said.

Penny returned carrying Venetia. She had put her into a nightdress, dressing gown, and slippers.

Detective Rossi introduced the policewoman Maria to Penny and Venetia. "She will ask you some questions, while I talk to Papa."

"Hello Venetia. Shall we sit on sofa?" Maria Bonetti's English was good, though accented. She asked to look at Venetia's arms. She took them both, turned them and saw the burns. Venetia gazed at the wall and said nothing.

Rossi wanted Gideon to show him exactly where he'd first seen Venetia. They left the flat and walked across to the lion. Rossi called the officers over from around the boat, and told them to start searching the area. Another launch arrived with the police doctor. Rossi waved and they took him up to the flat.

Maria Bonetti greeted him. "She is in shock. She is not speaking."

The Doctor and policewoman took Venetia into her bedroom for an examination. Penny went with them. Gideon waited outside with Detective Rossi.

Apart from the burns on her forearm the doctor could find nothing wrong with Venetia. He told the parents, knowing it would be on their minds: "She has not been sexually assaulted."

"Thank God," Gideon said.

"She will need to see a psychiatrist – a specialist. She has had some sort of mental breakdown," he said. "My diagnosis is post-traumatic stress disorder, but I'm not an expert in these matters. There is nothing physically wrong with her. Time is a great healer."

"She hasn't been well. She had the flu, has been sleepwalking," Penny said, "and our doctor wanted an MRI scan. They found something on her brain – a shadow, possible tumour. Could it have affected her speech?"

He asked who their doctor was. He rang Dr Gabrieli straight away to find out more. It was decided Venetia should go to the hospital the following day for a complete examination.

The police left the Mantell's flat in the early hours of the morning, taking the dress Venetia had been wearing.

After they'd gone, Penny and Gideon fussed over Venetia, getting her hot chocolate and biscuits. Gideon locked the door through to the hall and decided to keep the key safe under his pillow.

"Let's all sleep together," Penny said. "Mummy, Daddy and baby bear all cuddled up together. It'll be lovely and snug." She smiled at Venetia and picked her up in her arms.

The three of them got into the double bed together. Venetia lay between her parents and went straight to sleep. Penny and Gideon lay awake in the darkness thinking.

Penny thought the spirits were responsible for Venetia. They'd used her daughter and left her mind torn. Had they inflicted the burns – the supernatural light she'd seen surrounding her daughter. Did it burn? Whatever it was they were gone now – she felt sure of that. She would nurse her daughter back to health.

Gideon wondered who had held his daughter against her will. Had they done something to her – something that had made her brain shut down, or was it the tumour?

53

Another Scan

For the first time in days, Gideon woke without the feeling of empty hopelessness. His daughter was back. He shaved and dressed, and woke Penny and Venetia.

"Come on, you two – we've got to go to the hospital – I'll get breakfast."

They both opened their eyes.

"How are you feeling, sweetie?" He kissed Venetia on her head, and inhaled her smell. The smell he'd loved since she was born.

She looked at him curiously, as if she wasn't sure who he was.

Penny got out of bed. "I'll get dressed – then we'll get you up."

Gideon got the kettle on. While he waited, he phoned Carlo and Gianfranco to tell them the news.

Penny and Venetia arrived wearing matching red Guernseys, and jeans. "I had to dress you, didn't I?" Penny said, sitting Venetia down at a chair. She gave Gideon a concerned look. "I think we're going to have to do everything for her. She doesn't seem to understand. I gave her the clothes, but she just stood there holding them."

After breakfast, Penny phoned Elizabeta and told her Venetia was home.

"Such good news," she said. "How is she – what happened?"

"We don't know. She's had a breakdown. She's not talking; not doing anything. I'm not sure she knows who we are – who she is. We're about to take her to hospital. I don't know if it's the tumour." Penny could hear Elizabeta whispering to Isabella.

"Could Isabella and I visit? Isabella is longing to see her."

"Yes, I'll ring you later, when we get back."

They caught the vaporetto to Ospedale where they were met by Dr Gabrieli and taken up to the MRI unit. He told them the police doctor had given him more information.

"I don't think the tumour would cause the loss of speech. It sounds like a nervous breakdown – very rare in children. A disintegration of personality, usually temporary, it's as if the circuits have been overloaded, snapped under extreme pressure. We won't know what happened to cause this until she recovers. Until then, she won't be able to function."

"How long will it last?" Penny asked.

"Difficult to say – it could be weeks."

Dr Raphael greeted them in the MRI unit, and said he was pleased to get the chance to scan Venetia again. Penny helped Venetia get undressed, and onto the table in front of the machine. Once again she disappeared into the tunnel, and the clanks of the machine started up. Penny took Gideon's hand, as they waited for it to be over. Ten minutes, and it was done and Venetia was out.

Dr Gabrieli took her for a thorough medical examination. He looked closely at the burns. There were two distinct marks. It was impossible to tell what had caused them. "Do you remember how these happened? Did someone press something hot against your skin?"

Venetia gazed blankly at him.

"Well maybe you'll remember later. So that does it young lady," he said.

Outside the hospital, breathing in the crisp fresh November air, Gideon thought it would be good to walk back. "What about walking home with lunch on the way? What do you say to pizza and ice cream?"

"Yes, won't that be nice, Ven darling?" Penny said.

They walked towards Campo SS Giovani e Paolo and the statue of Colleoni on his horse. On the other side of the square opposite the church, they found a pizza restaurant. After lunch, they walked hand in hand, with Venetia between them, back to Arsenale. When they arrived in the Campo, Venetia let go of her parents' hands and ran over to her favourite old stone lion and hugged it.

Penny and Gideon looked at each other. It was the first thing Venetia had done of her own accord.

"It's a good sign," Gideon said. "At least she remembers him. She will get better. I'm sure of it."

She ran back to her parents, who stood watching her with absolute devotion. They returned to the flat.

Gideon was so full of hope, he was afraid to break the spell, but he had to know. "Are you going to rebook your flight? I wondered if you were still here on Monday, we could go with Laura and Gianfranco over to Madonna della Salute. We could bring them back here for a celebration dinner. I was thinking of doing roast beef and Yorkshire pudding. Something really English – What do you think?"

"I think it's a lovely idea, Gid."

"I'll ring him. So you're not going back England?"

She smiled at him. "Not yet, let's wait a week and see how Venetia is. If she's not any better, I will take her back. It may help to be in England — away from whatever happened here. We'll see."

Later in the day, Dr Gabrielli rang. He confirmed there were no signs of sexual interference, and apart from the burns, Venetia was in perfect health. He said they were still checking the results of the scan.

54

The Lido of St Nicholas

Cristofo paced his study. The words of the creature in the coffin prayed on his mind. He kept hearing them: *flesh of our flesh*. It was inside him, whispering unspeakable desire. He'd looked at Isabella with lust, woken in the night wanting to creep into her room. He was cursed with the perverted desire of that monster. He knew he could no longer control it. He dare not stay – he dare not risk himself with Isabella. His path was clear to him.

He opened the drawer of his desk and took out a box of matches he'd kept as a souvenir from a trip to London on the Orient Express. He put them in his trouser pocket, and left his study. He hoped he wouldn't see Elizabeta or Isabella. It was early afternoon. Elizabeta would probably be resting and Isabella playing in her room. He feared seeing them would break his resolve. On his way down, he picked up his overcoat and fur hat. No one saw him.

He walked through the hall of his ancestors without looking at them and opened the door that led to the passageway down to the boathouse. The familiar smell of damp and age invaded his nostrils. He heaved open the great iron door and entered. He pushed it shut with both hands. Its ancient hinges groaned, as if in complaint. He stepped down the mossy stones into his boat. He started the engine and steered out into the canal. It was a bright cold day. He rammed on his fur hat, and turned left. He wanted to take the canals that led to the Rio del Palazzo and go out into the lagoon under the Bridge of Sighs. It seemed fitting, the bridge where so many condemned men had had their last glimpse of Venice.

He motored out into the middle of the lagoon and turned left towards Via Garabaldi. He tied the boat up and crossed the street to a mobile phone shop. He bought the cheapest they had – he only planned to make one call. He returned to his boat and steered left, keeping near the shore. He past the Giardini, and turned under a bridge and on to the Campo San Pietro. He tied his boat to the stone ring by the steps, and got out the can of petrol he kept underneath the seat. He walked through the square with the can in his hand. He noticed an old couple going into the cathedral. He hurried on to No 2 Calle Frari.

The body of the woman still lay in the bedroom. He put the can of petrol down, and paused for a moment to look at her. He shook his head, and picked her up by the shoulders and dragged her out along the corridor, steeling himself to enter the room with the coffin. He wanted both bodies to be consumed by fire. He clenched his teeth and dragged her towards the altar. It was very quiet, only the sound of her shoes dragging against the floor. He dropped her down by the coffin and got the petrol. He unscrewed the cap and shook the contents of the can over the coffin. Then lit a match, knelt and touched it to the wood. He jumped back as it caught alight. The flames licked and crackled around the altar.

He watched as they became more intense. The coffin was well ablaze, and now the wooden cross above caught fire. Great yellow flames jumped around it. It rocked momentarily on its base, and then toppled to the floor, cartwheeling towards Cristofo. He jumped back, heart beating fast. It lay burning at his feet. He had to get out before the whole room went up.

He turned and ran down the corridor. It was done. Everything would burn. He left the building and returned to the boat. He motored back down the canal, and cut the engine, allowing himself to drift into the side. He got out the mobile and called the fire service. They would be in time to stop the fire spreading. He switched the mobile off and dropped it over the side of the boat. He restarted the engine and headed towards the lido of St Nicholas, the mouth of the lagoon. It was here that his ancestors had sailed out into the Adriatic. Within the lagoon lay safety, beyond lay danger, but also great fortune. For Venetians, the sea was life and death. He remembered the paper he had in his pocket, the page from the convent with the address. He tore it into pieces and threw it into the wind.

The creature whispered within him, "Turn back, you can have everything, all your desires. You cannot leave this world now. There is so much for you."

He fixed his eyes on the horizon. The sun was going down into the sea. It would soon be dark. "I am Cristofo," he said, "I am not you."

The wind got stronger as he entered into the Adriatic. In the distance, he could see the lights of the Lido. The boat rocked and bounced over the waves as he headed further and further out into the dark sea.

55

Festa della Salute

On Saturday morning, Dr Gabrieli phoned to say the shadow had gone. There was no trace on the new scan. It was a mystery. Dr Raphael suspected a fault in the last reading. He was confident this new scan was a true result.

"She doesn't have a tumour?" Penny said.

"There's nothing showing up – she's clear. When are you going back to England? I will write to your GP, no harm in a second opinion."

"I'm not sure now. We may stay on for a while. I'll let you know."

"And what about you – no recurrence of the panic attacks?"

"No – I'm fine – I'm still taking the pills."

"Good. Why don't you make an appointment and come in next week. You probably don't need them anymore."

"Thanks – I will." Penny said goodbye and ended the call. Could the shadow have been a trace of Elena? She thought about it. It was possible. Elena was gone and the shadow was gone. She would never know. Later she spoke to Gideon.

"Dr Gabrieli rang – the shadow's gone. He's given Venetia the all clear. I think it was Elena. She got inside Venetia."

"Let's not start that again, Penny," he said. "I thought you were getting better."

She looked at him, and decided to say no more. "Have you phoned Gianfranco?"

"I'll do it now."

He phoned and said they would meet outside the Gritti Palace at 5pm on Monday. "How about coming back to us for a celebration of Venetia's return? I'll cook you a good English dinner, roast beef."

Gianfranco hesitated. Gideon could hear Laura in the background. "OK," he said. "Laura wants to speak to Penny."

Gideon passed the phone to Penny.

"How is Venetia?" Laura said. "Has she said anything?"

"No – Dr Gabrieli says she's fine, the scan was clear. She doesn't have a tumour, but she's had a breakdown of sorts. Not surprising with what she's been through. She's going to have to see a psychiatrist."

"Do you still believe she was possessed?"

"Yes I do. Look, can't talk now. See you on Monday."

"I understand, looking forward to seeing you at the Festa della Salute. There'll be lots of sweet stalls, and people roasting chestnuts. Venetia will love it. Oh, and what's this about a good English dinner? Is there such a thing?"

Penny could sense her friend smiling. "Wait until you taste roast beef and Yorkshire pudding. You'll eat your words."

"I hope I'll eat more than that! Ciao."

Gideon rang Carlo, and invited him. "It's a celebration," he said. "Venetia's return. We're going to Salute with Laura and Gianfranco first for the Festa. Why don't you join us? We're meeting outside the Gritti Palace."

Carlo said he'd be there.

During the weekend, the pontoon bridge over the Grand Canal to Santa Maria della Salute was erected. It rained all Monday morning, but it didn't dampen their spirits. Gideon collected his meat, and pre-prepared as much as he could before they set off with umbrellas, waterproofs, and wellingtons for the Gritti in Santa Maria del Giglio. The wooden walkways had been put up all over the city and there were huge puddles in the streets and squares. San Marco had become a shallow lake, which they waded through to get across to the eastern corner. Venetia splashed about in the square, jumping up and down in her wellingtons. Penny and Gideon loved watching her enjoying herself again.

They went out of the piazza into Calle de l'Ascensione and made their way to the Gritti, sometimes using the raised walkways and sometimes wading through the water. The rain eased to a light drizzle. They entered the street, and in the damp air they could smell chestnuts being roasted. They saw Gianfranco, Laura, and Carlo standing outside the hotel, and there at the end of the street was the new bridge. They greeted each other with kisses, and Gianfranco led them across the bridge.

They crossed in a great crowd, chattering with excitement. Everyone looked wet but happy. On the other side, the streets to the Salute were full of tents and stalls selling brightly coloured sweets and long white candles to take into the church. Gianfranco bought them each a candle.

"We will make an offering, say our thanks for Venetia's return," he said, "and ask the Madonna for good health."

They climbed the steps into the packed church. Everywhere wet people mingled, and watched, and prayed. Steam seemed to rise off them. Carlo took them to a table to light their candles. Penny lit hers and gave it to an attendant in charge of placing the candles. Gideon saw her and did the same, and watched, as the others lit their candles, and handed them in.

In one of the chapels, a mass was being said for the Fire Service. About thirty firemen, dressed in yellow fire resistant uniforms, stood before the altar. It reminded Gideon of the fire he'd seen on the local news. A house had gone up in San Pietro and been almost entirely destroyed. They'd only just managed to stop it spreading. He wondered if these firemen had been there.

"Everyone comes to be blessed, the police, the gondoliers, the fishermen, and the firemen. There's a mass every hour, on the hour, today. I should bring the archaeology department," Carlo said, and winked at Penny and Gideon.

Gianfranco insisted they all took it in turns to stand under the lead chandelier. He said they must touch the words 'Unde origo inde salus' cut into the bronze disc with their right foot. He took Venetia by the hand and showed her what to do. He sat her down and pulled off her right wellington boot. She stood up and pointed her foot so her toe touched the word 'salus'.

Seeing her, Laura and Penny took off their boots and touched the word with their toes too. Venetia watched them, with her wellington boot in her hand.

"Mummy," Venetia said, "shall I'll put my boot back on?"

"What did you say, darling?" Penny turned, not believing her ears. She knelt beside Venetia.

"Put my boot on?" Venetia said again, as if it nothing had happened. She gave her mummy a curious look. "Why are you looking at me like that?"

Penny picked her up in her arms. "She's talking."

Gianfranco crossed himself.

They left the church. On the steps, Penny put Venetia down. She was full of sudden hope her daughter had recovered.

"Do you know who we all are?"

"Daddy, Laura, Gianfranco and Carlo," she said, pointing at them one by one, and laughing. "You are funny, Mummy." Then she frowned. "How did we get here? I can't remember."

56

The Mantell Secret

On a grey day, two weeks later, the Mantells walked to the little Renaissance church of Santa Maria dei Miracoli for Cristofo's funeral. It had been his favourite church. He'd described it as a little jewel box hidden in a maze. The church had been built to enshrine a painting of the Virgin and child, believed to have miraculous powers. Cristofo and Elizabeta had been married there.

His death had been a shock to everyone. He'd drowned somewhere beyond the Lido and his body had been washed up on the beach. Elizabeta couldn't understand what he could have been doing. He would never take his small boat outside the lagoon. The day before his disappearance, he'd been searching eastern Venice for Venetia. Lots of people remembered seeing him. While he'd been out, the Prior of the monastery on San Francesco del Deserto had delivered a small iron box. Cristofo had broken it open that evening and had been going through the papers. They belonged to the last abbess of the convent of Santa Maria delle Vergini. Elizabeta wondered whether he'd discovered something in them and rushed off without enough petrol in the boat. Without power, he would have been at the mercy of the tides. The police had taken the papers away.

The Mantells entered the marble church. It was very quiet. Elizabeta, Isabella, Aldo, and Maria were sitting in the front pew. Penny took Venetia's hand and they walked slowly up the aisle. Above the altar was the painting Cristofo had told them about. A bier, where the coffin would be placed, stood in front of the steps leading up to the altar. They sat down in the pew behind the Zancanis.

Elizabeta turned and smiled sadly at them. Her eyes were red with crying. "Thank you for coming," she said.

Isabella turned and kneeled on the pew to speak to Venetia. She had tears in her eyes. "Come and sit next to me."

Venetia looked at Penny. "Yes, go on darling," she said.

Venetia got up and sat between Isabella and Aldo. She took Isabella's hand, and looked into her tear stained eyes. "Your nonno was a very nice man," she said. "He was looking for me everywhere." They both began to cry and wrapped their arms around each other.

A priest appeared at the altar and a recording of Mozart's requiem began to play through the church's sound system. Six pall bearers approached bearing Cristofo's coffin on their shoulders, and put it down on the bier. The service began. The priest chanted and sprinkled Holy water on the body.

After the service, the pall bearers put the coffin on their shoulders and followed the priest out of the church. Elizabeta, Isabella, Venetia, Aldo and Maria walked immediately behind. Penny and Gideon took up the rear. The coffin was loaded onto a black motor launch. Another funeral launch took the mourners and they followed the coffin out to San Michele.

The priest led them through the cypress pathways of the cemetery island to the Zancani family tomb, where Cristofo was laid to rest. Elizabeta broke down. Penny comforted her as best she could. She didn't know what to say.

"I can't believe I'll never see him again," Elizabeta said, wiping her eyes with a handkerchief. "He was my best friend always."

344

Penny put her arm around her and helped her back to the launch. The others followed. In the launch back, everyone was quiet. Everyone alone with their thoughts of Cristofo and their eyes wet with tears. They returned to Palazzo Castello where they drank and ate and talked of their memories of Cristofo.

In December, Penny and Laura, on the pretext of a girls' night out, visited the medium. Venetia stayed with her father.

Signora Salvati, Sara Severi, Laura, and Penny sat in a circle. As before, the Signora went into a trance. The electric lights flickered and she spoke in the voice of a child. She spoke to Penny, but Penny did not understand. The Italian was complex. Then she stopped and opened her green eyes and smiled, "Tutto bene."

"What did she say?"

"A lot," Laura said. "All good! First, Venetia is safe. The danger is gone. The spirits have passed to the light. Elena says she did not mean to cause trouble. Venetia was the only one who could save them. Everything will be right now. Gideon loves you. There was more, but that's the gist. I think maybe you have a guardian angel now."

Penny sighed. She wished it were true, but she didn't think Gideon would ever believe Venetia had been possessed. It would always come between them. "Tell her thank you, I am content."

At the same time, in the flat at Campo Arsenale, Gideon and Venetia were playing Scrabble. The lights flickered.

Gideon said, "I hope we're not going to have a power cut. I want to get my revenge." He joined the letters E N G E R onto M E S S, getting a triple word.

"Oh Daddy, I wanted to go there." Venetia stroked her chin, and saw she could use the A in S T A N D. She joined E L E N on to it.

Gideon starred at the word ELENA with dread. "What made you put that down? It's a name. You can't have that."

"Elena was inside me, Daddy. I remember. She's gone now. She didn't hurt me." She got up and sat on Gideon's lap and put her arms around his neck and kissed him. "Everything is good now."

He kissed the top of her head. "I believe she was," he said. "I think this is a secret you, me and Mummy must keep, a precious secret that no one else must ever know."

He heard the door open. "Darling," he kissed Penny.

She looked at the scrabble board and saw the word ELENA.

"Venetia remembers," he said. "Elena was inside her. But we are going to keep it a secret. Aren't we Ven?"

"Yes, just you me and Daddy." She frowned. "And Elena, but she's not coming back. It's a Mantell secret."

After Venetia had gone to bed, Penny said, "Why did you say we must keep it a secret? Is it because you don't believe her? Don't want people thinking she's mad like her mum?"

"The opposite, I do believe. But imagine what would happen if the story got out, we'd be hounded for the rest of our lives." He took her in his arms. "I'm so sorry I didn't believe you. My God, what you saw."

She kissed him. "It's over now."

Epilogue

Detective Rossi had had a busy four weeks. The charred and blackened bones of two bodies had been found in the only occupied apartment at the house at No2 Calle Frari. Forensics identified them as the bodies of a man and a woman. It had been thought only one woman lived there, a Faustina Tarabotti. The apartment had been in the same family for over two hundred years.

The next day, he'd been contacted and told that Cristofo Zancani and his boat had gone missing. His policeman's instinct connected Zancani with the English girl. Had he abducted her, and now fearing being caught, vanished. He wondered when the girl's memory would come back.

On Tuesday, the body of Cristofo Zancani was washed up on the beach near the Hotel des Bains on the Lido. There were four theories as to why he had taken his boat out of the safety of the lagoon, into the open sea. The first and most plausible, that he'd been unable to restart the outboard motor and the boat had been pulled out into the Adriatic by the tides. The second that because of his age, he'd become disoriented and got lost. The third, that he'd committed suicide. And the fourth, and least plausible, he'd been murdered and dumped over the side of a boat. The post mortem had shown no signs of a struggle, or anything other than drowning. Signora Zancani had given them the papers he'd been working on when he vanished. They were a description of the closing of the convent of Santa Maria delle Vergini. She thought they might explain where he'd gone, but there didn't seem to be anything to take him out towards the Lido. The case remained open.

On Wednesday, the dress, Venetia had been found in was shown on television in the hope someone might recognise it, but no one had come forward. The key to everything was Venetia Mantell. Her memory had come back, but the crucial three days she'd been missing were blank. The psychiatrist could not get her to remember them. He'd asked her about the marks on her arms. She did not know how they happened. Someone had inflicted considerable pain on her. She had blotted the memory out. The psychiatrist wanted to use a hypnotist, but the mother had forbidden it.

Four weeks later, and Rossi was still nowhere with the case. The mother still refused to allow a hypnotist. She begged them to leave her daughter alone. She said Venetia had recovered, there was nothing wrong with her, and she didn't want anything to upset that. She wanted the past left behind. Her father, who originally had seemed in favour, had changed his mind and said going over the past would just open up a can of worms.

Without the girl, there was unlikely to be much progress. A week later, a body was found in a house opposite the Mantells. It belonged to Anna Mancini. Her neighbours had noticed an unpleasant smell emanating from the house, and realising they hadn't seen the woman for over a month, had reported it to the police. If it hadn't been for marks around her hands and legs, it would have been assumed the woman had died of heart attack. The pathologist was sure she had been tied up before she died.

The last person to have been with her was an old man who'd met her in the bar in Campo Arsenale. He was a plumber and had offered to help her with her washing machine. She'd told the barman the man's name was Federico and he lived over on the Lido. Rossi wondered if this man and Cristofo Zancani had known each other. Perverts were drawn to each other. Like attracts like, he thought. The kitchen of the flat overlooked Venetia's

349

bedroom and the table had had its legs sawn off. There were marks both on the table and window that showed it had been used as a platform to access the house opposite. Could they have abducted Venetia together? Could this man have killed both Mancini and Zancani?

The barman described the man as short and squat. He had a shuffling walk, and wore a black beret and blue quilted jacket. He had a strange gruff voice. He only ever drank brandy. He thought the man was probably about seventy. The description was put out on television. No one recognised him, and at the end of January, Comisario Gradenigo told Rossi to shelve the case. It would remain unsolved.

The End

19260588R00188

Made in the USA
Lexington, KY
12 December 2012